WOLF GOD

RUTHLESS GODS: WOLF GOD, BOOK 1

VERONICA DOUGLAS

Magic Side Press

REALM OF THE UNDYING COURT
SACRED GLADE
SARION'S PORTAL
SHIFTER VILLAGE
FROSTFALL
DEAD FOREST
MIST SEAS
THE 3 PYLONS
SHADOWSTONE
SOUTHERN ROAD TO AUREN'S DOMAIN
THE WOLF GOD'S REALM IN THE DREAMLANDS

PROLOGUE

Some monsters live only in stories, while others lurk in the shadows or at the edges of half-forgotten dreams. The Dark Wolf God lived in the space between nightmare and legend, and if we didn't stop him, he would claim our world as well.

The Dreamlands, Four Weeks Ago

Samantha

Gentle waves lapped against the shore of the little lake, belying the peril we were in. Crouching, I scanned the tree line for any sign of movement and sniffed the air. My werewolf senses would alert me the moment anyone came within a few hundred yards, but I was still on edge.

My heartbeat hadn't slowed since we'd entered the Dreamlands, a mystical realm woven from forgotten dreams. Everything was a little off, and I had the uneasy feeling that things changed each time I looked away, though I could never pinpoint exactly what.

It made keeping watch damned stressful.

A few weeks ago, I hadn't believed the Dreamlands were real.

But then again, I hadn't believed that the Dark Wolf God was real, either. He'd simply been a boogeyman, lurking in the stories the pack loremaster told to scare children.

I was dead wrong.

He'd broken free of the prison the Moon Goddess had made, and if we didn't repair the spells that bound him to the Dreamlands, he would tear his way into our world and lay waste to civilization itself.

I wasn't typically a pessimist, but the truth was, we were pretty fucked.

I glanced over at Jaxson, the alpha of our pack, and Savannah, a lone wolf who'd grown into my best friend. It was just the three of us in a desperate race to save Magic Side, Chicago, our home.

Savannah was perched on the top of a tall tower in the middle of the lake. A giant stone orb floated above her, sending a pillar of light straight into the air. It was one of three magical pylons that powered the prison that trapped the Dark Wolf God in the Dreamlands. We'd restored power to two. Only one left to go.

Of course, it was going to be the hardest one. The Dark God knew we were coming now.

There was a splash behind me as Savannah plunged from the top of the pylon into the lake and began swimming to shore.

I kept my eyes focused on the trees and toyed with the moonstone in my hand. It was like a little nuclear cell of the Moon Goddess's magic. Its power pulsed through me, and holding it made me feel alive for the first time in my life. I would kill to have magic like that.

But I didn't. I was just a werewolf.

The back of my neck tingled, and I froze. The forest was dead silent, but something was wrong.

"Jaxson, I've got a bad feeling about this," I shouted, but he was too busy pulling his sopping wet mate out of the water to notice.

And then I felt it—a low, rumbling vibration that swelled in the air. I began backpedaling. "Heads up!"

Trees cracked and groaned as the forest in front of me twisted into the shape of a tunnel.

And then the Dark Wolf God stepped out of legend and into my life.

The signature of his magic hit me first—the scent of wildfires and the taste of bitter chocolate. It roared around me and shook me to my bones, pressing in like the ocean depths and crushing the breath from my lungs.

I'd never felt anything like it.

The Dark God had taken the form of a man, but no human man was that perfect. His jaw was strong and shadowed by stubble, and tattoos of snarling wolves covered his muscled chest and shoulders. His glacier-blue eyes shone like diamonds, and his dark brown hair whipped in the breeze.

It was the only thing gentle about him.

Shadows trailed behind him in a cloak of midnight, and I trembled harder with every step he took. He was both beautiful and terrifying.

My mouth went dry, my entire body enraptured.

"Time to go!" Jaxson growled, snapping me from my hypnotic stupor.

I blinked twice, then bolted toward my friends. "Let's get the fuck out of here, Savy!"

She rushed to her bag to grab the teleportation charm the Moon had given us, and then all hell broke loose.

A fae witch with bark-like skin and flowers stuck in her hair burst from the underbrush and seized Savannah by the throat. They vanished in a sparkle of magic, appeared a second later by another tree, then vanished again.

The fae creature could teleport between trees? *Shit.*

My heart clenched. We couldn't leave without Savannah. I'd never abandon my friend. She was also the one of whom the prophecies spoke—the only person capable of stopping the Dark God from breaking out of his prison. Protecting her was all that mattered.

"Get Savy and open the portal," I shouted at Jaxson. "I'll try to buy time."

I swung around, and my muscles froze. The Dark God was only fifty feet away, striding deliberately toward me. Each step sent a wave of his power crashing over me. It was like trying to stand in stormy surf.

My knees went weak and my heart raced as I took in his beauty.

It was over.

I was just a bartender. I could fight like a cold-hearted bitch, but I had no doubt that he could kill me with a single glance.

Rather than terror, a wave of calm swept over me.

Magic Side was at stake, and Savannah was the one who could save them. I couldn't, but I *could* buy her time.

Jaxson shouted something at me, but I ignored it. Even a few seconds might be the difference between her and everyone I loved dying.

Clutching the moonstone in my right hand, I extended the claws of my left and stood my ground—just a werewolf speed bump as the Dark God bore down.

My heartbeat slowed as I accepted my fate, and I smiled. There was something in his eyes that wouldn't release my attention, that drew me in like the irresistible urge to look down while climbing a cliff. I'd always loved that feeling of vertigo.

The power of Jaxson's alpha presence slammed into me like a baseball bat as he roared, "Run! Now!"

That snapped me the fuck out of it.

I whipped my head around. Savy was back, and the fae creature was dead. I might just be able to make it to them.

I ran, and the ground thundered as the Dark Wolf God charged after me.

"Go now!" I shouted, but my friends didn't move.

Savannah used her magic to throw up a wall of darkness behind me, but as I glanced back, the god ripped through the shadows as if they were paper.

My foot caught. For a second, I hung in the air, and time slowed. Then I ricocheted off the ground. The moment I hit, I whipped around, and out of instinct, I threw the only weapon I had—the moonstone.

I put all my anger and hatred into the pitch, praying it would do something to stop him.

For a second, I saw surprise on his face, and then the world detonated.

Light blinded my eyes, and the shockwave flipped me through the air. Flying debris shredded my skin.

Ears ringing, I looked up from where I'd landed. A shimmering sphere of light wrapped around the Dark God, caging him like a beast.

Holy shit.

I hadn't expected that. I'd just thrown the thing, hoping it might blow up like a grenade. Yet somehow, the magic meant to power the walls of his prison had created a trap around him.

But how long would it hold?

The Dark Wolf God hammered against the shimmering wall with his forearm, over and over, until his skin was burned and rivulets of blood trickled down to his elbow. The ground shook, but the walls of the magic sphere held.

The Dark God met my gaze with eyes as cold as death, and his voice thundered through me. "Release me!"

"Fuck that!" I yelled as I scrambled to my feet, heart pounding, chest still aching from the impact.

Savannah darted to my side, and the god turned his hateful glare to her. "*You.*"

She skidded to a stop beside me. "Yeah. *Me.*"

The Dark Wolf God's blue eyes flashed with bright light, and a wave of his magic rippled outward.

Savannah screamed and doubled over, dropping the transport charm in the dirt. Jaxson was at her side in a second.

When she looked up, my heart skipped a beat. Her eyes were pitch black. Savannah was gone, and a dark presence had taken her place.

Her body began to quake, and then, with a sudden cry of rage, her fangs and claws slipped out.

"You will pay!" she said in a voice not her own, and she lunged at me.

Agony exploded through my body as her claws ripped across my chest. I screamed and landed in the dirt. My best friend flung herself forward, and with one swift blow, she sank her claws into my neck and tore.

Warmth flooded over my shoulders. There was blinding pain, and a sudden calm spread through me.

Jaxson was shouting. Then he was struggling with Savannah, but it was all very distant—echoes from far away. Why was he fighting with her? Wasn't she his mate? I would never fight with my mate. If I were ever lucky enough to find him, I'd stand with him against the world.

That was my last thought as the light faded. Then the pain faded as well, and the only thing left was warm darkness.

For a long time, I drifted downward. Voices echoed from the infinite shadows, calling my name. Or what had been my name. They didn't matter. Nothing mattered any more but the dark.

A howl ripped through my thoughts, calling me to return to

the pack—my alpha's call. Other wolves added their voices to the chorus. Savannah. The loremaster. All calling for a lost wolf. For me.

But the endless shadows pulled at me, entwining themselves around my essence. *Rest with us*, they whispered.

A part of me welcomed an end to the fighting, but my alpha was calling.

"Do you wish to return?" a young girl's voice said. I didn't recognize her—it echoed like three voices in one.

"Our world is in danger," I replied.

"There will be a cost," the voice said, but this time, it sounded more mature, the voice of a woman, of a kind mother cautioning her child.

The howls of my pack pulled on my heart, and I remembered I had a duty: to stop the Dark God. The lives of my friends were at stake. My city was at stake.

"Whatever the cost, I will pay," I whispered into the darkness.

An old woman walked from the shadows and stretched out her hand. She held a golden thread that trailed into the darkness.

"What is it?" I asked.

"The cost."

I couldn't see where the thin line led, and somehow, I knew she wouldn't tell me. For a second, I hesitated, then reached out and took the thread.

I gasped as sweet air filled my lungs.

My eyes fluttered open, and blurry shapes resolved into the concerned faces of my friends staring back at me: Savannah, Jaxson, even the Moon Goddess herself.

"Where am I?" I croaked, my throat as raw as I'd ever felt it. I was on my back, looking up at the roof of a temple instead of the blue sky. Then I remembered: the Moon's temple.

A sob tore from Savy's throat, and she folded herself over my body, pulling me up into an awkward embrace. "Oh, my God, Sam. I'm so sorry."

I was about to ask for what, and then, as echoes of agony racked my body, I remembered. The Dark Wolf God had used his power to force her to attack me. *The fucking monster.*

Savannah's arms tightened around me, and I looked around the temple. The Moon Goddess stood against the wall, watching me with wary eyes, as if something was troubling her. I could still feel her magic coursing through me.

Hell. I'd died. Or I almost had.

She must have brought me back from the brink. But who were the women I'd heard in the darkness? What had they said? I couldn't quite remember. It slipped from me like a dream. But it'd been important...somehow.

I pulled Savy tighter against me, trying to stop her from shaking. I knew the guilt and shame raging inside her were far more painful than those of my wounds. I would have been dying inside if the situation were reversed.

Savy pushed back and staggered to her feet, her eyes glistening. "Will you ever forgive me? I...it wasn't me."

"I know." I sat up and rubbed my blood-soaked chest. My skin was tender, but somehow, the Moon and her magic had healed the gashes that Savy had made, as well as those on my neck.

She wiped her eyes with her wrists. "He took control...my wolf, she went wild. I couldn't hold her back! I saw my claws..."

I reached out, took Savannah's hand, and squeezed, softening my eyes with all the love I felt for her. "That wasn't you. It was the Dark Wolf God."

And in that moment, I swore to myself that whatever it took, I'd find a way to make him pay.

1

———

Ten miles outside of Deerhaven, Michigan, Present Day

Samantha

"You from around here?" The young man behind the counter eyed me as he rang up my items.

The little gas station stank of cheap cologne and lemon air fresheners—that, and familiarity. The soft drone of country music piping over the speaker stirred memories of drinking cheap beer down by the river. High school in Deerhaven: the start of a lot of poor decisions and a shitstorm of consequences.

I slid a fifty across the glass-topped counter. "Not anymore."

"Didn't think so. You look like you're from the city." His gaze drifted to the newspapers stacked in front of the checkout.

I picked one up and grimaced at the headline: *Magic Side Rebuilds After Wolf God Wreaks Havoc on Chicago.*

"Glad those sorts of things don't happen up here," the man said, his eyes on the image of smoke rising from the burned-out skeletons of Dockside, the neighborhood of Magic Side that our pack controlled.

Magic Side was a magical suburb of Chicago, hidden from human eyes on an island in Lake Michigan. It was home to all kinds of Magica—supernatural people—vampires, sorcerers, demons, and werewolves like me. Most of the shifter communities outside of Chicago looked down on us city folk with suspicion. What kind of werewolf would trade living in the wilderness for the concrete urban jungle?

I'd thought the same once. Then the Deerhaven alpha drove me out, and the Dockside pack had taken me in—no questions asked.

They were my family now.

The newspaper photo didn't capture half the truth of what had been done to my home. It didn't show the corpses strewn through the streets of my neighborhood, or the brilliant magical wards that had shone like solar flares across the night sky. And it didn't show the feral faces of the werewolves the Dark God had forced to do his killing—werewolves who'd once been my friends and neighbors.

Just seeing the Dark God's name in print sent pinpricks down my spine. In their wake, they left an all-too-familiar knot of dread. I closed my eyes and reminded myself that I'd never have to see him again. Savannah had stopped him in the end.

Bing. The cash register slid open.

"You going to pay for that paper?" the attendant asked sharply, jolting me back to the present.

"No." I tossed the shitty excuse for a local paper down, and he wrinkled his nose in irritation.

"Shootings, sorcerers, and monsters... I don't know why anyone would choose to live in the city," the attendant muttered.

Because this town is hell itself.

I gathered my paltry gas station dinner as a burly man walked through the front door. His magical signature smelled like moldering earth with undertones of honeysuckle. The whole pack in Deerhaven had this scent, though it was stronger on the males. I used to find it comforting, but now it was sickly sweet and brought back bad memories.

I braced myself for the moment of recognition, but he just stepped around me as I shoved through the glass door with my head down.

As it swung shut, I heard him ask the attendant. "Who's the mutt? I got a hint of Deerhaven scent." Disdain and malice practically dripped off his tongue.

"Local girl come crawling back from the city."

"Magic Side should keep its trash, though I wouldn't mind having a fuck with her before shipping her back."

My fists clenched around the Styrofoam coffee cup and lukewarm burrito in my hand, and I took a quick glance at the jackass. Six feet tall, two hundred pounds, he was muscular but soft, with a beer belly protruding over his waistband. I could probably drop him in ten seconds.

The wolf within me stirred, then lazily retired. *Not worth it, Sam.*

I cast a death glare at the prick and headed to my truck. Deerhaven brought out the worst in me. I'd need to keep this trip as short as possible.

Ten minutes later, I pulled onto my mom's street. The pack still hadn't repaved it after last winter or repaired any damage from the blizzard.

"What's the point in paying pack dues if nothing ever gets fixed?" I muttered as I parked out front of my mom's off-white mobile home. The sun had faded the green trim around it, and weeds were breaking through the concrete drive and sidewalk.

I glanced at the manila folder on the passenger seat: ten pages of dirt on the local alpha. It might just be my mom's ticket out of this hellhole—for good this time.

Shivers skated down my spine, and for a moment, I froze. Was someone watching?

I scanned the street. No one stood in the shadows, and no curtains were moving in the windows. It was just my imagination once again.

Since returning from the Dreamlands, the uncanny feeling of being watched had become part of my daily life. I always checked, but there was never anyone there. It was probably just PTSD from nearly dying.

I rolled my shoulders and scratched the scar on my shoulder —another new nervous habit. Tucking the manila envelope under my arm, I grabbed my stuff and climbed out of the truck.

A door creaked, followed by my mom's gentle voice: "Samantha?"

I tossed the remnants of my burrito in a metal bin, then bounded up the stairs into my mom's outstretched arms and squeezed her tightly. "Hi, Mom."

"Hi, Sugar," she whispered, pressing a kiss to my hair. "It's good to see you."

She smelled of primrose and the garden, and her warm embrace immediately eased the tension I hadn't realized I was feeling.

"How are you?" I held her at arm's length, taking in her frail form.

Once graceful, she'd withered away these past two years. When the potion master in Dockside assured me that there wasn't a problem with the medication, I'd had to come to terms with Mom's new reality. Her sickness was progressing, and she couldn't live on her own much longer.

Werewolves weren't supposed to get sick that way. We healed from almost anything.

Out of instinct, I touched my shoulder. The Dark God had clawed me there, and while the wound had healed, the attack had left scars that burned whenever I thought of *him*.

"I'm good." She smiled faintly. "Things are good here."

A lie. There was nothing *good* here besides her.

She ushered me inside. Despite her illness, Mom still managed to keep a tidy house. A brown vase of sunflowers brightened the dingy beige kitchen.

As soon as the door shut, Mom began pestering me about every detail of my life. Work. Roller Derby. Lovers.

"No, Mom, there's nobody," I said for the third time.

"Well, it's only a matter of time before you meet your mate."

Bitterness tightened my throat. How could she believe that after my father had abandoned her when she'd been pregnant with me?

"I know, Mom." I smiled hopefully, a practiced reflection of her face. "Fates willing."

My mother only saw what she wanted to believe, and I didn't blame her. It was her way of holding on to hope when *everyone* else in life had shit on her.

The sick thing was that I'd told everyone in Magic Side that my parents had been fated—revisionist history that was easier for me to believe outside of Deerhaven.

I took a seat at the small dining table and set the bottle of her meds down. "I want you to come live with me in Magic Side."

Her expression froze, and I caught the scents of her shock and fear. The ability to smell emotions was one benefit of being a shifter, or downside, depending on the situation.

She looked away. "Sam, I...I can't. You know that I can't leave."

"You can't, or you won't?" My words came out more harshly than I'd intended, but maybe that's what she needed. "You shouldn't live in fear because of something I did a decade ago."

Her throat bobbed as she swallowed. "This is my home, darling. My pack, my friends are here. I can't abandon them. Besides, Wyland will never let me leave."

Heat crept along my jaw at the alpha's name.

"That's about to change." I slid the manilla folder onto the table and tapped it as I said, "This is your ticket out of this hellhole. You can come live with me in Magic Side, where I can take care of you. We have the best doctors and potion masters there. I'm sure we can find a cure—"

My mom slammed her palm down on the table. "Samantha, stop. This is absurd. I don't want to know what's inside that folder, but I'm guessing it's blackmail. Do you know what Wyland will do if you put him in a corner?"

I leaned back in the metal chair. "He'll try to save his ass."

She shook her head. "You may know Brent intimately, but Wyland is a different breed."

I flinched. Brent was the abusive bastard I'd been supposed to marry a decade ago—and Wyland's son. The coward might be a different breed, but he was just as evil as his father.

I had terrible taste in men.

My mother began compulsively tidying the house. "Wyland is proud and vicious. He'd sooner take the whole pack down than submit. I can't allow that to happen to my friends."

The chair scraped across the linoleum floor as I bolted to my feet. "These so-called friends, where are they? Why haven't they done anything to help you?"

The only sound was her washing pots that had been soaking in the sink. Her silence was all too familiar, and it meant the conversation was over.

She'll come around. She has to.

I shouldered my bag and headed to my old bedroom. Climbing gear and roller skates hung from hooks, and drooping posters of derby girls were still taped to my walls. I tried pushing one back in place, but it just curled back down.

There'd been a time when living here had been normal—comfortable, even. But that wasn't because things had been good. I just hadn't had anything to measure them against. And Brent, that bastard piece of shit, had torn my heart out.

That was when I'd learned that no matter what anyone promised, I was on my own.

My wolf stirred in my chest as old anger simmered, and I had to resist the urge to extend my claws. We were both a lot more vicious now than we'd been back then.

The box spring squeaked as I stretched out on the bed and stared at the cracks in the ceiling. How many nights had I laid awake, shattered and afraid, wondering how many more cracks it would take before I broke?

I sat up and ran my hand through my hair. The truth was, I'd probably still be stuck in Deerhaven if that POS Brent hadn't done those things to me.

Now it was my turn to get my mom out.

I dropped to my knees to stash the manila folder in the hidey-hole beneath my bed, but there were dozens of boxes in the way. "What the hell is all this shit?" I asked the silence.

I opened the largest and found my collection of Barbies and dolls. One wore a giant golden crown and a blue dress bedecked with sparkles and puffy taffeta sleeves. Princess Irrelevant, waiting for her prince to come rescue her.

Fates, I really played with these?

I scoffed and closed the box. The next had dozens of books. Rapunzel, Snow White, Beauty and the Beast. Nothing but fairy tales.

I shoved the junk away and pried up the loose floorboard. The hidey-hole beneath was empty except for a few chamber spiders. I slipped the folder in and covered the hidden panel with all the traces of the foolish little girl I'd once been.

It was time for us to cut ties with this place.

The first thing I needed to do was get a measure of Wyland. Hopefully, it had been long enough that his feelings toward me had changed. Probably not, but there was only one way to find out.

It was just past nine on a Friday night, which meant he'd be drunk and watching the fights at the Barn with everyone else in town. Unfortunately, it was probably the best mood I was going to find him in. Grabbing my leather jacket, I headed for the door.

Time to hunt down the alpha.

2

____

Cadean – the Dark Wolf God

The she-wolf slipped out of her truck and strode across the parking lot beneath the flickering lights.

Stabbing pain flared under the bandage on my arm, just as it did each time I watched her. It felt like sandpaper grating over my seared nerves. The muscles in my jaw tensed. *This. Woman.*

Every inch of her was hypnotic, like the fates had molded her just to torture me. Long sun-kissed hair. Sultry blue eyes that sent heat pulsing through me. Full pink lips that demanded to be devoured.

Samantha Bennet. My tormentor. My obsession.

Four weeks earlier, the she-wolf had unleashed the fucking fireball that had seared my arm and trapped me in a sphere of light. If that hadn't already been enough to draw my wrath, she'd also helped recharge the last of the pylons that powered the walls of my prison, locking me in the Dreamlands for good.

That, I would never forgive.

She made her way around the mass of parked cars, then paused with her hand on the door of the old building, looking around, suspicious. Like clockwork whenever I was near, she touched the scar I'd given her. Perhaps I haunted her like she haunted me. A cruel smile formed on my lips at the thought of it: *balance*—the only thing that kept the universe from falling into chaos.

For a second, her eyes settled on me, as if she'd spotted me lurking in the shadows. That was impossible, of course because I wasn't really there—I was seated on my throne in the Dreamlands, using my power to shadow-cast.

For me, all shadows were like dark windows into the waking world—the human realm beyond the Dreamlands. During the twelve hundred years of my imprisonment, it had been my only way to catch glimpses of the world beyond.

Usually, I only perceived hazy impressions of my target, but with Samantha, it was different. She was always easy to find, like a supernova drowning out a sky of stars. Maybe that was why she was so captivating.

I'd been stalking her for weeks, devouring every movement and expression.

At first, I was planning to seize her and take revenge. Then I contented myself with watching, hoping that I would learn something of the magic that she'd used to inflict the incurable curse on my arm.

But the more I watched, the more my fascination grew. I'd spent more time watching her in the last month than I'd spent watching any mortal during the millennium of my imprisonment. The truth was, I simply couldn't take my eyes off her. She was electrifying. Irresistible.

Yet, I still didn't know *what* she was, and watching her while being unable to touch or scent her was driving me to madness.

Somehow, the mortal little wolf had sunk her claws deep under my skin.

I moved to a closer shadow. Samantha shivered, then opened the door and stepped inside. I followed her like a specter.

What was this place? And why was she working so hard to hide the hate and anger hovering at the corners of her expression?

The rundown barn was packed with werewolves drinking and cursing. I imagined the stench of beer and sweat, but mercifully, my power only allowed me to watch and listen. The place was poorly lit, and I let my gaze coast along the deep shadows around the perimeter. The crowd was packed around an octagonal ring in the center, surrounded by a six-foot chain-link fence.

Some sort of fighting ring? Bile slicked my throat. The wolves here had clearly succumbed to the basest of human drives, brutality as sport.

What was she doing in a place like this?

It sickened me, but I couldn't stop watching her. She was so *vivid*. A mad part of me wanted to know everything about her, *had* to know. Even this part.

Frustration and rapture fought for control of my thoughts, but Wulfric's voice pulled me from my vision: "You're watching her again, aren't you?"

I inhaled sharply as my eyes flew open. Something dark and dangerous rose in my chest.

My most trusted general stood before me—a giant beast of a werewolf with black hair and a silver-tinged beard. Wulfric crossed his arms and shook his head. "You're obsessed, Cadean."

It wasn't the first time he'd raised that objection.

I leaned back in my throne of antlers and reined in the dangerous sensations that threatened to break free. "It's not obsession if it serves a purpose. She's the only one who has ever been able to give me a lasting wound. I need to understand her magic and how she did it."

I flexed my aching hand and glared at my bandage-wrapped arm.

She hadn't just burnt me. She'd infected me with some sort of curse. The strips of white cloth hid glowing lines of light that wound across my skin like roots. They always flared brighter after I'd shadow-casted with her.

I should have been able to heal any wound—I was a fucking god, for fates' sake. Yet this one persisted. Despite the attempts of healers, mages, and blood sorcerers, I still had no idea what it was. All I knew was that each day, it grew and left me weaker.

I rose from my throne. "I have to find the cure, and Samantha will lead me to the answer. I feel it in my bones."

I'd been drawn to her like a moth to flame from the moment I'd first laid eyes on her. That had to mean something.

Wulfric gave me an all-too-knowing smile. "Out of all the time you've spent watching her, have you learned anything about her magic? Or how heal to your wound? Or just what she eats for breakfast?"

Giving him a savage look, I began pacing the great hall.

A bagel with eggs and bacon from a shithole truck stop.

I ground my teeth in annoyance, one second from unleashing hell on my trusted companion. "Don't push me, Wulfric."

He had a point. I'd watched her mix drinks at the bar and repair burned-out houses. I'd followed her when she shifted into a wolf and ran through the city parks and when she went climbing in the small river gorges near her home. But I'd never once seen her use her magic. Not a flicker. Not a hint. It was beyond maddening.

"You need to focus on the high fae, not the girl," Wulfric growled from the dais. "Since your prison was restored, their attacks have grown more frequent."

Visions of decimated villages rose in my mind—my people, dead and dying and begging for help that I was increasingly powerless to provide. It sickened me to the core.

I glared at the werewolf. "Do you think I'm blind? I'm doing everything I can to protect our people. But this wound has weakened me, and the walls of the Moon's prison are closing in. That girl could be the key to both."

"Or she could be a wild goose chase."

Perhaps it was. Perhaps she would lead me nowhere.

As frustration raged through me like the earth splitting, I summoned my black axe from the ether and hurled it through the darkness. A *thunk* echoed through the cavernous hall as the blade sank into one of the enormous living trees that supported the roof.

"Once I'm free, I'll depose the Undying Court, drive the fae from shifter lands, and sow my realm with their blood. But to do that, I need to heal. I need to find a way to break out of this fates-damned prison again."

Wulfric knew better than to question me further, but he cleared his throat anyway.

"Was there something else?" I growled.

He shifted on his feet. "We may have another option. Auren sent word that he'll be arriving in five days."

Auren, my brother—never there when you needed him, always when you didn't.

I strode across the hall to retrieve my axe from the tree. Though I could've just summoned it back, a part of me wanted to wrench it from the trunk and listen to the wood crack. "Has my brother changed his mind about helping, or is he content to watch me wither while the fae feast on my lands?"

"He didn't say. Only that he's bringing wine."

Auren, the eternal diplomat, would refuse to help as always. We both fought to preserve balance, but we had very different interpretations of what that meant. His interpretation was to keep me hanging by my balls while he decided whether he had my back. It was a game and a complication I didn't need.

Placing my hand on the blade, I closed my eyes, trying to find calm in the darkness. But instead of darkness, she was there.

It was always her.

She was still in the barn but stood with fists clenched while the others cheered around her. I could almost feel her rage pulsing from the shadows.

She hated the place, and I couldn't blame her.

Werewolves crowded the octagonal fighting ring, shouting encouragement and insults at the pair inside. A girl ducked a blow from a boy, but she wasn't fast enough to land one herself. He danced around her before unleashing a double punch to her kidney.

They were barely more than children. Fury simmered in my veins. What kind of pack would allow this to happen?

3

Samantha

Nothing had changed in Deerhaven at all.

The girl in the ring was limping now. If she knew what was good for her, she'd throw in the towel, but by the way she squared her shoulders, I knew she wouldn't. The ring wasn't just a deranged form of entertainment—it was where young wolves established themselves in the pack hierarchy.

The crowd at the far end parted, and Wyland appeared, hands raised. "Let's see your wolf, Travis!"

My gut tightened. Things were about to get a lot messier.

I shoved forward to the edge of the crowd as the man in the ring flung off his shirt and removed his shorts with a smug grin on his face.

He was wolfborn like me. While some shifters could use their magic to change clothes and all, we did it the old way. The *hard* way.

With the sudden snapping of bones, fur erupted over his skin, and his body contorted into that of a wolf. The girl raised her chin defiantly, but I could smell her fear. She was in no shape to defend herself, especially not against that beast.

The wolf lunged and drove the girl to the ground. She screamed as he bit into her shoulder, then flung her across the dirt.

"Call it, Wyland!" I shouted, but the cheers drowned out my voice.

I knew he wouldn't. He liked seeing girls bleed.

The hair on my neck rose, and the tingling sensation of being watched returned, of being judged from the shadows. Before I knew what I was doing, I jumped on the side of the chain-link fence and flung myself over the top.

The crowd roared in outrage.

"You won," I said to the wolf. "Leave the girl alone."

The wolf's head snapped to me, a low growl reverberating from his throat as he slowly stepped off the girl.

The crowd erupted into a frenzy, people placing bets and hurtling curses at me.

"Get the fuck out of there!" Wyland shouted. "This match is over when I call it." Red in the face and snarling, he was perched on a worn leather sofa like a fucking gangster king.

The girl, shaken but alive, scooted to the corner as the young wolf rounded on me and bared his teeth.

"You don't want to do this, kid," I snarled.

He lunged straight for my neck, but I rolled to the side and was on my feet before he landed. "You won your match. It's over."

The young wolf charged, but I spun around him, and with a quick kick, flung him into the fence. He bounced off and hit the blood-caked dirt with a thud. He scrambled up, but I sidestepped and brought my elbow down on his skull.

I seized him by his throat, and although he whimpered, I didn't release him. "That's right, kid. You don't remember me, but I'm queen of this ring."

It wasn't a title I was proud of, but I pressed him into the dirt all the same. "Shift back and go home."

He was just young and stupid, much like I'd been at his age. I released the wolf and stood, dusting off my hands on my jeans. The boy shifted back to human form and gathered his clothes, then slunk out.

The crowd booed.

"Enough!" Wyland bellowed. "Get that bitch out of there!"

I turned to let him have a piece of my mind, but Brent stepped into the ring. No longer a gangly teenager, he'd filled out and become a man since I'd last seen him.

My mouth went sour as old hatred welled up.

"Samantha," he said slowly, as if testing my name after all the years that had passed. "You haven't changed, it seems."

"Neither has this shithole."

Dragging his eyes along my throat with a grin, he circled me. "You look good."

I knew what expectations came with his compliments, and old, forgotten bruises began to throb.

"Hands off." I backed around the cage, my fists clenched as I fought to calm the storm inside. "I came to speak with the alpha."

"I'm going to be the new alpha soon, and see that pretty blonde over there?" He tilted his chin toward a woman who was standing near the front of the crowd, frowning at the two of us. "That's my mate. If I'd known you'd be in town, I'd have invited you to the wedding."

How had I ever loved this guy?

"Does she know that you're an abusive, cheating bastard?"

He leapt forward, swinging for my jaw, but I ducked out of the way and elbowed him in the ribs. He grunted and stepped back as several pack members gasped.

Were we really doing this again? The old dance?

I stepped back and raised my hands. "Brent—"

My head snapped back, and pain seared my jaw. Two more blows in my gut knocked the wind from my lungs.

I doubled over, gasping. *Fuck. That's what I get for taking my eye off the ball.*

Brent spit blood in the dirt. "Yeah, you haven't changed. Still don't know your place."

"I'm not the girl you used to shove around." I charged forward, tackling Brent and knocking him on his ass. He rolled on top of me, his hands going for my throat, but I kneed him in the groin. Cursing, he rolled onto his side, but I was on him a second later, beating him with my fist. "Don't ever touch me again!"

"I said, get that bitch out of there!" Wyland said, but I didn't stop.

Seconds later, two pairs of hands seized me by the shoulders and dragged me back.

"One day, your daddy isn't going to be around to stop me," I shouted as two heavyset shifters hauled me from the Barn. They tossed me out on my ass and slammed the wooden door shut.

What was I thinking, coming here? This whole place was a minefield of memories and triggers I'd worked hard to bury.

Climbing to my feet, I rubbed the blood off my bruised knuckles, regretting everything. I headed to my car but froze as tingles erupted across my skin. I rubbed the scar on my shoulder, which had begun to burn.

I had the uncanny feeling of being watched again. Was there a wolf moving in the shadows at the edge of the light? It couldn't be. Too big.

Gravel chuffed behind me, and I spun around, claws out.

Instantly, my pulse slowed. It was the girl from the fight. Dirty blonde hair, skinny but tough. She reminded me of myself at her age.

She crossed her arms. "I didn't need your help. They won't respect me now."

I wiped the blood from my mouth. "They'll never respect you here. The sooner you figure that out, the better off you'll be. This pack is rotten to its core."

She winced. Yeah, she wasn't blind to the truth.

I pulled out the folded bills I was planning on giving my mom and held them toward her. "Get out while you can. If you want a job in Magic Side, catch a Greyhound and ask for Jaxson at Eclipse. He takes care of his pack."

Her eyes flashed at the cash, but she raised her chin defiantly. "I don't need your advice or your money."

No, she probably didn't need it, but if she was anything like I'd been as a teen, she could use it.

I pressed the bills into her palm. "I'm not doing this for you. I'm doing this for the girl I was once. If you want to stay here, fine, it's your prison. Take the cash and bet big on yourself next time."

With that, I headed toward my truck.

4

Samantha

The breeze rustled the changing leaves in the trees around the parking lot. Fall was here, and though I dreaded the impending brutal cold, the hot humidity hanging around in Chicago made my fur frizz.

Shouts and roars erupted from the Barn behind me. Another fight. Not my problem. What a fucking mess. Somebody had needed to step up and protect the girl, but I knew firsthand that the pack had lost all sense years ago.

And fucking Brent. It had felt damn good knocking him on his ass after all these years, but I'd lost my chance to speak with Wyland. Jaxson paid me to go into towns like these, keep my head down, and gather information. Except I couldn't do it here. There were landmines everywhere.

Well, I was going to step on a few more when I finally got a chance to talk to Wyland. He'd be fucking furious, but the dirt I had on him would make him let my mom go just to get me out of his hair. The details were bad, and she wasn't worth anything to him.

I paused with my hand on the door of my truck as a heady scent of oakmoss and freesia caught my attention.

I spun around. A tall man grinned back at me.

He looked like one of the burly Deerhaven werewolves on the surface, but for a second, the air around him flickered, revealing pointy ears, fine features, and an almost ethereal presence.

He was fae, hiding behind a glamour. Trouble I didn't need.

Pulse racing, I took two steps back and slid my claws out slowly, eyeing his throat. "Who are you? And why are you disguised as a werewolf?"

He raised his palms in a half surrender. "I didn't mean to give you a start, though I'm surprised you can see through the glamour. I'm trying not to draw attention. I figured the wolves around here don't take kindly to outsiders—or am I wrong?"

The guy felt powerful, and I had no doubt he'd be fast, which meant I had to make it count. I shifted one foot forward into a striking stance. "Don't come any closer."

He backed up. "I'm actually here for your help."

"Right. Most guys who sneak up on a woman in a parking lot at night are looking for help, just not the kind I'm gonna give. Back away slowly, or you'll regret it."

Sensing my alarm, his dark eyes narrowed, and his tone grew serious. "I'm well aware. I represent the Undying Court, and we know you fought the Dark Wolf God and wounded him. I'm here to find out if you're up to finishing the job."

My blood turned to ice, and terror took root in every corner of my body. Not again. I couldn't deal with this again. The Dark God had nearly killed me once and torn my shoulder apart the last time we met. The lingering scar still burned every time I thought of him.

That part of my life was closed.

"You're mistaken." I shuffled back a step and opened the

door of the truck without taking my eyes off the fae. "You haven't the faintest clue what you're talking about, and you'd better leave before the pack smells what you are."

"What happened in Magic Side is happening all across our lands. Villages destroyed. Families dead. We need help, Samantha. Our warriors have been trying to bring him down for centuries, but you're the first to give him a wound that didn't immediately heal."

My breathing turned unsteady, and my heart pounded against my chest. No matter what I did, I couldn't seem to escape the shadow of the Dark God. He was there back home in Magic Side, in the newspapers, and in my dreams. His presence lingered in my wounded shoulder and in memories that I still couldn't seem to shake. Hell, I was beginning to imagine him in the shadows, watching me.

And now this fates-damned fae had brought him here.

"I don't know what you're talking about." I slipped into the truck and locked the door.

The fae crossed his arms. "We heard that you cast a spell around him and trapped him in a burning orb. You weakened him. Could you do it again?"

Fuck. How would he even know about that? Questions tore at me, but I knew one thing: I needed to get out of there before every trauma I'd known in life came crashing on me all in one evening.

I turned the ignition and rolled down the window. "I'd consider helping you if I thought you were telling the truth, or that there was anything I could do, but I'm just a wolf shifter, and I don't have any magic. I threw a moonstone charged with the Moon Goddess's magic. You should track her down. She'll know how to help."

"She told us to look for you."

Gods *damn it*. The fates were definitely out to get me killed.

I leaned out of the truck window. "Look, guy, I don't know why she sent you. I'm sorry about whatever is happening, but that's not my fight anymore. I've got scars enough. Talk to Savannah Caine or Jaxson Laurent. It was Savannah's magic that stopped the Dark God. They're the heroes. I was just along for the ride."

"Maybe. But they're not you," the fae said.

"Lucky them." I hit the accelerator and peeled out of the parking lot.

The streetlights sped by as I did my best not to hyperventilate and run off the road.

I could feel those eyes on me, watching. Had it been the fae all along? What did I know of him or his problems? The bastard could've been sent by the Dark God himself, for all I knew. A trick.

Guilt and suspicion tore at me from every angle. I'd seen what had happened to Magic Side. If the fae was telling the truth—and that was a huge *if*—and the Dark God was attacking elsewhere, then the fae deserved help.

But I wasn't the one. I was just a wolf, not like my friend Savannah, who was part sorceress and knew how to wield shadow magic. My best skill was pouring a flawless Manhattan.

Maybe if I had power like hers, I'd accept. But I didn't, and I had a sick mother to look after.

The truth was, the fae had gotten the wrong wolf.

5

Cadean

Fury rippled through me. "She's talking to the fae."

Wulfric's shoulders tensed, and his expression flashed with surprise. "What?"

I strode out of the grand hall, the light from the sconces casting long shadows over the walls. "The Undying Court has sent someone to recruit her. She's now a liability. You need to grab her, now."

"Where is she?"

"Some shithole town. I'll send you through a portal. Grab her and kill anyone who gets in your way—especially the fae if he shows up again."

We snatched a charm of returning from the vault, then descended to the chamber of portals at the center of my citadel.

Twelve flickering arches stood around a central fountain. Hatred twisted within me. A dozen passages that led to all the realms but none which I could pass through—not while the Moon's prison still stood.

"What should I do if she won't come quietly?" Wulfric asked.

"Don't harm her," I said, with a force that surprised me.

"Take her quickly and go. I don't care who sees. No one in that town matters."

I closed my eyes and focused on Samantha. She was driving down a street lined by small, rundown storefronts—a downtown that had seen better days.

A thousand years ago, I would have been able to tear a rift into the sky and hurl myself through. Now, barricaded behind the Moon's spells, it was impossible, and it took all my power to tear a single hole in reality large enough for one of my subordinates.

I searched for a patch of woods. As a god of wilderness, some of my power could still eke through. Unfortunately, there was little of the wild left. The forests of pines were all planted in manicured rows, ready to be cut down for timber and planted again. They were no more a part of the wilderness than was a field of wheat.

How did wolves live like this?

Finally, I found a patch of gnarled pines by a bend in a river. They'd been left untended and now grew in their own patterns. It would have to do.

Focusing on that spot, I pressed my hand to the portal. Searing pain squeezed me like a vise, but slowly, a little tear in reality formed, connecting the patch of pines to the Dreamlands.

I glanced up at Wulfric. "It's open. She's in the town to the north. Do not fail."

Wulfric slipped through, and I let the rift collapse behind him. I flexed my fists as the discomfort eased.

What I would do for the freedom to leave like that.

Frustration took me as I stormed back to my throne room. I hated being trapped, having to rely on intermediaries. Having to watch from the distance when I should strike. I could have sent him to take her at any time. Why had I waited? What had watching gained me?

I braced myself against one of the tree trunks that supported the roof of my great hall and closed my eyes. As always, I found her almost instantly.

Samantha slipped out of the cab of her truck and pushed through the doors of a bar—the Mad Dog Tap.

I stepped from the shadows of the alleyway and into the dark bar behind her.

Anger boiled under my skin. She was so close, but I couldn't reach her.

There were a few patrons sitting around—one at the bar, and a few in the back. Wulfric would have to grab her in front of witnesses, but all that mattered was keeping her out of the hands of the fae.

Samantha paused and glanced around, then she looked straight at me. The hair on my neck rose. There was no way she should be able to perceive me, but her gaze didn't waver, and the wound on my arm began to burn.

She started to take a step forward, then a voice from the far end of the room tore her attention away.

"Samantha? Holy shit!" A woman rushed around the corner of the bar and pulled Samantha into an embrace.

"Katy? I can't believe you're still working here." Samantha's lips pulled into a smile, and an inexplicable warmth flowed through me, pushing away some of the shadows. As if I'd been holding my breath, waiting for that smile.

This woman was dangerous to me in more ways than one.

The bartender laughed and held Samantha at arm's length. "I can't believe you're actually here. Somebody said you showed up at the Barn and laid out Brent, but I assumed they were deep in the bottle."

Brent. The pathetic excuse for a wolf from the ring. If our

paths ever crossed, I would break his legs and string him up for touching her.

The bartender frowned, inspecting Samantha's bruises. "Oh, gods, it's true."

She shrugged. "Not my best moment."

It had been a fucking delicious moment, beautiful and feral. She'd stood up for that girl, then beaten that asshole into the dirt with her fists. Whatever their history, I would relish replaying that memory in my mind a thousand times. Nature sorting itself out. Balance restored.

The woman brought Samantha a drink, and they began to talk.

I didn't listen to their words. I couldn't take my eyes from her lips, studying them as they formed each syllable. Watching the way the line of her neck curved to her jaw. The casual way she pulled her fingers through her hair.

Wulfric would have her soon, but I had to admit, the shadows had their benefits.

The bartender's eyes went wide as the door slammed open and the prick from ring strode in—not the blond she'd beaten into the dirt, but the bastard alpha who'd lorded over the sick affair.

I stalked from shadow to shadow like a caged animal, wishing I had the power to reach out and tear out his throat. He was an alpha. His job was to protect his people, yet he reveled in their suffering. Everyone in the bar shied away as if he were something to fear, rather than their defender.

If I'd had my wits about me, I would've told Wulfric to take him out and rid the town of its burden.

The alpha stepped right up into Samantha's space, but my little wolf was not cowed. She took a long swig of her beer and pivoted on her stool. "*Wyland.* What a surprise."

"Cut the shit," he said with stifling arrogance. "You've got balls showing your face at the Barn. You're lucky Brent still has a soft spot for you, or it would have ended worse."

The alpha loomed over her, muscles tense with hate and menace, and a cold fury burned through me. If he laid a single finger on her, I'd rip his fucking heart out and stake him to the front of that barn.

But Samantha's glare didn't waver. "Why do you still hold those fights? They're barbaric."

His lip curled. "They made you what you are, girl."

Samantha's eyes were like stone. "*I* made me what I am."

I let out a low growl. *Good girl.*

~

Samantha

I shuddered as I felt a sudden sense of strength and approval, and I glanced over my shoulder—where it had come from, I had no idea. Everyone else in the bar had their eyes averted, studying their drinks or the grain of the table.

Wyland leaned in and spoke so low his voice was almost a whisper. "I want you gone by morning, Sam. My son and soon-to-be daughter will be mated this week. I don't need you stirring up any more trouble than you already have."

My gut twisted. The thought of his bastard son finding happiness after all the shit he'd done to me...

Werewolves heal.

"Trust me," I said, my voice cracking. "I want nothing more to do with this pack. I'll go, but I'm taking my mom."

The alpha raised his brows, and anger hardened his expression. "You don't get to dictate terms. Your mother is part of this pack, and that makes her mine. She stays put, and you leave tomorrow. And if I see you again, there won't be any conversation."

He turned to leave, but I blurted, "I know about your land deals."

Wyland froze, then slowly turned. "What the hell are you talking about?"

His face was as red as I'd ever seen it, and his fists were clenched in fury. But I could smell the fear.

I leaned forward and pitched my voice low. "Your trust is selling mineral rights out from under every landowner in this pack. Where the hell are people like my mother going to live when the bulldozers come? What do you think the pack will do to you?"

Wyland grabbed my jacket. "You dare call me out in here? I'll make this clear: if you open your pretty little mouth about anything, I will fucking kill you myself."

I bared my teeth. "Anything happens to me, and the Dockside pack will come looking."

He grinned. "We'll see about that."

"There's more," I whispered. "Pages and pages. But here's the deal: you let my mom leave, and I give you everything I have. You never see us again. Win-win. Think of it as my wedding gift to Brent."

"I should make your skin a wedding gift to Brent." His claws ripped into the leather of my jacket. "But because I want you gone, I'll make *you* a deal. You disappear, and I never hear from you again. In exchange, I don't break every bone in your mother's body."

With that, Wyland turned and left. It took every ounce of restraint I possessed not to take him down right then and there.

I could call my friends in Chicago tonight and drop the hammer on him. But what would Wyland's pack do? The pack trust would collapse. A lot of people might get kicked off their land.

Fuck.

I could have Jaxson deal with Wyland, of course. He'd do it for me in a heartbeat. But pack leaders were forbidden to meddle with each other's affairs. If the Werewolf Council found out...

I dragged a hand through my tangled hair and downed the rest of my beer.

"Wolf problems?"

I slammed my glass down, nearly choking. The fae man from earlier slipped onto the stool beside me, grinning. "What a coincidence. Me, too."

Where the hell had he come from? He was still shrouded in his husky werewolf glamour, though I could see the truth through it—but from the way no one else was paying attention, I mused that I must be the only one.

I leaned close. "I told you, I'm not who you're looking for."

He waved to Katy, who'd retreated to the far end of the room. "A gin, neat. Make it two."

Katy pulled a bottle of Hendricks off the shelf and rushed for a pair of glasses. By the way she kept her eyes down, I knew seeing the alpha and me like that had given her the shakes.

The fae leaned against the counter. "Let's start again. I'm Sarion, and it seems you have troubles of your own. If you assist me, I will weave a glamour on that alpha so strong, he'll treat your mother like she is the queen of Scotland."

Fear coiled in my chest. "You were listening? How long have you been following me?"

Katy set the glasses out, and he took one. "I went to find you in Magic Side. When you weren't there, I headed here."

But how had he known about Deerhaven? I'd buried my past. I was so ashamed of Deerhaven, I hadn't told anyone where I was going. But with the fae stalker, angry alpha, and uncanny feeling of being watched, nobody knowing where I'd gone was beginning to look like a major mistake.

He took a sip of his gin. "The Dark Wolf God's attacks on our kingdom have become more frequent and deadly. Innocent people are dying. You could stop that."

"And how's that? Savannah renewed the spells that bound him in the Dreamlands. He should be locked away forever."

"Not sure. We don't think he can enter your realm yet, but it might only be a matter of time."

My stomach tightened.

Sarion leaned forward. "Our spies told us that you did something that hurt him, even trapped him for a while. All we want to do is ask you some questions. Meet with our council. Listen to what they have to say, then decide."

His glamour couldn't hide the desperation in his voice. Hell, I could smell his fear and nerves. He truly believed I could help him.

"This sounds like a trap," I said.

"If I wanted to abduct you, I would have done so already."

Shit. Considering how easily his glamour had fooled Katy and the others, I didn't doubt it.

"Thanks for the warning. Or was that a threat?"

He started drinking my untouched gin. "Let me put everything on the table. The situation with that alpha and your mother? I can take care of that. In exchange, all you have to do is talk to the council. See what we're facing."

I didn't trust the fae one bit. Not many of our kind did. They had a reputation for being crafty and artful in distorting the truth. But if he was powerful enough to cast a glamour on Wyland, that could solve my Deerhaven problems for now.

And maybe I'd have a chance to get back at the Dark God for what he'd done to me.

The thing that made me nervous was how much I wanted it all to be true. That my mom might get out, that I might be able to thwart the Dark God, that I could do something to make a difference.

Deals made in desperation or hope usually ended poorly. If I could find some way to control the terms, I could solve all my problems.

The bar door burst open, and a rowdy group stumbled in. They were drunk, which was saying something for a shifter. Our metabolism ran high, so it took a lot to get shitfaced.

Sarion leaned in. "You're being wasted here. You could help a lot of people who are facing far bigger problems than a corrupt alpha."

Memories of what happened in Magic Side inundated my mind—bodies and burning buildings. Guilt tore at me. If I could help, how could I walk away?

A couple of males headed straight for the bar, and I swiveled to hide my face. One clapped his buddy's shoulder. "Hey, man, it's the bitch who busted up the fight."

"That's my cue," I said, sliding off the stool. The last thing I needed was to stir up more trouble that would likely blow back on my mom.

6

Samantha

The parking lot was already full, and plenty of werewolves were milling about their cars and laughing. Soon, the Mad Dog would be full of people celebrating their wins or drowning their losses in booze.

Definitely a good time to leave.

"These are your people?" Sarion asked disdainfully as he followed me out.

"Once."

I reached for the door of my pickup, but Sarion put his hand out and held it shut. "Do we have a deal?"

Leaning back against the bed, I fixed him with a hard stare. "Look, I want to help. I hate the Dark Wolf God with my entire soul, and if there's a chance to get back at him and help other places like Magic Side, I'm in. But I'll need assurances."

"I'll swear a blood oath not to harm you and to make sure your mother is taken care of. How soon can you leave?" Sarion extended his hand to shake, but I wasn't in the business of heading anywhere with strange men.

I shook my head. "Not so fast. I don't know you, and I'm not going anywhere alone. I want backup from Magic Side."

Sarion didn't respond. Apparently, that might be a sticking point.

I crossed my arms. "This is part of the deal for me, and it could be an advantage for you, even if it delays things. If Jaxson or Savannah can come with, they might have insights that would benefit—"

"Pretend we're done talking and get in the car. Don't look back," Sarion said, his voice deadly quiet but taut with apprehension.

I froze.

Was it Wyland or Brent? I sniffed the air and caught a strange scent and signature, like peat and amber, and there was a bitter, metallic taste on the tip of my tongue. It wasn't anyone from the pack, but for some reason, I recognized it.

Sarion bent his head down. "We've got company from the Dreamlands. Get in the pickup and peel out of here as fast as you can. I'll hop in the back."

Fuck.

I glanced covertly from the corner of my eye. An enormous werewolf was shoving through the crowd toward us. He had a deadly human physique and silver-black hair that matched the light glistening in his dark eyes.

I'd seen him before—after we'd bound the Dark God, this bastard had tried to take me.

Panic spread beneath my skin, and I spun and wrenched open the door, except it was still locked. *Fuck!*

I fumbled for my keys, but the whole damn truck lurched two feet away from me as the wolfman shoved it out of the way. In a blink, he'd seized Sarion and hurled him backward, and then went for my wrist.

I twisted out of his grasp and aimed a blow at his face, but he stepped aside, and my fist swung short. I ducked and spun, but he snatched my shoulder and pulled me backward. The keys flew from my hand as my back slammed into his chest and he locked my arms in place.

"This will go easier if you stop fighting," he said, his voice laced with menace.

"Like hell I will." I jammed the heel of my boot into his foot, and when his grip loosened just a fraction, I freed my arm and rammed it into his kidney. He grunted, and I darted toward the truck.

Halfway there, Sarion grabbed my arm and yanked me to him. "Sorry about this!"

I saw the werewolf's furious eyes as he lunged, then a wave of magic burst around me and cascaded over my skin.

The world spun. Deerhaven vanished, and I suddenly found myself whirling through the inky grayness of the ether. Seconds later, trees and bright sky appeared, and my feet hit hard stone. I stumbled forward but kept my footing.

Deerhaven was gone, replaced by a glen of aspens. We stood atop a stone dais, with a delicate, vine-covered archway over our heads. It hummed with magic—a portal.

Shit.

Sarion must've used a transport charm to teleport us here.

I spun around, taking in my surroundings. Besides Sarion and two horses, there was nobody else in the glen. That didn't suggest an ambush, but I wasn't about to let my guard down.

On the upside, there wasn't a massive werewolf trying to kidnap me anymore. On the downside, I'd essentially been abducted and had no idea where I was.

"Where the hell did you take me?" I kept my claws up in a fighting posture.

Sarion raised his hands apologetically. "Look, that got messy.

I know you were wanting backup and blood oaths, but we needed to get out of there fast."

The glen had a misty scent, and something was off about the way everything appeared—as if the trees were slightly different each time I looked at them. Dread churned in me as I recognized where we were. "This is the Dreamlands."

"Yes," Sarion said. "I had a gem of recall for this place. Isn't it beautiful?"

Beautiful barely described it. The trees were turning gold, and large white blossoms were blooming all around the bases of their trunks. But the Dreamlands were *his* domain.

My heart began beating stronger as apprehension trickled down my spine. "Are we outside of the Dark God's realm?"

"Yes. This is our kingdom. You're safe."

Sarion stepped forward, but I circled like we were in a fighting ring. "Let's not overstate the situation. I don't know or trust you, and you just teleported me to an unfamiliar location."

He shrugged and stopped trying to advance. "Well, it's not ideal, but I'm hoping you're still willing to help us—especially since the Dark Wolf God seems to be after you as well. That werewolf was one of his generals. Wulfric, I believe."

Fucking hell.

I retracted my claws but kept my distance. "I've seen that wolf before. He tried to abduct me right after we bound the Dark God, but my friends drove him away."

Sarion sat on the edge of the dais and pulled out a little tablet with a paper and quill. "He's a persistent bastard, apparently. Well, if at first you don't succeed..."

He began scratching out a message.

I stepped closer. "What are you doing now?"

He didn't look up or stop writing. "Letting the council know we've arrived and that you've agreed to meet."

Anger heated my neck, and I had to stop my claws from slipping back out. "Actually, we agreed that you'd swear an oath, take care of my mother, and let me have backup first. Then I was going to chat."

"All in due time," he said absently.

Frustration clawed at me. The unfortunate truth was that I didn't have many sensible options if he wasn't willing to concede. I had no idea how to operate the portal to get back to Deerhaven—not that I would want to head back there with a giant werewolf hunting me. The horses could be a means of escaping, but I didn't know anything about where I was.

When you fall in a river, you can either fight against the current or let the stream take you and gradually work your way to shore. I'd just have to work with the situation and look for ways to gain an advantage.

Sarion released the quill, which hovered in the air above the paper. I tried glancing over his shoulder to read his message, but I didn't recognize the script. After a few seconds, the quill began scrawling out a message of its own where his had stopped. The handwriting was different, and the short note ended with an official-looking flourish. Apparently, it was a form of enchanted email.

As soon as the correspondent signed off, Sarion leapt to his feet. "The council is sending someone to meet us about an hour's ride from here."

"How about we meet in Magic Side instead?" I prompted, without much hope.

Sarion just headed to the horses. "It's not safe." He unhitched one of the horses and held it steady for me. "I assume you'd prefer to travel as a wolf, but I can't, so mount up."

I headed over and warily put my hand on the saddle. I could ride a motorcycle, but horses were another thing entirely. "I assume you don't have a dirt bike?"

He smiled. "Not today."

7

Samantha

We mounted the horses, and Sarion showed me the basics. Within minutes, we were heading into the sparse woods. The horse seemed to recognize the fact that I was a novice and ignored any attempt I made to steer. Thankfully, it was content to follow Sarion's mount.

The leaves were turning scarlet and orange, and their last breath smelled of ozone and decay. The horses had to pick their way over a strange network of giant purple vines that wound their way across the forest floor. The woods were beautiful but vaguely uncanny, as if everything was on the verge of being an illusion.

I tried pressing Sarion for information about the council and what they expected, but he kept putting me off. "I was sent to recruit you. The council will fill you in on the details shortly."

The landscape began changing, shifting from leafy trees to large conifers, their dark green needles stark against the overcast sky. The purple vines still wove across the ground like alien tendrils reaching out. I breathed in the rich scents of sap and moss, my werewolf senses picking out the subtle woody undertones of crisp bark and musk.

Ever so slowly, the mist began to build around us, and the visibility soon dropped to twenty yards. Something about the thickening fog made my skin prickle. "The mist is unsettling. Is it natural?"

Sarion glanced back over his shoulder. "You're not very familiar with the Dreamlands, are you?"

"Many of our pack's legends mention the Dreamlands, but they don't describe what they are. To be honest, I thought they were mostly a myth until a few months ago, when I had the *pleasure* of meeting the Dark God."

He dropped back to ride alongside of me. "The Dreamlands are woven from countless dreams. When there are enough dreams of the same thing, they coalesce into islands of reality— a forest of pines, for instance."

"So, we're just riding through peoples' dreams?" I suddenly had the uneasy feeling of being somewhere I shouldn't.

"The dreams of animals as well."

"What about the mist?" I asked.

"When two dream-islands meet, they merge, but the mist always hangs around the seams." He raised his palms and brought them together to illustrate the principle. "The pairings don't necessarily make sense in a conventional way. You might find a desert next to tundra."

I inhaled deeply, reevaluating all the scents around me. The cool mist felt alive as it drifted over my skin, and the soft undercurrent of magic thrummed in my bones. The place had a strange sense of familiarity, like returning to an old home or a half-remembered dream.

A little tension released from my shoulders.

Had I ever dreamed of these pines? Were any of my dreams here?

Eventually, the mist began to thin, revealing a gnarled pine forest with little underbrush. My wolf stirred, longing for a run, but it would have to wait.

I noticed several dark shapes in the forest ahead. "What are those?"

Wordlessly, Sarion turned his horse, and we headed toward them.

The shadows slowly resolved into forms that were all too familiar: crumbled buildings. Their roofs had collapsed inward, and trees grew up from inside. The walls had been scorched by fire, and charred beams and crushed furniture lay rotting within.

"The Dark Wolf God's fingerprints are everywhere," Sarion muttered.

My muscles tightened, and I glanced around, half expecting to see the monster himself lurking in the shadows.

We rode through the burned-out village. Its streets and open areas were layered in needles, but I saw the reflection of Magic Side beneath it all. A patch of white drew my attention: bleached bones entangled in the roots of a tree. My gut twisted. Sometimes, I forgot that we'd been the lucky ones—that we'd survived the Dark God's attacks and had been able to rebuild. Whoever the inhabitants here had been, they'd died where they lived.

"This place looks like a hurricane hit it," I murmured.

Sarion gave a sad smile and turned his horse. "The Dark Wolf God is a force of nature, but this is an old wound on the land. You'll see what his wrath truly looks like soon."

Blue sky emerged ahead of us as we approached the edge of a cliff. Sarion stopped his horse a few paces off, allowing me a moment to gaze out over the landscape.

A long wall of iridescent light cut through the snarled forest. It was like the northern lights, rising from the ground as far as I could see. On the far side, I saw three faint columns of light shooting into the heavens. They formed a shimmering dome of magic over the Dark God's lands, trapping him inside.

"You've seen this before?" Sarion asked.

My heart clenched, and I nodded. "Just from the ground. When my friend recharged the last of the pylons, the Dark God was pulled away from us. There's a big orb—the nexus of the Moon's power—at the base of each column of light, but I never saw the dome like this."

The scar on my arm grew tender at the memory. That was the day *he'd* marked me. The wound had taken a hell of a while to heal, and even now, phantom pain tormented me.

Sarion turned his horse to face me. "It's the only thing that stands between us and him. Unfortunately, the spell that the Moon created only prevents him from crossing the barrier. His magic and allies can get through."

"Is that how he's attacking your towns?"

Sarion circled his horse to my other side so we were looking out together. "Before you and your friends restored the binding spells, the wall had grown weak, and he could force his way into our lands. Now that it's been restored, it should stop him, but he's found a hole or a way to circumvent it. We're not sure. When he comes, he leaves no survivors."

Dread crept up my spine, followed by an uneasy feeling. My scar began to burn, and I swore I could feel someone watching me again.

It was all in my mind, wasn't it?

My pulse began to beat a little faster. "He can't get us here, can he?"

"You're safe," Sarion said, but his confidence didn't meet his eyes. He turned his horse and headed down the slope perpendicular to the cliff. "We're not far now. We should go."

I watched the barrier warily as we rode, as if the Dark God

himself would come barreling out, but nothing moved. The forest of green pines stopped when they reached the magical wall. On the Dark God's side, there was a sea of dead and dying trees. Some of the pines retained patches of brown needles, but most of the aspens and birch were black sticks, like they'd been consumed by wildfire.

"What's wrong with the woods across the barrier?" I asked.

Sarion's face hardened, and he kept his gaze on the forest ahead. "The Dark Wolf God's realm is a place of death."

The division couldn't have been clearer.

I glanced up as a hawk flew overhead, and Sarion followed my eyes.

"We need to get a move on." He urged his horse into a canter, and my mount followed in stride.

"Is something wrong?" Panic fluttered in my chest.

"It's probably just a hawk, but I'm always cautious. He uses animals as spies," the fae said over his shoulder.

I glanced back toward the barrier. "You said we were safe."

Sarion turned his horse. "We'll be safe as soon as we get to the town. I just have an uneasy feeling, and around here, I've learned to trust my gut."

An uneasy feeling.

"Up on the ridge, I felt like we were being watched. I still feel it, do you?"

"We can't take any chances. Let's go." Sarion pushed his horse to a gallop. "Next time you get a feeling, warn me."

I'd felt the same feeling before, for weeks now, the tingling sensation and phantom pain from my scar. Had the Dark God been watching me this whole time?

Terror rose in my chest, and I fought to draw in air. *Focus, Sam.* We needed to get out of here. I bent low in the saddle as the hooves of our horses ripped into the ground.

"Almost there!" Sarion shouted.

Blue sky peeked through the trees ahead, like a small beacon of hope.

Then it was gone.

In a blur of limbs, the pines in front of us crashed together, blocking the path. Sarion's stallion veered off to the left, but my horse reared back in surprise. I seized the saddle and clung on for life.

"Samantha!" he shouted.

One of the pines between us shook and then crashed to the ground. With a frightened whinny, my horse backed up. It was frothing at the mouth and had a wild look in its eyes.

I was definitely no longer in control.

All around us, the trees began tearing their roots free of the earth and advancing.

"What's happening, Sarion?" I shouted, as the pines closed in.

The fae turned his horse and raced to cut around, but the living pines quickly filled in the gaps between us. Black shadows snaked along the forest floor, and my stomach dropped.

Then I felt the rumbling power of an earthquake, and magic searing the air around me like wildfire. The Dark God was here.

I had to get away. I yanked my mount's head around and kicked her side. With a lurch, she bolted forward through the trees as a hawk screeched overhead.

Flailing roots and pine boughs tore at me from every direction, the needles scratching my bare skin and sap sticking to my arms. For a second, I glimpsed Sarion on the other side of the trees. Then agony erupted through my chest, and I flew from the saddle. The wind exploded from my lungs as I hit the hard earth, and I arched my back, gasping in pain.

I scrambled to my feet, but a root lashed out and caught my ankles. My chin ricocheted off the ground, and stars burst across my vision.

No. I wouldn't go down.

Dragging myself up, I dodged another root. "Sarion!"

But there was no response.

I prepared to shift into my wolf form, but before I could, my feet were yanked out from under me, and I crashed down on my ass. I screamed in pain and rage and caught the next root that came at me with my claws.

Then something wrapped around my ankle, and the forest became a blur.

Dozens of roots and vines reached out and began dragging me. My ass, head, and spine cracked against the uneven ground, and I screamed in terror.

I dug my claws into the dirt and roots, but everything either slipped through my fingers or gave way. Then, without warning, a bright light flooded my vision, and unbelievable warmth coursed through my body. Something about it felt familiar and reassuring.

Then the feeling was gone. I blinked and stared up at blue sky and dead pines. I was on the other side of the Moon's barrier. *His* side.

Every muscle and joint in my body screamed with pain, and the wound on my shoulder burned, but I found the strength to flip myself over and onto my knees.

The shimmering barrier of light rose not twenty feet away, and beyond it, a sea of green trees. The fae lands, but no sign of Sarion or anyone else.

A shadow stepped into view, and I looked up—the hulking werewolf from Deerhaven.

Fuck.

Before I could react, he seized me by my tattered jacket and heaved me to my feet. For one second, I caught his bitter smile, and then he spun me around to face evil itself—the Dark Wolf God.

My heart clenched with fear.

The Dark God's eyes blazed like sunlit glaciers, and his strong jaw was set with iron fury. The signature of his magic smelled smoky and roared in my ears like a storm wind through pines. His power quaked my bones, and I tasted bitter chocolate on my tongue. He was unbearably close.

Sweat glistened on the muscles of his bare arms, and intricate tattoos peeked out his sleeves, right above the bandage on his forearm. He was both impossibly beautiful and everything that I had come to hate in the world.

I trembled beneath the crush of power that pressed in on me from all sides, and I struggled to fill my lungs with air. There was no point or way for me to hide my terror. He was a god, a blazing sun, while I was little more than a drop of dew clinging to life.

I was as good as dead.

The Dark God fixed me with a glare. "I've been waiting for you, little wolf."

The words thundered through me—a condemnation, a decree of unworthiness in a single breath. But beneath it all, there was the sound of triumph.

My throat was too tight to swallow, but I met the Dark God's icy blue eyes and gritted my teeth. "Fuck you."

The corner of his mouth ticked up in an exultant smile, and when he spoke, his words crashed down on me like hammers on an anvil. "I promised that I would hunt you down and make you pay. Consider this a promise fulfilled."

He reached out and gently touched my cheek. "Sleep."

8

Samantha

I woke in darkness, and a tightness squeezed my chest.

The Dark God.

I eased my breathing and reined in my panic. I was alone. And alive. How?

Rolling onto my side, I groaned. Being alive was only a small mercy. Every part of me throbbed with pain, from the back of my head to the bottoms of my feet. It wasn't all that surprising, since I'd been dragged two hundred yards by the roots of some not-so-gentle trees. At least it didn't feel like any bones were broken.

Something cold and heavy hung around my wrists. I reached forward, and chains jingled. Great, manacles. I was a prisoner.

Grunting with full-body discomfort, I sat up and slumped against the muddy wall. This was definitely a new low. Worse, I'd been so ashamed of my old life and how I'd grown up that I hadn't told anyone my destination, only that I'd be away.

I'm such an idiot.

My mother wouldn't know what to do. If she went to

Wyland, he'd laugh in her face. The truth was, I was on my own. But why was I alive?

I began to imagine the vindictive things the Dark God might do, but I clamped down on those thoughts. In the dark, imagination was the enemy.

I licked my parched lips. "Is anyone there?"

Silence.

I tried shifting into a wolf, but the manacles around my wrist began to tingle, searing my skin the more I strained to force the transformation. They were Magicuffs, designed to stop the use of magic. So much for that plan.

Thanks to my werewolf senses, my eyes were adjusting slightly to the nothingness around me, but they were still of little use. The air was damp, and water dripped nearby.

I rose and stumbled forward until I ran into an iron door with a small window. I was chained and caged like a feral animal.

I banged my cuffs on the unyielding metal. "Hello? Is someone there?"

After a few minutes of shouting, light appeared, and a man stepped into view. The torchlight cast shadows over his blond hair, sharp features, and fangs.

Vampire.

He wasn't alone. I caught the scent of the werewolf who'd tried to abduct me in Deerhaven.

The vampire grinned. "You seem to be in a predicament."

I grasped the bars. "I haven't done anything. Release me, please."

"We're not the ones to ask for that favor. But we'll take you to him," the vampire said, and chuckled.

Three metallic *thunks* echoed from the door, and then it swung open.

They were just silhouettes in the darkness. While the

wolfman was built like a brick house, the vampire was tall, lean, and lethal. He flashed me a grin that revealed his deadly incisors. "Something tells me you're going to try to do this the hard way."

He was right.

I fought and scratched as the vampire and werewolf dragged me along the hall and then up a flight of stairs. Soon, I began to feel the low rumble of *his* power and hear the wind blowing through pines—his signature.

My captors dragged me into a massive hall illuminated by floating lights. The roof was held aloft by two rows of enormous trees, their thick trunks covered with midnight bark. Their roots wove across the floor, while their limbs supported the rafters. They even had leaves. How was that possible?

From the sides of the hall, the musky scent of men and animals bombarded me—shifters of every kind: wolf, fox, owl, and more. Their gazes seared into me, but I didn't dare look to the sides. My eyes were fixed on the scene ahead.

The Dark God loomed before me at the end of the hall, perched on a throne of white-tipped antlers and bone. His eyes burned with icy blue light, cold and bitter and filled with hate. Stubble covered the sharp angles of his jaw, and the intricate tattoos on his forearms blazed with brilliant white fire.

My stomach tightened with despair. I stood before a god. His power pressed in around me, unimaginable as the sea. My lungs clenched, and I was certain that if I opened my mouth, I would drown. Yet I couldn't bring myself to look away from him—he drew my attention with an irresistible force.

My heart rammed against my chest. *Fates, I'm screwed.*

The wolf and the vampire released me, and I dropped to my hands and knees. For five longs breaths, I waited in terror.

At last, the Dark God spoke. His voice rumbled so low that it made my bones hurt. "I've shown you mercy because you are one of us, a shifter born. But you helped to bind me in this place, and you've been conspiring with the enemies of our realm. You are a traitor to your kind."

"Fuck that."

The Dark God leaned forward. "What did you tell the fae?"

I summoned every ounce of hate I had in my soul and hurled it at him with a biting glare. "That you're a fucking monster."

He smiled and leaned back, showing only the sinister curl of his lip. He flipped his hand, and dark tendrils of shadow wrenched me to my feet and then up into the air. I struggled against his magic, but it held me more securely than if I'd been stretched between iron shackles hanging from the walls.

The Dark God slowly rose from his throne and approached. The shadows and torchlight played over his form as he descended the stairs, highlighting the curve and strength of every muscle. He was what humans were meant to be; the men I'd met before were little more than poor copies. My mouth went dry as a damp heat spread through me, and I despised him for it. It was sheer madness, like longing for a train as it barreled down on you.

He circled me with predatory precision—each move deliberate and lethal. I struggled in my invisible bonds, the rising beat of my heart thundering in my ears.

"Samantha," he purred, testing my name on his tongue. "I know you've been meeting with the fae. What did they want from you?"

Hatred boiled up in my chest, and I clamped my jaw shut. I'd never tell this bastard anything.

He stepped unbearably close, and his aura burned my clammy skin. If my hands had been free, I would have clawed out his throat. But they weren't, and no amount of force seemed able to budge them, so I spat in his face. "You tried to destroy my city and forced my best friend to attack me. She almost *killed* me. I'm not telling you shit."

The Dark God's iron expression wavered, looking almost pained for a second—then it reset, harder than before. "I don't wish to compel you, little wolf, but my realm is at stake. You will tell me everything they told or asked of you."

His presence crushed in like an avalanche of concrete and steel. And even though a part of my mind tried to flee into darkness, his magic compelled the words to pour from my mouth, practically tripping over each other in their rush to get out.

I told him about Sarion, reciting every word we'd exchanged. Guilt and shame heated my neck, but I couldn't stop myself.

The Dark God stalked around me. "The fae wanted you because you'd wounded and trapped me with that magic of yours?"

"But I didn't!" I gasped. "I don't have any magic. I'm nothing, no one."

"That's not true," he snarled.

The speed and conviction in his words stunned me. Did he know something I didn't?

When I tried to read his expression, he looked away. "If you were *just* a wolf, the fae wouldn't have bothered with you."

I hung my head. "It was the Moon's magic—I had her moonstone, and I threw it. I didn't know what would happen."

His face darkened. "Then tell me about the Moon Goddess and her magic."

Shit. Was he going to make me betray everyone I'd ever met —or just the ones he was planning to kill? What truth could I give him that wouldn't harm her?

"According to our loremaster, the legends say that you were going to the destroy the world, so the Moon got you drunk on water from the river of dreams. Then she trapped you, and you've been stuck here ever since."

The Dark God gave a warning growl that sent terror racing down my spine. It wasn't the growl of a werewolf, but of something ancient—a monster that had survived and killed and hunted in the shadows of eons.

"I don't care about your fucking legends—they're just lies that have grown old. She betrayed me and left me here to rot. Was she the one that sent you?"

I tried to resist, but his power pressed in on me. "She warned us that the spells that bound you were weakening, and that we had to restore them. She gave us moonstones that were filled with magic—" I swallowed. "One of which I threw at you."

He flexed his hand and glanced down at his arm as another feral growl escaped his throat. "Why did she not repair them herself?"

His magic dug into my chest like a spike, and I blurted, "As long as you're trapped, she can't enter the Dreamlands. She's holding the door shut from the outside—at least that's how she explained it."

His eyes took on a distant expression, and my stomach curdled. Apparently, I'd just ponied up an important bit of information.

Fuck.

I needed to shut up, before I betrayed anyone else.

9

Cadean

Samantha hung in the air before me, suspended by tendrils of my shadow magic. Her eyes shone like hatred compressed to diamonds, while the fine lines of her defiant jaw were complemented by those damned alluring lips. My eyes drifted from her mouth down her elegant neck to the sheen of sweat that covered her heaving chest.

Whatever she believed, she was not simply a wolf. She was brave and strong and had a power racing through her, like wildfire just beneath her skin.

A reckless part of me wanted to reach out and touch the flames, but I fought down the urge. Not while she was bound before me. It wasn't right.

I tore my eyes away, yet I could still smell her sweet honey scent, and it clouded my thoughts.

I steeled myself against her intoxicating pull. I had to keep my mind clear. She'd just confirmed what I'd hoped was true—the Moon couldn't enter the Dreamlands. She couldn't repair the spells that bound me and had to rely on others. Had she taught them the intricacies of her magic? Could they reverse what they'd done?

I bent my head close to Samantha's ear. "You helped restore the spells imprisoning me. Can you release me?"

"I would rather die." Her voice was pure fucking smoke, and the malice that hung onto every word taunted me.

My fists tightened. "That can be arranged."

The she-wolf had plenty of fight, I'd give her that. And I liked a good fight.

I stepped back as fury heated my blood. "You and your allies altered the spells that form my prison. What did you do? Why is my domain shrinking?"

A flicker of surprise flashed in her eyes. "We didn't change anything. We just recharged the Moon's pylons."

She had to know something. I unleashed a wave of magic to compel obedience. "Tell me the truth, little wolf!"

"I am," she gasped. "I have no idea how any of this works! I'm a werewolf, not a sorceress, or can't you fucking tell?"

As the reverberations of her voice died away, we glared at each other in intractable silence. Finally, I released my hold over her. Breathing hard, I stepped back as a heavy weight settled on me.

She was speaking the truth. She knew nothing.

Fuck.

Then why did the fae send someone after her? Was she hiding something, or harboring powers she didn't realize she had? Or perhaps they'd also succumbed to a beautiful illusion.

Frustration lashed at me. There was something more to her. I could feel it, something hidden and deep. I closed my eyes and reached out with my magic, searching for a clue, but it was like a dream that slipped away on waking.

Whatever her secret was, I was certain the safety of my realm depended on learning it. If the fae thought they could get something useful out of her, so could I.

I released the spell holding her aloft.

The moment her feet touched the ground, her knees buckled. Slowly and hatefully, she pulled herself upright and glared back at me. "I've told you everything I know. Don't you ever use your magic to compel me to speak again."

I despised myself for using it, but she was my enemy, and my realm was in danger. The muscles of my neck tensed as I stared down at her. "And what if I do?"

"Don't." Her voice was iron, and I had to hide my approval.

Everything about her screamed strength: the way she carried herself wounded, the lean curves of her muscles, and the unyielding anger in her eyes. Yet as much as she hated me, I was bewitched by her presence.

I tore my gaze away. The woman was confusing my mind—a danger I couldn't risk. I motioned to Wulfric and Kassian. "Throw her back in the cell. I'll come for her later."

I turned my back and walked to my throne, though I didn't sit.

The she-wolf kicked and screamed curses at me as they hauled her away. Her pleas were like knives piercing my skin, and I pressed my palm against the point of the antler to stifle the guilt. The irony of it burned within me. All beasts deserved freedom. Didn't I know that better than anyone?

Snarling, I shoved the glimmer of regret away. My realm came first. I couldn't release the she-wolf until I was certain she wasn't a threat.

I stormed from the hall as my sorceress, Melanthe, stepped from the shadows. She fell in beside me as we headed toward my tower, her sweeping red dress brushing the floor with a soft hiss.

"What do you think?" I asked.

"She knows nothing. Considering how hard you pushed, I think we can be certain of that much, don't you?"

I stopped and growled low. "The fae would have pushed her harder if they'd thought she was a threat. They would have peeled the skin from her muscles until there was nothing left to hold her insides in."

Mel gave me a wry smile. "Feeling a little defensive, are we, Cadean? A little guilty, perhaps?"

I started walking again. "I will do whatever I must to protect this realm."

Mel tossed her hair. "Well, luckily, no one has to have their skin peeled. The girl was speaking the truth. She knows nothing of the spells that wounded or imprisoned you. Either the fae are wrong about her, or they didn't tell her the real reason they wanted her."

I released a bitter laugh. "They would never tell her. They play games with words, spinning truths into lies. They must know something. Though she may not realize it, she has power, I can feel it."

"Then how do we learn her secret?" Mel asked.

"We think of better questions." I paused at the entrance to the stairwell. "And if she's of any value, the fae will send someone to recover her. We wait, strike, and interrogate. If no one comes, then we send out warriors to seize members of the court until we find someone who knows something."

"If we start abducting nobles, the fae will increase the raids," Mel whispered.

"They'll do it anyway." I turned and stormed toward the wall. Two of the massive roots parted, revealing a hidden stairwell.

A thousand thoughts whirled in my mind as I ascended the staircase into the tower, but they left me no closer to any answers. As soon as I reached a window, I paused.

The Dreamlands stretched out before me. Far in the

distance, the ethereal walls of my prison flickered like an aurora. Beyond the border were the fae lands. One day, I'd be free of my chains, and I'd grind their kingdom to dust.

I stepped back, then hurled myself through the open window.

Wind whipped at me as I plunged downward along the face of the tower. I closed my eyes and let the spirits of the earth flicker through my thoughts.

Wolf. Stag. Lion. Eagle.

I seized that last form with my mind as my body burst into tendrils of shadow. I wove them back together, taking the form of a giant black eagle, and I soared into the sky. The joy of the form filled me as it did every time I shifted. Sun warmed my back as my lands raced by below.

I shot skyward along the face of my tower, and when I passed the tip, I began to count my wingbeats. One. A hundred. A thousand. Each beat drove me toward the infinite, shimmering sky.

Then a crackling wave of magic and agony raced over me as I slammed into the invisible barrier of my prison walls. I screeched in rage and fought to break through the dome of magic that covered my lands, but the harder I pushed, the stronger it became.

Fuck the Moon and her magic.

My ascent to the edge of the barrier had taken one less wingbeat than yesterday. Four less than the week before. Gradually, day by day, hour by hour, my invisible prison was shrinking.

The she-wolf and her allies had changed something. I needed to find out what it was before there was nothing left of my realm.

10

———

I fought back as my escorts, Fang and Wolfman, hauled me back down to the prison.

Finally, the vampire stopped short and spun around. He gripped the chain that hung between my cuffs and jerked me close. "Shut up and act civilized, for fates' sake. You are going back to your cell whether you like it or not, and I don't want to have to break your legs. Show some pride and come quietly."

I slammed my head forward. His nose made a sickening crunch as it shattered. The vampire shouted in surprise, and joy flared in my chest.

"Now I'll come quietly," I said.

Rage flashed across the vampire's face, but Wolfman gripped his companion's shoulder. "Cadean wouldn't want her hurt."

Fang pulled out of Wolfman's grip and glared at me. "He's obsessed."

Who the hell was Cadean? And what obsession?

Dread sank into my bones, and I allowed myself to be led down the halls. To distract myself from my increasingly dire plight, I counted my steps and took note of each twist and turn.

It was unlikely that I'd ever have a chance of getting out, but it paid to be prepared.

Fang shoved me from behind. "Keep moving and stop dragging your feet. I see you looking around every corner."

Dammit.

"How does everyone here speak English?" I deflected, my mood souring.

The vampire laughed with a sneer. "It's not English. It's dreamspeech—the language of intention. You just hear English because that's what you expect to hear."

I glanced back. "So how do you understand me? I don't know dreamspeech."

Only English and a slew of French curse words.

Wolfman's gaze softened. "You're speaking it now. You've known it since the first dream you ever had. While language tears your world apart, it's what holds ours together."

Had I really been dreaming in a different language my entire life?

At last, we came to a stop, and Fang flung the door to my cell open. It wasn't so much a prison cell as a cave gated off by an iron door. The torchlight reflected off root-covered walls, pale stalagmites, and a glistening blue pool.

"Your god has a strange idea of a jail cell," I muttered.

Fang shoved me hard from behind, and I stumbled through. "The Dark Wolf God has little use for prisoners. Consider it a custom conversion just for you."

A burlap sack landed by my feet, and then the door slammed shut.

I spun around. "Hold on! Aren't you going to let me out of these cuffs? It's not like I'm going anywhere."

The vampire tapped beside his nose. "I think you've demonstrated that you're going to make trouble. Consider them a precaution."

Shit.

I thrust my hands out. "Look, I'm sorry I hit you. I just have a thing about men hauling me around against my will. If you let me go, I promise not to bite."

"Yes, but I don't," the vampire said sharply. After a moment's hesitation, he slipped a key from his pocket and tossed it. "Catch."

It glinted in the air. I jumped for it, but my feet slipped on the smooth limestone floor, and the key deflected off the tip of my finger. It pinged off the ground and disappeared into the blue pool with a plunk.

Oh, hell, no.

I crawled over to the edge of the pool and began searching the shallows. "Where did it go?"

When I turned back, my captors were gone. I moaned in despair. "You've got to be fucking kidding me."

But no one was kidding. I was locked in a dank cave in the Dreamlands, the prisoner of the Dark Wolf God himself.

I must have really pissed off the fates. Maybe it was all the cursing. At least the assholes had left the torch, so I had some light.

First step was finding the key. With a grunt of annoyance, I sat down and yanked off my boots, then rolled up the cuffs of my jeans.

The pool filled a cleft in the limestone, and bioluminescent lichen covered the walls that weren't touched by the light. The pool was crystal clear, but it got deep quickly. The torchlight shone through the upper water, but below was darkness.

I shivered. *Super creepy.*

I dipped a toe in and sucked in a sharp gasp. It was also frigid. Wading into the water, I began searching the shallows for the silver key. I'd heard the plunk. It had to be somewhere.

Torchlight glinted off the surface, fooling my eyes again and again.

Soon, my feet were aching, and the limestone rocks underfoot felt like daggers under my frozen skin. As desperation sank in, I plunged my hands into the icy water and began flipping over stones. Sediment clouded the water, and after a couple of minutes, my fingers had gone numb, and I couldn't see anything. With a grunt of frustration and despair, I scrambled out of the pool.

"How about just a little help here?" I shouted to the dark ceiling above me.

No response.

Hands trembling with cold, I pulled open the burlap bag they'd left. Bread and hard sausage. At least they weren't trying to starve me. Yet. I flopped down with the bag in the corner of the cave, tore off a chunk of bread, and started chewing. It wasn't stale, so that was a plus.

I let my head thump back against the cave wall. "What the hell are you going to do now, Sam?"

No one was coming for me, so I was on my own. With the magic cuffs on, I wasn't going to be able to fight or claw my way out, so I had to get them off first. That meant going for a swim or making friends with Fang, the sadistic vampire. Neither was appetizing, but I'd do what I had to.

I glanced at the iron door set in the limestone wall. The reality was that I could daydream all I wanted, but my prospects for escape were dismal. I'd have to get out of the cell, evade the guards, escape the Dark God's fortress, navigate unfamiliar territory, and find a way out of the Dreamlands. The unsettling truth was glaringly obvious—I was going to have to convince the Dark God to let me go.

I took an irritated bite of the sausage. "Well, the good news is, you're not dead. Yet."

Apparently, he wanted me alive—at least for the moment. If my capture had just been about revenge, he would have killed me or tortured me, and gotten it over with. He'd wanted information about the fae, the prison the Moon had created, and the magic I'd used to attack him. Unfortunately, I didn't know jack shit about *any* of those things, so I couldn't trade information for my freedom.

The memory of his presence pressing into me chilled me to the bone. *He could just take whatever I knew, anyway.*

What did I have that he needed? The answer was *nothing*.

With a heavy sigh, I bundled up the bag of bread and meat for later. I was screwed, so I guessed praying wouldn't hurt.

Resting my head back against the wall, I closed my eyes. "Hey, there, Moon Goddess. I don't know how this works, or if you can hear me, but it's Sam. I'm trapped in the Dreamlands, and I'd really, really like it if you could help get me out of here. P.S.: My captor is the Dark God, and I get why you locked him away. He's an asshole."

I felt a little sheepish. I hadn't even really believed in the Moon Goddess until I met her in person a month ago. She was everything I wished I could be—beautiful, charming, powerful, and filled with radiant magic that had made me feel alive.

She also hated the Dark God and was the one responsible for trapping him in the Dreamlands ages ago, so if any god was going to help me out, it would be her.

Unsurprisingly, there was no immediate miracle. To be fair, it was a shitty prayer, but I didn't have much experience praying for things. I usually just bet on myself to get out of a jam. Unfortunately, this time, I was all out of chips.

I curled up in the corner of the cell, watching the dying torchlight flicker over the bright blue pool. After driving all day, fighting a handful of werewolves, riding through the Dreamlands and being dragged by my ankles through a forest, I was beyond exhausted.

If nothing else, I could sleep and heal. Maybe if I was lucky, I'd wake up back in Magic Side, and everything would have been a bad dream.

11

Cadean

The fae came for her three days later.

The first sign was a sentry murdered deep within my land. Then another.

I knelt by the third wolf the intruder had killed. His body was still warm, and a slender fae arrow protruded from his throat. Although the shot had silenced the wolf, the trail of blood crossing the glen meant he'd dragged himself to the base of the tree.

Had he charged his attacker with his dying breath?

I dipped my fingers in the blood seeping from the wound in the wolf's neck. *Very warm.* But I'd been too late to save him. I fought down the rage boiling inside of me and reached forward to close his eyes. "Rest. You belong to the ghost pack now."

Wulfric released a low and ominous growl, but I held up my hand to silence the large silver and black wolf beside me. "The wound is fresh, and the killer is close."

Despite my keen senses, I couldn't detect his scent, but a miasma of death clung to him like the stink of a rendering floor

—something that went beyond smell and could never be washed away.

I rose and scanned the clearing for signs of the intruder's passing.

My wolves patrolled in pairs, sometimes with mates. This one was dead, but there was another still out there. If I moved quickly, perhaps I could save her.

"Stay here until I summon you," I whispered. Wulfric bared his teeth but submitted.

I rose and headed into the forest.

The hunter had passed through my lands like a ghost, killing, then melting into the trees. Though his path had been circuitous, his destination was clear. My citadel.

After half a mile, I caught the scent of the other sentry. Was the killer close, stalking her?

I paused and listened. Silence. But that silence betrayed him.

Despite the gentle wind curling through the forest, a narrow swath of trees was still, and the birds among their branches didn't cry out. They were my hidden watchers, reporting his movements by ceasing theirs—a silent alarm that stretched across my lands and would lead me straight to him.

Now I was the hunter.

I moved quickly and quietly. He probably had a transport charm, and if he caught sight of me, he'd teleport back to his realm. So rather than moving as a man or wolf, I used my power to shadow-walk, blinking between the dark shade of one tree and the next.

I found the intruder creeping slowly through the misty woods. His movements were as precise and silent as the trail of death he'd left in his wake. The brush around him didn't rustle, and the dead leaves didn't scuff beneath his feet.

A master hunter, he'd even masked the stench of his fae

aroma with magic and scents of my forest—but both the forest and I knew he did not belong here.

Light brown fur flashed between the trees in the distance. The other sentry. The intruder raised his bow and nocked an arrow, preparing to take another life from me.

I shadow-stepped to a nearby tree, allowing me to see his profile. He had auburn hair and sharp features. The glint in his eyes didn't change as he aimed. There was no flicker of compassion for his prey, a child of my forest.

I would show no compassion either.

With a nod of my head, I commanded the white oak beside him. *Protect.*

Before the fae could release his arrow, the ancient tree whipped one of its heavy limbs down into the hunter's back, driving him to the dirt. The arrow whistled through the air, but the wolf bolted, and the shot flew wide of its mark.

The intruder's right hand flew to his belt pouch, but I leapt from the shadows and ripped it away. Grunting, he rolled over and thrust out his hands. A blast of magic seared my skin, but I gritted my teeth and drove my fist into his face.

"Bind and gag him!" I commanded the tree.

Roots surged from the ground all around the intruder, winding around his limbs and pinning him to the earth. He struggled and cursed as they spiraled up around his neck and choked his mouth until moans and grunts were the only sounds he could make.

The light brown wolf rushed to my side. She snarled and brought her teeth within an inch of the fae's face.

"You were lucky, friend," I said to the wolf as I crouched beside her. "But your partner was not."

The wolf's eyes widened, and she searched my face for the meaning of my words. When she found the truth, she choked out a mournful sound.

I ran my hand across her fur. "It's not your fault."

The wolf staggered away from my touch and gave a broken howl.

My arms quaked as a black and blinding rage poured through my heart. I wanted to become death and fall on the fae with fangs and savage claws. I wanted to pour my power over the border and stifle every one of the bastards.

One day.

But for now, I needed information. I wrestled my fury into submission and stripped him of his weapons. A sword. A dagger that thrummed with foul fae magic. Even two knives that he'd slipped into his boots. His pouch had a transport charm—probably what he had been reaching for—as well as lock picks, a garrote, and several unmarked vials. I popped the lid off one. Poison.

Not a hunter. An assassin.

Wulfric and three of his wolf warriors rushed into the clearing, summoned by the light brown wolf's howls.

I gestured to the bound bastard. "Is this the fae who tried to recruit that mortal woman?"

Wulfric dipped his head to sniff the intruder, then gave a low warning growl, his lips curling back from his fangs. *Yes.*

I ripped the ball of roots from my adversary's mouth. "What did you want with Samantha?"

The fae spat but didn't try to utter a spell. He grinned. "I don't know what you're talking about. Who's Samantha? I was just out looking for a couple of nice pelts."

I pulled my axe from its beltloop and used the blade to raise his chin. "Don't play fucking games. What is she? Why does she matter?"

He twisted to pull away from the blade. "Steady there. She's a bartender or pit fighter or kind of both. I'm not entirely sure."

I stepped back and let my presence blast into him—divine

willpower fueled by millennia of belief. The earth shook like it'd been struck by a falling oak, and the breath burst from my prisoner's chest. "You will only speak the truth."

My power burned away his will until submission finally glistened in his eyes. "Why do you want her?"

He choked beneath the onslaught of magic. "My queen sent me."

Queen Ayanna, ruler of the Undying Court. I twisted my hand to tighten the vines around him. "Why is the girl important?"

"I don't know, I swear!"

Truth. I could taste it on the air.

I pushed against his will until I found a glint of what I was searching for: the trace of a spell, emblazoned on his mind. "Did you know why she was important once? When you went to recruit the woman?"

Doubt flickered in his eyes, and he gritted his teeth. "I don't know... maybe."

I released my power and turned to Wulfric. "They've gated his memories with a spell. Melanthe will break it, and then we'll break him. Take him back to Shadowstone."

The silver-black wolf growled menacingly at the fae.

While my wolves guarded him, I searched the woods for his arrow. The reek of fae scent from his fingers clung to it, and it wasn't long before I'd traced it to a patch of overgrowth. I pulled the arrow out and examined the tip. Obsidian. I sniffed it, and my suspicions deepened. No trace of the poison in the vial, which meant it wasn't for taking out my sentries. Had he reserved that for breaking into my tower?

An irrational fury settled in my gut.

Was there a chance that the poison had been meant for the feisty she-wolf? He'd tried to recruit her once. If he'd failed to rescue her from my tower, was he supposed to take her out? The only reason to do that would be if she were a threat to the Undying Court or a boon to me. Might she have the power to heal me? Or even release my bonds?

My fist clenched. Even if that were true, she'd never agree to help.

12

Samantha

Splash.

I bolted upright and looked around. The day's torch had gone out, and the eerie light of bioluminescent moss revealed I was still in the godsdamned cave. Apparently, I was still a prisoner, and my abduction wasn't just a convoluted nightmare.

Fuck.

There was no sense of time in the cave. I'd suspected several days had passed, but the meals were irregular, and the guards that brought them never spoke.

I looked around, peering through the dim chamber. I'd heard a noise—had it been one of the guards?

A knot formed in my stomach, and I scrambled to my feet. The pool was black, but I could just make out a ripple. A shiver skated down my spine, and I was glad that I hadn't dived down to search for the key. Was it a fish? Or the probing tentacle of a horrific cave monster?

Please just be a rock falling from the ceiling.

When nothing in the water moved, I inspected the rest of my

cell for any sign of disturbance. The pit of my stomach dropped. My bag of food was gone, and in its place was a silver key.

My heart began beating double-time. Someone had swapped them while I was sleeping.

It couldn't have been Fang or Wulfric or even the Dark God—I would have heard the door. The tiny hairs on my arm rose as I turned in a circle. "Is someone there?"

I sniffed the air: nothing but the scent of the cave.

With a trembling hand, I grabbed the key and wedged it into the lock on the cuff of my manacles. It didn't turn at first, but at last, there was a metallic *snick*, and the metal band around my wrist parted. I shook my aching hand free, then unlocked my other wrist.

The manacles clattered to the ground, and the magic that had been restraining my wolf dissipated. It was like sucking in a gasp of air after too long underwater, and I immediately extended my fangs and claws. My magic raced through me, and I had to fight off the urge to shift right then and there. "Holy fates, I'm free."

Well, not *free* free, but fucking free enough. Had my half-assed prayer to the Moon Goddess actually worked?

"Thank you," I whispered, just in case.

I gave my wrists a shake, then searched again for any sign of the intruder. If they hadn't come through the door, there must be another way in.

The pond? Did the crack lead to another chamber? If there was a passage, could I find it if I could fit through—and crucially, not drown? Cave diving was a great way to die, and the last thing I wanted to do was jump in and get trapped in an underwater system.

But it was something, at least.

I went to the door and started clawing at the rock around the edges. Although it was soft, it quickly became apparent that I would reduce my claws and fingers to bloody stubs before I could make any progress.

I wasn't sure how long I'd slept, but I was famished. After I rinsed my hands, I pounded on the door. "Anyone out there? The least you assholes could do is bring me some more food. I'm a werewolf, for fates' sake. We get hungry!"

No response.

Apparently, if there were guards out there, they weren't bothered by my shouting or the sounds of digging. That meant I had a little privacy.

Unable to wait any longer, I stripped off my clothes and shifted. My back arched, muscles stretched, and bones snapped. Fur erupted across my skin. Within a few glorious seconds, I was a wolf again. My true form. The way I had been born.

I shook my fur out and stretched my aching limbs.

Nose to the ground, I investigated every corner of the cave. There wasn't any scent of prior occupation. It seemed that Fang had been telling the truth: the Dark God hadn't used the room as a cell before—or not for a very long time. I investigated the edge of the pool but didn't venture in. There was a different scent leading out of the water to where my bag had been. Kind of fishy.

Please don't let it be a tentacle monster.

Eventually, I gave up searching, shifted back, and put my clothes on.

Now what?

Shifting had used up a lot of my strength. It had been worth it, but with no prospect of an immediate meal, I'd need to conserve energy. With nothing else to do, I laid back down and fixed my eyes on the pool.

Nothing moved in the eerie light, and soon, I began to drowse.

Clink. Clunk.

My eyes shot open, but I didn't move a muscle. Something was in the room with me.

Pulse racing, I slowly turned my head.

About eight feet away, there was a bald little creature with gray-green skin. Less than two feet tall and dressed in trousers and a tunic, the creature had a huge nose, wonky fangs, and beady little eyes that glinted in the faint phosphorescence of the cave. The thing was so ugly, it was almost cute. A goblin?

He was gingerly lifting my manacles off the ground, link by link.

I fought down the urge to leap up and grab him. The gobbo obviously knew a way in and out of my cell, and maybe he could help me escape. More than anything, I needed to make friends.

"You brought me the key, didn't you?" I asked, heart pounding.

The goblin jumped back and clutched the manacles to his chest.

I sat up and stretched out my hand. "Don't be afraid. I want to thank you for helping me."

He bared his horrid little teeth and backed up, dragging the heavy manacles with him. But he didn't flee into the water. That was something.

I gave him the warmest smile I could muster. "I'm trapped and locked in here. Do you know a way out?"

The creature just glared at me with abject hatred.

"Did you come in through the water?" I asked, pointing to the pond.

He shook his head and shivered. Apparently, he understood human speech.

"What about the door? Did you come through there?"

He shook his head again. Well, shit. "You found my key and took my food. Why?"

As the goblin held up the manacles, he pulled a large fish from the pouch at his side. He raised one, then the other.

"You wanted to trade?"

He threw the fish to me. It slapped across the stone floor, still gasping. Had he heard my shouting? My heartbeat accelerated as my brain spun with the possibilities.

"Look, thank you, but I don't need a fish. I need a way out. If I give you the manacles, can you find the key to this door?"

He clutched the manacles tighter, raised two fingers, and then pointed to the fish.

"I don't need two fish, I need—"

His head whipped around, and his eyes widened. With an alarmed yelp, he vanished into thin air.

Holy crap. Could he teleport? It would explain how he got in and out. That could be very useful if my new friend ever returned.

But what had I done to frighten him?

I started to rise, and then I felt *his* presence roaring down the hall like a rogue wave. The scent of fire and the rush of wind in the pines. The taste of chocolate, bitter on my tongue. The scar on my shoulder tingled, and then burned.

The Dark God was coming for me.

The wave of his power pushed me step by step until my back was pressed against the wall. Panic tightened my chest, and I struggled to draw a breath.

Light filled the hallway, and a large shadow moved in front of the door. The lock clicked, and my pulse raced as the door swung wide, revealing the silhouette of a god. What did he want?

My throat went tight, leaving my voice paralyzed. All thoughts I had of bargaining with him dissipated into nothingness. It didn't matter. There was nothing I could say to change his mind about what he was going to do, whether it was to kill or torture me or... I didn't dare consider what else. My screams for help wouldn't matter.

He stepped into the cell but left the door open.

I could run, but of course, the god would be faster. The truth was that he was the door and the key. There was no escaping except through him.

Sucking in an unsteady breath, I mustered my courage. "Why am I here? I've told you everything I know. Please let me go."

A muscle in his jaw ticked. "You helped restore the walls of my prison, little wolf. So long as I remain trapped in the Dream-lands, so will you."

My gut sank. That meant forever. The rest of my life, spent in a dark cave. A life without feeling the sun or the breeze or being able to run among the trees.

Fury heated my neck. "This cell isn't the same thing at all. You're free to breathe fresh air and can see the sky. The Moon didn't take that from you."

His lip curled and the muscles of his shoulders tightened with restrained fury. "I've been trapped more than a thousand years. No mortal can comprehend what *you* took from me when you denied me my freedom."

"I can't free you, and I can't tell you how to get free. Keeping me imprisoned in this lightless cave serves no purpose. So if you value freedom as much as you claim, then you should let me go. I have far fewer years to spare."

For a second, I thought I saw doubt flicker in his eyes. Then it was gone, replaced by ice and steel.

He slowly unwrapped the cloth strips that wound around his right arm. "When you attacked me with your magic, you gave me this wound."

His voice was laced with a viciousness that made my insides want to crawl out, and I understood why, when I glanced down at the wound. His skin was scarred as if by fire and covered with blue tendrils that glowed in the darkness of the room. It was a curse, with a strange ethereal magic that I didn't recognize.

I met his eyes. "Does it hurt?"

"Intensely," he growled.

I thought of all the people he'd killed and the ruined buildings of Magic Side. I thought of the wound he'd given me, and even though terror clawed at my chest, I couldn't help the smile that formed. "Good."

The Dark God's gaze didn't waver from mine. "Can you heal it?"

"No. I told you, it's the Moon's magic."

He stepped forward, and my heart pounded so hard, I felt it in my temples. I was inches from the Dark fucking Wolf God. His power thrummed around me and through me, and my nerves exploded with a kaleidoscope of sensations—heat, terror, and an overwhelming sense of him being beyond human. A divine being. A god. His presence was so intense it was almost pleasurable, like the rush of falling through the sky.

He placed his hand against the wall and bent his head close to mine. "I've been trapped here for centuries by the Moon's magic, and I know it as well as my own. This was you. What did you do to me, little wolf?"

The warmth of his breath on my neck sent goosebumps rippling over my skin, and I shuddered, fighting the delight that I somehow felt. I raised my chin in defiance. "I did less than you deserve."

With a brutally swift motion, the Dark God shoved away from the wall and stalked to the other end of my cell. He was a shadow only, which made him only more terrifying to behold. "You have no idea of the harm you've caused."

"The first time we met you *nearly killed me*. The second, you gave me scars that still haven't gone away." I pulled the edge of my jacket back, revealing my shoulder.

His eyes drifted down, and my scars tingled beneath his gaze. He stepped forward and reached out his hand. I flinched and he hesitated. "May I see?"

There was almost guilt in his eyes, but I doubted the monster could feel anything, and if he could, I prayed that the guilt would eat him from the inside out.

His fingers hovered over the scars, almost as if he was reticent to touch me. I could feel the heat of his hand above my skin. The millimeters between us sparked with electricity, and my nerves were suddenly so sensitive, I could feel every piece of fabric that I wore dragging over me like sandpaper.

We hovered there, his hand a finger's breath from my skin. Not the hand of a man, but of a god. I could feel the magnetic pull of his power, and my breathing hastened. His scent, his power, everything about him was too much to process. They filled me with a fear that was too close to desire.

Sucking in a sharp breath, I stepped away, pulling my jacket back over my shoulder. "Those scars are nothing compared to the people I lost, so I have no pity for you or your realm. I hope your wound drives you out of your mind. I hope the suffering never ends."

His face was a mask of cold fury.

For a long moment in which I didn't dare breathe, the Dark God studied my face with a gaze that felt like the hammer of judgment. "You despise me so much, yet you'd help the fae—the sick bastards who are killing my land and people."

The disdain in his voice heated my neck, and my claws extended. "You're the sick bastard. You would've destroyed Magic Side if we hadn't stopped you. Our legends—"

"Fuck your legends!"

I flinched at the force of his words. I kept my head turned

away, but I still spoke, defying his attempt to silence me. "You would have devastated our world, just like this one. I saw the ruined village along the border and the desolation of your magic corrupting everything on your side of the Moon's barrier. You're a monster, and you deserve to be bound until the end of time."

He circled me with predatory steps, backing me away from the wall and up against the edge of the glistening pool. "Is that what they told you? That the blight is mine?"

When I didn't speak, he continued. "The fae lie. They're deceivers, bending truths to fit their needs. It's fae magic that's bleeding the life from my land. *They* are the ones who send monsters across the borders. And you would have blindly helped them, spreading devastation like you've never imagined."

"I don't believe you." I knew who the Dark God was—he was death and destruction and hate. Nothing more.

His expression flared, and step by step, he closed the distance between us. "You will soon. I will prove it to you, little wolf."

13

Samantha

My heart pounded as the Dark God led me down the corridors of his citadel. It was hewn from the rock, but the doorways were framed with elaborately carved wood. The complex was severe, primitive, and beautiful, much like him.

It wasn't the empty fortress of solitude that I'd imagined, either. There were people everywhere. They gravitated away from us, not in fear, but in awe and wonder as the god strode through their midst.

I turned his words over and over in my head. *It's fae magic that's bleeding the life from my land. They are the ones who send monsters across the border.*

It couldn't be true, could it?

The Dark God thrust out his hand as we approached a massive set of doors. They swung open without a sound, revealing bright sunlight beyond.

My eyes strained as my heart fluttered. I couldn't believe it. Actual sunlight. A part of me had feared I'd be trapped in that cave for the rest of my life. Maybe I still would.

We descended the stairs into a courtyard, and I sucked in a deep breath of air as if it were my last.

"Bring me Vega, if he's fresh," the Dark God said to a boy who awaited at the foot of the steps.

The boy hurried off and I slowly turned around, craning my neck upward as I was overcome by awe.

A black basalt cliff ringed around us in all directions—the remnants of an ancient volcano. The center was a massive lake bordered by trees, and four white stone towers soared above me into the sky. Built into the face of the black cliff, the towers were curved, like claws tearing their way up through the earth.

Fitting.

"Welcome to Shadowstone, my home."

"Why does a god need a castle?" I asked.

He glanced down at me with a mix of curiosity and annoyance. "It's not for me."

"Right."

The Dark God turned, and the danger in those icy blue eyes had me taking a step back. "This place is a refuge. It offers protection and reminds my people that *I* control these lands. That as long as they are within my borders, they are safe. Or that they should be."

I shuddered.

The protectiveness he felt for his people was unexpected, and the intense emotions in his voice stirred something deep inside of me. How could a monster like him care for anything?

The clop of hooves and scraping of claws sounded from the forecourt, and I turned. A man was approaching, leading a ferocious animal that I could barely comprehend.

Part falcon and part horse, it had a pair of horns and a lethal beak that looked like it could crush a person's head with a single bite. Its taloned forelegs could have easily opened me from neck to belly in a single swipe, yet its hindquarters were of a horse, except for a scaled, feathered tail.

I backed away as the creature sniffed at me. It gave an earsplitting screech and reared.

I ducked out of the way of its talons. "Excuse me!"

Its handler stumbled back, but the Dark God strode forward, his hand raised. "Steady, Vega."

With a sharp cry of annoyance, the beast dropped back down and gave me a disdainful look.

The Dark God patted its beak and brushed his hand over the feathers of its head. "I know you don't like her, but do this as a favor for me."

I was too shocked to be offended. "What is it?"

The creature clacked its beak as the Dark God began adjusting its tack. "This is Vega, a griffstrider—he's part eagle, part horse, with the most aggressive aspects of both. He's also extremely intelligent and occasionally moody, so watch what you say."

I swallowed. "Wherever we're going, I think I'll go as a wolf."

The Dark God looked back and gave me a dangerous grin. "As much as I want to meet your wolf, you'd be too slow. And I want you close."

Fuck. By the threat in his voice, I knew there'd be no negotiating.

"Where are you taking me?" I asked.

"To see the border. And the truth." With that, he put one foot in the stirrup and swung himself up. Then he held out his hand.

I shook my head. "Oh, hell, no. I'm not getting up there with *you.*"

His hand didn't waver. "It's not a request. If you want to see the truth, then you will ride with me. If you'd prefer to sit in the cave for the rest of your days, then that is your choice."

A month ago, I'd burned that hand, and he'd nearly killed

me. Now I was going to sit next to him? Impossible. But what choice did I have? Sit in the dark, and wonder if he could be telling the truth?

Fuck that.

Grinding my teeth in annoyance, I placed my foot in the stirrup and grasped his hand. Electricity sparked between our skin. His energy swirled around me and over me, sending a blast of heat through my body.

The Dark God's eyes dilated with surprise as my breath hitched with a flurry of inexplicable emotions. For several silent seconds we took the other's measure, then before I could say anything, his expression hardened, and he heaved me up into the saddle in front of him.

His grasp was iron, and the motion was effortless, as if I weighed no more than a feather. I dropped into the saddle, and my blood went cold as my back pressed against the strength of his chest.

I couldn't count how many times I'd woken from nightmares, terrified that one day, I'd see him again. And now, here we were, nothing more than an inch separating us.

The heat of his body was overwhelming. I arched my back to create space, but he placed his hand on my belly and pulled me close. *Oh, fuck me.*

My breathing halted, and every muscle in my body tensed. I could barely think. My chest began to rise and fall with quick breaths, but my brain felt depleted of oxygen. Mortals weren't meant to touch gods.

I have to get away.

But I couldn't. I was pressed against him and could feel every curve of his hard, muscled form. My mind whirled, and I tried to stop myself from trembling—whether with fear or elation, I wasn't sure.

His breath heated my neck. "Stay still and don't yank on any of Vega's feathers. He's not shy about nipping."

"Nothing with a beak that big nips," I said, my voice cracking.

"True." His words did little to relieve my terror. The Dark God pressed his legs against the griffstrider's side. "Let's go. Take us by the northern road."

Before I could beg him to put me down, we were in motion. The griffstrider galloped through the gateway and shot over the narrow causeway that crossed over the lake and through a cleft in the looming basalt wall. The ground fell behind us, revealing the blue waters churning hundreds of feet below.

The gracile bridge didn't seem capable of holding a man, let alone a giant griffstrider with two riders, and I tightly gripped the Dark God's thighs out of sheer panic.

He bent his head to my ear. "Relax, little wolf."

My spine stiffened, and I extended my claws into his legs. "I *will* when I'm on the other side."

My heartbeat hammered in my ears as the griffstrider charged across the end of the bridge and into the trees at a lethal speed. But that wasn't what had me panicking—it was *him*. Although the Dark God was suppressing the power of his signature, it was like flames licking my skin. I felt him with every nerve in my body, stirring a rush of sensations within me—panic, anger, and a primal heat that had my core clenching.

I tried to concentrate on synchronizing my body with the strider's movements, on the landscape flashing past, on savoring what might be my last moment of freedom—on everything and anything to distract from the fact that I was pressed up against him.

I scooted forward, but the beast at my back pulled me closer. "Vega's not used to two riders. Stop moving."

Every impact of the strider's hooves drove me into the firm

strength of the Dark God's body. His proximity was dizzying and intoxicating, and although I hated the Dark God with every fiber of my being and my instinct told me to get the fuck away, my body had other preoccupations.

His hand tightened around my stomach as the griffstrider leapt over a massive, felled tree. The feathers under its front legs opened, carrying us a good ten feet before it landed gracefully.

My thighs ached, and my heart pummeled my ribs. Fucking hell.

"Your heart is pounding, Samantha," he whispered, the closeness of his body unleashing a cascade of shivers down my neck.

I jammed my elbow into his abs and twisted forward. "You're a god, and you're too close."

It didn't have any effect. His hold on me was unyielding, and I couldn't get separation or ignore the way the hard angles of his body seemed to mold around me. I closed my eyes and muttered a silent prayer to the Moon Mother: *Kill me now and spare me from this misery.*

We continued in silence, and I tried to focus on the trees and griffstrider's thundering hoofbeats.

The forest quickly became inundated with shadows and mist that wove between the trunks of the trees, as if the sun there wasn't strong enough to drive it away. Every so often, strange shapes appeared in the mist. Some moved away as soon as they spotted us. Others stood still. I couldn't discern if they were piles of rocks or broken, gnarled trees. Maybe they were creatures, content to watch us pass, unafraid.

Further into the woods, I barely made out the broken face of a wall. Gray haze shone through the empty windows. There were ruins all around us—brick, glass, and charred wood.

"What was this place?" I whispered, nervous to disturb the memories lurking in the mist.

The Dark God turned the strider away from the crumbling town. "Something that didn't belong in the wilds. It's been reclaimed."

I shuddered and looked away. It was just like the destruction on the fae side of the border. I couldn't ever let myself forget that he intended to wipe humanity off the face of the earth and cleanse the world of its human blight.

Bile and anger rose in my throat. Was this what Chicago would have become if he'd been released? I gave thanks to the Moon Goddess under my breath that we'd been able to stop him and prayed that he would never break free.

The woods changed the further we went. Withered birch and ash trees became more and more frequent until we were passing through a dead forest. The only things living were patchy grasses and shrubs clinging to life and the same dark vines with purple leaves I'd seen on the fae side of the barrier.

This was the true face of the Dark God: ruined buildings and dying forests. He was a harbinger of destruction, and our world had barely escaped.

14

Samantha

After a silent hour, the Moon's barrier finally loomed above the dead trees. Something about the mesmerizing wall of green-blue light called to me. I closed my eyes and focused on the thrum of magic emanating from the barrier. It radiated across me in waves, warming my skin and clearing my mind like a summer breeze in a smoky room.

Freedom was on the other side. So close.

Across the barrier, vibrant green and gold ash, birch, and alders stretched as far as I could see, while on our side, the forest was dark and twisted, and several of the trees had shattered as if they were made of glass. The contrast made the Dark God's desolation seem even worse.

The griffstrider slowed to a halt a hundred yards away.

Before I could get my bearing, the Dark God lifted me out of the saddle and dropped to the forest floor beside me.

I gave a wistful glance at the barrier, and he caught my arm. "Whatever you think is on that side of the wall waiting for you, it's far worse than I am."

"I doubt that."

"The fae are not your friends." He knelt and lifted a splinter of one of the trees from the forest floor. It was brittle, and he crushed it into dust. "This is what they have done to my land."

"The fae said that the barrier blocks your magic. That you're the one spreading the desolation. Why should I believe you over them?"

The Dark God thrust his hand to the side, and black mist took the form of an axe with a lethal crescent blade.

I stepped back, hands raised even though I was hopelessly outmatched.

He lifted one of his brows, almost amused. "I know you will not believe me, little wolf. That's why I brought you here, so you can see with your own eyes."

Without warning, he raised the axe over his head and brought it down, cleaving through one of the purple vines. He kicked the sections apart, and purple-black ooze dripped like blood from the cuts onto the olive moss below. Where the drops of blood fell, the green of new life suddenly appeared. The vine blood kept flowing, and the moss brightened into a vivid green patch in the desolation.

"What is this?" I asked.

The Dark God swept his axe in an arc, gesturing to the hundreds of vines twisting through the forest. "These vines are draining the life from my lands. Everything they told you is a lie —or a truth, twisted in on itself."

I shook my head in disbelief as I looked around, tracing the path of a large vine. Smaller spurs branched off it and snaked through the desiccated undergrowth, sprouting tendrils that wound around the trunks of dead trees.

"Why would the fae do this?" I pressed. "What do they gain?"

The Dark God adjusted the axe in his hand, then slammed it down to sever another spur from the cut section. "The Undying

Court lost their immortality when they were exiled. They siphon the life force from my lands to keep from aging."

My blood chilled at his words. "I thought they were trying to defeat you."

His expression grew icy. "I am a god of wilderness and wolves. The more shifters the fae kill and the more wilderness they destroy, the weaker I grow. By killing my land, they are slowly killing me."

Fuck. It could still be a lie, but if it wasn't...

Disgust soured my mouth. I'd agreed to help take down the Dark God, not to slaughtering shifters or sucking the life out of forests.

I let out a shaky breath as I tried to calm my nerves.

Part of my heart had suspected that Sarion might've been deceiving me. The other part—a furious, angry, hateful part— had wanted, had *needed* it to be the Dark God who was the monster. The bastard had devastated my city. Everything would be so much easier if the desolation here were his fault as well.

I backed away from him. "I rode through a decimated village on the other side of the border. They claimed it was your fault."

The Dark God wrenched his axe free of a vine and gave me a brooding look. "I'm in a war, and I will always maintain the balance. When they send warriors and beasts to kill my people, I retaliate."

So yes, he'd destroyed it.

The truth was, I had no good reason to believe the Dark God or what the fae said—or even my own eyes. If the fae could cast glamours or deceive without the scent of a lie, so could a god. He could probably twist the truth, or even create illusions. Hell, he'd compelled me to speak before—couldn't he be using his magic now?

One thing was clear: there was no one I could trust in the Dreamlands, not even myself. What the fuck was I supposed to do, trapped between a murderous monster and a fae kingdom of lying bastards?

"What sort of fucked-up war is this?" I muttered beneath my breath.

"One they started long ago." The Dark God turned his back on me and cut through another heavy vine. "After I was imprisoned by the Moon Goddess, the Undying Court seized the land beyond the walls of her prison and drove the shifters out. But the fae were not content with the land they stole, so now they're draining the life from mine."

He ripped the vine free of the tendrils that anchored it to the ground, then chucked it forward. It curled over like the body of a sea serpent, then crashed down deeper into the forest. "If these vines prove nothing to you, I can show you burned-out husks and abandoned villages as well. There are just as many on this side of the barrier."

My stomach tumbled. Everywhere the vines bled, life sprang from the dead earth.

The Dark God slipped his axe back into its loop. "The wound you caused weakened me. I need you to heal me so I can heal my land."

I swallowed, shaking my head. "I don't know how."

He closed the distance between us, and my breath caught as I stared up into his face. The scent of his sweat and the blood of the vines mingled in a heady cocktail of musk and sweet fruit.

"I know you don't think you have magic, but you do. Maybe it was the Moon's magic you used, but you shaped the spell that wounded me. Work with my sorceress. Find a way to reverse the curse you put on me. That is all I ask from you."

Holy fuck, he was close.

Maybe not as close as on our ride, but there was no way to pretend he was anything other than a dangerous beast. He gazed down at me from his lofty height with a fierce expression that made me want to flee for my life, but my feet were rooted in the dirt.

My throat was too tight to swallow. Even if he was telling the truth, I couldn't consider healing the bastard we'd fought so hard to stop, could I? What if he won his war? What would he do to the fae? To Magic Side?

Trembling, I said, "I'm sorry about your land and your people, but nothing about what you've shown changes the fact that you're a monster and bringer of death."

The Dark God cupped my jaw, his cool magic spreading as his thumb rubbed my cheek. "I may be a monster, but you're my prisoner. Yet I'll make you a deal. Heal me, and I will let you out of the cave."

I shivered. "That's not enough."

"Then you're your own prisoner." He released my jaw and stepped away

I sucked in a sharp breath as whatever hope I had in my chest evaporated.

He pulled his axe from its loop and slammed it down to cleave one of the spurs from the massive vine. "I know you despise everything I stand for, but spending the rest of your life in a cave will change nothing about the world."

With a quick yank, he tore the large vine free from the tree it was wrapped around, shattering its desiccated branches. "If I can't defend my borders, this blight will spread, and many of the animals, shifters, and even fae who call my lands home will die."

The weight of the world crushed in on me, and I felt more trapped than when I was in the cave. It wasn't just my freedom that hung in the balance. My own life didn't matter. I'd already risked it once to stop him. I was on borrowed time, but my mother depended on me. If I didn't get back, no one would give her medicine.

And he was right—if I sat in a cave doing nothing, the world would move on. He and the fae would fight their war. People would die. If I healed him, maybe I could stop some of it. He was still trapped in his prison. He couldn't cross the border, even if his armies could.

It wasn't like I was setting him free. Magic Side would still be safe.

And if he let me out of the cave, maybe I could find a way to escape. I could go to the Moon Goddess. She would know what to do. She had the power to change all the things I couldn't. I wanted to spite him, but freedom meant more—to me, my mother, and any hopes of stopping him in the long run.

I fixed him with a hard stare, trying to search for every hint of truth hidden beneath his expression. "If I try to heal you, you'll let me go?"

"If you try, I'll let you out of your cave. If you heal me, I will let you go, little wolf."

My heart raced. So that was the devil's bargain I'd have to make.

I glanced at the shimmering wall—so close to where I stood. All my instincts told me to run, but I knew there was nowhere to go. Even if I made it across the border, he'd make the trees pull me back. Taking the deal was my chance to get out of here.

I raised my chin. "How do I know you'll keep your bargain?"

The Dark God smiled and drew the blade of his axe across his palm. Bright crimson mixed with the purple-black sap of the vines. "I am a god. I keep my word."

Not likely, but what other choice did I have?

15

____

Cadean

The stars were out by the time we reached Shadowstone.

Samantha's head drooped forward, and her weight shifted to the side. I'd used my presence to calm her like I would any of my wolves, and slowly she'd succumbed to the rhythm of the ride.

I curled my arm around her waist and eased her back into me as I slowed Vega to a walk. The little wolf leaned her head against my shoulder, and though her eyelids fluttered, she didn't wake.

It was almost too much to bear, having her so close.

I memorized the soft curves of her cheekbones, the small indentation above her lips, the delicate lines of her neck...

She was such a fragile mortal creature. I couldn't understand how she'd managed to wound me so gravely. Or torment me so endlessly.

Vega brought us to the courtyard, and Samantha jerked awake. "Where are we?"

"Back at Shadowstone."

She leaned forward. "I fell asleep?"

"You've endured a lot."

Cheeks reddening, she began to struggle. "Let me down."

The greedy bastard in me didn't want to let her go, but I helped her dismount, then led her back to the depths of my citadel.

Her eyes widened as soon as she recognized our path, and she turned on me with a furious expression. "You're taking me back to the cave? I thought we had a deal?"

I gave her a gentle push forward. "We do, but you have to earn each step of your freedom. Tomorrow, you will meet with Melanthe, and by then, I will have a room prepared. But tonight, you will sleep where I know you are safe, under lock and key."

Fury quaking in every step, she glared back at me. "Safe? From what?"

My lips curled up into a wicked smile. "You mean other than me?"

Her chest rose and fell, but she showed no fear. "Is there anything *else* worth fearing around here? Not your vampire, that's for sure."

Living nightmares. Fae assassins. Knives in the night.

She cocked her head, inspecting my expression. "Why are you hesitating? Am I not safe here?"

I slowly strode toward her, and she backed away from me. "The Dreamlands are perilous. You're safe as long as you're in my citadel. And tonight, that's in the cave."

I'd enchanted it as soon as I'd sent Wulfric after her. I hadn't known what to expect from her powers, so at the time, it had been as much for my protection as hers. But with the fae looking for her, it was the safest place. In the morning, I would enchant a room for her with protective wards. The other option was my chambers, of course, and as much as that intrigued me, I knew she'd choose death first.

Samantha marched along. Although she was trying to hide it, I caught the faint scent of doubt and dread beneath her anger.

Good. She *should* be afraid. The Dreamlands were a dangerous place for a little wolf, especially one willing to help me.

I had many enemies, and not only among the fae.

We wound our way through the deep hold and stopped at the door of her cave. I unlocked it and swung it wide. "This is for tonight only. I'll send someone for you in the morning."

She hesitated but finally stepped in. "We made a deal."

"And I'll honor it." I shut the door and locked it as she slumped against the wall.

Guilt tugged at me as I walked through the small complex that served as my makeshift dungeon. I delt with problems one way or another, so I had little need for prisoners, nor any desire to keep a creature in captivity. Samantha was an exception, and so was the fae bastard we'd captured in the woods.

Melanthe and Kassian met me on the way to his cell. "You were gone a long time. Did you two have a pleasant ride?" Kass asked.

"I showed her the vines. She doesn't trust me, but she's agreed to try to heal me in exchange for some freedom."

He drummed his fingers on the giant *Book of Confessions* he had tucked under his arm. "I don't like this, Cade. She could be looking for an opportunity to attack you again."

"She had plenty of opportunity to do that on the ride out. She has no idea what she did, nor what kind of power she possesses." I turned to Mel. "I want you to meet her tomorrow. Figure out a solution to bring her magic out and teach her how to heal me."

Mel bowed her head. "I'll test her blood. I have my suspicions. If I'm right, I'll know a way forward."

We stopped in front of an iron door. "Have you prepared the prisoner?"

"He's pliable." She unlocked the door and swung it wide.

The fae intruder hung inside, tightly wrapped in roots.

Mel gestured to the purple smoke rising from the brazier at his feet. "The fumes should weaken his mental barriers. I lit the fire the moment you returned, so he should be pliable now."

The intruder's head lolled to the side, and his glazed eyes stared reverently at Mel. "I'm ready, Your Highness."

I raised my eyebrows, and Mel let half a smile creep across her lips. "Just a small side effect."

Finally, I would have some answers. I stepped forward and reached out with my power. "Who sent you? Who do you serve?"

"The Undying Council and the high queen herself. Her, most of all," he slurred.

"Why do they want the she-wolf?"

Hesitation.

I felt the mental gate then, halting his words, hiding his own memories from him. But Mel's incense had weakened his shields, leaving the traces of the original spell exposed.

"You remember." I pressed some of my magic against the spell and let a little of my power into his mind, breaking the wards that protected it. He strained against the roots, but I wouldn't be stopped. My realm depended on it.

"She's dangerous!" he shouted as I felt the tug of his memories flooding back.

My skin iced, and I seized a root around his neck. "How?"

He fought me with his will, but he was intoxicated with Mel's magic, and his wards were nothing against my power. Eventually, he submitted and bowed his head. "Queen Ayanna asked the oracle about the she-wolf when we heard that she'd wounded you. We hoped she would be a weapon, but the oracle said she is a coin, cast by fate."

The oracle? My heart pounded. "What does that mean?"

The fae smiled. "Heads, she has the power to save you, but tails, she will bring you to your knees and bind you with bonds that cannot be broken."

Dread tightened every muscle in my body. The Moon's prison was already constricting around my realm. Would the woman take my very freedom?

I spun away as fury seized me. *I will not be bound.*

As my anger swelled, the scars on my arm began to burn, unbearable flames racing over my skin. No one had ever wounded me like she had. No wonder the fae coveted her.

I stepped closer to the dangling prisoner. "Did the oracle say which way the coin would fall?"

He shook his head. "She is spinning on an edge. My queen wishes to make sure the answer is tails, or no answer at all."

A low growl rose in my throat.

The poison.

I tightened the roots restraining him. "What would you have done if the woman had refused to come with you? Would you have killed her?"

The fae squirmed and shook his head. "No! My queen commanded that I was to kill her if you'd corrupted her or I failed to capture her, but I wouldn't have done it! I swear."

The dark, malicious beast swelled inside of me, and my hand tightened on the haft of the axe that hung at my hip. I fought back against the black rage and forced my hand to release it. Even in this grim work, I had to preserve the balance.

I stepped forward so that we were inches apart. "You swear that you would have let her go?"

He tried to pull away from me. "Yes, I swear. Maybe I would have found a way to help her escape, maybe not. But I wouldn't have killed her. I fear defying the fates more than I fear my queen. Or you."

Truth.

I inhaled slowly and released a little of the tension from my limbs. "And that answer is the only reason I'm going to let you draw another breath."

Kass put his hand on my shoulder. "You're not going to like this, Cade, but if Queen Ayanna is willing to kill the girl to ensure which way the coin falls, then maybe we should consider that option as well."

A torrent of rage exploded through me. I seized my friend and drove him up against the wall of the smoky room. "No one lays a hand on her, is that clear?"

The vampire grinned broadly. "My mistake. I was just setting out an obvious option, but message received. No harming the girl."

"Good." I released him.

Kass dusted himself off. "As much as I care for your well-being, I'm more than happy to overlook the ominous bit about her bringing you to your knees if it makes you happy."

I knew he had my best interests at heart, but I ground my teeth in frustration. "Didn't you hear the other side of the oracle? She has the power to save me. Maybe that means she can heal me, or even release me from this damned prison."

But I knew it was more than that. There was something captivating about her. Untarnished. The thought of the fae hurting her filled me with an almost blinding rage.

Frustrated, I turned toward the door. "His mental wards are broken. Mine him for everything he knows about the she-wolf, the oracle, and the Undying Court."

The vampire's expression twisted with a cunning smile, and he pulled out his knife. "With pleasure."

I paused at the door. "And Kass, you can ask questions, but don't harm him. I'm going to send him back to Ayanna with a message, and I don't want him becoming a martyr."

He opened the *Book of Confessions* and laid it on the table. "Sometimes, Cadean, you really do take the fun out of my job."

"Content yourself with the knowledge of what Ayanna will do when she finds out."

The prisoner squirmed. "She'll take my wings."

Kass dipped a quill in ink and grinned back at the fae. "Time to tell me everything you know about Ayanna. If you behave, maybe Cadean will be merciful and let you stay permanently at the Dark Wolf Hotel."

Mel followed me out of the room. "If the queen and council believe she's a threat, they'll send more assassins. We'll need to be vigilant."

My hand instinctively dropped to my axe as I strode down the hall. "We'll prepare a safe room for the she-wolf tonight. We can enchant it with wards and renew the ones on your workshop as well. I don't want her anywhere that isn't protected."

16

———

Samantha

I spent the night on the cold stone floor, tossing and turning and questioning my decision.

There was no doubt in my mind that I wasn't going be able to heal the Dark God. No matter what he said, I didn't have magic. But I'd play along, pushing for more and more liberties until I had an opportunity to escape. Hell, if I could just get a note to Jaxson and Savannah, that might be enough. But to do that, I'd have to manufacture some allies, and I needed a lot of luck.

At least for the first time in days, I had a little hope.

Pounding on the door woke me from restless dreams, and I sat up and looked around. Torchlight illuminated Fang's face at the door. "The Dark God wants you to talk with Melanthe."

She must be the sorceress.

He dropped his torch in a sconce. "Get up and put on your manacles."

Aching, I rolled to my side. "The manacles fell in the pond. You can go look for them if you like."

The lock on the door clanked, and I scrambled to my feet as

the vampire shoved his way in. "I'm surprised you found the key. But I came prepared." He held out a rope. "Turn around."

I flexed my fingers, tempted to take him out right there. But vampires were fast, and I didn't want to wreck my chances of freedom on day one.

Fang gave me a wicked grin. "We can make this as difficult as you want."

Sighing, I turned around and played the nice prisoner. "The Dark God didn't make me wear manacles. Are you afraid your reflexes aren't fast enough, or that I'll knock you out and go running through the citadel?"

He bound my wrists and yanked the cord tight. "The Dark Wolf God might let down his guard around you, but I answer to him. If I lose my temper and happen to sink my teeth into you, he'll have my head on a spike."

I was about to hit Fang with a snappy retort when he yanked a burlap bag over my head. "What the shit!"

The vampire jerked me close. "What's that? You want a gag, too? I don't like it when food talks back."

My wolf stirred, and every instinct I had screamed for me to fight, but I forced myself to relax. I was going to behave, meet the sorceress, and get a better room. After that, all bets were off.

"I'm going to stake you one of these days," I muttered under my breath.

Fang marched me down a long corridor and up a series of stairwells. Finally, he jerked me to a halt and ripped the bag off my head, pulling out some of my hair.

"Asshole," I grunted.

He pounded on a heavy oak door with no handle. "I've brought the woman. Please fucking take her before I snap her neck and get us all in trouble."

The door creaked as it swung open, though there was no one there to guide it.

A woman in a scarlet dress leaned over a stone table, her long, dark hair falling in curls over her shoulder. She looked up and gave me a sly smile. "Welcome to my workshop."

Fang shoved me in.

Three tall windows lit the pentagonal room, and the scent of juniper and pepper tickled my nose. The vaulted ceiling tapered to a point thirty or forty feet above my head, giving me the uncanny feeling of being on the inside of a beehive. A section of it was glass, letting the sunlight filter in.

Wooden shelves lined the walls most of the way up. They were populated by a bizarre assortment of jars, boxes, books, and animal parts—from wings to shells and bones.

The sorceress approached me, then anger darkened her face. "You bound her?" Marching over, she pulled out a long knife from a sheath at her waist. "Hold steady," she told me, then sliced through the rope and turned me around. "I'm sorry about that. Kassian is a sadist."

I shook my wrists out. "He's got a sad amount of self-confidence as well. Imagine being afraid of a little ol' werewolf."

The vampire extended his fangs with a snap, but the woman in red gave him a look of death. "The Dark God will not be happy."

She waved her hand, and the chicory taste of her magic tickled my tongue as the door slammed shut in the vampire's face.

"Please don't be nervous," the woman said in a tone that made the hair on my neck prickle. "I'm very sorry about all that. As Master of Information, Kassian is suspicious and highly protective of the Dark God's interests. Ridiculously so."

"Thanks for telling him off. He's an ass."

A smile formed on her full, seductive lips, and she held out her hand. "I, on the other hand, am happy to meet you. Melanthe, high sorceress to the Dark God."

After a moment's hesitation, I shook her hand. "Samantha."

"Have you eaten? You look…"

Mercifully, she didn't finish her thought. I had a decent idea how I looked, with filthy clothes, baggy eyes, and lines of exhaustion pulling on my cheeks.

I shook my head. "Not since a couple days ago."

Melanthe wrinkled her nose in disgust. "I expected as much with Kassian looking after you."

She grabbed a basket from below the nearby table and spread the contents out before me—some type of drop biscuit, fresh butter, three different jars of jam. A nut butter. Honey. The savory aromas had my mouth watering.

"I hope this is okay. I don't eat meat—probably the only one in the entire citadel—but that's what happens when you make your home with vampires and wolves."

My hand floated over the basket. "May I?"

"It's all yours."

I grabbed a biscuit and slathered it with butter and honey. I bit in, savoring the flavors and warm steam. "Thank you," I said, my mouth full. "I really mean it. I'm used to coasting on empty, but I was so hungry."

Maybe they were playing good cop/bad cop, but I didn't care.

"You can take that with you. And I promise you'll never go hungry here again," she said.

Once I'd finished two more biscuits and a glass of cold milk, Melanthe hopped up on a small ladder and began pulling jars from the shelf. "We should get down to business. Tell me about the spell that wounded Cadean."

"Cadean," I whispered, the syllables rolling off my tongue like a prayer. So that *was* the Dark God's name.

As she worked, I circled the room, inspecting the shelves and savoring the freedom to just walk around. "I'm afraid I'm going to disappoint you, but I didn't cast anything. I just threw a moonstone at him. It was infused with the Moon's power. That's what burned him." Despite the temptation, I didn't add, *Though I wish it had been my doing.*

She set a collection of jars on the table. "I've studied the wound you gave him, and I know the Moon's magic well. That was no uncontrolled blast of moonlight. It was a curse, and a complicated one at that."

I clenched my teeth. "I'm telling the truth. If you were a wolf, you'd be able to smell it."

Melanthe studied my expression for a long time. Her gaze was so intense, it felt like her eyes were stripping away my skin layer by layer. "I don't need to be a wolf to smell out a lie. In this case, you're lying to yourself. That much I know already."

My stomach tightened. "What the hell are you talking about? You people think I'm something I'm not."

"That's what I want to find out. Since you're not familiar with your magical heritage, I want to test your blood. You're not the squeamish sort, are you?"

Suddenly, I discovered I was.

Backing away, I shook my head. "Look, I have a bad history of blood sorcerers wanting to drain me dry, so maybe let's try something else."

Melanthe set a brass brazier down in the middle of the table. "I promise not to hex you or do anything unsavory with it, and I'll only use a little. All I want to do is learn about your heritage and magic. You must want that, too, in some way."

I swallowed with trepidation, but I had a feeling that the Dark God wouldn't give me the option to refuse. And if there was any chance that I had magic—which I severely doubted—I had to learn what it was. If I could master it, I might be able to use it to escape, or even against the Dark God.

At last, I nodded. "Fine, but I'm holding you to your word. No funny business."

"Good." Melanthe tipped the brazier over a wooden waste bucket and beat the back with a wooden spoon. Ashes and chunks of charcoal tumbled out. "Whoops. Forgot to clean it. We wouldn't want to be inhaling *that*."

I swallowed, and my skin crawled.

She clanked the brazier back down on the stone table and dropped in a few briquets. Then she waved her hand, and the charcoal burst into green flame. Traces of pungent purple smoke began to rise from the fire, and I leaned away.

"Don't worry about that," Melanthe said absently. "It will burn off quickly. It's probably not too debilitating in small quantities."

Not too debilitating? What the shit was in there, lady?

She added a few pinches of powder and leaves from each of the jars. They let off puffs of smoke that smelled like burning aluminum and changed the flames from red to pink, blue, and finally green.

Melanthe unsheathed the knife from her belt and held out her hand to me. "Now, the not-so-secret ingredient. Time to give up the goods." She wiggled her fingers in what I assumed was supposed to be an inviting gesture.

I sucked my teeth, and after a moment, thrust out my hand. "Fine. Take my soul."

She clasped my hand and made a small, thin cut in my palm with the razor-sharp blade. "Let it drip into the flames."

I fisted my stinging hand over the fire, and drops of blood sizzled as they pattered onto the coals.

After a moment, Melanthe gently guided my arm away from the fire and cleaned my cut with a white cloth and some ointment. "Sorry about all that. I'm a blood sorceress, so I'm used to it by now, but I know it can be disconcerting. Keep pressure on it."

My skin began knitting together instantly, even more quickly than normal. I pulled the bloody cloth away and examined my hand in surprise. "That ointment works really fast. What is it?"

"Eye of newt and eagle dung."

I gaped.

Melanthe laughed, a hearty belly laugh that filled me with sudden delight, but I still wasn't quite sure if she was kidding. I never got sorcerer humor.

As the flames began to die down, Melanthe sat down, closed her eyes, and began fanning the smoke toward her. "Now for some analysis."

For a long while, she just sat there, fanning the fumes into her face, and breathing. Her eyes rolled back in her head for a moment, and then she stared at me with a shocked expression.

My stomach flipped. "What is it?"

Melanthe licked her lips. "You have magic, though not a type I expected. What can you tell me about your parents?'

Only her first words sank in. I had magic.

The world rocked slightly, and I put my hand out to brace against the table. After a moment, I stammered, "My mother is a werewolf. I assumed my father was, too, but...I never met him. He left before I was born."

Lines of what I assumed was anger hardened the corner of her mouth. "I'm sorry."

Melanthe waited patiently while I processed what her question implied. Had my father been some other kind of Magica? If so, why had my mother never told me? Had she not known?

A sudden weight settled over my shoulders. "Do you know what my father was? Can you tell me anything about my magic?"

She rose. "Not as much as I would like. But your powers are definitely influenced by the Moon. Maybe your interactions with her brought your magic out. You said that you carried an object imbued with the Moon's power?"

I nodded.

"What was it like to use it?"

I scrunched up my brows as I tried to remember exactly. "It felt like I was glowing from the inside out, cool and warm all at the same time. I've never felt anything like it. It was all I ever wanted to feel again. Do you always feel that way—aglow with the magic in you?"

Melanthe smiled softly and shook her head. "Not always. But you'll want to reach for that feeling when you call your magic. Try to focus on those same sensations."

When I called my magic.

It was still overwhelming. I rubbed the nearly healed scar on my palm. "What...what can I do? Do I have powers?"

"I'm not sure, and I don't know who to ask. But that sphere of force you made around Cadean—you did that all on your own. You could begin by practicing that."

My shoulders dropped. "I wouldn't know how."

She stood and began cleaning up. "Well, the first thing you *must* do is accept that you have magic and that you actually used it to shape a spell. Once you come to terms with that, the magic will flow. Healing the Dark God is a good place to start. Now that I have some direction, we'll make a balm that I hope will draw out your magic."

"We?"

"Mainly you. You cast the spell. You need to make the cure." She pulled a book off her shelf, flipped through the pages, and opened it to reveal an ink and pastel sketch of a white flower. "I even want you to gather the materials yourself. These are moon blossoms. I'll have the Dark God take you out to collect them tomorrow."

Suddenly I had magic and was picking ingredients for potions. What was the world coming to? I shook my head in a haze of wonder and confusion. "I still don't understand what I did to him."

"I don't know entirely, but I have a better idea now." Melanthe returned the book to her shelves and grabbed a sheaf of paper. She spread them out on the table, revealing sketches of the Dark God's arm. "I've been trying to cure his wound for a while, but I haven't been able to do it." She pointed to the lines working their way up his arm—the ones that glowed blue in the darkness. "What do these remind you of?"

I shrugged. "Maybe veins. Or lightning?"

"Or vines?" Melanthe offered.

Recognition dawned.

"Whatever you did to Cadean is affecting him like the vines you visited last night, sapping both his strength and magic. The vines have been invading our realm for years, but what you did to him is new. Somehow, I think you made him susceptible to the blight."

My mind whirled, and I didn't know whether to be proud or horrified or scared. Maybe all three.

I shuffled through her drawings, but they didn't hold any answers. "How would I have made him susceptible to the blight? I don't know the first thing about curses or the vines."

A dark expression crossed her face, but she quickly pressed her lips into a forced smile. "I don't know. But I've been making wards to prevent the vines from spreading. I want to try a variation of that with you and the Dark God in the form of a balm imbued with moon blossom extract."

I was certain there was something she was hiding, but there was so much I didn't understand already. I was surprised at how forthcoming she was, considering I was the one who'd wounded him in the first place. "Why tell me all of this? Aren't you afraid I could use it against him?"

Melanthe lightly touched my arm, and I looked up to meet

her smile—a true one this time. "I want to trust you, Samantha, and I want you to heal him. You'll be able to do that better if you have some idea of what you're trying to achieve. Most of all, I want you to find your magic. It's your birthright."

Swallowing, I nodded slowly.

My birthright.

That left the burning question: what was I?

17

Samantha

Melanthe whisked away the pile of drawings and put them back on the shelf. "I'll clean up later. Let's get you situated in your new accommodations."

Right. I was going to be rewarded for my docile cooperation.

The truth was, anything would be better than lying in a dank, dark cave. I didn't care if the Dark God put me in a spartan monk's cell as long as it had some kind of bed. And running water.

Please let there be a window. That alone would change everything.

Melanthe gathered up the basket of biscuits, then led me out into the citadel. She didn't bind my hands or put a sack over my head. It was almost like they were willing to treat me like a person now that I'd agreed to help.

We navigated the hallways, then spiraled up into the tower. There were people everywhere, and all of them were looking at us. No, looking at *me*. Was it my clothes? Or did they have some idea who or what I was—the prisoner who'd hurt their god? My skin prickled beneath their judging gazes. *Maybe the burlap sack wasn't such a bad thing.*

I kept my head down, and instead of meeting their eyes, I focused on reading the scents of the people we passed. A panther shifter who smelled of baked goods, and a werewolf with the scent of rivers and watercolor paint. Where did they all come from, and what tragedy had happened to make them take up allegiance with the Dark God?

I paused on the stairs as the aroma of warm pepper and amber overwhelmed my senses. Not a scent, a signature. It was almost as strong as the Dark God's, though this one felt like a kiss of warm sunlight and rang like steel clashing on steel.

A man—tall, fierce, and powerful—watched us from an adjoining hall. He looked every inch a classical Greek god. A sword in a golden scabbard hung from his side, though I doubted he'd ever need to draw it, not with a physique like that. His features were sharp and elegant, though eerily familiar.

I gaped for a second, and then recognition sent a shock of alarm though my body. Something about his eyes and the cut of his jaw reminded me of the Dark God.

Melanthe jerked me forward, and I stumbled up the stairs.

"Who was that?" I whispered.

"No one you need or want to know," Melanthe said, barely hiding the venom in her voice. Her tone made my stomach drop, and I reminded myself that not all beautiful things were safe to touch.

The Dark God certainly wasn't.

The godlike man kept my thoughts whirling as we spiraled upward. I was out of breath by the time we exited into an arched chamber and stopped in front of a plain wooden door.

My muscles tensed with anticipation. I knew the Dark God was on the other side. His overwhelming presence radiated through the door: the scent of warm fires, wind in the pines, and an earthquake of power.

Melanthe swung the door open as I gave her a nervous look. "Welcome to your new quarters, Samantha."

I didn't see the room at all. All I saw was *him*.

The Dark Wolf God leaned by a window with one arm braced against the wall, staring out at his domain. When he turned to face me, I shuddered with both fear and delight. He inspected every inch of me with diamond eyes that threatened to tear right through my clothes. My heart quickened, and a sheen of sweat beaded on my skin.

Why did his attention have such an effect on me?

Because he's a god, that's why.

A smile threatened to bend the corner of his lips. "Are you going to come in or just stand in the hall?"

I glanced down at my feet, then hesitantly stepped inside the room and looked around.

My chest rose in surprise. Sunlight filtered in through three wide windows, falling softly on the puffy duvet covering the large four-poster bed. The pillows and comforter looked unbelievably soft, and my back groaned just seeing them. A door led to a private bathroom, and I caught the glint of a large mirror. It was paradise.

Yet somehow, the whole place felt infused with his magic. Why? Suspicion tugged at me. "Is this a trick?"

The Dark God crossed his arms and leaned back against the window, a subtle grin on his face. "No tricks. This room is yours as long as you keep your side of the bargain. You approve, I hope?"

I looked around again and nodded, my throat dry. "It's more than I expected."

"You're more than I expected."

My head snapped to him, a question hanging on my lips. What did he mean by that? My magic?

Fighting against an irrational flutter in my chest, I cast a glance at the heavy set of locks on the door and tried to use my anger to ground my thoughts. "Don't think I have any illusions about what this is. This room may be fancy, but it's still a prison."

The Dark God inclined his head. "For now."

Everything had a double meaning with him. Did his response mean that it wouldn't be a prison for long? That he'd let me come and go freely if I kept cooperating? There were so many people in the citadel. If I could get freedom of movement, I might be able to find someone willing to help me escape, or even my own way out.

"If you'd prefer the cave..." the Dark God purred.

I shook my head. "No. This is good. Thank you."

I was tempted to add, *And thank you for your mercy, oh great god*, but held my overly sarcastic tongue. This was progress, and I was truly thankful.

The Dark God turned to look back out the window. "Join me."

With a little trepidation, I stepped into the heat of his presence.

Outside the window, wild lands stretched in all directions. Mist rose from the hills and forests and hung low in the valleys. I'd never seen anything like it. It was unruly—a patchwork of landscapes that didn't seem like they should go together, but that all blended with seams of mist.

"It's beautiful, isn't it?" the Dark God said in a soft, almost soothing voice. There was even a hint of pride.

I nodded, not trusting my eyes to look at him or my throat to answer. I was so grateful just to be able to see the sky.

He smiled down at me. "I love this view more than anything.

You should see it at night. We have few cities here to drown out the stars."

His gaze burned into me, and I fought the shiver that worked down my spine. The Moon's barrier stretched like a shimmering band of light across the distant hills and mountains.

He followed my eyes. "And *that* is the wall of my prison, reminding me that I will never be free."

Message received. *So long as I remain trapped in the Dreamlands, so will you.*

I felt the Dark God's eyes drift down my body, and my pulse raced. He was devouring me with an intensity that I felt all the way to my core. Suddenly, he seized my wrist. "You were bound?"

A current of electricity snapped up my arm, and I sucked in an uncertain breath, but his attention was locked on the dirty rope marks around my wrists.

Melanthe crossed her arms. "Kassian thought it safer to bind and put a bag over her head while bringing her up. I told him you would not be pleased."

Fury flashed in the Dark God's eyes, and the heat of his signature increased an order of magnitude. I stepped back, feeling the lick of flames and the roll of thunder.

He released my hand. "I'll speak to him. This won't happen again."

His gravelly voice grazed my skin. It sounded like a death threat.

"Easy, Cadean," Melanthe whispered.

He turned away and strode to the other side of the room.

Why by the fates did I have the inexplicable urge to go to him? Because I was an adrenaline-seeking lunatic? Luckily, fear rooted my feet in place.

After a moment, the fire in his expression calmed, and he

tilted his head and scrutinized Melanthe and me. "Was your time together fruitful, at least?"

Melanthe danced her fingers over a carved bedpost. "Quite fruitful, though I'm not certain of all the implications. After testing Samantha's blood, I believe we can craft a balm to prevent the curse on your arm from advancing, and maybe even heal it. We'll need to gather moon blossoms to brew it, however."

"Finding someone willing to do that might be difficult," the Dark God muttered.

Melanthe balanced her fingers on the post and looked between the two of us. "Samantha can."

The Dark God's expression hardened, and the aura around him became ice. For several breaths, the two of them stared at each other, speaking in the silent language of old allies.

"We should talk about this privately," he said, his voice cold as an arctic wind. "Once you have Samantha settled in, find me in the aviary."

Melanthe nodded. "I will."

He strode to the door but paused with his hand on the frame. "Make sure she has whatever she needs. I'll post guards on the door."

With that, the Dark God swept out of the room.

The gravity of his presence subsided, and I felt the whiplash of his moods sink into my bones. Amusement, fury, and ice-cold anger. It was exhausting, and I was tempted to collapse onto the bed. "What was that about?" I asked.

Melanthe set the basket of biscuits atop a small table. "Moon blossoms grow on the fae side of the border. That means to pick them, he'll have to send someone over. That should be you, but I don't think he's all that receptive to the idea yet. I'll work on him."

She wanted to send me over the border into fae territory? My thoughts whirled with the potential.

Melanthe gave me a wry smile. "I see what you're thinking, and don't get any ideas. Whatever Cadean decides, he will not let you get away—that much I can guarantee."

Was I that fucking transparent? Of course I was. I wanted to get away from him more than anything. But until then, a room with a bathroom and a bed and a window would do.

I tested the plush bed with my hand and tried to sort out my thoughts as Melanthe disappeared into the bathroom. There was a squeak, followed by a rush of water. I looked in to find her dumping dried lavender into a hammered copper tub.

I blinked. "There's running water and a bathtub?"

She laughed. "We can't all live in caves."

"I can take a bath..." I whispered, trying to process the glorious reality.

Melanthe leaned closer and gave me a conspiratorial wink. "I wasn't going to mention it earlier, but you need one. Along with some new clothes."

I looked at myself in the wide mirror, and my jaw dropped. It was worse than it had appeared in the dark reflections of the pool. My favorite leather jacket was gashed, while my shirt and jeans were full of holes and stained with blood. I probably smelled like sweat, cave slime, and griffstrider.

Fuck my life.

I'd been pressed up against the Dark God during our whole ride, sitting right under his nose. His senses had to be even better than a werewolf's. My faced flushed in mortification. I tried to believe that maybe if I was lucky, the stink had burned his sinuses.

She patted my shoulder and headed to the door. "Don't worry, I'll have one of our seamstresses make you some new clothes, but in the meantime, let me see if I've got something that will fit you."

I poked my head back out of the bathroom. "I don't know how to thank you."

"I'm glad to help."

I bit my lower lip. "Do you have something that's not a dress?"

Melanthe paused for a second, then laughed. "A dress? No, honey, I don't think that's your style at all. I'll be back in a bit."

My face heated as she slipped out the door.

I'd worn dresses before. I *could* pull them off. *If* I wanted.

The locks clicked shut, one by one, each a thundering reminder that I was still a prisoner. I tested the door just to be sure. It was sealed shut, and the windows were, too. But at least I had food, a bed, and a bath. That was something. And if I focused on mastering my magic and healing the Dark God, maybe I'd get a little more freedom.

As the bath finished filling, I wolfed down another biscuit, then stripped off my clothes and inspected myself again in the mirror. "I've got to be honest, Sam, you look a little worse for wear."

My hair was in tangles, and my face was caked with grime that made it two shades darker than the rest of me. The scars from being dragged through the forest had already faded, but the ones that the Dark God had given me weeks ago were still sharp and well defined. Would those savage claw marks ever go away?

Maybe if I scrub hard enough.

Shuddering, I raised my leg high and awkwardly dunked one toe in.

Damn, it was toasty.

I climbed into the copper tub and sank down. As the water rushed over my shoulders, I let out a deep moan. For a blissful moment as I inhaled the lavender steam, I let myself forget the Dark Wolf God and the bargain I had made.

18

―――――

Cadean

Mel found me deep in the aviary, tending to Elowyn, one of my favorite striders.

With a knowing smile, she leaned against the wall and crossed her arms. "I got Samantha settled in and took her a couple of my riding outfits—though I'm surprised you put her so near your own quarters."

I didn't meet her gaze. "The woman is trouble, and I want to keep an eye on her."

We both knew I was playing with fire. The safest location for Samantha was close to me, but would I be able to sleep with her only a few paces down the hall? The woman who'd cursed me and refused to leave my thoughts alone?

But there were new questions I had to face.

I put down the preening brush and patted Elowyn's neck before turning to face Mel. "You said Samantha could enter the glade. Only fae can enter the groves where the moon blossom's grow."

She nodded. "I'm not certain, but after testing her blood, I think she's part fae. She never knew her father..."

Fuck.

Whatever hope I had that she was only a wolf drained from my heart. *Of course* she would end up having fae blood. Just like Ayanna and her Undying Court, Samantha tormented my days and longed for my destruction.

The fates had a twisted sense of humor.

Things fell into place. The fae interest in her. The wound she'd cursed me with. Even Vega's behavior—the griffstriders could probably smell her blood.

Fae.

That made everything a lot more fucking complicated. I tightened my fist, trying to hold on to reason in a sea of frustration. "You can't tell her the truth, Mel. She can't find out."

"She should know."

"No," I said sharply. "We need her cooperation, and she already hates me. I might be able to get through to the wolf part of her, but if she finds out she has fae blood, she'll turn on us without hesitation."

"This is a bad idea, Cade."

"It's not negotiable." I held up my hand to stop her protest. "When the time comes, I will tell her, but on my terms. Not before."

She bowed her head in acceptance.

I opened the gate to Elowyn's roost and heaved her dinner in —a deer I'd caught for her in the woods. She clacked her beak appreciatively and tore into it.

I cleaned my hands off and turned back to the sorceress. "Did you learn anything about the wound she gave me? Is it a fae curse, then?"

Melanthe shrugged. "Maybe—Samantha has innate magic but no idea what it is or how to use it. She was carrying a stone infused with the Moon's power when she attacked you. I think she instinctively drew on that source without knowing what she was doing, then hit you with a powerful curse that's made you susceptible to the fae blight."

"The blight? You're certain?" The implications strained the muscles of my neck.

"I suspected, but now I'm almost certain. Your wound is draining your strength, just like the vines are draining your land." Her eyes dropped to my hand.

Blue veins of light crept out from under the bandages, just like the vines were crawling over my border. Were they really one and the same? If so, I was fucked twice over.

"How do I cure it?" I asked.

"If anyone can, it will be her. I think if we use moon blossom extract, we can draw her power out. She seems attuned to lunar magic, and the blossoms absorb it from the barrier. It will be slow, but I think it will work."

My jaw set. "Absolutely not. I'm not taking her across the border, and I'm certainly not going to let her go into one of the sacred glades alone. They're perilous to begin with, and the fae are actively hunting for her. I'll force the bastard in the dungeon to do it."

Mel shook her head. "It won't work. She needs to pick them with her own hands for the spell to have any effect. It's why I gather all my own ingredients—and why I can't be the one to make the balm."

I scrubbed a hand over my jaw. "There has to be another way."

Melanthe sighed and circled to the other side of the aviary. "We could let her draw power from the moonshard, or even the pylons, but considering what happened the last time she drew that much of the Moon's magic..."

"No." She'd seared the skin from my arm and given me the wound in the first place. It began to burn just at the memory. I flexed my fist against the pain. "You think she'd actually be able to spread the curse or cast the spell again?"

Mel shrugged. "Maybe. Are you willing to risk it?"

Never, and that left me royally fucked.

First, I'd been imprisoned. Then the fae had begun to prey on my land. Now Samantha's wound was draining me dry and haunting me with unending pain, and the only person who could apparently cure it couldn't control her own magic and would probably incinerate me alive if she could.

Fury tightened every muscle in my body, and I spun and rammed my fist through one of the posts supporting the roof.

The rafters groaned, and I yanked my hand from the splintered crack. Lines of bright blood trickled down my arm.

"Easy, Cade," Melanthe said, a wry smile on her lips.

Elowyn swished her tail, unimpressed. I glared at the strider. "I could bring this barn down in an instant if I wanted to."

The griffstrider gave a soft screech, then went back to her dinner.

"There must be another option. I'm not sending her to a fae glade, and I'm not going to risk her eviscerating me with the Moon's magic again. Find another solution."

Mel's expression hardened, and she approached. "Those *are* the solutions, Cade. But you need to do something and do it soon. There's less risk to you if we use the moon blossoms."

"I don't care about the risk to me," I growled. "I care about the risk to her, and what happens to this realm if I can't protect it. Find another way."

She put a hand on my shoulder. "You *are* the realm, Cadean. You need to protect yourself as much as the people in it. Send Samantha into the fae glade. Let her heal you slowly."

The shadows lengthened and began to creep down the walls as my mood darkened. Every path out of my predicament seemed to mire me further in it.

I wasn't a fool; I knew Mel was right. I had to heal the wound before the fae pressed their advantage and learned exactly how vulnerable I'd grown. But I couldn't risk the woman, especially if she was the solution to healing me.

Or if she was destined to bring me to my knees.

I turned from Mel and strode out of the aviary. "I'll think on it. Give me time."

"You don't have time, Cade," she called to my back.

Two days later, I met Mel in the courtyard. The sun blazed high overhead and reflected in silver flashes across the great lake that filled the center of the caldera. The tranquil scene belied the turmoil in my head. So many things could go wrong with our plan.

I frowned at the sorceress as I walked over. "I don't like this at all."

She pursed her lips. "Do you want a shot at being healed or not? You've been debating this for two days, and your wound isn't improving."

My jaw ticked with irritation. "I debated because it's risky. I don't like the idea of sending Samantha into the fae lands—not with them hunting her. And into one of the sacred glades, moreover."

Mel crossed her arms. "This plan kills two birds with one stone. If she can enter the glade, it will confirm she's part fae. And while she's there, she can gather the moon blossoms I need to heal you."

Before I could argue further, Samantha's voice echoed from inside the entrance hall. "I swear to all the gods, I will drive a stake through your chest the first moment I have a chance!"

A smile tugged up the corner of my lips, and I turned as Kass shoved her out the door.

She was wearing one of the riding outfits Mel had selected, and I couldn't help but inspect every inch of her: the elegant sweep of her neck, her silky blonde hair, and her sleek curves. I drew in a slow breath, trying to calm my thoughts, but my blood was on fire. What was it about her that was so captivating?

I called to the aviary master, and a moment later he and his apprentices led three griffstriders out. My own steed, Vega, screeched in recognition and reared in greeting. The other mounts were agitated, likely by the scent of Samantha's fae blood. They bucked against their handlers, snapping with their beaks and clawing the ground with their talons.

I released a wave of my power to calm them, and grudgingly, the striders settled down. Vega clacked his beak in mild irritation, looking suspiciously at the woman.

"Does your room suit you?" I asked.

"Other than the part where it's locked all the time? Yes. Though I appreciate the opportunity to get out." She brushed her hair to the side and gave me a suspicious look. "I'm surprised you've agreed to take me along."

"Would you like me to change my mind?"

She didn't reply.

I cocked my head toward the sorceress. "Mel says you're the one who must harvest the moon blossoms. That's why."

Kass grinned and leaned close. "It's also because you're expendable, and if you die retrieving the flower..." He gave a noncommittal shrug.

I gave him a warning glance. She was *not* expendable. Not in any circumstance. I turned and strode toward Vega. "We should go."

Samantha looked from Mel to Kass, and then back to me,

suspicion burning in her eyes. I could smell the scents of her mistrust and anger, but also faint hope and excitement.

I swung into the saddle and motioned for her to take my hand.

She backed up, shaking her head. "No way. I'm not riding with you again. I want my own."

I tightened my fists on the reins. She should be terrified of Vega and his siblings, but it was the prospect of riding next to *me* that gave her pause.

Kass laughed and cast her a devilish grin. "And here I thought you didn't have a death wish. Their beaks are designed to crack skulls like millet seed. You'd never be able to handle a griffstrider."

The she-wolf glared back at him, and her claws came out. "Kiss my ass, Fang."

Melanthe snorted. "Fang? She calls you Fang? Fates, that's amazing."

I ran my hand through the steel gray feathers along Vega's neck and looked down at her. "Kass is right. Griffstriders are difficult to handle. They honor us by carrying us into battle. You haven't earned their respect yet, which is why you will ride with me."

She looked from Vega to the aviary master and back to me. "Then let me try to earn it."

A dark mood settled over me.

Fine. She would learn quickly enough.

I gestured to the master. "Bring Elowyn. She's level-headed."

He turned pale but hurried back to the aviary anyway. He knew what one of the beasts could do if it got out of control—but he was also a superb trainer.

Kass approached Vega cautiously. "I can't believe you're doing this. I thought that you didn't want her harmed, on pain of death?"

I gave him a wry smile. "You learned to ride somehow, didn't you?"

The master returned with the gray griffstrider with turquoise plumage on her neck. I trotted Vega alongside of her to calm her. "Elowyn, this is Samantha, who has my protection. She would like to ride. Be gentle." I nodded at the little wolf. "Go ahead. Make friends."

Samantha stepped forward and tentatively placed a hand on the beast's sleek hide, gently tracing its shoulder as she cooed at it. Kass just shook his head.

Tentatively, Samantha reached for the saddle horn, put her foot in the stirrup, then heaved herself up into the saddle.

Elowyn reared, the feathers of her forelegs splaying as she released a piercing cry. Samantha held fast, clenching her thighs against the strider, refusing to give up.

I shifted Vega out of the way as Elowyn keened and bucked, sending gravel flying, while Samantha clung on like a monkey. Time slowed as her hand tore free of the pommel and the strider reared again. Samantha was flung from the beast and landed in the dirt on her back. She lay there motionless for a heartbeat too long, and a spark of panic rose in my chest. I rose to dismount, but she sucked in a gasp of air and released a long trail of expletives.

Elowyn stalked over and placed one of her obsidian talons on Samantha's throat. My pulse quickened, and I shifted Vega to her side. "Elowyn, enough."

The beast would heed my order, but every muscle in my body tensed.

Samantha's eyes were wide, her body pressed into the dirt. "Okay. Message received. We've got a long way to go in the respect department."

At last, Elowyn removed her claw and primly stepped over Samantha before returning to the aviary.

I maneuvered Vega to Samantha's side. She glared defiantly up at me with an undaunted ferocity I had to respect. Not many would mount a griffstrider without an invitation—or ride it so long. "Are you injured?" I asked.

She sat up and dusted off her palms. "Only my pride."

"What Cadean forgot to mention," Kass said without hiding his glee, "Is that griffstriders are extremely intelligent, understand our speech, and really don't like to be treated like horses."

"Duly noted." Samantha climbed to her feet and looked between the two of us. "I'll ride with Melanthe. Or Kass, if I have to."

Fuck that.

I extended my hand and pushed her with my presence. "You're riding with me. Now."

Her jaw clenched, but at last, she clasped my hand, and I pulled her up in front of me. The warm curves of her body settled against mine, and the rise of her breasts stirred a fiery heat inside of me. Her hair and neck were so close, I couldn't help but consume the scents of her skin and sweat—warm, salty, and sweet. I had to seize control of my breathing to keep it steady.

What was it about this woman? It was all I could do to keep my mind intact around her.

She shifted in the saddle, and I had to dig my nails into my wounded arm just to keep from going stiff.

"How long to the border?" Samantha asked as I nudged Vega into a canter and headed over the causeway.

Too long. Way too fucking long.

19

———————

Samantha

My heart pounded as we raced through the forest, and a sheen of sweat formed on my chest. I'd figured out how to synchronize myself with the motion of the strider, which made the pounding gait of the beast smoother, but it was almost worse that way. The Dark God and I rose and fell as one, my back to his chest, with each impact driving us closer together.

It was maddening. My skin was flushed, and my mind kept slipping off to places I'd forbidden it to go.

I have to learn to ride my own griffstrider, even if I get bucked off a hundred times.

There was no way I was going to keep my sanity if we continued riding around, pressed tightly together.

After two agonizing hours, we finally descended out of the dead forest into a wide valley bisected by a shallow stream. The magical barrier rose just beyond the opposite bank, sending hues of yellow and purple swirling upward like the northern lights.

As we drew near, the signature of the Moon's magic rolled over me in waves. It felt like a warm fire on a cold winter night and tasted like honeydew. It was so strong that it pushed back against the darkness of the god behind me, and I felt like I could breathe freely for the first time in ages.

The Dark God's muscles tensed as we approached.

"Does her signature hurt you?" I asked.

He didn't respond, which I hoped meant, *Yes, it burns me like hellfire itself.*

We stopped ten paces from the barrier, along the oxbow of the stream. It was clear and shallow, though I imagined it flooded in the spring, if there were even seasons in the Dreamlands.

There was so much I didn't know.

As before, the vegetation on our side of the wall was twisted and dead, while the other side was lush and vibrant. Thriving grasses flowed over the hills, and trees shimmered with the shades of fall.

The Dark God dismounted and helped me down. "The glade is at the center of the forest on the other side. We'll enter the forest on foot, then you'll proceed into the glade on your own."

Sudden dread iced my veins. "We? As in, you're coming with?"

"Just me. Kass and Mel need to repair the wards that keep the vines from infesting this section of land."

Suspicion crept up my spine. "But the barrier...I thought you couldn't cross it."

Everything depended on him being locked away in his prison. The implication that he could slip through was horrifying. I recalled what Sarion had told me weeks ago: *He's found a hole or way to circumvent it. When he comes, he leaves no survivors.*

A devilish smile tugged on the corners of his lips. "I can't cross it, but I can push it outward temporarily. Not far, but in this case, far enough to join you."

"How?" I asked, steadying my voice. As least he couldn't break out. It wasn't great, but not the disaster I feared.

Kassian grinned and held out a splinter of stone that flickered with silver light. "We have our means."

It was so beautiful that my breath caught. "What *is* that?"

The Dark God tugged on a heavy gauntlet covered with arcane sigils. "*That* is my most prized possession: the moonshard."

I took a step closer, drawn by its captivating light. Magic radiated off it, cooling and warming me at the same time. The Moon's signature. "Did the Moon Goddess create it?"

The Dark God's eyes hardened. "In a way, I did. After I was imprisoned, I spent a year attacking the pylons with every ounce of magic and strength I had. Finally, I broke a single shard off one of the orbs—though the explosion of power nearly killed me. It was worth it. The moonshard allows me to manipulate the barrier."

I glanced at the stand of trees on the other side of the wall as my stomach dropped. "Then you're coming with me into the glade?"

The Dark God shook his head. "Unfortunately, no. Even with the moonshard, I can't enter there. None of us can, which is why it must be you."

Hope fluttered in my chest. Was there still a chance?

"Why?" I asked. "Why only me?"

An emotion I couldn't place flashed in his eyes, and he hesitated. "Because you're not of this realm, little wolf. The rules that apply to the three of us don't apply to you."

Trying to restrain my heart, I took another glance at the trees. Somewhere, deep in the swath of green, might lie my freedom. Perhaps I could find Sarion. I didn't trust him, but I didn't trust anyone in the Dreamlands.

The Dark God gave me a wicked smile. "I know what you're thinking, little wolf. Don't."

My blood iced, and I shook my head. "I was thinking that I'd better watch my ass out there."

"Liar." He stalked toward me, dark purpose in his eyes. "I know because I think of the exact same thing every time I look across that wall. Freedom."

My pulse raced. I was screwed.

I tried to back away, but my foot caught on a dead tuft of grass overhanging the stream. Flailing with both arms, I tilted backward, but he lunged forward and seized me, pulling me upright and close. His magic raced across my skin, leaving it tingling.

"We had a deal, little wolf. You heal me, and I let you out of the cave. Are you planning to renege on your end of the bargain? To run off the moment you set foot in that cursed land?"

His expression was volcanic, churning with fire, rock, and steam.

"No," I stammered, and I knew he could smell the lie.

"Good."

Maybe he couldn't? For a second, I relaxed in his grasp. Then he traced two fingers lightly along my neck. "Unfortunately, I need to make sure."

Electricity raced from his fingers to my throat, and suddenly, there was a metal choker around my neck, a cold weight of iron stinging my skin.

I tore away from him and staggered back along the bank. Grasping the iron band, I clawed and tugged at it, but it was locked. "What the hell is this? A collar?"

Regret and guilt shone in his eyes before his expression hardened. "You were intending to run. I could see it in every glance, every motion, and every breath you took. Or am I wrong?"

Hell, yes, I was.

I bared my teeth. "What are you planning to do? Hook me up to a five-hundred-foot chain while I weave my way between the trees?"

"It lets me summon you back from anywhere." He snapped his fingers, and a bonfire of his magic roared around me.

Suddenly, I was standing inches away from him.

Oh, holy fuck.

Rage consumed me, and I hauled back and slapped him. My claws raked across his face, leaving jagged lines of red in their wake.

I struck again, but his hand stopped mine a finger's width from his face. "Once is enough, little wolf."

My chest rose and fell with furious breaths as white-hot anger simmered under my skin. I narrowed my eyes at him and wished I could claw both of his out. "You're an asshole."

"I'm not going to let you go into a sacred glade without protection and some means of getting you back."

"Protection? Are you serious about yourself?"

"Deadly. You may think the fae are all pretty elves like the bastard who came for you, but they're not. The moment you enter that glade, you're in peril. I will not see you harmed, and I can't protect you in there. Monsters beyond your imagination stalk these woods."

I bared my teeth and yanked my hand free of his grasp. Of course, that worked only because he let me. The only reason I had any freedom at all was because he let me.

Spite boiled within my heart. "The only thing I need protection from is you."

Guilt and doubt haunted the corners of his eyes, but his voice was as cold and inflexible as the iron around my neck. "You asked me if you were in danger the other night. You are. The fae sent someone across the border to either bring you back or kill you. They are not your allies. You won't find refuge on the other side."

My stomach tumbled. The fae wouldn't actually try to kill me, would they? Although I didn't smell the scent of deceit, it had to be a lie or a half-truth at best.

"You're not my ally, either," I said. "This collar isn't about protection. It's about control."

"It's about both." The Dark God glanced at the forest beyond the wall, the corner of his mouth turned down.

I followed his gaze. Every muscle in his body was taut like he was ready to strike. What was he looking for out there? Was it really so dangerous?

Even if it was, I knew his concern for my safety was only because of what he believed I could do for him.

When the Dark God finally looked back, the conflict raging in his eyes was gone. "I'll make another bargain with you, little wolf. Wear the collar while you're outside of Shadowstone, and when you're within the walls of the citadel, you may wander freely—so long as you're accompanied by me or my guards."

My heart hammered against my chest. Another deal with the devil?

If I tried to heal him, I could have my own room with windows and a bath. If I agreed to wear the collar, I could move freely about the citadel. And if I refused, then I couldn't get the flowers and couldn't heal him, so it would be straight back to the cave for me.

Some choice.

I closed my eyes, knotted my fists, and tried to calm my raging nerves.

The goal was to escape. And as long as I was in the cave, I couldn't. He was offering me freedom inside the citadel. It was what I was hoping for: incremental liberties—each one another step closer to finding a way out.

I opened my eyes and fixed him with an ice-cold stare. "You said that I have to wear it as long as I'm outside of Shadowstone. Does that mean I get to leave the citadel again?"

The touch of a smile softened his expression. "Perhaps. If you gather the blossoms and start trying to heal me, I might even let you run your wolf in the forest—in my company, of course."

My wolf stirred in my chest, longing for a chance to stretch her legs and smell the scents of the world.

He had me on the hook, and I could tell by his smile that he knew it.

I turned and headed toward the bank of the stream. "If that's part of the deal, I'll do it. But this is still fucked up, so let's get this over with."

20

———

Samantha

The Dark God reached up with his gauntleted hand and took the moonshard from Kassian. Light leaked between his fingers and from the tip of the knife-like blade, making the shadows that clung to him seem all the darker.

The stone pulsed with the signature of the Moon, and I was drawn to it in some indefinable way, almost like it was calling to me. My hand reached out to touch it, but the Dark God lifted it out of my grasp. "Considering what you did to me the last time you had an object infused with the Moon's power, I'd rather you keep your claws off it, little wolf."

I scowled to hide the pleasure of that memory.

He'd also just given me crucial information: he was afraid that I could hurt him with it.

The Dark God had to wear an enchanted gauntlet to wield the moonstone, which suggested just touching it was dangerous for him. If I knew how to use my magic, maybe I could use it to do more.

"You're still staring," he growled.

"It's beautiful. I don't think I've ever seen anything so beautiful."

It wasn't a lie.

"Neither have I," he said, staring back at me with an intensity that filled my stomach with flutters. Then he tore his gaze away and turned to Melanthe. "Any final instructions?"

Still mounted, she maneuvered her strider forward and handed me a sack. "Pick as many of the flowers as you can carry, because I don't know how many we'll need. And pull them up, roots and all. The most important thing is the bulb. It will have the most residual magic."

"Got it," I said, and started walking toward the barrier.

"And be safe," she called. "Cadean wasn't lying. The glades are treacherous, home to many dangerous creatures. Trust no one you see and nothing you hear."

Kassian smirked. "Basically, try not to get eaten. Good luck."

"Don't fall on a sharp tree, Fang," I shouted over my shoulder.

Melanthe laughed, and they turned their striders for the hills.

"Ready?" the Dark God asked, holding the glowing stone aloft.

I felt his magic flare as we walked forward, and suddenly, the shimmering wall began to move—slowly at first, then rolling before us like a wave of light.

The moonshard had to be how he was attacking the lands across the border. Did the fae know that that was what made it possible? My stomach knotted, but I kept going. Perhaps I could get them a message.

We made our way through lush grass that reached my ankles. The air smelled sweet and fresh, and everything felt like midsummer.

"I like this side better," I muttered.

Anger flashed across the Dark God's face. "All of it is stolen, the land and the lifeforce that makes it so lush."

Suddenly, the air didn't taste quite as sweet.

The Dark God held up his hand, and I stopped in my tracks as he looked around. Then he let it drop and continued forward.

I scanned the trees ahead. "Is anything the matter?"

"Many things, but there's no immediate threat. Still, if any creature approaches you, I want you to run and call for me."

"Can't you just yank me away like a yo-yo?"

He took my arm and spun me to face him. "I'm not playing games, little wolf. You met a fae in the bar. *One* of them. The fae that stalk these woods would rip you to shreds, then feast on your blood and slowly drain your soul."

How had he known that I met Sarion in the bar? I yanked my arm free of the Dark God's grasp. "Right. And it makes a lot of sense running back to *you*."

"It does if you want to live."

I followed him as we continued into the stand of trees.

The woods were musty and smelled of rich earth and moss. Old growth trees rose around me, blocking the light, and particles of luminescent pollen floated in the air. Every so often, we passed through a beam of sunlight that filtered through gaps in the thick canopy, giving the forest an ethereal feel.

"This place *is* beautiful," I said.

"It is," the Dark God grudgingly replied.

After twenty minutes, we came to a tall, slender stone protruding up from the earth. I paused in front of it. "What is this?"

His expression darkened. "A line that I cannot pass."

Facing him, I smiled wryly and stepped backward to the other side of the stone.

The corner of the Dark God's mouth ticked up. "And that is why you have a collar."

I opened my mouth to fire a retort, but a whisper of voices carried on a silent breeze. I didn't recognize the words, but for some reason, I felt drawn to them. I looked around. There were more standing stones in the distance, but no movement.

The Dark God stepped toward me. "Is something the matter?"

"No," I said, still searching the trees for the source of the sound. "Just a tingle of magic."

"Be quick. Shout if you see anything out of the ordinary. I will be watching, too, through the shadows."

I shivered. That was right. He was somehow *always* watching.

Ducking under a low branch, I headed toward the patch of light ahead.

"Be safe, Samantha," the Dark God said. I couldn't quite place the tone of his words, but his voice made my skin prickle.

Making my way downslope, I moved quietly and cautiously among the trees. More and more light appeared as the forest thinned, and after sliding down a shallow, leaf-covered incline, I emerged into a small glade. It was ringed by ashes and alders, which stood guard like sentinels.

A single, ancient ash dominated the center of the glade. Its trunk was several arm spans around, and its twisted branches made it look like an alien octopod. My destination was impossible to miss. Dozens of white flowers grew thickest around the old ash where the sunlight was unobstructed.

All around me was a sanctuary of safety from *him*, and I was going to steal from it.

"I'm definitely working for the wrong people," I muttered as I headed in.

The magic of the glade tickled my skin. It was almost alive, searching, and caressing me. I looked back but couldn't see the

Dark God. And yet, I felt his familiar gaze on me, watching from the shadows.

I knelt beside one of the white moon blossoms. It had a long stem and velvety soft leaves, and its petals were closed. Curling my lip in frustration, I grasped one of the flowers by its base and pulled it up, bulb, roots, and all. I held my breath, but no monstrous fae creatures burst out of the woods. Still, I couldn't shake the feeling I was doing something very wrong.

I sighed and brushed the dirt off the surface of the acorn-sized bulb with my thumb. Could such a small thing really be the antidote to the wound I'd caused? Could it really be the key to my freedom?

Well, I guess I'll find out.

After a quick check of my surroundings, I began uprooting moon blossoms one after the other and laying them gently in the sack.

Suddenly, a shiver worked down my spine. The Dark God was watching. For a second, I swore I saw him moving among the surrounding trees. It was like seeing his reflection in the shadows, each patch of darkness a fragment of a broken mirror. I blinked quickly, and it was gone. It had to be an illusion. He'd said that he couldn't cross the boundary of the glade. Melanthe's warning played on repeat in my mind: *Trust no one you see and nothing you hear.*

Heart beating a little faster, I worked double time, stuffing in as much as the sack could hold. I paused when I spotted a beautiful purple flower peeking out from the cluster of white. With vivid purple petals cupping a yellow stamen with sticky pollen, it was breathtaking in contrast to the flowers beside it.

I reached out to pluck it—

"Don't touch that," the Dark God growled. "You'll not wake up again."

I jumped back, terror ringing through me as I spun. Where was he?

But no one was there. Either I was losing my mind or the magic of this place was toying with me. I slipped the sack of moon blossoms over my shoulder as the grass rustled behind me.

I extended my claws and turned. A young woman beamed back at me with a hypnotic smile. "Hello, friend. Do you like my garden?" she said in a lark's voice.

I backed up. "It's beautiful."

The woman leaned down and plucked the purple blossom. "Don't be afraid. I don't mind you picking my flowers. I see you like the moon blossoms, but the dream lily is my favorite. It has such a beautiful scent."

She held the purple flower out to me.

Pointed ears poked through her long, straight black hair. She wore a silver dress that shimmered like mist and gently smiled.

Except she didn't.

I could see through her glamour, and it terrified me to my core. In truth, she was a tall, slender creature that towered at least a foot above me. Her pale green skin stretched thin over her sinuous muscles, and she had three-foot talons instead of fingers.

She smiled, revealing a row of serrated teeth.

The fae that stalk these woods would rip you to shreds then feast on your blood and slowly drain your soul.

In retrospect, that suddenly seemed a little too close to the truth.

21

———

Samantha

The creature's black eyes studied me as it tilted its narrow, almond-shaped head, and its slitted nostrils flared.

I slowly grabbed my sack of moon blossoms and started backing away. "Don't come near me."

The creature advanced toward me, talons flexing. "Don't be afraid, little princess. We can be friends."

"I see through you," I whispered. "I know what you are."

The lids of her obsidian eyes narrowed, and her body coiled. "And I see your heart, thief—stealing my moon blossoms! You're a traitor to your kind!"

The creature leapt forward and reached out with her gruesome talons. She was fast, but I was faster.

I ducked to the side and swiped with my claws out, tearing into her skin. She screeched and struck back, but her talons just missed my chest. I kicked at her knee to spin her around, but she contorted her body in impossible ways and was on top of me in a second.

An instant before her talons ripped into me, magic exploded

through the collar around my neck. It surged through me like a tsunami, and suddenly, the glade and the fae creature were gone.

I collapsed onto my ass at the feet of the Dark God, the sack of moon blossoms spilling beside me.

Axe in one hand, he dropped to my side with a wild look in his eyes. "Are you hurt?"

"No. I'm okay," I panted, sure my heart was ready to explode from my chest.

That fae had been fast, and I didn't want to even consider what might have happened. Even though the collar chaffed against my neck, I was glad I'd been wearing it. Not that I would admit that to him in a thousand years.

The Dark God held out his hand to help me up.

I scrambled to my feet on my own. "What the hell *was* that?"

"A close call," he said, his voice deep and low. "The briarwitch was offering you the gift of endless sleep. Dream lilies are toxic, and briarwitches are the only creature immune to its poison. They plant them among other flowers and bushes to trap their prey. Just touching it would have knocked you out, and she would have fed on your entrails while you lay sleeping."

Prey, that's what I'd been—like a foolish rabbit sitting exposed in a patch of flowers. I dusted off my pants as best I could. "Maybe next time, warn me *specifically* if there will be things like that."

The Dark God's expression of concern hardened into anger. "There are countless perils on this side of the barrier, especially in the sacred glades. I told you to shout and to fucking run if any creature approached."

"And I thought you said you'd be watching. You were a little late on the trigger."

He gestured to the trees around us. "I was watching the

entire forest. That wasn't the only creature lurking in these woods, or the most perilous."

Irritation heated my skin, and I crossed my arms. "I feel like this is more information I should have been given. What's the most dangerous thing out here?"

The Dark God stepped close and fixed me with a lethal stare. "I am."

My breath shook as his power rolled over me.

Of that, I had no doubt.

It was definitely time to get out of the godsdamned Dreamlands.

He looked around, axe at the ready. "That said, let's get out of here before any more fae disguised at young women show up."

I ignored the jibe and shoved the spilled moon blossoms back into the bag. "Actually, I could see through her glamour. It was the same way with the fae I met in Deerhaven. He disguised himself as a werewolf. While it fooled the others in the bar, I could still see his true form."

As we headed for the edge of the woods, the Dark God muttered, "Then you should count yourself lucky."

I narrowed my eyes at him as I trudged along beside him. He didn't seem surprised at all. "Why do I have that ability? Is there something you're not telling me?"

He didn't meet my gaze. "Perhaps it has something to do with your magic gifts."

He was lying. I could sense it like a hot iron pressed against my skin. But why? What was he hiding?

It didn't take long to reach the edge of the forest. The Dark God had moved to a different location than where we'd parted. What had he been up to? Hunting fae? I took a quick glance at his axe. It was hard to see against the black blade, but there was the glint of dried blood.

A shudder raced down my spine.

Still, I'd been glad he'd saved my bacon. Clearly, not all fae could be trusted. Could any of them?

I glanced back over my shoulder. The Moon's barrier moved through the forest behind us like a massive wave of light, held back by the Dark God's magic.

"How far out can you bend the barrier?" I asked.

"Far enough."

Fine. Don't give up state secrets, then.

Vega was still waiting for us beside the oxbow of the stream, along with Kassian and Melanthe on their mounts.

"Success?" Melanthe asked. I held up the bag, and she beamed. "And you look unscathed."

The Dark God scowled as he handed Kassian the moonshard. "There was a close call with a briarwitch. I took care of the rest."

Now that he was in the sun, I could see the streaks of blood on his dark clothes, and my stomach tightened.

He glanced over at Melanthe. "How about you? Did you renew the wards?"

She turned her strider toward the hills. "They'll hold the vines back for a while, though I'm not sure how long."

The Dark God placed his gauntlet in the saddlebag. "Good. We should get out of here before the fae arrive. They'll know I crossed, and you can bet your ass there is a flight of deathwings headed our way."

What the hell were deathwings?

I watched him as he mounted up on Vega's back. His expression was pained, and exhaustion dragged at his movements.

My heart tightened. I'd never seen him like that before. Was it from fighting off the fae in the woods? I imagined he could fight for a thousand years without tiring. Was it from carrying the moonshard? He couldn't touch it directly, and I realized now he had Kassian carry it in his saddlebag instead of ours. Did being near it hurt him? Had using it sapped his strength? If so, how long and how often could he use it?

There were so many questions that I knew he would never answer.

And what about seeing him in the shadows of the glade? I racked my brain as I tied the sack of moon blossoms off on one of Vega's saddlebags. I realized that sometimes, I'd caught a glimmer of movement before.

I glanced up at him. "When you watch through the shadows, can you hear as well?"

The corner of his mouth ticked up in a weary smile. "You never stop probing for information, do you?"

"Just wondering if I should shout *fuck off* the next time I feel you watching me."

He held out his hand to pull me up. "You could, but it wouldn't change a thing."

Of that, I had no doubt. And he'd just confirmed my suspicions—he *could* watch me from the shadows.

He heaved me up, and I settled down in the saddle in front of him. The heat of his body warmed my back, and the rich scent of his sweat addled my brain. He leaned close, and his breath skimmed my neck. "Thank you for doing this, little wolf."

A weight settled on my shoulders as guilt tugged at me, and I wondered if he'd heard what the briarwitch had said.

You're a traitor to your kind.

The next step was to make the balm to heal him, the very beast whose magic had killed many of my pack. Would my pack-mates see me as a traitor? Would Jaxson, my alpha, or Savannah, my best friend? I was helping the very monster we'd risked our lives to stop.

I shut my eyes and tried to steady my breath as anger and regret pierced my chest. What else was I supposed to do? Lay down in a cave and die? If I could just find a way to get free, I'd be able to warn the pack about him. I could bring back intel and maybe even find a weakness we could exploit, like his wound or the moonstone. Maybe there would be a way to rein him in for good.

Would that be enough for them to forgive me?

22

———

Samantha

I was exhausted by the time we passed across the bridge to Shadowstone.

As soon as we were in the courtyard, I slipped off the griff-strider, grabbed the sack of moon blossoms, and headed toward the door.

"Samantha," the Dark God said from behind.

I paused. "What?"

He dropped off Vega's back and strode over, a haze of shadow clinging to his cloak. "Forgetting something?"

He reached up and touched the iron around my neck. I stiffened. There was a click as he unlocked the collar, and then he pulled it from my neck and slipped a key into his pocket.

My pent-up breath slowly escaped. Although a weight had been lifted from my shoulders, I suddenly felt more exposed and I couldn't explain why.

Fucking mind games.

The Dark God turned back toward his strider, unwilling to meet my eyes. "I keep my word, little wolf. We're back. You're free to explore Shadowstone as long as you are accompanied."

The freedom to explore the citadel. I was one step closer to finding a way to escape or a means to get word to my friends. Although it chaffed, that was easily worth the price of the collar.

I followed Melanthe to her workshop with the bundle of flowers in my arms. As soon we were inside, I asked, "What do I do with these?"

She pointed to a long wooden workbench at the far wall. "Put them there, and we'll get to work. Well, mostly you. A sorcerer puts a little of their soul into every potion they brew. While you're no sorcerer, I'm hoping that it will work the same way with you."

I dropped the flowers off and frowned. "I'm afraid I don't know the first thing about crafting." The only thing I ever brewed was moonshine.

"I'll walk you through everything. It's going to take a lot of work." Melanthe held out a basket of pink and green fruit. "We're also going to need some of your blood, so eat up. You want to keep your blood sugar high."

Every muscle in my body tensed. "Again, I'm really not comfortable with blood magic. I have a traumatic past."

She pushed the fruit at me. "Tough. I'm a blood sorceress, and it's what I do. And until you master your own magic, that's how we're going to harness your energy."

Fuck. My. Life.

But it was either this or the cave. I took one of the fruits and bit into it. The sweet juice tasted a bit like a cross between a watermelon and an apple. It was amazing, and I bit off another big chunk.

"These are really good," I mumbled through a succulent mouthful.

She set out a knife and mallet on her wooden workbench. "First step: cut off the bulbs, pound them with the mallet, and grind them up in this mortar." She gestured to a giant stone mortar and pestle beside the bench. "We don't need the rest, but I'll hang the flowers to dry. You never know what's going to be useful in the magic business."

Hoarder mentality. It definitely explained her overflowing shelves.

I picked up the knife and took a deep breath. No big deal. Chop, pound, grind. Heal the Dark God. I could do this. It wasn't much different than muddling an old-fashioned. A pang of sadness knotted my stomach as I recalled my bartending days in Magic Side not that long ago.

How had this become my new life?

Pushing away the memory, I set to work.

It was a lot more difficult than making fancy cocktails at the bar. The bulbs were tough as all hell, and by the third one, my shoulder was sore from pounding them with the mallet. And when I crushed them in the mortar, they let off a pungent scent of melon that was so strong, it was almost stifling.

Melanthe *thunked* a small cast-iron cauldron down on her massive stone worktable. She pressed her fingers to one of the runes carved into its surface, and green fire leapt up beneath the cauldron, like turning on a supernatural gas burner.

"When the bulb mash is as fine as mashed potatoes, scoop it out and dump it in the cauldron," she said.

Melanthe gathered up the flowers as I started beating another batch of bulbs. After a while, I asked, "Why could I enter the fae glade when no one else could?"

The Dark God had already given me his answer, but I wanted to hear hers.

She tapped the pollen from each blossom into a very tiny jar, then hung the blossoms in bunches on a string. "The fae enchanted it so that no one from our realm can enter."

There was an awkward pause while she continued her work, and I waited for her to elaborate. The subtle scent of deception tickled my nose. She hadn't told a lie, but she wasn't telling the truth, either.

I paused pounding. It was the first time I'd caught the scent of Melanthe being dishonest, and that intrigued me. There was something there. "Have you tried breaking the spells that keep you out?"

"It doesn't work like that."

I dropped the crushed bulbs into the stone pestle and began grinding away as nonchalantly as I could. "Are there other places in the fae lands that the people from this realm can't enter?"

Melanthe looked up from her flowers and scrutinized me for a second, then smiled. "You're just fishing for information on how to escape. No offense, but my lips are sealed. I won't cross Cadean."

She returned to hanging the flowers to dry, and I kept grinding. There was another awkward silence.

What was his hold over her? Granted, Jaxson had earned unwavering loyalty from me. A god could probably demand blind devotion, deserved or not.

I paused and rolled my aching shoulders. "How can you work for a monster like *him*?"

"He's not a monster," she said, far too quickly.

I set the pestle down harder than I'd intended. "He's the very definition of a monster. A murderous bastard intent on destroying my world."

Melanthe put down her bundle and fixed me with eyes that were as dark and hard as obsidian. "You have no idea who he is. Many people here owe everything to him, me included. You're in a shitty situation, and I will do my best to make life easier for you, but do not ask me to betray his trust."

"What's his hold over you?"

She looked down at her hands, uneasy for a moment. "I lived

on the other side of the barrier once. When my powers manifested, the fae came to kill me. My family fled here because we had nowhere else to go. Cadean protects his people."

The fae again. She'd been persecuted, and he protected her. I was nauseous and uncertain of what to say. How could I reconcile her perception of him with the monster who'd devastated Dockside and left so many dead and wounded? Bitterness twisted inside of me. "I wonder, if the Dark God had succeeded in destroying Magic Side, would he have offered the same protection to my people?"

Melanthe looked away, regret shaping her expression. "I get why you're angry, Samantha. I would be, too. But there is a lot you don't know about the Dreamlands. Or this war. Or Cadean."

The sadness in her voice tugged at my chest, and a lump of guilt formed in my throat. We were survivors on opposite sides of a war. I hated the Dark Wolf God with my entire soul for what he'd done, but not her. She'd shown me kindness and was the only other woman I'd met in this place. And even if she wasn't willing to betray him, I needed her on my side. I needed a friend.

I rubbed my forehead. "I'm sorry, Melanthe. I'm angry at him, not you."

She nodded. "I understand. And I'm glad you're willing to help, despite everything."

Sighing, I went back to work, but Melanthe rose and placed her hand on my shoulder. "Everything you feel is valid. But for the moment, you need to let go of your anger and hate, or you'll put it into the balm."

I looked down at the bulbs. "I'm not sure I can do that."

"You told me that when you held the Moon's power, you felt like you were glowing, that it was all you ever wanted to feel again. Well, these flowers grow by the barrier and feed on her magic. Each bulb is filled with her power. Concentrate on that. Concentrate on how happy it made you feel."

I took a deep breath and closed my eyes, focusing on the soft sensations of the Moon's magic, the cold and warmth, prickling over my skin. Slowly, it pushed the anger away, and I returned to work.

The cauldron was bubbling when I scooped the last of the moon blossom mash in. Melanthe walked me through the next steps, and we added precisely measured amounts of elderwort extract, cannis bark, and a variety of herbs. The redolent scent went from sweet and floral to downright horrible.

Melanthe sniffed. "Ah, that's coming along nicely. Time for the final ingredient."

She drew a long slender knife from her belt and offered it handle-first to me.

Right. The final ingredient.

I'd known it was going to come to this, but that didn't make it any more palatable. Blood magic was forbidden by our pack, and I was going to use it to heal the Dark God. Fucking insanity. But what else could I do?

Reluctantly, I took the knife, and she passed me a slender brass cup. "Fill it halfway. We don't need much."

Here we go, girls.

I made a tiny cut and watched my lifeforce drain out. I'd donated blood before to help sick people. This wasn't any different, was it?

When the cup was half full, she blotted the wound and smeared on a dab of the healing ointment. "Very good, you'll heal quickly. Eat another fruit."

"Do I pour it in?"

She shook her head. "Not yet. I want you to close your eyes, raise the cup high, focus on your intentions, and push your magic into it. Envision the balm healing his arm. Make yourself believe it will work—*know* that it will work."

It was hard to imagine anything but burning the bastard's skin further. *That* I would delight in. A smirk tugged on my lips, but Melanthe's sharp gaze wiped it right off.

This was my best shot at keeping what freedom I had and staying out of the cave.

I lifted the cup and forced myself to imagine the flesh of his arm becoming smooth and the glowing veins fading away. *Please make this fucking work*, I silently prayed to the Moon Goddess.

Eventually, I lowered the cup. "I'm not sure anything happened—"

She touched my hand to quiet me. "It will work. Believe it, and pour it in."

I tipped the cup and watched as my blood drained into the burbling brew. The concoction began to hiss and turned a pale orange.

After a moment, she shut off the flame. "Very good. The brew will take an hour or so to coalesce, so now we clean up."

I helped her pack the rest of the flowers and dumped the detritus of our work in a bin. We scrubbed the table, then scooped the balm out of the cauldron and into a couple of little jars to cool. It smelled fruity, like persimmons—nothing like the stinking brew from earlier.

"Do you think it will work?" I asked.

She smiled. "You did a good job. It may not cure him completely, but if it can even just halt the advance, it will be a victory."

A little disappointment set in. I didn't have high expectations, but a part of me had hoped that it would be one and done.

"Don't worry. This is a first step, designed to draw out your magic. The more you discover about yourself and your magic, the more effective it will become," she said.

"How does it work, anyway?"

"You'll apply it to the wound and push your magic into it. My hope is that the balm will be the perfect conductor, drawing out your magic and transferring it to him."

The world dropped out from underneath me, and I steadied myself against the table. "No way. I'm not rubbing this on him."

"It's how the balm is designed to work. It has to be you."

Everything in the room began swimming around me. The cauldron, the jars on their shelves, even Melanthe, round and round. This was my nightmare.

Just riding next to him had nearly broken me. I loathed the way my breath shortened when I was near him and the way my skin tingled every time he touched me. It was fucked up how I couldn't tear my eyes from him, how his scent aroused needs I couldn't let myself contemplate.

He was a monster. Nothing more. I couldn't forget that.

Panic seized my mind. "Maybe it will work if someone else does it. We could try. Even if it's not as strong, maybe eventually..."

The certainty in her features brought my words to a stuttering halt.

"You told the Dark God that you would try," she said. "This is it."

I swallowed and closed my eyes. I'd gone so far already. Was I really going to bail? This was one step in the direction of getting out of here. Every part of my soul rebelled, but I reined it in and steeled myself. I had to get home.

You can do this, Sam.

Melanthe took my hand. "I know you dislike Cadean, but put aside whatever you feel about the man and be a healer. He is hurt, and you can help him. That's your obligation here. Treat the wound, not the Dark God. You're taking away someone's pain, and that is a good thing, no matter who they are."

I licked my dry lips. "So I—"

I couldn't say it.

"Just apply the balm to the burns you gave him, and when you do, I want you to focus on that feeling you had when you held the Moon's power. Reach for that power and push it into the wound. Imagine his skin healing, believe in it with all your soul."

My pulse was racing. "I don't know if I can do this."

She gave me a warm smile. "I know you can."

Melanthe led me out of the room and through the winding passages of the Dark God's citadel. We spiraled up into the tower and emerged near my room, then headed down a long hall that terminated at a pair of ornate wooden doors.

I swallowed. "Where are we headed?"

"To his chambers."

My heart tumbled. "He lives on the *same floor* as I do?"

"You're the only one who's up here besides him. Normally, your room is reserved for his brother."

My throat tightened. I would never be able to sleep at night again.

She stopped in front of the door, which had been carved with a hundred different beasts—wolf, eagle, stag, even dragon. They were so realistic that the longer I stared at the intertwined sea of bodies, the more they seemed to move.

I glanced around. "No guards?"

Melanthe gave me a flat look. Oh, right. He was a god, not a king. Top of the food chain.

Before she could knock, the door swung open, revealing a place where the light seemed to hide from the shadows.

The Dark God's chambers.

23

———

Melanthe nodded for me to go on in and softly nudged me forward, but I held my ground.

The Dark God's presence poured out of the room like a river, and my thoughts spiraled in the eddies. The fear he struck in me was so intense, it bordered on desire—like the edge of a cliff, tempting you to lean out as far as you could.

My chest constricted, but I tightened my grip on the balm and craned my neck to see inside the dimly lit room.

I can do this.

Although one side was completely open to an expansive balcony, the light from the sky didn't penetrate far beyond the vaulted arches. It was like a cave overlooking a broad horizon.

The Dark God stood at the balustrade, silhouetted against the sky. His hands gripped it with such force that an irrational part of my mind feared the whole tower would collapse if he let go.

"I've been waiting for you." His voice rumbled low through the chamber and seemed to reverberate unnaturally out of the shadows clinging to those impossibly dark corners.

Now would be a good time to wake up from the nightmare.

But it wasn't a dream, and there wasn't anything I could do but push on forward. Swallowing hard, I stepped inside.

The Dark God didn't turn around. "You've brought the balm?"

I took another step. "Yes."

The door thudded closed behind me, leaving Melanthe impossibly far away. My heartbeat raced. It was just him and me. Alone.

"Join me, please," he commanded, gesturing to the balcony.

I hesitated.

"You don't need to be afraid. I'm not going to hurt you." The low, gravelly tone of his voice tugged on me like an invisible thread. I strained against it, drawing on anger for strength.

"Don't be afraid? That's rich, coming from you." This man had wounded me, killed me, and imprisoned me, and now I was locked in a dark room with him. "Just what should I feel?"

His eyes glistened with diamond light. "Since I took you captive, I haven't hurt you, or tried to. That's a good indication you are safe."

"Said the fox to the hen," I whispered.

After a long pause, he stepped away from the balustrade, slowly stalking toward me as he flicked his hand. A fire spang to life in a hearth at the back of the room, and torches sparked along the wall, yet their warm light did little to dispel the shadows. For a second, my eyes flicked to the bookshelves lining the wall and the thick white fur in front of the fire, and then my wary gaze was back on him.

"As long as you are in my care, I'll never harm you. And you are free to leave this room whenever you wish." He raised his hand, and the door behind me cracked open ever so slightly.

I looked at the thin sliver of light, and I couldn't shake the feeling that if I panicked and dashed toward it, it would disappear like a mirage. "*In your care* is a funny way to phrase it."

"You are. I wouldn't have let anything happen to you in the sacred grove, and nothing will happen to you here. You are safe." He held his hand out, gently motioning me forward.

Here we go.

I sucked in a slow breath and approached one footfall at a time. Every instinct I had told me to run, but he had a dark gravity that pulled me forward. My pulse raced as the dark silhouette slowly resolved into the man. Standing half in shade and half in light, it was like a sculptor had chiseled the Dark God from night itself. His shirt was unbuttoned, the sleeves rolled up his thick forearms, and the way the shadows accented his strong jaw and sculpted muscles made it impossible not to let my eyes drift down his abs and beyond.

He was magnificent, and I couldn't suppress the awe and treacherous desire that filled me.

I swallowed hard as I realized I was going to have to touch him, skin to skin. It was almost too much, yet a vile part of my mind wanted to trace my fingers over those hard angles, just to be certain he was real. My fingers wanted to feel the strength of his flesh and the smooth touch of his skin.

A subtle warmth pooled at my center. I dug my fingers into my palm, reminding myself that I hated the evil, wicked, beast of a god.

Heart racing, I paused at the seam between light and shadow. He took a step closer so that we were only five feet apart. Even at that respectful distance, the radiant heat of his body licked over my skin, raising goosebumps in its wake.

His eyes flicked down to my hand. "Is that the balm?"

My fingers tightened on the jar. "Yes."

He held out his hand expectantly. "Then may I have it, little wolf? Or is it your intention to keep it for yourself and force me into another bargain?"

I licked my dry lips as my stomach went on full retreat. "Actually...I have to put it on." He raised his eyebrows, and I stammered, "On you, not on me. Because it wouldn't make sense the other way around. That is, with putting it on me, instead of you."

His expression was dark.

My stomach flipped. "Sorry, I'm—"

"Babbling," he finished.

"It's what Melanthe told me to do..."

"To babble?"

I blinked. His words had brought me to my senses like a slap across the face. Fates above, had that been a joke? There was no way the monster had made a joke, though the slight tug at the corner of his mouth claimed otherwise.

I seized on my anger before my thoughts could go in another direction. He was a sadist, that was all. He was savoring this— probably drinking in my terror like a cocktail and relishing the way I squirmed beneath his gaze.

Fear and embarrassment distilled into fury, and for one second, I slipped out of the terrified shell I'd become and into the old me. The real me, the one that wasn't a prisoner and terrified she'd never be free.

I held up the ointment. "Here's the plan. The shit in this jar goes on your fucking arm, and I have to put it there because of magic. So let's get this over with."

"I see," he said, his gentle amusement clear. I glared, but he motioned to a crystalline bottle of golden liquid on the railing beside two glasses. "Would you like a drink? You seem like you could use one."

"No," I said sharply. "Let's get on with it."

Actually, I needed a drink very badly, but I sure as hell wasn't going to turn this into cocktail hour.

Without a word, the Dark God unwrapped the bandages around his arm, revealing the burned skin. The blue-white lines running beneath his skin glowed like they'd been lit by a blacklight.

I glanced at the gorgeous god that stood before me—the architect of my misery. *Treat the wound. Not the man.*

I unstopped the jar and tucked the cork in my pocket. Then I dipped my fingers in the balm and set the jar aside on the wide balustrade. Shaking, I reached out and grasped his offered wrist with my free hand. A soft surge of electricity flowed between us —not like a shock, more like a low hum. My breathing quickened, and his eyes dilated.

He'd sensed it, too.

I blobbed the translucent orange balm onto his skin, and he jerked slightly. Then, closing my eyes, I slowly rubbed the ointment over his skin and concentrated on remembering the warm glow of the Moon's magic. It had filled me with such light that I thought I was going to explode.

If only I could find that feeling again—but it was almost impossible to think of the Moon's magic with his dark presence wrapped around me, blotting out her light.

I tried to focus on what mattered. I had to heal the Dark God and get home to my mother. To Savy and Jax and Magic Side and my pack. I prayed to the Moon Mother as I began massaging balm onto the other side of his arm.

Please heal, for fates' sake.

But nothing changed. The only thing I could feel was the monster, watching me work.

"Everything okay?" he asked.

"Fine," I said, opening my eyes and scooping more of the

balm on my fingers. "Just trying to do magic or something. Do you feel anything?"

He cleared his throat. "As far as the wound goes, it stings. Burns, really."

I sighed. What a fucking joke. They had the wrong girl for sure.

The Dark God raised his other hand. The lights in the room swelled, then dimmed. "I never concentrate on my magic or force it. I concentrate on what I want to happen, and the magic does the work."

"You're a god. I'm not."

"That doesn't matter."

I steeled my mind and forced myself to imagine those lines receding and the skin becoming smooth—despite how much I enjoyed seeing him suffer. But there was no tingle of magic, no change in his skin. The truth was clear as day. No matter how much I was trying to will it into existence, I didn't want to heal him. I wanted to burn him, hurt him, and drive him out of my life.

Eventually, he pulled his arm away. "We can try again another day. Maybe the balm will work its magic at night."

But I held on, and his expression flashed with surprise.

"I'm not a quitter." I dipped my fingers and set to massaging it into his bicep and the faint lines that crept up his shoulder. I wanted to be free. Craved it with all my soul. If I had any magic in me, that would be what would wake it up.

I imagined him releasing me, his arm healed and pure. I begged with my fingers as I rubbed the balm into his wounds. *Freedom, freedom, freedom.* I repeated it like a mantra, over and over and over, and then, after a moment, a soft warmth began building in my fingertips.

I held my breath, not daring to let myself think about the tingling sensation or risk breaking my concentration. I just poured every ounce of willpower I had into that wish for freedom and the magic that would make it possible. *Freedom, fates, give me freedom.*

I lost myself in the motion and forgot everything but the sensation of touch. Sight, sound, taste—I was lost to them all. The only thing that existed were my fingertips tracing along his skin. My fingers turned wildly sensitive as every nerve in my body switched on.

I forgot where my skin ended and his began. I forgot how much I hated him or that I was even a prisoner. I forgot everything, except my hand that was pressed against his skin.

For a second, we were the only thing in the world. And then there was a spark. A jolt of electricity racing through me like a lightning bolt, like someone had flipped a breaker that I had no way to shut off.

My eyes flew open as I gasped and looked down. My hands glowed with radiant light that was pouring into him.

24

———

Cadean

For an hour there had been nothing. And then my nerves exploded with pleasure as Samantha's magic flared and her light raced over my skin.

She rocked forward, mouth open in a silent moan, and I had to grit my teeth to stifle a growl. Her touch was almost more than I could bear. It was cool and warm, and it overwhelmed my senses, like stepping into the daylight after living your life in the dark.

What was happening? Wherever there had been pain, there was ecstasy...and then the sensation was gone.

She stumbled away from me, shock etched on her beautiful face. "Holy shit."

Holy shit was right.

I raised my arm and marveled. The scars had begun to heal, and the glowing lines had receded. But most importantly, the pain was almost gone. After a month of nearly endless agony, I could think. The pain had been like a waterfall roaring in my mind, a ceaseless noise that had made it hard to concentrate or even think. But it was gone now, replaced by blissful silence.

I turned my arm over in awe. "It's working...your magic works."

We locked gazes, our chests heaving like we'd both run up a mountain.

It hadn't just worked—it had been overwhelming pleasure pouring through my body. I hadn't wanted it to end. I was beyond aroused and painfully stiff, and I couldn't tear my eyes from the sweat glistening on her neck and chest.

She was the answer.

A dozen witches, mages, and fae creatures had all tried to treat the wound with their potions and incantations, yet Samantha had succeeded where the others had failed.

Her magic was doing more than healing me. It had woken wild desires, the need to drink in the scent of her exertion, to drag my lips over her body and taste the sweat that had formed on her skin. To worship her in ways that would make the maenads blush.

The seduction of healing magic.

There was no doubt, Samantha felt it, too. Her eyes flickered with surprise and desire, and I could smell the need rising within her, demanding to be set free.

For a second, she took the slightest step forward.

The animal within urged me to pull her close, but I fought back with what little restraint I had left. As much as I craved her lips, I would never take advantage of her. Her soul was too pure to be tainted by mine.

Regret tearing at me, I pulled my hand from her grasp. I opened my mouth to explain, but Mel's voice echoed from the corridor: "He's occupied. Come back later."

"But the door is open," Auren said.

Anger drowned every other emotion swarming through me. My brother. I cursed the fates that made him. The bastard had impossible timing and was the only one brazen enough to disturb me in my chambers.

Confusion flashed in Samantha's eyes as she realized how close we were, and she retreated to the other side of the room. "I should go."

I lifted my hand to shut the door, but Auren pushed through, despite Mel's protests. He stopped short when he saw Samantha, his eyes blazing with curiosity and intrigue. My hand dropped to my belt, but my axe wasn't there.

Samantha looked enraptured, and white-hot rage raced through my veins. "I'm busy."

"I can see that," my brother mused in an approving voice, his eyes not wavering from Samantha.

She backed up, swallowing. "I was just leaving. Excuse me."

Before I could protest, she slipped past Auren and out the door. Her sudden absence sucked the breath from my lungs. I took a step in pursuit but stopped myself. Mel exclaimed something from outside, and I heard them leave down the hallway. I inhaled deeply, trying to clear my mind—yet it did the opposite. Her honey and lavender scent lingered in the air, an aphrodisiac that sent my head spinning.

Auren grinned. "I'm so sorry to disturb you, dear brother. I didn't realize you had a new mistress. Either she's very good or you're out of practice. She wasn't in here long."

Fucking ass.

I flicked my hand, and the door slammed shut. "Prisoner. Not mistress. I was mining her for information."

Auren met my furious gaze with a broad grin and scoffed. "I doubt that very much, given your penchant for blondes. I spotted her and Melanthe in the hallway. She doesn't look like a prisoner."

I turned my back as I wrapped the bandages around my

wound. The last thing I wanted was for my brother to know the extent of how much I now depended on her.

She had some type of power over me that I didn't understand. I was certain of it now. I'd felt a connection between us—the chilling sensation of someone else being in control. The power to heal, to wound, and to bend my mind. I had no doubt that in the hands of the fae, she would bring an end to me.

I had to find a way to control her, to keep her away from them. And away from him. The truth was clear: I could never let her go free.

Tucking my arms behind my back, I turned to face him. "She's simply working to earn her freedom. Providing me with intel. Nothing more."

Auren joined me on the balcony. "I don't believe that for a second, unless we have a very different interpretation of *working*. I know that look in your eyes. You've scented her, and you're on the hunt. You even gave her my room, for fates' sake. I must admit, I'm a little hurt."

Part of me wanted to crack him over the head and hurl him off the balcony—not that it would do any good. He'd just take me with him or turn into an eagle. We shared similar magic and were so evenly matched, fighting was pointless.

Instead, I uncorked the mead I'd set out to put Samantha at ease and poured a glass of the golden liquid for him. "You have no idea what you're talking about, as usual."

Auren took it and raised it in salute. "I'm your brother. I know you better than you know yourself, unfortunately." After a sip, he held it out, appraising it. "What is this? It's marvelous."

Pouring a drink for myself, I halfheartedly saluted him in turn. "Elderflower mead from the Summerlands, made by Bacchus himself."

Auren gave a low whistle and sniffed his glass in appreciation. "How did you even get a bottle? Your guest must have provided you with very special assistance, indeed."

Rather than respond, I took a sip and let the mead play across my tongue. It tasted like sunlight and soft breezes and smelled of flowers rustling in the wind. And without persistent pain tearing through my thoughts, I was able to actually savor it.

Or I would have if my brother hadn't intruded. With a sigh, I set down the cup. "Prisoner. And we didn't drink."

He laughed and looked out over the balcony. "That only means you offered, and she turned you down. You should summon her back. A bottle like this should be enjoyed with a beautiful woman. Perhaps I might be able to persuade her."

Auren reached for the bottle, but I put the stopper back in and held it in place. "You're right. This would be better enjoyed with a woman. And as long as you're here, you're forbidden to go near her."

He released the glass neck of the bottle and gave me a wolfish grin. "Now you've got me really interested. You're jealous...and if it's not about her raging sex appeal, *as you claim*, then why be so possessive?"

"That's none of your business." I returned the mead to the shelf and searched for the right bottle. It had to be something strong and bitter and complex, like our relationship. Hopefully, I could get him drunk enough to forget all about this. I pulled down a dusty, dark brown bottle of cedar bark wine made from my own forests and filled our glasses.

My brother gave me a sour look. "Come on, Cade, you know I'll find out eventually."

It was true—my brother had spies everywhere. Still, I wasn't going to give up the information so easily. Not without getting something in return.

I drummed my fingers on the balcony railing in annoyance. "Just *how* long are you staying?"

He snorted and downed half his drink. "Until I get bored."

The heat of frustration began to creep up my neck. "Don't you have your own kingdom to attend to?"

He leaned back casually against the railing and topped his glass. "My kingdom is tedious. I know everything that's going on there, while you clearly have something exciting on your hands. I can't help but investigate."

Samantha.

I stepped close to my brother and locked his gaze. "You're not to go near her. That is my condition for allowing you to stay."

"Your condition? That sounds almost inhospitable of you. When did we stop sharing?"

He knew exactly when.

"You're lucky that I enjoy your company," I snarled, baring my teeth.

Auren took the bottle and topped my glass. "Only when you're drunk, so let's drink."

25

———

Cadean

I woke in pain. My arm burned as if someone was flaying my skin from my body, one layer at a time.

With a low growl, I threw off the bearskin and examined my wound beneath the light streaming in from the balcony. My scars had worsened, and the blue-white lines had advanced back up my arm—almost to where they had been before.

Fuck.

The treatment had failed.

On top of that, my head was pounding, but that part was my own fault. My brother was one of the only beings in existence who could give me a hangover. Why the hell had I even lifted a glass with him?

I threw on my clothes and stormed through the tower until I reached Mel's door. Between the omnipresent pain and the hammering in my head, it was nearly impossible to think. I had to do something.

I knocked three times, then waited. Minutes ticked by.

Finally, the door swung open, revealing Mel, bleary-eyed and in a bathrobe. "Do you have any idea what time it is?"

"The sun is up."

She motioned me inside. "Well, I had a late night. It looks like you had a late night, too."

"My brother stopped by."

"I saw." Her lips tightened with disgust. "He's the last person you want around here right now."

"Don't you think I know that? But we need his help against the fae. I can't put him off."

She yawned and lit a green flame beneath her kettle. "Is this about him?"

I showed her my arm. "The balm didn't work. Last night, I thought Samantha had almost cured me. I could think and feel again. But now, the pain is worse than ever."

Her expression turned grim as she took my arm. We both knew what was at stake.

"Well, your hangover probably isn't helping the pain," she muttered. "Fortunately, the wound is slightly better. The scars have improved, and the tendrils have retreated."

I sucked in an unsteady breath as frustration tore at me.

"If you want to get this under control, Samantha will need to attend to you each day—though I suspect she's not going to be happy about it," Mel said.

I pulled away. "I don't give a damn. I need a cure. Fates, I need to be able to think."

The devil only knew how I was going to keep my mind around that woman. Her scent addled my thoughts, and her touch had been beyond maddening, stirring a ravenous beast inside me. When she'd stepped toward me, it had taken all my willpower not to press my mouth to hers.

What kind of monster would she think me then?

Mel turned her back to me and poured herself a cup of tea. "If you want a cure, we'll need to teach her to harness her magic and use it properly. Until then, everything else will be a stopgap."

"Absolutely not." I began rewrapping my arm. "She gave me these wounds in the first place. You heard the fae bastard in the dungeon: Samantha has the power to bring me to my knees. To bind me with bonds that cannot be broken. If she knew what she was doing..."

Mel turned around and leaned against the table. "She just wants to cure you and get free."

I met her eyes with a grim look. "She wants to destroy me. If she could harness that power, do you think she would walk away? She despises me with her entire soul. She risked her life twice to stop me from taking Magic Side, and she agreed to help the fae bastards as well. If she has a chance to cripple me, she'll take it—or do you assess the situation differently?"

Mel was silent for a long time. We both knew I was right.

She looked out the window at the land beyond. "It's a risk. But you to need to decide whether you're more afraid of Samantha developing her magic or the fae invading your realm. Because if we don't cure your wound, they will come and make prey of us all."

I ran my hands through my hair. "What am I supposed to do?"

She shrugged. "Convince her you're not a monster."

My stomach sank, and I set my jaw. "But I am."

She turned and gave me a sad smile. "Then start by convincing yourself."

$\sim$

Samantha

The scent of warm biscuits stirred me from my sleep. I sat up, blinking in the sunlight.

There was a basket on the table, along with a pitcher of milk. I hadn't heard the door, so who'd been in my room? Melanthe?

Fates, I hoped it had been her.

Hunger rumbled in my stomach, and I massaged my temples. I'd been pretty shaken up after healing the Dark God, so Mel had calmed my nerves with a cocktail of wine, fruit, and herbs that she'd brewed. Sorceress sangria. It was delicious and refreshing, and we'd drunk way too much. Hopefully, I hadn't run my mouth.

I wasn't prone to the best decision-making while under the influence. And I'd been under the influence last night, drawn in by the magnetism of *his* power, my senses dulled by the elation of finding the magic inside me and by the sudden, overwhelming connection between us.

It had left my mind spinning with desire and an unshakable need to embrace the moment, to feel alive. I shuddered, thankful that we'd been interrupted.

Healing magic was a notorious aphrodisiac, and my mind had been fogged, hadn't it? Yet for some reason, I couldn't shake the uneasy feeling of sudden clarity, of that magic cutting through a fog I'd lived with my whole life.

No. It was just the magic and wonder of it all. That was it.

I shoved the ridiculous feeling out of my mind, slipped out of bed, and wandered to the table. The basket was overflowing with jellies and honey, along with a tub of butter. It had to have been Mel. Who else would know I liked them?

For a second, I felt the Dark God's gaze on me, hot and tingly, and I spun toward the shadows.

My breath eased out. No one was there, and the sensation of being watched faded. Maybe it had just been my imagination.

I dug into my breakfast, and my thoughts churned. The night before, I'd healed the Dark God. Not completely, but partially. The ramifications were almost too staggering to contemplate. If I could heal him completely, would he let me go?

Of course, there was the other part. Almost the *bigger* part: I had magic. My soul had come alive as it flowed through me. And this time, it had been *my* magic, not the Moon's. I was certain of it.

There was no hiding from the truth any longer. I was more than just a werewolf. But that just created more questions. Was it from my father? What had he been? What could I do? How could I even use it?

I suddenly felt overwhelmed and sick to my stomach—though that might have had something to do with overeating. I looked down at my crumb-covered plate and then at the diminished basket.

Fates, how many biscuits had I wolfed down? Half a dozen, at least, all slathered with butter and honey and jam.

I looked from the bed to the tub to the pile of food and shuddered as I recalled the dank darkness of the cave. *Cooperation has its perks.*

Crossing the room, I tested the door. Locked.

So much for that promised freedom.

Then the lock clicked, and it partially opened.

"Yes? Did you wish to go somewhere?" an unfamiliar voice said.

I slammed it shut. "Who are you? I'm not dressed!"

"I'm one of your bodyguards. If you wish to explore the citadel, uh, after you put some clothes on, of course, we're assigned to accompany you."

Holy shit. Freedom was back on the menu.

My heart raced with excitement. "Yes. I want to, just give me a moment. And keep the door locked."

The lock *clacked* back in place, and I breathed a sigh of relief.

"Who brought the food?" I asked through the door. "I don't want anyone in here without my permission, even Melanthe."

"What food?" the guard asked. "Do you need breakfast?"

I glanced over my shoulder. The basket was still there, and I was stuffed, so it wasn't an illusion. Maybe she'd used magic?

"Never mind. I'll be out in ten." I crossed to the room and tested the windows. Still locked.

Well, I'd sort it all out later. I selected one of the outfits Mel had loaned me, then rushed into the bathroom to change. As I pulled the shirt down over my head, there was a clink from my room. My heart skipped. Someone was there. I could hear them breathing and moving quietly.

I extended my claws and flipped around the corner.

The little goblin's eyes went wide, and he clutched a pile of biscuits to his chest and bared his pointy teeth.

I relaxed. *Him.*

"What are you doing in here? Did *you* bring the biscuits?"

He looked at me in confusion. Of course not—he was trying to steal them.

Giving me a guilty look, he dumped the biscuits back in the basket and backed away. They looked...slimy. My stomach turned.

Then the little goblin dug around in his satchel and pulled out a frog. It croaked and squirmed. He pointed from it to the basket, then offered the frog to me.

"No. I don't want a frog," I snapped. Then again, I didn't want biscuits covered with goblin cooties. I dropped to one knee. "How about we trade? I'll give you all the biscuits if you can bring me a key to this room. Or even the windows. Can you do that?"

He hesitated and shrugged. Then in a blur of motion, he leapt onto the table, grabbed the basket, and vanished with a pop.

"Hey!" I shouted, but the little thief was gone. I put my hands on my hips and sighed. "Fuck. I should have asked him to teach me that trick."

When he didn't return, I went back to getting ready, then pounded on the door. "I want to see Mel. Can you take me to her?"

The door unlocked, revealing a pair of hulking warriors in chain mail with swords hanging at their side. They had the scent of shifters, panther and wolf.

The panther shifter inclined his head. "Follow me."

26

———

Samantha

We wound our way down through the tower, but partway there, a voice called out behind me: "It's Samantha, isn't it?"

My heart jumped, and I spun around, claws out, as my guards went for their blades.

The man who'd interrupted us last night was leaning against an archway, crossing his sun-kissed forearms. He was tall and handsome, and a slight shimmer of golden light emanated off him. The scent of toasted wheat and amber wound around me, and my breath stilled. His aura was almost as strong as the Dark God's.

The guard on my right relaxed slightly, but I didn't sheathe my claws. "Who are you? Why do you know my name?"

"My name is Auren—or it's the one I use here. I heard that my brother had a new prisoner, and I wanted to see what all the fuss was about." Amusement flickered across his face. "Now I know."

Brother. My blood turned cold. There were two of the bastards?

He took a step forward, but the wolf shifter stepped in front, hand still on his blade. "Lord Auren, my apologies, but no one is to speak to her without his permission."

"No one? Or just me, I wonder?" His lips curled up into a deadly smile. "I understand that you don't want to disappoint your master, but he's not here, and if I read your posture correctly, you are openly threatening a god."

His signature washed over us, bringing to mind ripe wheat on a hot summer's day. The tension in my shoulders relaxed slightly, and both guards backed down. The wolf bowed his head. "Of course not. I am sure you're an exception."

They stepped to the side, leaving me standing in the middle of the hall. Auren slowly walked around me, a tiger circling his prey. I backed away but suddenly bumped against the wall, and I swallowed as I looked up into his hungry eyes.

He gave me a soft smile. "I know my brother is a bit of a beast, but we're not all monsters. You don't need to be afraid."

Suddenly, there was a wave of magic, and I relaxed as my thoughts became clearer. Of course I didn't have to be afraid of him. He was immensely powerful. If he'd wanted to hurt me, he would have done so already.

Feeling foolish, I retracted my claws. "I just didn't know who you were. Do you live here as well?"

"Me?" He laughed. "Fates, no. I have my own kingdom. I visit from time to time to see how my younger brother is doing— being locked up in a prison can be so stifling. We used to have such a good time, roving the countryside and spreading mayhem together."

His searching gaze sent a shiver down my spine. "The more interesting question is, why are *you* here? At first, I'd assumed he was keeping you around for fun—he has a penchant for blondes, you see—but now I'm not so certain."

Although his power was intoxicating, I turned my cheek to the side. "Why don't you ask your brother?"

One god was too much already, and I didn't want to draw the attention of another.

Auren inclined his head, and his signature washed over me again, calming my nerves. "Cadean likes to play games, and sometimes, he forgets to tell me things. For instance, what does he want with you, Samantha?"

The way he purred my name made my insides flip. What was it about these brothers that was so damn alluring?

"He thinks I can heal his wound," I blurted, immediately regretting it.

"Can you?"

"Maybe. I healed it a little."

"That's a relief. I was afraid that it was causing him great pain. Do you know how he got it? He hasn't been very forthcoming."

His presence tugged the words from my lips. "I gave it to him."

Auren smiled broadly. "Ah. No wonder the fascination."

I had the peculiar feeling of having said too much. Was I supposed to keep what I was doing a secret? From the Dark God's own brother? Yet for some reason, the words kept flowing from my lips. "If I can cure it, he'll let me go."

"Is that so?" he asked, a mischievous tone to his voice. "My brother has been able to get his hands on all sorts of unusual things lately. I doubt he will want to let go of you, though. Not something so clearly unique." His bright eyes dipped to my lips for a moment, and he grinned.

Bile rose in my throat, and something within me shouted that this *was not right*. No matter what I was feeling, these thoughts were not my own.

"I'm getting out, one way or another," I muttered, then immediately regretted it as Auren's eyebrows lifted. Why was I was running my mouth? Normally, I was very tight lipped.

The voice inside screamed at me, dispelling some of the comfortable warmth, and I gave Auren a suspicious look.

He opened his mouth, then shut it. "Well, I'm afraid I must run. It was wonderful meeting you. Please, if you need anything, don't hesitate to search me out. You're in my old room, after all."

He gave me a wink and headed toward the archway, but right before stepping through, he put one hand on the stones and looked back. "Just a warning, young wolf. My brother is the jealous type, so I think for your sake, you might want to keep our conversations secret." He looked from me to the guards. "All of you."

His energy rolled over me, and I shuddered as his point rammed home. I *definitely* didn't want to give the Dark God any excuse to be pissed at me or throw me back in the cave.

I breathed a sigh of relief after he left and turned to my guards. "Let's go."

My pulse pounding in my skull, we continued on our way.

How were the two brothers even related? I could see the surface resemblance, but in every other aspect, they were wildly different. While the Dark God was brooding and severe, his brother was jovial and suave. Auren's signature was like sunlight, while the Dark God's was all shadows and fire.

Both were trouble. I shuddered.

I suspected Auren had been mining me for information he wasn't supposed to have. That was a problem, but also an opportunity. I had something he wanted. Perhaps I could win him to my side. It could be very useful—or perilous—to have someone that powerful in my corner.

It was, of course, a foolish game to even contemplate. Just like dream lilies, not everything that was beautiful was safe to touch.

～

As we approached Mel's workshop, the door opened, and the Dark God stepped out. His frown was hard and almost pained, and the shadows of the hall clung to him as he moved. He froze when he saw me, and a touch of a smile threatened to crack his grim expression. "Already roaming the corridors, I see."

I stopped fifteen feet away. After last night, it was almost too close. The scent of him, even at a distance, threatened to muddle my mind, and I couldn't help but remember the sensation of gliding my fingers across his skin. Of pouring my light into him. Of being overwhelmed with confusion, desire, and something else.

Neither of us moved.

I gestured to my guards. "I thought I'd take the opportunity to get out and about before you took it away from me."

It wasn't entirely banter. Now that I had the room and a little freedom, I was terrified he'd withdraw it all.

The shadows trailed after him as he began to walk toward me. He inclined his head in acknowledgement. "You keep your part of the bargain, and I will keep mine."

I let my gaze drift from his powerful jaw down to his bandaged arm. "Are you feeling better?"

His fist clenched. "Some of the veins came back. It will take more treatments, I'm afraid. But thank you for what you did. It was..." His Adam's apple rose and fell as he swallowed. "It was a relief."

Was.

My shoulders dropped. Although I hadn't admitted it to myself, I'd hoped that the magic would keep working through the night, and he'd wake up healed. Instead, it sounded like the wound had regressed.

I licked my lips. "Does it hurt?"

The corner of his mouth twitched up. "We've done this song and dance before. Yes, it hurts. Happy?"

Remorse for my earlier barb lanced through me, and I shook my head. "No. I want you healed." He raised an eyebrow, and I quickly added, "So that you'll let me go."

A glimmer of guilt flickered across his face, and he looked down at his hand. "That may be some time."

"I understand," I said, a little too sharply. Maneuvering around him, I headed for Mel's door. "I'll see if there's anything I can do to speed up the process."

He gently took my arm, and a shiver raced up my spine as I stopped to meet his eyes. His touch was electric, and my nerves woke with anticipation. "Is there something else?" I asked.

"There are problems on the border. I'm heading out on patrol tomorrow, and I'll be gone all day."

My throat tightened, and I pulled from his grasp. "To do what? Murder fae?"

"No. To inspect the border and look for signs of activity." He hesitated and glanced from me to the guards and back. "You could come if you wished to get out of Shadowstone."

My wolf leapt in my chest. *Hell, yes, I do.*

"Would I be able to run my wolf?" I asked.

He released me. "I want to get eyes on the border as quickly as possible. But maybe on the way back."

"I'll come."

The Dark God fixed me with a hard, unyielding stare. "You recall the conditions?"

The collar. Fuck. The sweet taste of his signature turned bitter in my mouth. I wanted nothing to do with that thing, but this was my chance to get out of the citadel and see more of the Dreamlands. Maybe it would lead to more freedom, or at least a little trust.

Swallowing, I nodded. "I remember."

27

———

Samantha

True to his word, the Dark God sent for me the next day. His guards brought me down to the aviary where they kept the griff-striders. It was a lofty stable, built into the side of the basalt cliffs. Each of the griffstriders had their own cave in which they lurked.

Dozens of falcon-like eyes watched me from the shadows as I entered. The Dark God was tending to Elowyn, the strider who'd bucked me off the other day.

He turned and his gaze dragged across me with a hungry intensity that made my stomach flutter.

I steeled myself and strode over. "No chance Elowyn agreed to let me ride on my own today?"

He tore his eyes away, though a hint of a smile graced his lips. "I think the two of you have a way to go yet. We'll ride together. You ready?"

"I was ready yesterday."

Guilt flashed in his eyes. "We have a bargain..."

I tensed and my wolf thrashed in my chest at the thought of

wearing the collar, but in this fucked up world, that was the cost for a chance to smell the scents of the woods and feel the caress of the sun and the wind. "A devil's bargain." I pulled my hair away from my neck. "But go ahead. I'm ready to get out of here."

He hesitated, then slowly slipped the collar around my neck, raising goosebumps across my skin. His intoxicating magic washed over me as the iron collar locked beneath his fingers, cold, heavy, and unyielding.

My mind swam with emotions. I was furious, but his touch was gentle, almost kind, and I'd felt a pang of longing as his fingers dropped away. I drew in a quaking breath. "Well. Here we are again."

His hand dropped, and his expression turned foreboding. "Even in my realm, the Dreamlands are dangerous. This is for your protection, little wolf."

"And your control," I whispered.

His jaw hardened. "That, too."

The Dark God handed me a long knife in a leather sheath. "You should be armed. The danger is no illusion."

What the hell were we riding into?

I took it and strapped it to my belt. "I guess this means you're not worried that I'll stab you in the back?"

"Compared to what you've done to me already, I doubt I'd even bat an eye."

Good to know. Don't try to kill a god with a steak knife.

We mounted up on Elowyn and rode deep into his lands. Her pace was quick, though not a hard gallop. I tried to focus on memorizing the path and savoring the scents of the wild, but it was almost impossible to think of anything but the Dark God's body moving against mine. Stride by stride, heat built in my core.

My heart was pounding by the time the Dark God slowed Elowyn. He tensed and sniffed the air.

I craned my neck to look up at him. "What is it?"

"Vines. New growth—they weren't here two weeks ago."

The Dark God maneuvered Elowyn down into a gully, where we spotted the first tendrils. "We'll follow them north for a while and cut them off where they thicken."

We crossed through one of the heavy banks of mist that separated the patches, and his gripped tightened around me, pulling me against his hard body. I could feel every inch of him, and my skin flushed despite the cold, damp air.

As ruins emerged from the mist, we wove between piles of ancient rubble. The crumbling houses were covered with thick vines, and trees with golden and red leaves grew in their midst.

"We'll stop here," he said. "The overgrowth of vines is new."

The devastation wasn't. The place looked like it had been hit by a tornado and reminded me of the village I'd visited with Sarion—the one where I'd seen bones twisted in the roots of trees. Would it be the same here?

As we slowed to a stop, my stomach lurched, and I tasted bile in my throat. The Dark God slipped out of the saddle and reached up to help me down. "Is everything okay?"

My chest ached as I surveyed the ruins. "Is this your handiwork or the fae's?"

His expression turned cold. "This was the fae."

I slipped over the other side of Elowyn without his help. "How am I supposed to tell the difference? They destroy your villages, and you destroy theirs. The people on the land lose. You and the fae, you're just the same."

He stalked around the back of the strider, and his signature burned with flames of fury. "They stole my lands and are draining the life from what is left. They attack across the border to weaken me, unprovoked."

Unfazed, I crossed my arms and fixed him with a stone-cold stare. "And what about Magic Side? That was unprovoked."

The ruins beneath the trees could have been Dockside. I could imagine the beautiful fall trees growing up from the heart of Eclipse, the bar where I worked. Would I find the bones of our patrons bound up in the roots, or just broken liquor bottles?

The Dark Wolf God paused, and a pained look flashed across his shadowed face. "You would not understand, little wolf."

With that, he raised his hand, and his axe appeared in a burst of shadow magic. He turned and stalked toward the vines as the sky overhead darkened.

That was all he had to say?

I hurried after. "I watched my people die, so there'd better be a fucking explanation."

He stopped in his tracks, but he didn't look back. "Before the Moon locked me away, I roamed the earth freely. I protected shifters and the wilderness. Once I'd amassed enough power to see into the waking world again, I was horrified by what I saw. A rage took me."

"And so you thought that a great way to come back was to take out your anger on Magic Side?" I said, each word pointed like the blade of a knife.

"Twelve hundred years ago, your continent was wild and beautiful. But everything has been leveled with farms and roads and cities, and the people who'd once lived in the wilderness had all been murdered and driven off their land. I went insane with fury. I wanted to restore the balance to the way it had been."

I swallowed. And that was only one part of the dark past of our continent. Disgust and sadness churned in my gut, but I shook my head. "Those changes happened long ago. The people you killed had nothing to do with them."

"Those changes are still happening," he growled, and swung his axe wide, cutting through three vines as thick as my leg. The strike sent purple-black liquid spraying across the walls. Splattered with vine blood, he looked back at me with piercing blue eyes that made my heart stutter. "It doesn't matter. I've given up on your world. I have my own domain to save and my own people to protect." His voice rang with anger and a deep sadness. The sense of his loss and failure was overwhelming.

Guilt tore at me, but fury as well. He wasn't wrong about what had happened, but everything he'd done was wrong.

He threw the cut vines by the base of a tree and moved further into the ruins. Had he really given up on our world? The words lit the slightest glimmer of hope in my soul. Did that mean Magic Side was safe?

The Dark God brought his axe down, cleaving through another vine and reducing the wall it covered to a pile of rubble. A dreadful certainty settled in my chest, extinguishing the flame. *As soon as he's done with the fae, he'll return, just as angry as before.*

With nowhere else to go, I followed him. He seized another vine and raised his axe, but he froze mid-strike. A six-foot-long chrysalis clung to the side of the vine, and it was open.

The hair on my neck rose. "What is that?"

The Dark Wolf God scanned the forest with his axe at the ready. "It's the chrysalis of a broodling."

Well, that sounded fucking bad. I slipped the blade he'd given me out of its sheath. "Do you want to tell me what the hell a broodling is, or is this another surprise like the briarwitch?"

He scowled. "Broodlings are the hounds of the fae, used for hunting and raiding. Thankfully, this one is long gone. You can sheath your weapon."

I realized I was holding my breath. "What do they look like?"

"Spidery, with long legs and many eyes. They're blood drinkers."

With a shudder, I knelt and inspected the chrysalis with the tip of my knife. "They go through metamorphosis? What do they start out as? Giant worms?"

The Dark God inspected the other vines. "The mature form lays eggs that hatch into giant white and purple larvae. They feed off the sap of the vines and carrion. Once the grubs get to the size of a bear, they form a chrysalis and become a broodling."

Bear-sized grubs. *No, thank you.*

"The final stage of their lifecycle is a deathwing. Silent as the night, they can fly up behind you and inject you with a lethal toxin, then they carry you off to feed on you."

Well, hell.

I rose and backed away from the chrysalis. "You know, I think I'm finding that I'm not a fan of the flora and fauna in the Dreamlands."

He laughed softly—such a strange sound to come from the dark and brooding god who moments before had looked ready to lay waste to the world.

I narrowed my eyes at him. "Something funny?"

"I'll admit, you haven't seen the Dreamlands at its best."

"I have a hard time imagining what that's like."

He closed his eyes and reached up with his hand. His signature rolled through the forest like a rustling wind, and I tasted chocolate on my tongue. A shiver of pleasure ran down my spine as his magic spread around us. Then the leaves of the trees around turned from yellow to green, and tiny white blossoms formed.

I smiled in wonder. It was like he'd reversed fall to spring.

The Dark God opened his eyes and gave me a mournful smile. "You haven't seen me at my best, either."

Apparently not.

He picked a flower and held it out to me as all the other petals began to fall around us like snow. I swallowed, and not knowing what to do, I took the flower. "If you can do this, why not restore all your dead forests?"

A look of sadness crossed his face. "I don't have the power to bring back the dead, and the vines kill. Luckily, cutting them can restore a little life."

"Then we should cut some more."

He gave me a look that I couldn't quite read. It was scrutinizing, as if I'd just done something quite strange.

I frowned, feeling suddenly uneasy. "What?"

"Nothing. Just glad for the help." With a long strike, he cut the chrysalis from the vine. "Another benefit to killing the vines is that it kills the grubs."

I grabbed hold of a small vine that was strangling a nearby tree and sliced through it with my blade. Rivulets of opalescent purple blood welled up from the severed vine and flowed over the back of my hand. Spikes of pain rippled over my skin in its wake, and I frantically wiped the sap off on my clothes. "Fuck, that stings!"

The Dark God glanced back. "The vines don't like being cut. The pain will fade, but I'd suggest you don't get the blood on you in the first place."

"You don't seem to be having any issues."

"It burns me, too. I just have a more painful wound to worry about." He lifted the vine he'd just cut and hurled it over the side of the house. "Try to drop the vines so that their blood nourishes the plants."

Shaking off my hand, I set to work carefully freeing another patch of trees. "Why not send your minions to clear these from your lands?"

"Because the vines don't die—they just regrow and spread, so in the end, it will only make them stronger."

I stopped with my blade against the side of another tendril.

"Then why do any of this if it makes it worse? Just to starve the broodling grubs?"

The Dark God let his axe drop and looked at me with a pained and distant expression. "Because I have to do something, even if it's only to buy my people a little more time."

28

____

Samantha

It took another hour of work to cut through all the vines. I took out my anger and frustration and confusion, and by the end, I was breathing hard. It looked like we'd massacred a giant squid, and I was also covered with purple-black sap or blood or whatever it was. I hoped Mel wouldn't be pissed at the state of her clothing.

When I rejoined the Dark God, he was standing still, watching the sky through a patch in the canopy. My shoulders tensed, and heart pounding, I scanned the clouds. "Deathwings?"

"A messenger."

I followed his gaze and finally saw it: a black speck against the late afternoon sky. A hawk. It soared down, heading straight for us. The Dark God raised his arm, and the bird landed, drawing blood where its talons sank in.

It screeched at him, and the Dark God's face hardened. He jerked his hand into the air, and the hawk took flight. "I was a fool to bring you along."

"What is it?"

"I should have brought Kass or Wulfric along so I could send you back." He whistled, and Elowyn cantered over through the ruins.

I wiped the knife off on my ruined pants, sheathed it, and hurried to his side. "Wait, why?"

"We need to hurry. The fae have sent a swarm of deathwings across the border up north to attack a shifter village, and it would have taken the hawk an hour to reach us."

My stomach twisted. A swarm of flying monsters whose sting could kill.

The Dark God swung himself into the griffstrider's saddle, then held out his hand. "Get on. I'll drop you at the citadel and pray to the fates that I can make it in time."

"No. I'll go with you. I'm not going to be responsible for an entire village dying just because you had to take me back."

"I'm not putting you in danger. Get on."

I took a step back. "I can fight."

"Not deathwings," he growled.

My fists clenched. "Then fucking protect me so that you can protect your village. Or do you think you can make it to Shadowstone and back in time?"

His eyes flashed with fury. Then, with a snarl, he leaned down and snatched my wrist. "Climb up!"

I popped my foot in the stirrup, and he hauled me into the saddle behind him. He kicked the griffstrider into a gallop before I was even settled. "Keep your head down and hold on."

Unsure of what that implied, I wrapped my arms awkwardly around his waist. The heat of his fury seared into my skin, hot and wild and relentless.

Elowyn surged forward as if hell itself were on our tail, yet the Dark God was like a man possessed and kept driving her faster and faster.

The breakneck speed and lethal god in my arms had my

pulse pounding. His scent and heat mixed with the terror and exhilaration that were rushing through me, and the cocktail made it impossible to keep my head clear.

"Are we going to the citadel or to save lives?" I shouted into his back.

"You do not leave my side," he growled, his voice laced with warning. "Do not try to take on one of them."

The hawk soared in front of us, showing the path, but soon fell behind.

"Don't we need to follow it?" I shouted.

"This is my land. I know exactly where the deathwings will be."

Soon, the dying forest gave way to brittle brown pines sinking in a sea of mist. Even though the ground disappeared beneath her feet, Elowyn didn't hesitate or slow.

The pine branches should have ripped us to shreds, but the Dark God's magic flowed ahead of us, bending the trees out of our way and creating a straight path through the forest.

I swallowed. Even in death, the wilderness bowed before its dark god.

I felt his magic pulsing in the air—not the harsh force that had become familiar, but something different, primal and wild.

Before long, we crested a rocky ridge and plunged down the other side. Rusty needles gave way to patches of dark evergreen, actual living woods.

"This is deeper than they've ever struck before," the Dark God rumbled beneath his breath.

The scent of smoke rose in the air as the trees diminished in height and thinned.

Suddenly, Elowyn burst out of the pines into a plain of dense moss and patches of tall grass. She turned right, barreling toward a little village of sod-covered houses. Pillars of smoke streamed from the center, and strange creatures whirled in the air above.

Deathwings?

"Hold on," the Dark God said as he spurred Elowyn into a charge.

She lunged, and we soared over a low stone wall. My teeth cracked together when we landed, and I dug my claws into his side, not feeling the slightest bit sorry.

Chaos and death surrounded us. The sod roofs of several of the houses had been cratered in, and bloody bodies lay slumped near the doors and windows.

A man raced between a gap in the low buildings in front of us. Like a diving falcon, one of the circling monsters swooped down and pinned him to the ground with saber-like legs. Its wings spread wide to reveal a horrific mothlike pattern, and it had a tail like a scorpion—a thing of nightmares.

Its tail struck with blinding speed, and the man screamed.

We crashed into it a second later, and Elowyn ripped through the creature's wings with her talons. It thrashed wildly and released an unearthly wail as she hammered it into the dirt.

My head snapped up as a shadow blotted out the light. A second deathwing dropped out of the sky and, with a flick of its tail, plunged its stringer straight for my chest.

I braced, but the stinger stopped an inch below my throat, seized in the Dark God's grasp. He roared and cleaved straight through the monster's tail with his axe, splattering hot white blood across my chest and face. Then Elowyn finished it off.

I gaped in shock and horror.

The Dark God turned Elowyn, and we barreled toward the sounds of screaming and the scents of blood, smoke, and terror. "Don't let them get near you."

I twisted to glance behind us. "That man—"

"Is already dead."

Deathwings whirled above us, diving down to strike at fleeing men and women. One ripped chunks off a sod roof, while a second thrust its stinger through a window.

A pair of white foxes darted out the front door, and realization dawned.

This is a shifter village.

The two deathwings leapt from the side of the house and dropped on their prey.

"Hold on to Elowyn!" the Dark God growled. A second later, his body shifted into curling whisps of shadow, and I lurched forward in the empty saddle.

He reappeared fifty feet away and crashed into the monsters in a whirling vortex as he reappeared.

"I thought you said not to leave your side!" I shouted, unsheathing my knife.

But of course, he couldn't hear me over the sound of battle.

His blue eyes burned with rage, and the steel of his wicked black axe flashed as it sank into a deathwing's skull. White blood splattered across his body, and an unearthly scream split the air.

I clamped my hands over my ears, and Elowyn reared with a shriek, launching me from the saddle.

Pain exploded through my back and shoulders as I slammed into the ground. Adrenaline surged, and though I could barely draw a breath, I rolled to a crouch.

One of the deathwings dropped on a girl with silver hair who'd taken shelter behind a detached door. Its stinger buried into the wood, and girl fled from behind.

I shouted and lunged as the creature wrenched its stinger free. I seized a wing with my claws and rammed my blade between the gaps in its carapace, over and over. Warm blood drizzled down my arm, and the thing released a death screech as it twisted free and toppled to the ground.

Pain blasted through my eardrums, and my vision swam

with vertigo. I staggered and fell on my back.

A shadow flashed above. I blinked, my stomach roiling. One of the deathwings marked me with a hundred pink, glowing eyes. My heart stopped as its wings spread wide, revealing a kaleidoscope of dazzling, iridescent patterns—and a skull, staring back at me.

Death.

It dropped and struck, but I rolled out of the way and sank my blade into the tip of its tail.

That's right, I've got a stinger, too.

The monster ripped its tail free and coiled back to strike. Then a wave of white blood splattered over me as the creature exploded out of the air.

Where it had been stood the Dark God with his bloody axe. Chest heaving, he met my gaze with a look so intense, it took my breath away. I couldn't read it. Protectiveness? Anger? Desire? Hate? It was a dozen different emotions crashing into me like a tidal wave. Heat pumped through my body as my mind and senses tumbled.

"Thanks," I croaked.

The Dark God scooped me up from the ground.

Shock slapped me to my senses, and I struggled in his arms. "What are you doing?"

He heaved me onto Elowyn's back. "Sending you to safety. One strike of their stingers is death."

I wrestled and pulled my wrists free of his grip. "No way. I can fight!"

Then I saw them: three tall men in silver armor. Not men— fae. One turned his gaze toward me, and cold terror bit into my heart as he smiled.

I'd met the hounds. These were their masters.

The Dark God slapped Elowyn on the rump. "Take shelter in the trees, and protect Samantha with your life!"

29

———

Samantha

I shouted in protest, but Elowyn catapulted forward. In two shaking breaths, she was at the village wall, and then over it in another. Deathwings dropped from the sky toward us, but she was faster.

In seconds, we were inside the dense pines, with the deathwings trapped above the treetops.

"Stop!" I shouted as I fumbled with the reins. "They can't get us in here."

She slowed, and I twisted to look back at the town. All I could see were glimpses of green sod roofs, streaming smoke, and deathwings circling in the sky—though their number had been greatly reduced.

"Damn it!" It wasn't my pack or my fight, but gods be damned if I wasn't going to help those people. The echoes of the screams and chaos rising from the village twisted my gut.

But there I was, cowering in the trees and powerless to help.

One strike of their stingers is death.

Well, I'd been fucking dead before, and I'd made it back. I yanked the reins and tried to turn Elowyn back toward the village. "The Dark God says you're a warrior. Don't you want to do something?"

Elowyn screeched and snapped her beak at me. My stomach sank. Something about her look said, *I'm a warrior and follow orders. Now I'm babysitting you when I should be out fighting.*

I had no doubt that if I tried to head back on my own, she'd pin me with her talons like she'd done the first time I'd tried to mount her alone.

The truth was, I was way out of my league. The Dark God was...well, a god. Hell, he could move through shadows and had a magic axe that could blow monsters to pieces. Elowyn had savage claws and a skull-cracking beak. In a bar fight, I could hold my own, but that had been no bar fight. Still, the bitterness twisted inside me. Was there nothing I could do?

I scanned the woods and took a deep breath, then froze. We weren't the only ones out here. I could smell the musk of were-foxes. Young ones. That, and something else, sickly sweet and horrible.

Not a deathwing, but like it. My legs tightened against Elowyn's flanks. "We're not alone."

My heart accelerated as we listened and watched. Silence. Stillness.

Patting Elowyn's neck, I squeezed my legs—unsure how to steer a highly independent griffstrider. She snapped her beak at me.

I repositioned and pleaded, "Just work with me here, Elowyn. I smell shifter cubs—or kits, in this case. And something like one of those things. We need to find them before *it* does."

She hesitated, then headed deeper into the trees.

The forest floor was mossy and open, but between fallen trees and craggy outcrops of rock, there were plenty of places a kit fox could hide. I guided the griffstrider toward the scent of the kits, scanning the woods until I spotted a patch of white behind a fallen log.

I pulled her up short. "I see them, but I don't want to scare them out. They'll bolt if we approach. We'll just stand guard."

Heart pounding, I sniffed the air. The thing was close, but the forest was still.

Minutes ticked by.

Then there was a flicker of movement—an iridescent glimmer beside a tree.

"Something's over there," I whispered.

Elowyn raked at the ground with her talons. I tilted my head, searching for that strange patch of color among the dark trees. Nothing. Yet I couldn't shake the feeling of being watched. The hair on my neck rose, and I twisted around in the saddle.

A motionless creature stared back at me with a hundred phosphorescent eyes. Only ten feet away, the tall, spiderlike thing stood on blade-thin legs. Its iridescent blue-green carapace was almost beautiful. Almost.

This is why people hate spiders.

These had to be broodlings. I twisted my fingers into Elowyn's feathers. "Behind us!" She swung around and screeched a challenge, but something flashed in the corner of my eye. "Another on our right!"

Elowyn wheeled as a second spider-thing burst from the trees. It lashed out with serrated legs. She reared back on her hind hooves to dodge the blow, and then she lunged, ripping into the creature's pink eyes with her talons.

Pain lanced through my shoulder, and I crashed out of the saddle and onto the ground with a scream. The side of my head cracked against a rock, and the world tilted. Stomach swimming, I flipped over.

For the second time that day, a face with a hundred glowing eyes peered down at me. The broodling's three sets of drooling jaws began chittering. My mind wanted to crumble in horror, but I latched on to the white-hot fury boiling up inside me and scooted backward, reaching for the knife, which had been flung from my belt.

The towering thing rammed a leg down into the rocks and moss inches from my skull.

I rolled sideways. *Okay, just claws, then.*

Tumbling out of the way of another strike, I sprang to my feet behind it. The thing wheeled around, but I was ready. I lunged forward, ripping through its eyes with my claws. It let out one of those ear-shattering screams as it staggered back into the trees.

I pursued, snatching up my knife from where it had fallen in the rocks. I charged, dodging between its legs and ramming the blade into its side again and again. White gore splattered over me, but I didn't stop until it was still.

I looked for Elowyn. She was tearing into a third creature. I checked the log where I'd seen the kits, but they were gone. *Fuck!*

Frantically, I searched the forest. Three small flashes of white darted through the woods—and ahead of them, a motionless broodling lay in wait.

Cadean

The deathwing rammed its stinger into my leg, and pain eviscerated my senses. My muscles seized in rebellion, and I staggered to the side of the house.

Their poison would paralyze a man and stop his heart, but I wasn't a man. I was a god defending his lands. The agony of the poison just added to my rage.

The enormous deathwing lurched back, but I seized it by the

tail and sliced through its wing with my axe. Blood splattered across my chest as the creature's discordant scream tore at my eardrums. With a growl, I wedged my axe into its eyes, silencing the fiend forever. Before it hit the ground, I flung myself off the top of the wall and toward the fae bastard it had been protecting.

Moving fast as lighting, he blocked my axe, then spun and rammed his blade into my side. Pain exploded through my torso, but I seized his wrist with my left hand.

He jerked away, but I didn't release him. Instead, I cut off his hand.

The fae screamed and staggered back, staring at his bleeding wrist. I pulled the sword from my side, then thrust my hand out, and vines of shadow wrapped around him like a constrictor. He struggled, but he was nothing before my magic.

"Leave my lands." I clenched my fist, and the shadows constricted. His armor crushed in on itself, silencing his cries.

I had no mercy for his kind. Not after the hell they'd brought with them.

Breathing hard, I looked around.

They were all dead. I'd decorated the village with the blood of three fae and eight of the winged horrors. Their dismembered bodies littered the ground. Among them lay many of my people, werefoxes and werewolves alike.

Samantha.

The compulsion came unbidden: *find her, protect her.*

Shaking off the wounds and poison, I closed my eyes and searched for her through the shadows. I could feel her: Fear. Anger. Determination. A thousand emotions, drawing me toward the forest.

Then I was looking at her, though my body was still in the village.

Her blonde hair flashed as she darted through the trees. Her fear tore at me, but she wasn't fleeing like a deer. She was the predator. She bounded over the rocks with a lethal precision that made my heart skip.

White and red blood streaked her clothes. She was in danger. But from what?

A flash of iridescent carapace moved through the trees. Fucking hell. *Broodlings.*

An inexplicable terror took me. I reached out with my magic, grasped her collar, and pulled. But instead of Samantha appearing beside me, the world shifted, and suddenly, I stumbled into a pine forest like I'd shadow-stepped.

I extended my claws and spun around. *What the fuck just happened?*

Blonde hair glinted between the distant trees, and shock rocked me as Samantha met my gaze with wide eyes. Had she pulled *me* to *her*?

I ran, leaping between shadows where I could.

The spidery broodling was on her in an instant, but Samantha dodged and swung her claws with a savage yell, spraying white across the stones.

"Run!" I shouted.

She spun beneath the creature and rammed her blade upward. "We can't leave them!"

Leave who? And where the fuck was Elowyn?

Pain lanced my side, and I crashed to my knees. A broodling ripped its claw back, shredding my flesh. I spun and split its head with a blow from my axe. I poured my magic into the cruel obsidian blade and blasted the creature into a hundred fragments.

The pain coursing through my body meant nothing. The mad drive to reach Samantha was the only thing in my mind. I had to call the trees. I climbed to my feet, but not quickly enough. Two broodlings were on her. She fell, and one sprang with its claws raised high.

I threw up my hand, but a flash of searing light drove me back, and the wound on my arm scorched. I sucked in a sharp breath as a white orb blazed in the center of the pines where Samantha had been. The broodlings struggled against it.

Fuck. She'd called her magic—the same spell that had once trapped me and given me the wound. But how long would it last?

Urgency and anger pulled me into a sprint. I hurled my axe at the broodling on the left. The blade sank into its back as I charged for the one on the right. Hatred like I'd never felt before exploded through my muscles, and I ripped it limb from limb, spraying blood across the forest. I poured my magic into my axe, and the other broodling exploded in a cloud of black and white mist.

Samantha.

I spun toward her, terror pulsing through my veins. She was crouched on the ground, head down and arms raised, light pouring from her hands. I let out a shaking breath, and then my throat tightened.

Cowering behind her were three terrified white foxes. Kits.

Fucking fates. She'd saved them.

Emotions raged through me. Relief. Fear. Pride. And gratitude above all else.

30

A blinding heat exploded through my body, filling every space and threatening to tear me inside out. Head down, I knelt, trying to hold up the shimmering dome of magic. There was only one thought in my mind: *Protect.*

The word echoed through my soul again and again. Were they *my* words? Or a thousand voices, speaking in distant whispers?

Then I heard another voice, deep and low: "Samantha, you can let go. It's over."

I slowly pulled my head up. Beyond the dome of light, I could make out the blurry outline of the Dark God.

He's here.

Relief poured through me, extinguishing the radiance that felt like it could easily split me apart. The kits would be safe. I would be safe.

My shoulders sagged, and the magic within me sputtered and ceased. The dome dissipated into sparks, and I collapsed onto my palms, sucking in ragged breaths as my limbs shook.

Then the Dark God's arms were around me, pulling me to my feet. "Thank fates you're all right."

Relief and dread rang in his voice, but I was too exhausted to interpret it. I turned to look at the fuzzy white foxes emerging from behind the rock.

My legs buckled, but he pulled me into his arms. The heat of his signature raced over my skin, and I clung to him, craving his warmth and strength. I wasn't above it. Not ashamed. Whatever I'd done had drained every ounce of energy I had.

"Those foxes are safe because of you." Gratitude laced his voice, and his touch was gentle as he ran his hand down my back. It was like a summer breeze caressing my skin or falling into bed after a long day. After a moment of silence, he asked, "What happened? How did you call your magic?"

I leaned against his shoulder and trembled. "I don't know."

An hour later, I was perched atop the low sod-topped wall that encircled the village with a thick woolen blanket over my shoulders. The trembling in my limbs had stopped, but I hadn't cast the blanket off—its weight was like armor draped around me.

I needed that. The three fae warriors, the deathwings, and the broodlings were all dead or gone, but I still felt their residue in the village: a stench of despair and death.

I was weary to the bone, and my limbs had been completely drained of strength. Even my brain hurt. Whatever magic I'd released, it had taken everything I had.

But what had I done?

One second, I was throwing myself between the freaky spider-crabs and the kits, and the next moment, radiance exploded through me. I glanced down at my palms as if they'd have some sort of answer. They didn't.

I was going to have a lot of questions for Mel when we got back.

Back.

I shuddered. *Enjoy the freedom while you can, Sam.*

Drawing in a lungful of fresh air, I turned my attention back to the fox kits yipping and chasing in the grass beyond the wall. While the villagers attended to the dead and temporary repairs, they'd sent the children out to play so that they didn't have to see the reality of what had transpired. A dozen others had joined the three I'd saved, though I had no idea where they'd been hiding.

I was keeping watch. I didn't mind—this way I'd know that the kits were safe, and it gave me a chance to be useful and alone at the same time.

The gaggle of little werefoxes had their own version of tag. One took the form of a fox and chased the others. As soon as she'd caught one, they'd shift and help her chase. The last human standing got to be it, and they worked backward until everyone had shifted into human form again.

I shook my head in wonder. Just an hour ago, they'd nearly been lunch. I could really use resilience like that.

The hair on my neck rose, and my scar tingled. *He* was watching. I turned to look back at the village and saw the Dark God striding toward me. His presence practically plowed the air ahead of him, and the muscles in my legs inadvertently tightened.

He'd come for me. I'd been close to failure, and then he'd been there, and I'd known he'd protect the kits. And me.

I sucked in a slow breath. I couldn't let that affect the way I felt about him. He was a living nightmare that had tried to reduce my city to dust, that had pretty much murdered me and made me his prisoner. I despised everything he stood for.

Unfortunately, the horrid truth was that as much as I hated

him, having him near made me feel protected in a fucked-in-the head kind of way. Even wearing the fucking collar had felt like armor among those trees.

He'd fought like a man possessed to defend the little village. I could respect that if nothing else about him. He cared for these people. I'd sensed it in his scent and the desperate tension of his body in battle: fury and a desire to protect.

I was grateful for it.

I realized that I was tracing my fingers over the scars on my shoulder, and I jerked them down to my lap.

The Dark God stopped a few feet away. "You've been through a lot today. Are you feeling better?"

"Yes, thanks," I said, trying not to meet his eyes.

He held out a steaming mug. "I'm not sure what this is, but the village apothecary said it should help get rid of the shakes."

Embarrassment flushed my cheeks, and I dropped the blanket from my shoulders. "I'm fine. They're gone."

The Dark God glanced back at one of the nearby houses, where two or three villagers were peeking out the window. "Drink it for their sake. They're all desperate to show their thanks for what you did."

I sighed, then took the piping hot brew from his hand. It was musky and tasted of licorice, dandelion root, and sweet honey. Also, a bit of booze. I wasn't going to say no to that.

Sip by sip, the tea washed a little of the weariness from my bones.

The Dark God lingered. Streaks of white blood coated his chest and arms, mixing with the blood of the vines and his own.

I brushed a rogue lock of hair back over my ear. "You look like you survived Armageddon. Didn't you say that deathwing stings were fatal?"

"For a man, but I'm a god."

I grunted. "Really? I hadn't noticed. Should I be impressed?"

The corner of his lips twitched. "You're getting your edge back. The tea must be working."

I set the half-empty cup down on the wall beside me. "It's helping, but I feel like a used-up bar towel—like somebody dipped me in whiskey and vodka, then wrung out every last drop."

"You have a way with similes."

I shrugged. "I've just spent too much time tending bar and cleaning up after drunks."

"You're no bartender," he said with a soft certainty. "You're a warrior. You proved that today."

My mouth opened, then shut. I had no idea what I was.

When I didn't respond, the Dark God nodded toward the laughing kits. "You've been watching them play a long time. Fond memories?"

My stomach knotted as the reality of my youth crashed down on me: jeering packmates, bloody noses, and broken bones. Bouts in the ring where I'd wanted to kill everyone I'd grown up with.

"No," I said flatly.

His expression hardened into concern. "I didn't mean to open old wounds."

I shook my head. "It's nothing. These kids lead such a different life here. I'm just having trouble processing."

He angled his head. "It's a game of tag—no different than what any shifters play."

My nose twitched. "In my town, games like this usually ended with someone getting the shit kicked out of them. Often me."

A wave of heat and anger rolled off him. "I've seen how your pack plays. I saw you in the pit, fighting for that girl. How does your alpha allow that to happen?"

It was like someone had dumped ice water on my back. The

Dark God *had* been watching me that night in the pit. It had been *his* unwavering gaze on me the whole time.

I suddenly felt ashamed for my youth, and bitterness tightened my throat. "The alpha encourages it. He claims that he's training us to face a hard world. In reality, he's just training more bullies like him."

"If he lived in my lands, I'd strip his hide and send him across the border as a lone wolf. I'd watch the deathwings tear him apart and thank the fae for the first time in my life." The Dark God's voice was like a knife, and the savagery underlying his words caught me off guard.

His claws were out. It was like he'd taken it as some kind of personal offense. What did he care? The Dark God was just another bully, wasn't he?

I glanced back at the children wrestling and laughing. "The past is the past and doesn't matter. What kills me is these kids nearly got eaten an hour ago, and they're playing like they don't have a care in the world. I don't think I've ever felt carefree like that, and I didn't grow up on a dangerous border."

There was a long silence before the Dark God spoke. "Danger tends to remind people of what they have and what they could lose."

Something about his tone made my skin prickle. He was looking at me with an intensity that sent heat rushing over my shoulders and down somewhere low in my belly.

That comment hadn't been about me, had it? It couldn't have been. I was nothing more than a tool to him.

He raised his hand, then plucked a twig from my hair. "I'm not surprised that the kits feel safe. They have you watching over them. What you did means everything to these people, and to me. You have my gratitude."

My pulse raced at his touch. Where had the big bad wolf gone, and who was this? I looked down, rattled by the uncharacteristic tenderness of his words and touch. "It's what anyone would have done."

"It's not. I saw you out there. You were fearless. Impressive. Magical."

His words melted over my skin, and butterflies fluttered in my stomach. Though I didn't need or want his approval or praise, it felt good. On instinct, I reached for my simmering anger to strangle the shameful emotions welling up, but it wasn't there.

"What happened in the woods? How did you make the sphere?" he asked.

"I don't know. The broodling charged for the foxes. I threw myself between them at the last second, but I knew it was going to be too late..." My words faltered, and I bit my lip until I regained my composure. "Then it was like fire poured through me. Before I knew what was happening, I was on the ground with this ball of light protecting me and the kits. But I didn't know how to maintain it or push back against the broodlings..."

I let my shoulders slump and the words die away. The horrible truth was that I'd been finished, about to give in, and the shame of that cut me to the bone. I sank my claws into the turf as anger welled up. "I need to learn to control it. We wouldn't be having this conversation if you'd come a moment later."

The Dark God's power swelled around me, and I felt his admiration like a searing flame. "You did well. We're pack animals, Samantha. No one expected you to take on a horde of broodlings on your own. You held out long enough, and that made all the difference."

I slipped away from him and hopped off the wall. I knew he was right, but these people weren't my pack. *He* wasn't my alpha. I had all of that back in Magic Side. My home.

All around the town, people were bustling, patching houses,

carrying casks and baskets of food, and in the distance, stacking logs for a pyre. Bitterness stung my throat.

"Well, we were still too late for many," I whispered.

When I looked back, the Dark God's expression was as hard as iron. He met my gaze with blue eyes cold as frost. "You're capable of more than you know, and saving those kits today proved it. It's easy for everyone to see, even if you can't."

I felt a sudden lightness in my body, like a great weight had been taken from my shoulders, but I shoved it down. I wouldn't let his words keep having this effect on me. It was wrong.

"I have no idea what I'm capable of," I said.

A smile crept into the corner of his mouth, and he leaned closer. "That's something I am supremely interested in discovering."

The sultry tone of his voice had made nerves fire all around my body—nerves that should not be reacting with excitement toward a murderous dark god who'd nearly wiped out my city.

He was talking about my power, right? That was *all* he meant, wasn't it?

Not by the tone of his voice. Panic took me, and I backed away. "Thank you, the tea helped. Maybe there's something I can do around the village to help with repairs."

An unreadable expression crossed his face, and he motioned to the village. "I'm sure we can find something."

31

———

Samantha

The town was the nightmare I feared. I could still see where the dead had fallen in my mind, even though they'd been taken away. Yet despite what had happened, villagers descended on us, hugging and thanking me. The more they pressed, the guiltier I felt.

I could have done more.

The Dark God introduced me to the head steward of the village. She suffocated me with thanks, but at last, I was able to get a word in edgewise. "I want to help. Is there something I can do?"

"What do you do?" the steward asked.

"Back home, I'm a bartender."

The Dark God's mouth twitched in what I assumed was annoyance, so I added, "And I can swing a hammer as well as anyone. I had to help rebuild my town recently after it was viciously attacked by a monster."

The Dark God's eyes went ice cold, and his jaw stiffened. Although I couldn't read his expression, I hoped he was being torn apart by shame and regret.

She pressed my hands firmly into hers. "I'm so sorry to hear about your town. These are troubled times. I just wish there was more I could do to thank you."

"Put me to work."

She smiled. "I have just the spot for you."

The head steward led us to a long, low building that had a doorframe decorated with carved bees. She rapped loudly. "It's the steward! I've brought help!"

The door swung open, revealing a girl about my age with silver hair and a flowing blue dress. Her signature tasted like wildflower honey and smelled like a crisp breeze. A light sheen of sweat glistened on her brow, and the wild expression in her eyes confirmed that she was overworked.

"Yes, steward? What do you need?" She pushed her hair out of her face with an irritated gesture, and then she paled when she noticed the Dark God next to me. She dropped to a knee. "Lord Wolf, I'm sorry. Thank you for everything you did for us. Is there anything I can do for you?"

"This is Samantha. She's looking for a way to help," he said.

The girl looked up, and her eyes widened as she noticed me. "You saved my life from a deathwing today, and my little brother as well!"

She started forward like she was going to hug me but stopped in her tracks and fumbled with her hands. "Oh, I'm sorry, I didn't mean to presume. I'm just so grateful for everything you did. I don't know how I'll ever be able to thank you."

I smiled. "Just put me to work. I've had a rough day and need to clear my head."

"Of course! You'll have saved me a third time because I'm about all worn out."

The Dark God narrowed his eyes at her. "I have to ride the perimeter, so I'm leaving her in your care."

The woman swallowed. "I understand. I'll take good care of her, Lord Wolf."

I breathed a sigh of relief as soon as he was gone.

The young woman looked at me with wide eyes. "You travel with *him*? You must be really important."

I squeezed my eyes shut. "I'd rather not talk about that. What can I do?"

She ushered me inside and brushed her fingers through her messy hair. "Welcome to Frostfall Meadery. We make the best mead in the Dreamlands—though I'll admit, we're a little understaffed right now. I'm Selene, by the way."

I shook her hand. "I'm Samantha. Is this your place?"

The interior was dimly lit with jars of what appeared to be yellow-orange fireflies. There was a low counter, a few tables, and hundreds of stoneware bottles. Through a door, I could see dozens of racks of wooden casks.

Selene uncorked one of the bottles sitting on the counter and filled a mug. "I run it with my father, and I taught him everything I know." She quickly looked over her shoulder. "Don't tell him I said that. My grandmother started this place. It's a family tradition. You like mead, don't you?"

I took the mug. "I haven't had much, honestly."

She touched my arm lightly. "You'll love it, and if not, don't tell my father. He'll die of shame."

I lifted the mug to my lips. "And what about you?"

"Let's just say you'd better love it."

The mead smelled strongly of honey and melon, with hints of flowers and something else I couldn't place. It rolled over my tongue, sweet and smooth, with more body than wine. Energy instantly flowed through me. "It's divine."

"Good. Drink up. We've got a lot of work to do to get ready for the feast tonight."

"Feast?" Disbelief widened my eyes. "After everything that happened? Don't people...need time to grieve?"

"Of course. We'll drink and dance and eat for three days to help the dead on their way. They shouldn't have to wait in the mists while we dry our tears and get our shit together." She smiled and laid a hand on my arm. "Of course, we'll also be celebrating that our town was saved by the Wolf God and you."

Three days of feasting.

I opened my mouth, then snapped it shut. Who was I to say anything? When our pack lost members, we ran together along the lakeshore and howled at the moon. Everyone had their own traditions.

She must have caught the stunned look on my face because she blushed slightly. "Maybe things are different where you're from."

I gave her a soft smile. "It's a beautiful tradition. I wish our pack did something like that."

"We believe all life should be celebrated. Death is a chance to remember the good, and with all the festivities, for the younger people, it's a chance to make new life. Or at least, many will give it a go." She winked. "Who knows, perhaps you will find a male that catches your eye. See where the spirits of the mead take you."

Heat flushed my face. "I think I'll pass. My life is complicated enough as it is."

As soon as I'd finished my mug, we set to work. I helped Selene finish loading a cart with small casks of mead and ale, and then we pushed it toward the great hall, which was perched on a hill in the center of the village. Despite the wreckage, the little village seemed like such an idyllic, if rudimentary, existence. Simple homes, sweeping expanses of grass and trees.

"Do the fae attack often?" I asked between labored breaths.

Maybe I'd been a little too enthusiastic loading the cart. Even with shifter strength, this was overburdened.

She shook her head and dug her feet in as we shoved the cart uphill. "This was the first time here. But we used to live across the border. Some of the high fae considered us no better than animals and hunted us for sport. The Wolf God offered us refuge and this land on the condition we act as stewards."

"Aren't you isolated out here? No roads, or electricity, or…" I trailed off, not sure what these peoples' lives were like.

Selene laughed—a beautiful and light sound, despite how hard we were straining. "Who needs roads? We have a portal in the center of the village. That's where everyone was running to. Our children go to school in a large city, and we can trade there with ease."

"Sorry, I just assumed…"

"Because it looks primitive?" She smiled. "We honor the Wolf God's gift by curating this land as best we can. The sod houses keep us warm in winter, cool in summer. We light them with magic and have fresh running water from one of the mountain lakes. Everything is designed so it doesn't break up the beauty of the landscape here."

I felt the pull of the land—the sweeping grass and snowy mountains in the distance. "It really is beautiful. It gives me a sense of peace, despite everything that happened."

"Us, too. Our elders chose this place because it reminded them of the home we fled, and we'd rather do anything than despoil it."

Finally, we reached the great hall. It was a long, elegant building with a sod-covered roof and sides constructed from intricately carved panels of wood. I couldn't begin to calculate how long it would have taken. The enormous front doors had been carved with playing foxes. Unlike much of the geometric decoration that covered the building, they were so lifelike, it was a wonder that they didn't dash off to play with the children in the field.

"My grandfather carved those," Selene whispered proudly.

I traced my fingers along the raised wood. "They're extraordinary."

"It represents his hope for what this place would be. And thanks to all the woodwork, he'll always be a part of the village. He and my mother carved much of our house, so it's like he's right there. They tried to teach me, but I just don't have the talent for it."

A deep sense of sadness weighed down on me, but before I could respond, Selene dusted off her hands and grabbed one of the handles of the cart again. "But I *am* good at making mead. So rather than being remembered forever, if I've done my job right, nobody will remember anything at all. Let's drop this off and get another load."

My eyes practically popped out of my head. "This is *a lot* of mead already!"

She laughed. "Clearly, you've never drunk with werefoxes—and trust me, you won't be wanting to push a cart tomorrow."

Two hours later, I collapsed on a chair in the meadery, soaked in sweat. We'd spent all afternoon running around the great hall, setting up casks and helping prepare.

Selene bustled in from a back room and held out a bundle of clothes. "These are for you. It's not much, but I want you to have something nice to wear tonight for the feast, and your outfit... well, it looks like you fought tooth and nail to save a village from deathwings."

I looked down at myself and frowned. "You're very kind, but you don't need to do that. I was happy to help with prep, but I think I might just curl up somewhere for a nap. I'm bushed."

"After a long ride, a battle, magic, and a little hard labor? Of course you're tired, but it's nothing that a proper meal, a lot of mead, and a little dancing won't cure." She pushed the bundle toward me. "You're going to the feast, and you're going to wear this."

Hesitantly, I accepted the gift and inspected the pale white blouse and blue corseted dress. They were simple but had delicate embroidery on the chest and shoulders. "They're beautiful. Thank you."

"It's the least I can do." She clapped her hands. "But before you try those on, we'll need to get you cleaned up."

Selene took my arm and towed me into a back room that was modestly decorated with a bed, dresser, and small desk below a mirror. She pointed to a divider opposite us as she slumped onto the edge of the bed. "The water isn't hot, but it's warm enough not to get a chill."

A shower? Just the thought sent shivers of delight through me. "That sounds amazing."

I set the clothes down beside her and stepped behind the divider, which was made from waterproofed animal hide stretched between wooden panels. I hung my dirt- and blood-stained clothes over it and turned the small faucet on the wall. How in the gods did they have plumbing and heated water here?

The cold stones dug into my bare feet, but the warm water that rushed out of the showerhead was enough to make me moan. "My gods, Selene. This is exactly what I needed."

She handed me a washcloth and a dark brown bottle. "Use this, it's much better than the soap in there."

After I'd scrubbed myself clean and washed my hair twice with the heavenly lavender soap, I wrapped myself in a rough towel that Selene had hung beside the divider. "I don't think I've ever enjoyed a shower so much."

Selene laughed. "You look infinitely more relaxed. Now, you get dressed while I shower."

"Do you live here alone?" I asked as I inspected the underwear and woolen knee socks she'd laid out for me.

"Yes. My mother and father live a few houses down. I moved in here last year." She peeked her head around the divider and grinned. "It was too weird bringing guys home with them sleeping in the room right next door."

I slid the blue dress over my hips and laughed. "Yes, I suppose that might be awkward."

Selene had grown up in a totally opposite world from mine, and yet, there was so much that was the same. I had to loosen the laces of the corset, and the bust was still snug. I frowned at myself in the mirror and tugged on the sheer white top, which did very little to conceal my chest. Otherwise, it fit perfectly. The delicate embroidered swirls dipped down the front and cupped my hips.

"Wow," Selene said, bundled in a towel and hair dripping. "You look divine! And your boobs do, too."

Warmth flooded my cheeks. "You don't think it's too much? They're practically spilling out."

What would the Dark God think?

"Please. They were *made* for that dress." She shrugged on a robe and smiled at me in the mirror as she drew my hair back and pulled a brush through it. "Your necklace is beautiful. With all the interwoven patterns, it reminds me of my grandfather's art. Where did you get it?"

All the warmth drained from the room, and I pressed my fingers against the cold iron around my throat. Beauty? Was that what she saw?

I let my hand drop. "The Dark God. I'm his prisoner."

The smile on Selene's face melted away. "What do you mean? I thought by the way he looked at you…"

I dug my nails into my palms, then met her eyes. "He abducted me. As much as you worship him, he's a monster in my eyes."

Maybe, some small part of me insisted, that wasn't entirely true anymore, but I still saw the destruction in Magic Side every time I looked into those icy blue eyes.

"I…I didn't realize. I'm sorry." There was an awkward silence as she kept brushing my hair.

Her scent told me she meant it, but I knew that hearing the truth pained her. She obviously worshiped him, like everyone in the village. At least she didn't try to convince me I had it wrong, or that he was some kind of knight in shining armor or misunderstood saint.

She tugged the brush down with furious strokes. "Maybe after what you did today, he'll let you go. He treats us as if we're his children. I could petition him on your behalf and my brother's behalf—"

"No," I said softly. "I appreciate it, but he's made our arrangement clear. I could've saved this village singlehandedly, and it would never be enough. Unless I heal him, he'll never let me go. The problem is, I don't think I can do it. Not permanently at least."

She put her hands on her hips. "Then how can I help?"

I gave her a weak smile. "I don't know."

She popped the cork on another bottle of mead and topped off my glass. "Well, then, I'll start by making you look irresistible, and I'll give you some of my strongest mead. Between the two, he won't have any choice but to let you go when you ask him."

"Hold on, are you trying to get me to earn my freedom or get me a date?"

Selene brought out a box of makeup and set it on the table. "You're ravishing as it is, but a little spice never hurts the look."

As she dusted my cheeks, my thoughts churned. I appreciated everything she was doing, but he'd never just agree to let me go. I had to find my own way out.

"You mentioned there was a portal in this town. Does it lead to Magic Side?" I asked.

She paused her work and glanced back at me in the mirror. "It only leads to the city, but they have portals there that lead to places all over the Dreamlands...and even into the waking world. Your world. Maybe you could find a way through."

A sliver of hope blossomed in my chest. "Could you show me where it is and how to use it?"

She swallowed and nodded. "After what you did for me, I'd do anything."

My stomach dropped, and I gave her a sad smile as the reality hit me. "Thank you, but I shouldn't have asked you that. He'd probably imprison anyone who'd helped me. Or he might even kill them. I don't want to put you in danger."

"You saved me and my brother."

I placed my hand on her arm. "I know, and I don't want all of that hard work to go to waste. I don't even know why I'm even thinking about running. The collar is enchanted. The instant the Dark God noticed I was gone, he'd use it to pull me back. I'm stuck until I find a way to get it off."

Selene pursed her lips as she outlined my eyes with liner. "I want to help. First step, I'll take you to meet Sigrun the seer. She'll be at the feast tonight and is always happy to help in exchange for a bottle of mead."

"But would she go against the Dark God?" I asked.

Selene grinned. "I think so. She likes to make trouble. You'll have to meet her to understand."

32

———————

Cadean

The funeral pyres burned bright against the deepening twilight. Their rising ribbons of smoke carried the dead on their way to the netherworld, where'd they'd join the ghost packs.

The journey would be fraught with danger, but I'd promised the head steward to ease their passage through the underworld. That meant that later tonight, I'd have to make a deal with the Opener of Ways—a cold and calculating bastard of a god.

The soft sobs mixed with the scents of birch and bone were a testament to my failure. I'd been too slow to arrive and too complacent with the fae across the border.

As if it were some sort of atonement, I'd cut the trees for the pyres myself. It would've taken the werefoxes too long to gather enough wood, and I had to work out my anger before it consumed me.

I would've prepared to bury my axe in the fae across the border, but I hadn't brought the moonshard with me. Sooner than later, their time would come. The moment we returned to Shadowstone, I'd take the moonshard, sweep back over the border, and restore the balance through blood and fire.

But now was the time for grieving and memory.

I left the villagers to their wake and headed back toward the flickering lights of Frostfall, where *she* was waiting. I felt her presence tugging at my chest like a slowly spinning whirlpool, drawing me to my salvation, or perhaps my doom.

I strode up the hill toward the great hall. I'd enchanted the building with a dozen protective wards following the battle, turning it into a fortress that would keep the fae out for a time. It had taken more skill than usual, as I had to craft the spells so that they wouldn't keep Samantha out as well.

The protective sigils glowed with a bright light that only I could see, but Samantha outshone them all. She was like a beacon on a hill, shining fiercely, drawing me in. My heart beat faster with each step that brought me closer to her.

Her bravery had moved me in unexpected ways. It wasn't just that she saved the kits—it was that she'd acted without hesitation. It hadn't mattered that she didn't know my people. It was who she was.

She had the instinct to protect. The *drive*. That was something I could respect and understand, even if we stood on opposite sides of an unbridgeable chasm. She'd never forgive me for what I'd done to Magic Side, nor would she ever understand. And for nearly killing her—I doubted that either of us would forgive me for that.

Dark memories plagued me as I climbed the hill, but the moment she came into view, all thoughts vanished from my mind. There was only room for her.

She was a vision of beauty, leaning against the wall of the great hall, bathed in flickering torchlight. Her hair tumbled over her shoulders in loose curls, and that dress. *Fuck.* My throat tightened. The soft blue fabric hugged her body, accentuating each enticing curve and dip.

"Gorgeous." The word escaped my throat like a whispered

prayer.

"What?" Her lowered eyes flicked up to me, and my heart skipped a beat.

Stepping into the circle of torchlight, I cleared my throat. "The dress suits you."

"I'm not sure how I should take that."

I took up a spot along the wall beside her. "That you look beautiful."

A faint blush rose in her cheeks. "I'm sure I look exhausted."

"Not exhausted. Radiant."

She looked away.

I dug a single claw into my palm, using the sharp pain to gain control of my senses. The woman was a trap, and I was playing a dangerous game.

She will bring you to your knees and bind you with bonds that cannot be broken.

Yet with every breath I took, I drank her in like a cup of fine mead, and it sent my head spinning as if I'd gone deep into the bottle. What was it about her? Her scent, her beauty, her fearless strength, all seemed crafted to ensnare my attention.

Unwilling to meet my eyes, she dipped her head to the burning pyres in the distance. "Is the wake over?"

"I wanted to give them a moment to grieve without me looking over their shoulders. They'll start filtering back soon enough."

"Do you think they'll be offended that I didn't attend?"

I turned toward her, unable to pull my gaze away. "No. Their ceremonies are not for us, but for them and the dead."

Samantha wrung her hands nervously. "I've seen too many dead today already."

"So have I." It was always too many. The old anger rose within me, but I reined it in. Tonight was about celebrating lives, not vengeance.

She studied me carefully, apprehension and doubt in her eyes. "How long has this war been going on?"

"Centuries." Dark memories swept around me, and the shadows followed, creeping across the ground and defying the torchlight. "It wasn't a war at first. Once, they kept to themselves, occupying unprotected patches beyond my border. But after they drained those dry, they began to spread, and now...now it seems no part of my lands is safe."

There was a long silence before she looked up again, a softness in her gaze. "I'm sorry. About the fae. That your people are suffering."

The sadness in her words took me by surprise, and my breath stilled. That simple statement was far more than I'd dared hope for.

Pushing off the wall, I stalked to the edge of the torchlight and stared out over the village I'd failed to defend. Dozens of golden lights glowed in the windows, a happy contrast to the pyres beyond. "It wasn't my intention to bring you to this place or for any of this to happen. But I'm glad you were here. You saved lives today. And now you know the truth: the fae are deceptive and ruthless."

"So are you," she whispered.

Her words twisted in my back like a blade. She'd said as much a dozen times before, but for some reason, it was bitter wine coming from her lips.

I turned to face her, bringing my shadows with me. "Yes. I'm a monster. But it's what they need me to be—a monster that can protect their families. One who will burn, pillage, and do anything to keep them safe."

"And does that include keeping me on a leash forever?" Her words weren't laced with malice or anger—they were matter of fact.

I hung my head. "You know I can't let you go. Not yet."

"I saved three kits today. If you care about these people as much as you claim, then that should be worth my freedom. Or at least your trust."

A great weight pressed down on me, and my shoulders tensed to bear the burden.

"I'm grateful, but our bargain is bigger than individual lives. It's about healing my wound and breaking my bonds so that I can protect this realm, whatever the cost." Reluctantly, I met her eyes. "Even if that cost is your freedom, for a time."

"I guess my freedom is a small price for *you* to pay." She looked away. The bitterness in her words was worse than the sting of a dozen deathwings.

Silence stretched between us until I could no longer bear it. I looked out at the pyres on the horizon. "Even if I can't change my decision, I'm sorry—for all of it. For wounding you and keeping you here."

"Are you?" Suspicion cut through her words like a razor. "What would that even mean, coming from you?"

Frustration tightened my jaw, and I turned back to her. "Do you think I'm blind to the irony of our arrangement? I chafe at the walls of my eternal prison, and yet I'm keeping you prisoner. I despise having to do it, despite what you think."

"Then get rid of this collar. For good."

But I couldn't. I didn't trust her not to run, and I couldn't leave her exposed to capture. She wouldn't understand it, but that collar had me trapped as well as her.

"It's not just to stop you from running. It's armor to protect you when I'm not around, like in the glade."

"And what will protect me from *you*?" The venom in her voice was palpable.

I slowly stalked toward her, my throat tightening at the protectiveness that surged inside me. "You're right, little wolf. I *am* the most dangerous beast that prowls this land, but that doesn't mean you shouldn't fear the other things that lurk in the shadows."

Her breath faltered, but her sharp gaze remained steady. "If you had pulled me out of danger today, those kit foxes would be dead. So armor or no, I want you to take it off."

A deep unease settled in my gut, and indecision tore at me. Despite what she thought, she was not safe here. But I needed to gain her trust and bring her to my side. I needed to compromise. "If I gave you more freedom, would you stay and help me? Or would you shove a knife in my back and flee?"

"I would—"

I pushed my magic toward her, compelling the truth with my presence. It cut off her words instantly, and understanding flashed across her face.

She gave a low snarl. "That's a dirty trick."

"But a useful one when the truth matters."

Samantha looked away, and I could smell the scent of her shame and anger.

Frustration and guilt raged within me. I hated compelling her, but what choice did I have? I couldn't trust her. And if I couldn't give her the freedom she craved, how was I supposed to build a bridge between us?

I had no idea how to navigate this woman, let alone convince her that I wasn't a monster. Yet I could see her so clearly. Fierce, brave, and loyal, she embodied everything I respected most.

I would find a fucking way.

We shared the instinct to protect. Could I speak to that?

I closed the distance with her, savoring her scent and delighting in the fierce set of her jaw and the undefeatable presence that she wielded. "Your time in the Dreamlands can be about more than our bargain. You saved innocent lives today. You could make a difference here. Not just by healing me, but for all the shifters in my land."

A flicker of something crossed her features before they hardened. "This isn't my fight, and these aren't my people. I belong in Magic Side."

I inclined my head. "Are you sure of that?"

Her brow furrowed. "Of course I am. What the hell are you talking about?"

Her energy was so different than when I'd watched her in the waking world—more vibrant and alive. Was it because of her fae blood or something else?

I called the shadows into my hand, where they slowly spun into the shape of a black rose. I held it out to her. "Your magic has only ever manifested in the Dreamlands, and it's grown stronger since you've been here. You're tied to this place, whether you like it or not."

She looked at the rose but turned her head away. "My magic has nothing to do with where I belong. My pack does. My friends do."

I dismissed the rose into darkness. "But it does. I saw the way you looked out at the mountains today. Tell me you don't feel this place in your bones, feeding your spirit. You were starving in a soulless land of concrete and glass. The proof is in your magic. You belong here in the Dreamlands."

With me.

"I don't." She shoved away from the wall and opened the door to the great hall. "You're telling yourself stories to justify keeping me prisoner."

Underneath the denial, I sensed the uncertainty that battled with her convictions.

"And you're hiding from the truth," I said.

She hesitated for a moment, a glimmer of anger and trepidation on her face before she turned and disappeared into the hall.

33

Samantha

I leaned against the door. *Please don't follow.*

A huge wooden bar awaited to lock it shut, and I was tempted to drop it into place. If only I'd had nails and a hammer as well.

You belong here. His words had sent my stomach spiraling down the drain. It was too close to the truth.

There was something about the Dreamlands that I just couldn't shake. The trees and the hills and even the mists—beneath them all, there was a low murmur, a susurrus calling to me that I was doing my best to ignore. The level of confidence in his voice told me the Dark God wasn't just guessing, but that he knew.

I took a deep breath and closed my eyes. *I belong back in Magic Side with Jaxson and Savannah. And I'd bring my mother there, too.*

The Dreamlands was death.

Opening my eyes again, I searched the enormous hall for Selene. She was the only safe harbor I had in a dark and hostile sea.

The hall itself was enormous. The peaked roof above me was supported by intricately carved pillars and rafters, and I wondered if they'd been crafted by Selene's grandfather or mother. While there were a few separate rooms, most of the space was occupied by a single chamber with tables along the side. A dais stood at one end, and another platform with huge drums. Mouth-watering aromas rose from giant hearths with simmering food.

"Samantha!" Selene called from a side room. She hurried over with a pitcher and poured me a mug of mead. "For a second, I was worried you were going to skip the feast."

"After all the work you put into freshening me up? I wouldn't miss it." I took a long swig of the sweet honey wine, then pulled the pitcher from her hands. "I'm here to help."

"No way." She laughed. "You've helped enough. You should sit with the others and celebrate!"

I shook my head as I surveyed the vast room. "You're the only person I know here, and I don't want to meet anyone else. I'm overwhelmed as it is. Put me to work, I can keep up."

Taking my arm, she led me to a tall table piled high with bottles and casks. "All right, but just to warn you, I'm a hard taskmaster, and this place will be hopping."

"No worries. I'm a professional."

But Selene wasn't kidding. As the villagers began to pour into the hall, we rushed around double-time, hauling in fresh casks of beer and mead, and pouring drinks.

I was clearly a curiosity to the villagers, so I moved as quickly as I could so that I didn't catch too many questions—I'd had all that I could stand. Even back in Magic Side, I was always happier behind the bar than in the crowd. The work was a safety net.

The hall grew noisier, and a band of musicians set up in one corner. Soon, drumming and strings filled the place to the rafters. People kept coming, and it became deafening. Eclipse had never been packed like this. Where had they all come from? It had to be the entire village, and then some.

In the midst of a wild jig, a sudden hush fell over the hall, and I froze mid-pour. I didn't need the quiet to tell me what had just happened—I could feel *his* presence burning all the oxygen from the room. I glanced over my shoulder, and where there should have been an open doorway, there was only shadow.

My mouth went dry, and I was surprised that half the people didn't bolt for the exits.

The Dark God strode down the center of the hall, shadows trailing like a cloak behind him. My emotions pulled in a dozen directions. Once, he'd been the monster that haunted my nightmares, but now, he'd become an inescapable part of my life. Someone with whom I had casual conversations while sitting atop a wall.

Or maybe not so casual.

For a second, his eyes were on me, though it felt like minutes. I had to fight with all my will not to let his gravity pull me toward him.

Someone rose and began to cheer, and then the room exploded with voices. Everyone was suddenly on their feet, and the deafening sound of their voices reverberated off the walls and filled every inch of the space. Even Selene was cheering.

Of course she was. He was their god and savior.

So many doubts tore at me. Who was he? A monster who would have leveled my home if he'd had the chance? A cruel beast who had imprisoned me?

Or was he a tragic king under siege within his own prison? When Mel had been hunted down for her powers, she'd fled to him. When the fae had first come for Selene's people, he'd offered them refuge in his lands. And today, he'd fought to protect them with everything he'd had.

Not only them. Me.

He'd been like an avenging fury fighting off the deathwings, and when my magic shield threatened to fail, he'd been there in the nick of time to slay the deathwings trying to kill me and the kits. I'd never forgive him for nearly killing me, but it was more than once now that he'd saved my life.

I found myself touching the collar and cursed. The blasted piece of metal may have saved me from the briarwitch and even the broodlings, but I still wanted to melt it into scrap.

Slowly, the cheering and applause died away, and the sounds of the feast returned. Drumming and music, laughing and dancing. The Dark God took a seat behind a thick oak table on the dais at the end of the hall. Sitting like a king enthroned, he made the room feel small.

I didn't know what to make of him. He'd called me gorgeous and stopped short the moment he saw me in my new dress. I hated how that had sent my pulse racing and made every effort Selene had put into my hair seem worthwhile.

Each time I looked up from my work, he was staring straight at me. My shoulders tensed as the smoldering curiosity of his gaze heated my cheeks. It melted straight through me and made me feel like I was the only one in the room.

I'd tried to ignore it, but there was no denying that he was intrigued. The knowledge was intoxicating and terrifying, and every look between us became a dance between predator and prey.

I held his gaze a moment too long, and he motioned me forward with a subtle gesture. I meant to turn away, but I found myself drifting toward him, step by step. His will was absolutely magnetic, and I couldn't deny the call of his eyes. He wasn't the only one looking. The whole room was.

Please, no.

As I stepped up to the dais, he gestured to a chair at his side. "Samantha. Join me, please."

The low tones of his voice skated over my skin, and I had to force myself to shake my head. "This place is for you, not me."

"The steward has assigned us both a place of honor. After what you did today, you deserve to be up here with me. I want you at my side."

He was referring to the spot beside him, but I couldn't help but wonder if there was an underlying meaning to his words. I poured the pitcher of ale into his flagon. "I'm your servant, aren't I? I'm content to serve."

His hand tightened on the flagon, and I was afraid it would break. "Am I so abhorrent to you that you can't sit next to me for a night?"

Although I hated him, that wasn't why. I bit the corner of my lip, and his gaze followed. "That's not it."

It was because he was toying with my mind. I needed him to be a villain, but instead, I was thinking about him as a protector. *And* I was thinking about his hands lifting me up and pulling me close. His gentle words and longing looks, and...his very presence played with my mind. It was infuriating. Even six feet away, the scent of his body and the vibrations of his power were driving me wild, and a tight ache was blooming low in my belly.

I backed away. "I really have to go. I promised Selene I'd help."

He raised a questioning eyebrow and swirled the mead in his glass. "I could order you to stay."

My hands tightened on the jug. "I'm not a pet to be ordered about."

"You're a shifter, and I am the Wolf God."

Anger strengthened my resolve, and I gave him a coy smile. "Until you let me go, you won't be anything to me but my jailer."

With that, I turned and rushed away.

34

———

Samantha

All through the night, as I carried mead, wine, and ale, people approached the Dark God to pay their respects or ask for boons. There was a constant line, and yet I swore that every time I looked up, he was watching me, an amused smile hovering on his lips. Even when I had my back turned, the heat of his gaze dragged over my skin, lighting my nerves on fire—appraising, desiring, relentlessly observing. It was all I could do to keep my mind on the work.

Had that been his plan all along? Provoking the fae so that he could trick me into seeing another side of him? Heat crept along my jaw. I had to get my head on straight.

Two hours in, I was soaked with sweat, but the revelers and musicians were still going strong. As the werefoxes began to push tables out of the way to make room for more dancers, Selene grabbed my arm. "Hey, there, busy bee. I think it's time we took a break. When's the last time you ate?"

"I can't remember."

She forced me to set down my pitcher, then hauled me over

to the vast table laid with food. My stomach groaned at the rich aromas, and I mounded a plate with dark bread, venison, fish, and several dishes I didn't recognize.

"Come on, I want you to meet Sigrun, that seer I told you about," Selene said as she grabbed an unmarked bottle from under a serving table.

I followed her through the developing chaos toward a table near the hearth, where an old woman sat watching the dancers. She had long silver hair, leathery skin, and a deep green dress woven with elaborate patterns of orange and white. When she turned toward us, I halted for a split second. A scar tore through the socket where her right eye should've been.

Selene did a curtsy that I wasn't going to dare attempt, so I smiled and dipped my head.

"Grandmother, this is Samantha. She saved my brother."

"I'm not your grandmother, so don't call me that. It's Sigrun." The woman's face erupted in a broad smile. "As for you, Samantha, I've heard you are very brave. We all owe you far more than we could repay."

"Do you mind if we join you?" Selene asked, holding up the bottle. "We've got strong mead and a question."

She waved us forward. "Sit, sit, and open the bottle. You're always welcome."

Just holding the plate of food was torturing my tastebuds, so as soon as my butt was on the bench, I dug into the succulent meat while Selene and Sigrun talked.

"Mmmm," I moaned through a mouthful. "Either this is so far beyond amazing, or I'm tipsy and starving. Or all three."

"All three, by the looks of it." Sigrun chuckled. "I saw that you passed on sitting at the table with the Wolf God. You could have been far more drunk and far less hungry and exhausted by now."

My fork paused halfway to my mouth. "I'm fine right where I am."

Selene uncorked the bottle and filled the weathered old woman's empty mug. Sigrun sniffed the mead, then took a long drink, eyeing Selene the whole time. "Did you brew this, or did your father?"

"My father—though we really work together."

She gave a soft harrumph and adjusted in her seat. "It's fine. And I owe Samantha already, but I wouldn't be opposed to you bringing me a bottle of one of your batches. You can always tell when it has a woman's touch."

Selene glanced at me. "She means I brew it stronger."

"That's not what I meant at all, though it's true." The one-eyed woman glanced at me and smiled in a way that made me feel like we'd known each other for decades. "All right, then, what do you want to know?"

"She's a seer," Selene reminded me.

"I'm not." The woman adjusted her beautiful dress. "I traded my eye to the fates so that I could see the future. Why the hell the fates would want an old woman's eye, I don't know, but it's not for me to question."

My jaw dropped, and my fork clinked on my plate. She'd traded her eye? I fumbled for some kind of coherent response. "Wow, that's...I mean, thank you..."

After letting me squirm for a few seconds, Sigrun grabbed Selene's arm and started laughing. "Oh, look at her face, she bought it!"

My cheeks heated, though I wasn't sure what was going on.

"That old story is a load of goat shit—though that's what I tell the kits when they're small." The old woman chuckled. "It's good to have someone around who doesn't know the truth. The fae took my eye long ago because I mouthed off, and what they take, they don't give back. Trading it to the fates is a much better story and helps build the brand."

I licked my lips. "So, you *are* a seer?"

Sigrun took a sip of her mead. "No. I'm just very insightful when I've had a few. Ask me what you want to know."

"She's a seer," Selene said again between mouthfuls, and the woman scowled.

I leaned forward. "I'm the Dark God's prisoner. How do I get free?"

She steepled her fingers and leaned back. "Well, that's rather awkward. Have you tried asking him to let you go? He's a wild beast but can be reasonable from time to time—at least with *me*."

I gave the non-seer an incredulous look. "I've asked, begged, pleaded, and demanded. He says he'll release me, but only if I heal him or free him from the Moon's spell. The problem is, I don't know how to do either, and I'm not sure I want to."

She nodded with all the attentiveness of someone who wasn't listening at all.

"That's a pickle, but the hard truth is, we're only ever prisoners to ourselves." Sigrun smiled broadly, then took a big swig of mead, as if she'd just dropped an earthshattering insight bomb on me.

The hope in my chest came crashing down. "That's categorically false."

Maybe she'd earned great respect somehow, but I was going to call out bullshit when I heard it.

The woman waved her hand. "Not literally, honey-dear. But the reality is that being a prisoner *to him* is the least of your worries. The real problem is that you're a volcano. You've got magic bubbling up inside of you and no idea how to use it. If I had that kind of power, I'd bet my good eye would be glowing like a lighthouse."

I blinked. How did she know that? "Look, I don't know what's going on. I couldn't do magic before I came here. I'm just a werewolf. Can you help?"

Sigrun held out her hands. "Well, I didn't have gas until I was sixty-three, and then one day, poof. There it was."

I opened my mouth, then shut it sharply. Her wounded eye made it seem like she was always winking, and I didn't know if I should take her seriously.

She stared at me with her good eye. "What I'm saying is that you need to change your perspective. Stop hiding. Learn your magic and figure out where it came from. Once you master your power, no one will be able to control you. Not even the Wolf God."

"I don't know how to begin."

Sigrun nodded at the dais. "I'd suggest going straight to the top of the food chain and begin with him. He's a god and the most powerful being in a thousand miles. If anyone can help you learn your magic, it's him."

I followed her gaze to where the Dark God sat. His glacier-blue eyes were fixed on me with a keen intensity.

My stomach dropped, and a slow-building heat spread across my exposed skin. Fucking hell.

Suddenly, he stood and started striding over. The crowd flowed out of his way like waves around the bow of a ship.

I turned back, frantic. "He's coming over!"

My hands grew clammy, and my heart began thumping against my ribs. Had the Dark God heard what we were talking about? His senses were far more powerful than mine, and Sigrun wasn't exactly being quiet. What would he do if he thought they were trying to help me escape?

I tugged on the laces of the corset, certain the tightness of it was the cause of my lightheadedness. "What do I do?"

Sigrun narrowed her eye at me. "In regard to your magic?"

"No. About *him*."

Wasn't it painfully obvious?

"Honestly, from what little you've told me, it sounds like he needs you more than you need him. Seize your power and flip the script! He wants you to heal him, or whatever, so make him train you and set you free first. And I bet he knows more about your magic than he's telling you." She clenched her fist and grinned.

Easier said than done.

"He's a *god*. I can't make him do anything."

With a toothy smile, she sat back and swirled her mead. "When a woman harnesses her power, she's unstoppable. He might be a god, but he's still just a man."

"Just a man, am I?" the Dark God said from right behind me.

The blood drained from my face, and I slowly turned around. He was just a couple of feet away, standing with arms crossed.

When had he gotten so close?

Sigrun shrugged. "I mean, I always assumed you were. You have a rather obvious build."

He inclined his head. "It's good to see you again, too, Sigrun. And Selene."

He knew their names?

Turning his attention on me, he fixed me with a withering stare. "Samantha."

The way my name rolled off his tongue, smooth and languid, sent a shiver down my spine. He inspected me from head to toe, and I became aware, once again, of how painfully constricting Selene's dress was against my chest.

That, and the fact that everyone's eyes were on him and me and our table.

"Hi?" I said, unable to cover up the anticipation in my voice.

His brilliant blue eyes were awash with amusement as he

held out his hand. "The people here honor the dead by drinking and dancing. You've taken care of the first. Would you join me for the second?"

My jaw dropped as my thoughts slowed to a glacial pace. Did the savage and brutal Dark Wolf God just ask me to dance?

Oh, hell, no.

I swallowed. "I just sat down. I've been on my feet all night."

The uptick at the corner of his mouth became a knowing smile. "You've spent the whole night dancing around the hall, pouring ale and mead, just to avoid sitting with me, and now you're going to sit to avoid dancing?"

There was a slow and steady tug on the back of my dress as Sigrun pulled me back for a conference. "I've only got one eye, honey-dear, and even I can see that it's foolish to turn down a god when he asks you to dance—especially when you want something from him."

He raised an eyebrow at that, and heat flushed my cheeks. Of course the treacherous old seer said it in a stage whisper so *everyone* could hear.

The Dark God stepped closer, hand still out and waiting for me to take it. "Sigrun is wise beyond her years. I'd listen to her."

A hundred eyes bored into me from around the room, and the weight of their expectation sent panic coursing through my system. "I can't, I don't know how to dance. Where I come from, we just jiggle around and wave our arms without much rhythm. That's how I dance—not like this..."

"Don't worry, I have thousands of years of practice."

Silently cursing myself, I took his hand. My heart fluttered as the electricity of his touch raced through me, and yet apprehension still tightened my chest.

He bent his head close, the warmth of his breath kissing my neck. "We're here to celebrate the lives that were lost and lives that were saved—lives *you* helped save. For just one night, stop fighting me. Come and dance."

His soft words raised goosebumps over my skin, and when he tugged me to my feet, I let him. Something about his touch made me feel lighter, like I was made of clouds. The room applauded, and I was certain that I'd turned a deeper shade of crimson. "I can't believe I'm doing this."

"One dance doesn't have to change anything between us. You can still despise me all you want. This is for them, not me." The Dark God placed his free hand on my hip. "Just relax and let me lead."

The music started, and before I could speak, he pulled me onto the dance floor. The beat was too fast, and yet we were somehow moving with it. The room spun around us, and I pressed my eyes closed, dizzy.

"Look at me, little wolf," the Dark God said, his voice low and gravelly.

I opened my eyes to find his riveted on me, and I couldn't look away even if I'd wanted to.

Almost instantly, I stepped on his foot, and he gave me a sly grin. "They really don't have dancing where you come from, do they?"

"Look, it's different, okay?" I turned right as he tried to bring me around to the left.

He pulled me in gently. "You're still fighting me. Relax."

Of course I was fighting him. He was the fates-damned Dark God, and we were dancing. *Together.*

A wave of his magic rolled over me, and the shadows rose from the floor, winding around us like tendrils of smoke. They moved across my skin and gently guided me to where I needed to be. It was like having his hands everywhere on my body at once.

I stifled the soft moan before it left my lips, but by the way the Dark God's pupils dilated, I was certain he'd noticed.

Fuck the fates.

Slowly—painfully so—I started to find the rhythm. But when I glanced over my shoulder as we turned, the panic returned. "Everyone is looking at me."

"They're looking because you're beautiful and brave and inspiring," he purred. His words lit a warm glow in my chest, and by his scent and the timbre of his voice, I could tell he meant it.

Why did he have this kind of sway over me? Why should I care what he thought?

When his hand moved to my lower back, I melted into him, letting his body direct mine. We moved together, our bodies in sync, gliding over the dance floor like we were the only ones in the hall.

"They'll be talking about my terrible dancing for years, is what you really mean," I said breathlessly.

"That's a lie. Everyone here wonders who you are. Even me, little wolf." He dipped his head slightly so that his lips were mere inches from my ear. The heat of his breath warmed my neck and sent goosebumps cascading over my skin. "I must admit, you're a mystery that I am very keen on unraveling."

Mysterious or not, I *was* unraveling. Confusion spun in my mind, mirroring the dancers on the floor. The song ended, and I pushed away.

"The night is young. Stay," he said.

My heart was beating too fast, my chest had gone tight, and I caught myself looking into his eyes, trying to measure the man. Why was I admiring the strength of his shoulders and hard lines of his jaw? He wasn't a knight in shining armor. He was a brutal warlord and god of destruction. Yet dancing in his arms, I felt safe and protected when I should have been terrified. His light touch along my side sent fire across my nerves, and it was all I could do to keep my thoughts on course.

It was too much.

I took a step back. "I can't do this. The dancing and laughing. The good god/bad god routine. I'm your prisoner, nothing more."

With that, I spun and hurried out the back of the hall with panic on my heels.

35

Samantha

I let out a deep breath the moment I was outside and free of the Dark God's intoxicating presence. Cold air greeted my flushed skin, and I felt a little faint.

Too far. That had gone too far.

The dancing, the praise, the desire. It couldn't happen. He had to stay the monster, or I would lose my mind.

I could still hear the music and laughter and sound of revelry inside, but I was suddenly glad not to be a part of it. Whatever the people inside the hall were feeling, it didn't matter. I was an outsider, imprisoned in someone else's story.

Not certain where I was heading, I stalked toward the low stone wall where I'd watched the kits earlier. The ascending moon cast silver highlights over the grass-covered roofs, but the rest of the town was deep in shadow. I stumbled on a loose stone and nearly lost my balance.

Was it my dizzying thoughts or the mead? I'd only had three flagons. Well, three and a half, maybe four. No, it hadn't been the booze—it had been *him* and the jumble of conflicting feelings that he'd awakened inside me. The truth was that I was beginning to see another side of him, and that scared me. The Dark God could be ruthless and brutal but also kind, and when he smiled at me, it felt like I was glowing.

It was all too much to sort out.

The fire in my belly pushed me onward despite my wobbly steps. Once I'd reached the wall, I stuck my boot into the gaps between the stones and sank my claws into the sod covering the top.

But before I could pull myself over the wall, the Dark God's voice rose behind me. "Just in case you're looking, the nearest portal to Magic Side is the other way."

My heart skipped, and I whipped my head around as he stepped out from under the overhanging roof. The shadows of the night clung to him as he strolled toward me.

I dipped my head back and sighed. "Can't you give me one moment of freedom?"

"Obviously not. Three minutes away from me, and you're already trying to make a run for it."

"I'm not trying to escape." I tightened my grip on the sod and prepared to haul myself over. "I want to let my wolf run a bit and clear my head. But maybe after that, I'll walk back to the border and see how long it takes you to stop me."

"It's not safe." He wandered closer, moving slowly, as if I might bolt like a wild animal. Not like I'd have any chance. "I drove off the fae, and Elowyn is patrolling the woods, but I can't be certain there aren't deathwings out there still. They hunt at night."

"Fuck my life," I muttered under my breath.

He braced himself against the wall and stared out across the starlit grassland. "If you want to run, I'll join you."

It was very tempting.

I looked over at him. "What are you even doing out here?

Can't you just watch me from the shadows? Must you follow me everywhere?"

"I've come to make another bargain."

My breath caught as he held up an ornate brass key. "If you'll stay in the safety of the great hall, I'll make an exception for tonight only. You should feel free to dance and drink unburdened. I should have taken it off earlier."

He was offering to take the collar off? The earth swayed beneath my feet.

Regret and shame shone in his eyes, and he almost looked pained by it. "I don't want to be your jailer, but I can't let you go. You're in danger, and I won't risk losing you. I'm only considering this because I enchanted the great hall to act as a refuge in case the fae return. It's the same deal we have in the citadel."

I'd definitely accept, but could I push it? I crossed my arms. "Tonight's not enough. I want it off for good."

The key disappeared into his fist. "It has to be enough. You've seen what kind of danger is lurking out there."

I wanted to take a stand and push back, but temptation tore at me. With it off, I could sneak out of the hall and find the portal. It was a one in a thousand chance, but I had to take it. This could be my only shot.

Sorry, Wolf, you'll have to wait for a run.

"Are there strings attached—other than returning to the hall?"

A wry smile graced his lips. "None. Just don't run off. And *don't* betray my trust."

I nodded. "I won't."

A lie.

"And one more thing." He stepped forward, towering over me as his fingers grazed the skin beneath the collar. "No dancing with any man but me. Do you understand?"

I narrowed my eyes up at him, the wolf in me daring to challenge him. It was tempting, but I wouldn't waste this opportunity. And truth be told, there wasn't any other man I wanted to dance with. "Fine."

He slipped the skeleton key into my collar, measured my eyes for a moment, then turned it. There was a click, and the collar parted.

A wave of relief washed over my shoulders as he removed the heavy iron around my neck. It was like a crushing weight had been lifted from my chest. Even if I couldn't find my way through the portal, I would still have one more night without the cursed thing. That was a win on its own.

"Thank you," I said, and then I took a step back. A part of me was terrified that it was all a game, that he'd lunge forward and snap it on with a sly grin. But he didn't, and deep inside, I knew that wasn't who he was.

Instead, he sighed and leaned against the wall. "You were talking a while with Sigrun. She said you wanted something from me?"

I sucked in a deep breath. "I want you to teach me to use my magic. To really use it."

He raised his eyebrows. "Melanthe is teaching you already."

Shaking my head, I looked at him and pleaded with my eyes. "Healing isn't enough. I want to master the spell I cast today. I have no idea where the magic came from or how I was supposed to control it. I want to know what other powers I have. Will you help me?"

The Dark God closed the distance between us, and his heated gaze dragged along the line of my jaw. A part of me wished it had been his fingers. "One step at a time. Concentrate on healing for now."

"Why won't you teach me? You saw what I did today. Imagine if I could control it. I could help instead of being a risk. What are you not telling me?"

His jaw tightened, and the heat of his signature flared. "The spell you used today is the one that wounded me. As soon as I was near you, my wound began to burn, and when I reached out, the curse spread."

My stomach dropped. "It got worse?"

He glanced down at his arm and flexed his fingers as if they were aching. "I can't risk training you. Not until you master healing."

Frustration weighed down on me, and my hands began to tingle. Cool and warm energy built inside.

And then, like a dandelion in the wind, it was gone.

I looked at my open palms. "My magic is going to come out. It's hovering at the surface. If I knew how to use it, I could find a way to reverse the curse. But if I don't learn, there's no way for me to control what happens."

I raised my eyes and watched the shadows of foreboding creep across his face.

He inclined his head. "Was that a veiled threat, little wolf?"

I lifted my chin. "It's the reality of a very complex situation. Train me or risk the consequences."

Resting back against the wall, I smiled as a conflicted expression shrouded his face.

That's right. I may not have much power, but I'll use what I have.

He measured me with his eyes, letting them drift from my lips, along my neck, and down my body. The approving smile at the edge of his mouth had heat flaring in my belly.

The Dark God took a single step closer. "How about you let me train you to fight with a sword and a knife? Any weapon you want."

I crossed my arms. "I can already fight. I want to learn magic."

"You're good but not experienced enough. Fighting werewolves in a ring is one thing, but in the Dreamlands, you'll need to learn to fight monsters—monsters like the deathwings. Monsters like me."

A cold shiver skated down my spine.

I pushed off the wall and pressed my palm into his chest to create some space between us. Shit, he was solid, and my stomach was suddenly doing flips. "I can handle myself just fine. I killed a deathwing today."

He lazily brushed my hand away, and with an effortless move, brought my wrist behind my back. He pulled me close so our bodies were nearly touching, his gaze lingering on my lips. "And you were almost stabbed by another. Their sting would kill you."

I looked away, but he gently lifted my chin, not letting me escape his scrutiny. "Let me train you, Samantha. I could teach you to use your body in ways you never thought possible."

I sucked in a sharp breath, the fire in my belly dipping lower.

His sultry words were an invitation to try things I didn't dare let myself imagine—though I easily could. I was already lost in his presence, and my mind danced with the possibilities he was offering.

My chest tightened, and I swallowed hard. "We're not talking about fighting anymore, are we?"

His eyes blazed with something dark and feral, and he leaned down, his breath grazing the shell of my ear. "Every conversation with you is a fight."

He released my wrist, yet I didn't back away. The warmth of his body so close to mine sent prickles across my suddenly sensitive skin, and every movement of my dress set my nerves alight. I wanted his hands on me, even though I knew it was wrong.

He must have read the truth in my rising desire because he leaned close, and whispered, "Today, we triumphed. Let's stop fighting each other, even if only for a night."

I desperately wanted to. I was drowning in need, a madness I couldn't help.

Why did the bastard have this effect on me? Was it because when I looked up, I didn't just see the Dark Wolf God, but a ferocious protector, a god that could change fall into spring? Was it his scent or his presence or the way his low voice vibrated through me? Or was it because I could still feel the rush of battle and him coming to my side?

It took every ounce of my willpower to slip my hand between us. "I should go."

His hand lightly pressed against my back—not restricting but affirming. "I want you to stay. The little wolf who fought bravely at my side is the only person I want to be near tonight, and there are a million things I'm desperate to discover about her."

My breaths were short, and my heart was beating fast. He was the devil manifest—a tempter whispering in my ear, asking me to abandon my senses and morals.

I wanted to give in to that desire, to let down my guard and get lost in the music and joy flowing from the hall beyond. I wanted to throw my inhibitions to the wind and melt against him.

"Stay," he whispered again. The sinful curve of his lips was an invitation to bring my world crumbling down.

It was impossible. It was wicked. He was the antithesis of everything I stood for. It was too much to contemplate, and yet, when he leaned down and brushed his lips across mine, all hope was lost.

36

Samantha

Before I knew what I was doing, I leaned into him, tasting his lips with mine. Traces of smoke and bitter chocolate mingled with his rich male scent, sending tingles all the way to my toes.

The kiss began slowly at first, tentatively, as we explored how we fit together. But when I dipped my tongue into his mouth, I felt his hunger grow, like he'd been waiting for me to make the first move all along.

He growled low and pulled me against him, the hardness of his body and the firmness of his grip on my waist turning that fire in my belly into a dull, aching throb. I didn't know if it was his signature or pheromones, or maybe the cocktail of chemicals that was flooding my system, but this felt right, like I was exactly where I belonged.

We fit perfectly, the hard contours of his body molding with the soft curves of mine. Heat and delight raced through me as I melted into his kiss. His lips were neither soft nor sweet, but had become hard and consuming, drinking me in until there was no breath left in my lungs.

I pushed back, gasping when our lips parted. "I can't believe I'm doing this," I said breathlessly.

The Dark God's pulse thrummed against mine, and heat flashed where our bodies touched. His fingers tangled in my hair, sending a shiver along my spine. "Stay and savor the night with me, Samantha."

Shadows shrouded his face, but even in the starlight, I could see through them. It wasn't the face of the god I'd learned to fear, the savage destroyer. Instead, it was the warrior who'd fought for his people, the man who'd come to my defense.

They couldn't all be one and the same, could they?

I should have fled right then and there, but when he placed both hands on my hips and brought me closer, I didn't pull away. The collar was gone, but I was trapped by something else. Something thrumming and vibrating deep inside of me. A force of need that had never been there before—that *he* had awakened.

His lips drifted downward to meet mine again, and when his tongue dragged slowly against mine, I moaned at the promise of what it might do to other parts of me.

Gods, he felt good.

I bit down hard on his lip, making him growl with pain and pleasure, and something about that sound made me lose control, urging me on. The world spun around us, and all my worries and regrets slipped away. I forgot about what he was, who I was, and everything in between. Every sensation felt new and right.

Breaking the kiss, he looked down at me, his lips pulling into a devilish smile. "I should have kissed you sooner, little wolf."

I gripped his hair, the pulsing heat between my thighs threatening to tear me in two. "I would have ripped out your throat."

"But you haven't yet. I wonder why?"

His eyes blazed with desire, and the way he looked at me made me feel like every inch of me was awake. Alive.

Although I'd fought it, the pull between us had been building since I'd set foot in the Dreamlands. Every touch, every look, every time we rode together, it grew. Even in my restless dreams at night, he was there, protecting and wild.

Before I could respond, the Dark God's hands curled around the back of my thighs, and he lifted me, our faces inches apart. He was hard everywhere, and my body instinctively moved against his. I'd been with other men, but this was different—like dumping kerosene on a fire, he was fueling the flames building inside me. I wanted to be grasped and taken and consumed by this fierce god of a man.

"Fuck, Samantha," he growled against my lips.

What would the villagers think if they caught us? The danger and thrill of that sent shudders through my body.

But then another thought floated into my sex-addled mind. What would my friends at home think?

The door of the great hall burst open, and laughter filled the night behind us.

Reality and burning shame crashed in on me, disintegrating the heat of the moment.

I was kissing the man who'd nearly killed me. Who'd unleashed hell on my city and would have done worse. Who'd threatened those I cared about most.

Had I gone mad?

I shoved away from him and staggered back toward the hall.

His eyes burned with desire, but he let me go.

"This can't happen," I said. "Collar or not, I'm your prisoner. Don't ever kiss me again."

He dragged his thumb over his lower lip, a flicker of amusement in his eyes. "You kissed me back, if I recall."

Almost quaking, I shook my head. "That was the mead. Nothing more."

We both could smell the lie, but I needed it to be true.

Adjusting my dress, I spun and hurried toward the great hall. When I reached the door, I paused and looked back. He was gone, like he'd never been there. Like it all had been another dream.

I touched my swollen lips and knew that it wasn't. *What have I done?*

Shame and guilt assailed me like arrows raining down from the sky as I pushed back inside the noisy hall.

I clutched my forehead and groaned. Had I really just kissed the Dark God? What was it about his presence that made me completely incapable of rational thought? He was a ruthless bastard who'd kidnapped me. He was using me for his own sick plans for retribution.

And I'd kissed him. Had I gone *absolutely* insane? Clearly, yes. The gut-wrenchingly horrible part was that I'd wanted more. I'd *needed* it.

I grabbed a mug of ale from a server and drank it down. It wasn't my fault. I'd drunk too much mead. I had Stockholm syndrome. I'd hit my head in the battle.

Hell, he was a *god*, and his sexy god voodoo had to be corrupting my thoughts. How could any woman be rational around *that* kind of divine magnetism? He probably had that effect on everyone. He'd just chosen to exploit it with me, his prisoner.

Bastard.

I grasped for a thousand excuses as I jostled my way through the crowd of rowdy werefoxes. Finally, I found Selene, right where I'd left her, drinking with Sigrun.

Her bright smile faded as it dropped to my neck. "You convinced him to remove the collar! Well done!"

I touched the bare spot on my neck and grimaced. "Just for tonight."

"Considering how swollen your lips look, I would have asked for a week, at least," Sigrun muttered.

Oh, gods.

"It's not like that. He took it off, and then when I turned to go back in, he asked me to stay, and...we kissed." I put my elbows on the table and rubbed my temples. "It was the mead. It won't ever happen again."

More lies.

"Uh-huh," the old woman said. "And where is our extremely handsome and brave lord and master? Recovering?"

I glared at her. "I don't know where the bastard has gone. When I turned back, he'd just vanished into the shadows."

Sigrun shrugged. "Ah, he's probably gone to speak to the Opener of Ways. He promised the town council that he'd do it tonight."

"Who?"

The one-eyed woman gave a big sigh. "No one ever pays attention to the old stories. The Opener of Ways oversees the transition from this world to the next. The Wolf God is going to ask him to guide the souls of our clan to safety—though if memory serves, the two gods aren't on friendly terms."

"I thought this feast was to help guide the souls of the dead," I said—not that I understood how *that* was supposed to work.

Sigrun waved dismissively. "When you've got a god to intercede on your behalf, the rest really doesn't make much difference. He's doing us a great honor. That means tonight can just be about celebrating memories, drowning our sadness with drink, and for the young folk, getting laid. Very dour stuff."

I blinked, unable to get a measure on her.

Selene knocked back the rest of her mead and grasped my hand. "So your collar is off, and the Wolf God is away. Maybe you can't be completely free of him, but you're free for tonight. That's something, isn't it?"

Her words sent ice water plunging into my veins, waking me from my stupor. The collar was gone. And so was he.

My pulse quickened. The confusion of the kiss had overwhelmed everything else, but this was my chance to run. I looked around the hall. Should I risk it? Could I slip off through the crowd and down to the portal?

Don't betray my trust.

Fuck that. I knew he didn't trust me just as much as I didn't trust him.

It could be a test, though. All around us, dancers spun in circles while werefoxes laughed and drank throughout the hall. Yet everywhere I looked, I thought I caught glimpses of people watching me.

Was it because I was an outsider or because their god had ordered them to?

The hair on my neck rose, and I glanced up. High above us, a pair of owls sat perched in the rafters, looking back at me.

He uses animals as spies.

Dread coiled in my gut. Should I risk it? Or should I stay and prove I was trustworthy? I'd pushed him, and he'd agreed to take the collar off tonight. Maybe he'd do it again the next time we were beyond the citadel, and the next, until eventually, I found a way out.

The truth was that this was a golden opportunity, but I didn't know enough about the Dreamlands to take advantage. And there might be deathwings lurking in the forest.

I sighed.

"Are you okay?" Selene asked. "You spaced out. I thought you'd be happy."

I smiled weakly. "Sorry. It's been a long day."

She grasped my hand and tugged. "The day's done. Come and dance and forget the rest until tomorrow."

Too exhausted to resist, I let her haul me into the mass of people that had filled the center of the steward's hall.

Echoes of the Dark God's words rang in my mind: *No dancing with any man but me.*

I shuddered. Was he watching even now? The tingle of his gaze had returned. But Selene shoved me along, and as the crowd pressed in around me, I gave up fighting and let the beat and the mead carry me away.

It might be the only night I had to live for a long time.

37

———

Samantha

Five hours later, a voice woke me from a restless sleep.

"Samantha."

I sat upright.

The embers in the central hearths pulsed slowly, bathing the great hall with warmth and dim amber light. Selene was curled up on the ground a foot away on a heavy blanket. I had mine on top of me. Where had they come from?

All around us, werefoxes lay sleeping. Some were in human form, wrapped in blankets, but most were cuddled together in their furry forms. All slept soundly, assured that their god was watching over them.

Except he wasn't there. I didn't feel his presence.

When I'd first arrived in the Dreamlands, I thought it was just the feel of the place. Now that he'd vanished, I realized how much of that low vibration was his power, pressing down on everything from all sides.

Was he still speaking to the Opener of Ways, or out hunting the fae?

No one stirred in the shadows of the great hall. Perhaps the whisper had only been my imagination.

Lying back down, I closed my eyes and tried to get comfortable, but my mind kept spinning with the events of the day. Life-draining vines. Fae warriors. Deathwings. Burning pyres. Dancing with a god. Kissing him beneath the stars. Shit. It was enough to keep a girl awake for a week. All that, and I had to pee.

Stretching my stiff limbs, I sloughed the heavy blanket off and stood. My muscles moaned in protest as aches erupted all over my body. After riding, fighting, dancing, and then sleeping on the ground, my body was in full-on revolt.

So was my head—I'd drunk way too much of Selene's mead after I'd returned to the hall.

After I kissed the Dark God.

Burning with shame and desperate to escape the much-too-hot memory, I tiptoed around the sleeping werefoxes and made my way toward the rear door of the hall. It grated softly on its hinges as I pushed it open and slipped outside. Two males stood guard.

"I wouldn't wander. Not tonight," one whispered as I emerged.

"Call of nature. I'll be quick."

He nodded.

I rounded the side of the building and took a quick squat in the grass behind a nearby house. The entire world was still, though the scent of smoke and fire hung in the air.

When I was done, I headed back to the hall.

"Samantha," a voice whispered, and I froze in place, every muscle tense. I recognized it but couldn't quite place it.

I extended my claws. "Who's there?"

"We need to get you out of here! There's not much time," the voice said from the darkness.

"Sarion?" I slunk forward, ready to pounce. There was no fucking way he was here.

I rounded the corner and froze.

Sarion stood in the soft moonlight, a pair of lacelike wings extending from his back. He motioned for me to hurry. "I can fly you out of here and across the border."

Except it wasn't him.

Beneath the glamour, I could see that he was someone else. His hair was brown and cropped short, and he stood at least a foot taller than Sarion. I could see both the truth and deception at the same time.

Sweat slicked my palms, and my heart pounded in my chest. I thanked the fates that for whatever reason, I was immune to their glamour.

But not their lies.

I flicked my eyes right and left, my gaze landing on the moth-like pattern of a deathwing lurking in the shadows of a nearby house. I was fucked. There were two of them and one of me. I might be able to fend off the fae male, but one sting from the deathwing would do me in. And if I called the guards, I'd be leading them to their deaths as well.

Now would be a great time for the damn Dark God to pop out of nowhere.

I slowly backed up.

The fae pretending to be Sarion crept forward. "Where are you going, Samantha? I promise not to hurt you."

"I know you're not Sarion, so stay the fuck back."

The glamour he'd cast faded, revealing his true form. He wore the same dark leather armor as the warriors who'd attacked the village. "I thought his form might ease your fears. We don't want to hurt you. We want to help you escape."

"Who are you?" I backed up another couple of steps. "And why should I believe anything you say?"

He smiled, though it didn't reach his eyes. "The Undying Court. We need you. You know how to defeat the lying god. You are safe with us."

Yeah, right. I'd watched them murder villagers right in front of my eyes. The rising fury in my chest almost compelled me to ram my claws straight into his face, but that would just get me killed.

Violence wasn't the answer, but if I could keep him talking, I might be able to buy myself time to get some information while figuring a way out. "I can't leave. He has the power to summon me back any time he wants."

The fae male tilted his head, no doubt searching for a lie. "Our masters are powerful. They can break the magic, but he mustn't know you're gone. Come now, I won't hurt you. We'll even spare this village as a down payment for your assistance."

If it had actually been Sarion, and if I hadn't lost all trust in him, I would've gladly traded loyalties to protect the werefox village and to be free of the Dark God's leash forever. But I knew I couldn't trust Sarion or the fae. Not after the chaos and murder and lies.

"You promise not to harm the village?" I whispered, inching closer toward the corner of the building.

"Yes. I promise."

"I want the Dark God dead as much as you do. Let me get my things."

"You're lying," the fae said, impatience blooming in his eyes.

A scraping noise stole my attention. I snapped my head up. A deathwing clung to the roof, its pink eyes trained on me.

I pressed my back into the side of the longhouse.

"Come now," the fae said calmly. "If you resist, this village will pay, and I'll take you anyway."

"Samantha?" a woman's voice carried through the dark. Selene.

Fuck, fuck, fuck.

Her shape rounded the corner. "Is that you?"

I bolted toward her. "The fae are here. Get inside!"

Selene froze as a dark shadow blotted out the moonlight illuminating the side of the hall. I twisted and barely ducked the grasping pincers of the deathwing. Lashing out with my claws, I tore into the freak's wing, and it dropped like a stone. "Run, Selene!"

Legs and claws tore at my limbs, shredding the bottom of the dress she'd given me. Stifling the pain that erupted across my calves, I sank the claws of my left hand between the plates of its carapace and ripped through its eyes, just like Elowyn had taught me. It crashed onto its back, legs twitching.

Strong arms grasped me from behind, and my body lurched off the ground. I fought and kicked as the fae beat his wings upward.

"Settle down!" he growled, his sharp teeth grazing my neck.

Selene seized my ankles. "You're not taking her!"

The fae grunted, and we dropped several feet. For a second, I dangled between them. Then fabric ripped, and I crashed.

"Come on!" Selene grasped my hand to pull me up, and we ran.

Silent wings beat the air around us, and Selene cried out in surprise as we rounded the corner. The two guards were dead.

We pounded on the door, but it was locked. Selene shouted as she beat it with her hands, but the second deathwing was already behind us, its shimmering wings making the pattern of a skull in the air. It coiled to strike, and fire pulsed through my veins.

"Selene!" I shouted as I yanked her down. A searing heat raced over my arms, and a wave of white light rolled over her body.

She collapsed on top of me as a sparkling ball of energy

spread around us. The deathwing stabbed at it again and again, but its stinger couldn't break through.

Selene rolled over and gasped. "This is your magic?"

"Get the door open. I can't hold it for much longer!"

The forcefield I'd created was taking everything from me. My skin tingled with radiance as the warmth and strength were pulled from my body. It was glorious, but whatever reserve the light was draining, there wasn't much left.

Selene kept pounding on the door and shouting. "Let us in!"

My arms quaked with exhaustion, and the light started flickering.

Iron and wood grated behind us, and the door cracked open. Hands grabbed at me as the dome of light protecting us crackled and dissolved.

But then the fae gripped my ankle, tugging my legs out from under me. Unrelenting pain exploded from every cell in my body, and the world went white.

38

———

Cadean

The bonfire burned blue against the night sky, crackling and popping as it consumed the sap.

A dark form flickered amid the flames: the Opener of Ways.

Seated on an ebony throne, the death god had the head of a wolf and body of a man. I could feel his magic creeping into my world, calling to all living things.

I would destroy him if I could.

"Why have you summoned me, Wolf God?" he growled.

Clenching my fists to restrain my hate, I fixed him with an iron glare. "Many werefoxes from my realm will cross your land tonight. I've come to petition you to give them safe passage."

"Those that cross the veil must do so on their own. It is the way."

"They were murdered by fae sent by the Undying Court—creatures you hold no sway over, though you should."

"They will be mine in time." He shifted forward in his seat, eyes burning. "As for your request, you have something that belongs to me—a woman. The Moon pulled her from my grasp.

Give her to me, and I will guide the souls of your village safely into the night."

Protectiveness surged inside me. I would never let her go. Never give her over to that beast. Though deep down, I knew that one day, she would have to cross his lands.

"No," I snarled, surprised by the ferocity of my voice. Something had changed. Had it been the kiss, or was it the growing bond between us?

The Opener of Ways sat back and spread his hands wide. "Then we have no deal."

If I could have reached through the flame, I would've ripped out his tongue. "She's the key to my freedom. I will not relinquish her."

It wasn't the entire truth, but I wasn't going to let him know that.

"The lords of death do not take kindly to thieves."

"That is the fault of the Moon, not me," I said. "Take from *her* all that you will."

A jackal's grin formed on his face. "Yet you have what I want."

As I opened my mouth to speak, searing pain rippled along my spine. My wounded arm clenched in agony, and I staggered back from the flames. Vision swimming, I summoned my axe and spun around, scanning the clearing. No one was there.

"What is it?" the Opener of Ways asked from within the fire.

Then the truth struck: it wasn't my pain. It was *hers*.

"This conversation isn't over," I growled, and dismissed the magic oracle. As soon as it was gone, the bonfire collapsed inward and diminished to low flames licking around the ends of the charred logs.

Closing my eyes, I searched the shadows for her.

The village.

The shadows resolved into an image. A fae male was dragging her body from the door of the longhouse, a deathwing at his side.

Violence blurred my vision. I reached for the magic of her collar to summon her to me, but it didn't respond.

Fuck, I'd taken it off.

Fury blazed through my veins, and I called on the primal spirits held within my soul. I searched through the thousand forms I could command. Wolf. Owl. Raven.

Peregrine.

I seized the form and exploded into the air in a whirl of shadow and feathers. Beating the air with my wings, I soared into the sky as if the gods of hell were driving me onward.

The village appeared in seconds, and I whirled to scan the sky. The moonlight highlighted the fae and two deathwings racing low over the village. The form of a woman dangled between them.

Fucking hell.

My razor-sharp eyes trained on Samantha, and I reached out with my power, connecting to her through some inexplicable bond. A glimmer of life. Flickers of cool magic in the darkness.

Hope.

I climbed higher and higher, and as the pair turned north below me toward the forest, I dove.

The world blurred as I hurtled down. Moments before I hit, I seized the form of a giant eagle. Tendrils of shadow wrapped around me, and my wings unfurled to twenty feet across.

I crashed into the back of the first beast and grasped it by its wings. It struggled, but before it could free itself, I swooped and impaled it on the top of a dying tree. The thing screeched, but I was already soaring away.

The fae jerked back to the south and started to climb, but he couldn't evade me. Seconds before I tore into him, he released Samantha.

Fear clenched my heart. I tucked my wings as I rammed into him, then dove in pursuit of her.

She plunged into the canopy of yellow birch, and I seized her in my talons. The branches ripped through my broad wings, breaking bones and tearing through flesh and feather. I paid no head to the pain. My only thought was for her.

I called on the form of a man, and the shadows poured around us. Human again, I crashed out of the tree, clutching her in my arms.

My spine slammed into a protruding root, and I let my body absorb the weight of our fall. Above, the deathwing spiraled toward us through the hole I'd made.

Agony thundering through my back, I rolled on top of Samantha to block its strike. Its poisoned barb lanced my skin, and I felt the toxin burning through me.

It would have killed her, but I was a god. The pain only fueled my anger.

I seized the deathwing by its tail and sank my axe into its thorax, releasing my magic. The creature shrieked as black lightning tore its body apart.

Silence settled around us.

I dropped to Samantha's side. She'd gone comatose, and *fuck*, I was a hunter, not a healer. I could regrow the forest, but not flesh.

Desperation tore through me, and I pulled her to my chest. I had to try.

I called on my power of regrowth, but instead of imagining a tree healing and springing back to life, I imagined her wounds vanishing and her eyes flying open. Every bit of strength I had, I pushed into her, but my magic didn't respond.

"Please," I whispered. "Heal."

But there was nothing.

And then the thrum of wings rose overhead.

Samantha's pulse grew more erratic, and a panic and dread I'd never felt settled in my bones.

The deathwing's toxins coursed through my veins, weakening my power. I could shift and fly her back to the fortress, but that was a risk I wasn't willing to take. Not while two more deathwings were currently headed our way.

I scooped her up, my broken bones and lacerations screaming. Cursing the damn deathwing that had stung me, I stepped into the shadows of the trees.

The darkness swallowed us, and I shadow-stepped through the forest, putting as much distance between us and the fae creatures as possible, hoping the exertion would purge the toxins more quickly. When I no longer felt the magic of the deathwings, I stopped.

Certain we were safe, I cast a veil of shadows around us. I knelt under an ancient white ash, holding Samantha in my arms. A column of moonlight cut across her soft features. "Samantha, wake up."

Her breaths were shallow and fast, her pulse irregular. My chest tightened, something painful lodging in my throat. "I command you to wake."

Her heart fluttered briefly, but she didn't stir. I needed to recover from the noxious sting so I could get her back to a healer, but I sensed there was no time. I had to fix her.

Shadows glided across the leaf litter and moss, twisting around us as I drew my power inward. Agony flared as the poison worked through my system, searing every nerve and sapping my strength. Gritting my teeth, I pressed one palm to Samantha's chest while sinking the other into the damp soil, calling forth the connection that pulsed between me and every living organism in my realm. It was faint at first, a flickering of electrical charges that grew into a steady stream of energy that flowed between the forest's network of roots and me.

The verdant energy surged up my arm, grounding me and restoring my power. I'd never tried to transfer this power to another, but my magic seemed to gravitate toward Samantha, as if she were somehow calling it.

I let a trickle of it pour into her, careful not to overwhelm her.

At first, there was nothing. Then a faint glow of magic pulsed between us—not that of the forest but of something unfamiliar. I couldn't be sure if it was coming from her or me, or in the space between our bodies, but it was there, and building. The power roared between us, and like a whirlpool flowing backward, a luminescent energy poured forth. Heat raced over my arms and crashed into her.

She gasped, her body arching as her head tilted back in a silent moan. Sensations of heat and light overwhelmed the connection burning between us. Every nerve in my body blazed, no longer with pain but with awareness of each movement she made against me. I could smell her desire, and every muscle fiber in my body tightened. What the fuck had just happened?

Her eyes flew wide. "Deathwings!"

I tightened my grip. "It's all right. They're gone, and you're safe."

She struggled in my arms. "But the village—"

"Is safe," I whispered, brushing the loose hair from her face. "It's just you and me."

I relinquished the forest's power that was still coursing within me, unspent. Whatever the magic had been that healed her, it wasn't mine or that of my land. Had I somehow triggered hers?

My skin had never felt so sensitive, and the dark colors of the night were all the richer. The magic had left me exhausted and alive and filled with wild desire.

A sudden dread filled my heart. There was another explanation… but it was impossible.

I'd heard of the effects caused by the triggering of a mate bond—the heightened senses, the shared emotions, and the ability to heal. But I was a god, and she a mortal. The fates never forged such bonds because they could never last.

It had to be something else. But what else could explain the thunderous pain in my chest, or the terror I'd felt seeing her wounded?

Samantha's chest rose and fell in heavy breaths as I searched her face for impossible answers. She gazed up and smiled. "You came for me."

That uncomfortable tightness squeezed my chest harder. "I will always come for you, little wolf."

The words were out of my mouth before I knew what I was saying. The shock of them cut deep. They were true. How could I ever let her go?

Her expression darkened. "Because I'm the pawn in your game."

Her voice was thick with an emotion I couldn't discern.

"No." I dragged my thumb along her cheekbone, her skin heating under my touch. "Because you're the queen."

"Why should I believe that?"

"Because it's the truth."

I craved her and wanted to protect her, but it was more than that—far more than I could explain. She made me want to be better, to be the man I'd once been before I'd been consumed by rage, before I'd been trapped behind the walls of the Moon's magic.

My thoughts drifted to her lips and to the damp heat I sensed rising between her luscious thighs. She was just so damn beautiful and strong, and I'd never felt such shameless desire for a woman. By the look in her eyes, I could see that I was not alone in that desire.

She fisted my shirt and slowly pulled herself up. "Then prove it. Show me what a queen means to you."

I sucked in a sharp breath at her sultry invitation, and my body tensed. I could taste her need, and I felt it in every word that rolled off her tongue. Her lips were mere inches from mine, her sweet perfume clouding my judgment. I wanted to worship every inch of her. Prove to her that what I felt for her was real.

Would that be enough to convince her that there was goodness inside of me?

I ran my fingers up her side, and she moaned softly in a way that sent shivers of pleasure racing over my skin. My hand froze inches from her cheek as an unfamiliar emotion pulled at me. She deserved better.

"I need to take you back to Shadowstone," I growled. "You're still hazy with the aftereffects of the healing."

And if she kissed me again, I wasn't sure my heart could take it.

"My mind has never been clearer," she said, her voice steady and eyes focused. I could sense the truth of her words, but I didn't want her to regret what might happen between us. Both for her sake and mine. I was a selfish bastard.

I started to rise—

"Cadean," she said, desire thick in her voice.

I froze, paralyzed by the invitation on the tip of her tongue. She'd never used my name before, and I swore to the first gods that I'd never heard anything sexier from a woman's lips. My cock stiffened, my trousers painfully constricting. I silently cursed under my breath, begging whatever spirits inhabited these woods to give me strength.

But the greedy bastard in me brushed my lips against hers. "You know my name."

She traced her mouth across my jaw. "I know you want me."

My blood became fire, and I thanked the fates that she didn't know how much sway she held over me in that moment, because she could ask me anything right there, and I'd give it to her.

"Do *you* know what you want?" I asked, my voice raw and gravelly.

"To be kissed by the man who woke me," she said breathlessly as her chest rose and fell against mine.

Whatever restraint I had crumbled into dust. My hand clenched her hair, and I took her mouth in mine, not softly or gently, but hungrily and wantonly.

She arched against my body, and I knew in that moment, Samantha had been sent by the heavens to destroy me.

39

———

Samantha

The Dark God's lips crashed against mine, violent and all-consuming.

Like thunder cracking, the world shifted. Something deep inside of me burst, spreading through my every fiber like an explosion of champagne bubbles. I gasped, breaking our kiss as electricity jolted between us, heating my skin and setting alight every nerve.

What the hell was that?

It was utter madness, and I didn't care. I wasn't drunk on mead or high on healing magic, I was alive. Present. And in that moment, I knew what I wanted—*him*.

A dull ache spread low in my belly, and dampness slicked my thighs. My skin was raw, and even the heat of his breath against it was almost too much to bear.

"Tell me to stop, little wolf," the Dark God rasped. "Tell me to bring you home."

I pressed a kiss to his cheek. "Why?"

"Because you deserve better." A thousand emotions played across his face as he wrestled his demons.

I deserved what I wanted—to be wild and unrestrained and to be able to satisfy the pulsing heat at *my* core. The fucking world could wait. This could be a one-time thing. Nobody would have to know.

Part of me knew it was crazy, and yet...

"Show me," I said. "Show me what I deserve."

His expression turned almost feral, and gods, I didn't know why, but it made the heat building at my core even worse.

"Are you sure?" he asked, his fingers caressing my side.

My nerves exploded beneath his fingers, and I moaned. "Yes."

Gods, yes.

He lowered his lips to my neck, grazing my sensitive skin. His touch sent a shiver of ecstasy along my spine, and I arched against him. When he kissed me this time, it was tender and gentle, every flick of his tongue against mine a reverence.

My body burned with sensations I couldn't describe—a kaleidoscope of scents, tastes, and emotions humming through me. If this was what kissing a god felt like, I feared that fucking him would demolish me.

"Cadean..." I moaned as one of his hands cupped my breast. Like a beast unleashed, he dragged his tongue against mine, inciting something deep and primal inside me.

Whatever heat had seized me, I couldn't stop it, didn't want to. I slipped my legs on either side of his and rolled my hips, seeking the friction of his body. He growled low, and when my core brushed against his hardness, I nearly lost my damn mind.

"I don't want you to stop. Please," I begged.

I'd never felt this before, but if I didn't get release soon, I was going to die.

"Fuck, Samantha." His hands lifted my hips, and he lowered me onto the damp ground. One hand cradled the back of my head as the other slipped under my dress and gripped my ass.

"What is it about you that is so fucking irresistible?" he said against my lips.

I was too focused on seeking release from the mounting pressure at my center to worry about that. I ground against him. "I think it must have something to do with my traitorous pussy and terrible taste in men."

He fixed me with a hungry gaze. "Good thing I'm a god."

"Just fuck me already." My hips rocked against his, demanding friction.

"Not tonight, little wolf." Before I knew it, he'd pinned me down, his lips pressing a soft kiss against my belly. "But I *will* take care of you."

I glanced down my trembling body, meeting his heated stare with a mix of desperation and anger. Was he serious?

"Please..." I begged, reaching for him. "It's what I want."

He traced a slow circle against my inner thigh with his tongue. "I *will* fuck you, little wolf, but this isn't the place," he continued, his lips grazing the sensitive bud of nerves under my panties. "And when I do, I'll worship every inch of you before I bury myself deep inside."

I clung to his words like a promise, but they only fanned my desire and desperation. I didn't want to wait—I needed him in me now. I twisted under his hold. "You bastard. You're going to leave me like this? Another game?"

"I would never leave you wanting," he whispered against my skin as he slipped his hand between my legs.

I whimpered as his fingers traced the fabric over my entrance, then sucked in a breath as they slipped under my panties, ripping them away with a quick tug.

"Gorgeous. And so wet," he purred right before he dragged his tongue down the entrance of my sex.

My hips jumped at the contact of his mouth, delight and torture shuddering through me. Pulling my hips forward, he tucked my legs over his shoulders as he took me further in his mouth, devouring me like a godsdamned ice cream cone.

Stars flashed behind my eyes, and my head fell back on the damp mosses and leaves. Between the deep strokes of his tongue and the friction of his lips, I was panting and bucking, the intense pressure at my core rising.

"My gods," I moaned, my fingers clawing at his hair as the muscles at my core clenched. This man was going to destroy me. A tautness spread through my chest, and I swore that my heart was about to give out.

Mortals weren't meant to experience such pleasure.

As my climax neared, the Dark God slipped two fingers inside me, and holy fuck. He found that sensitive spot deep within, working me until I was on the brink.

"I want you to say my name when you come, Samantha," he growled, looking at me with a possessive heat in his gaze.

My head fell back as I tried to stifle a moan. I wouldn't say his name because that would mean something. This was just sex. A moment of—

His mouth returned to my sensitive flesh, setting off an explosion of pleasure that ripped through me.

I pitched and rolled my hips, my hands clawing at the ground, and before I knew what I was doing, I was screaming his name over and over, until my voice had grown hoarse. Convulsions of pleasure and bliss rippled through me, and my stomach dropped like I was freefalling. When I'd returned to earth, and the aftershocks of my orgasm had eased, I glanced up at the Dark God. "I think you broke me."

He gently tugged my dress down over my bare legs and met my gaze, a wicked curve gracing his lips. "Then you'd better rest up, because I haven't even begun."

40

Samantha

Warmth crept across my cheek. My eyelids fluttered open, then closed against the column of morning light that streamed through the large window beside me. Groaning, I turned over, the heavy vestiges of sleep beckoning me.

My eyes flew open, and panic coursed through my veins. Where was I?

Although my heart was still pounding, I relaxed. I was in my bed in Shadowstone. A warm sense of security rolled over me.

Then it shattered.

The memories came flooding back: the deathwings, the feast, dancing with the Dark God, kissing him, the attack, and—

"Oh, my gods," I said in a hushed voice.

The world crashed around me, and my chest ached. I'd let the Dark God himself go down on me. I'd *begged* him to do it... and even more.

I yanked the soft comforter over my head and screamed. What was I thinking?

Clearly, I'd gone insane or had been drunk on danger. I'd nearly died, and he'd healed me with his magic. I knew healing magic was sensual, but *his* had been intoxicating beyond anything that I'd ever imagined.

And *Cadean* had been beyond anything I'd ever imagined.

How fucked in the head was I? He was the bastard Dark God. A monster. A brute. The person I hated most in the universe.

My treacherous pussy had gotten me in some tight spots before, but this made my soul hurt. I'd betrayed everything I stood for. Everything we'd fought for.

Please, fates, just kill me now.

Even as I cursed myself to hell and back, I couldn't drive out the memories of what we'd done together. I replayed every moment in my mind as guilt and shame burned my soul.

His kisses had been soft at first, then hungry. A deep ache settled low in my belly as I recalled the way his broad shoulders had flexed while his head was pressed up between my thighs. Those sinfully delicious things he'd done with his tongue and fingers.

Heat flooded me, and I let my fingers slip deep between my legs—

No. Nope. Nuh-uh. Last night was a one-night fling. I wouldn't let it happen again.

My pack, my *friends*, would disown me if they knew the sins I'd committed. My wolf, who had a more fluid sense of morality, stirred in my chest, still basking in the afterglow. *Well, he* was *a god.*

Oh, yes, he was. And he was good. Really good. Things had gotten way out of hand, but hell, I couldn't deny that that had been the best orgasm of my life.

I make the worst decisions when it comes to men.

I sat up, whipped the thick duvet off my legs, and slipped out of bed, cringing at the midnight blue chemise I was wearing. I definitely didn't remember putting that on. I began pacing across the cool stone floor like a caged animal, my mind searching for some rational form of control.

The thing had happened, and there was nothing I could do to change the past. But I could take a stand. Whatever his expectations were, *that* would be a one-time thing—a result of the attack and his healing magic. Near-death-experience sex. That's all it was.

I ran my fingers through my hair. "Fuck my life."

What I feared most was the glimmer of sympathy and respect that had formed in the pit of my stomach. The way he'd protected Selene's village, and the way he'd honored those who'd been killed. He'd revealed a side of him I wasn't expecting, brave and relentless in his defense of his people.

In defense of me.

I took a hot bath, but rather than washing away the foolishness of the night before, I found myself reliving the moment.

This was going to be a major problem.

I had to get out of the Dreamlands as soon as possible and away from the god. I couldn't be trusted around him, and if he thought I was amenable to his advances, he might never let me go.

And I had to go. I had been gone a week and a half at least. My mother would be worried, and so would Jaxson and Savannah. I had to find a way to heal the Dark God more quickly. That meant forcing him to teach me to master my magic. And if that didn't work, or he doubled back on his promise, I had to be ready to run. I needed to learn the landscape. Find other portals like the one in Frostfall. And most importantly, make allies like Mel, Sigrun, and Selene. Even the little goblin.

Speaking of whom...

I hustled over to the table where the biscuits had been, and my heart leapt. There was a tiny brass key in the corner.

Hand shaking, I tried it in the window. The lock clicked, and with a hard shove, I was able to crack it open. Fresh air whistled in, and I took a deep breath. "Good job, gobbo."

The sky was blue, and the morning fog had burned off, but the seams of mist that separated the patches still remained. How many villages were out there nestled among the trees? How many cities?

There was so much I needed to know, and I needed a damn map.

I stuck my head out the window, and my gut spun with vertigo. It was a long, long way down, and would be a dangerous climb. Thankfully, I had claws and was a hell of a climber. And if I ever did have to go out the window, I could probably find access through another opening lower down.

I closed the window and locked it, then hid the key in the back of a drawer.

Next, it was time to test how much freedom I actually had and make sure the Dark God hadn't forgotten his promise to train me. Though he'd only agreed to training me with a sword and knife, if I could earn his trust, he might help me with my magic.

I opened the dark mahogany wardrobe and froze. Where there had been three of Mel's outfits before, now it was full of clothes—trousers, riding pants, tunics, and underwear. Where had it all come from? I'd never had a wardrobe like this in my entire life, and it scratched a deep, forgotten itch that I'd shoved deep under my bed in high school. Six gorgeous dresses in rich hues of plum, cherry, and sky blue hung on hangers. I examined each in turn, holding them up to the mirror and deciding which color suited my skin tone. Somehow, all of them did.

I could almost feel the Dark God's approving gaze on me from the night before. It had been relentless and had sent warmth rushing to my core. He made me feel beautiful, like I was one in a million. The truth was, I was just a mortal little wolf with unpredictable magic.

Nope. No more dresses for me. I'd send them all to Selene to repay her for the one I'd destroyed. Well, almost all of them.

I shoved the beautiful things back into the wardrobe and selected a simple tan and black leather riding outfit. Then I headed to the door and jiggled the handle.

Still locked. At least I didn't have to wear the collar.

I pounded on the door. "Take me to see the Dark God."

It was time for us to have a frank talk, and it was best to get it over with.

41

Cadean

I lunged forward and swung my axe, trying to tear through Auren's neck.

He slipped to the side and let the keen edge of my axe glide down the blade of his sword, then spun right and thrust for my gut.

I slammed the sword away inches before it pierced my skin. "I need help, Auren."

My brother switched grips and took a new fighting stance with his blade held high. "With your form or your sex life? Maybe there's some hope for the first, but I don't think anyone can fix the second."

"Neither." I dropped low and swept his feet from under him with my leg.

He landed on his back with a crack and quickly rolled out of the way of my strike.

I loomed over him, axe pointed at this head. "My fucking realm is stretched to the limit. The vines keep pushing deeper into my land, and the fae attacks have doubled in the last month. They've even sent assassins across the border."

He rolled over and snatched his blade, and I stepped back to dodge the blow. It gave him time to spring to his feet and swing twice more. "What were they after? They know better than to try to kill you or sweet Melanthe. Was it the blonde? The little flower you've been hiding from me?"

Anger surged through my veins. I deflected his blade and stepped inside his guard, then slammed my fist into his chin. He staggered back, and I gave him a wicked grin. "Don't worry about the woman. I need you worried about my realm. I'm dying here, and you've sat on your hands for a decade."

"You know it's not as easy as that. You're not the only one who shares a border with the Undying Court. I have to be careful." He rubbed his jaw, and then, moving like lighting, he made three quick strikes. One grazed my thigh—the first blood either of us had drawn today.

I tightened my hands on the haft of my axe and lunged forward, driving him back with wide sweeps. "You'll let the crows feast on my bones to protect your own hide?"

"Their time will come." Auren's sword clanged off my axe, and then he swung the blade so that it passed inches over my head. "We just need to make the end swift and final. No protracted wars. That's why you need to neutralize the barrier. I'll come to your aid the moment you're free to ride into their territory with me."

He drove home the attack, jabbing with his sword, keeping me on my back foot.

But I'd had it with his constant delays and excuses and plotting. I stepped into the blow and then brought the flat of my axe down on his hand. The sword flew from his grip. "I need help *now.*"

He shook out his hand. "Fuck, Cade, that actually hurt." Auren switched hands and pointed his sword. "Why do you insist on such a short view of time? What does another decade or century matter to us? We're gods. We can afford to be patient."

"My people cannot," I growled, and batted the tip of his blade away.

He just brought it back and slowly circled the point, as if to tempt me to attack. "You worry too much about mortal lives."

It was true. And there was one in particular.

I lashed out twice with my axe, but Auren deflected and stepped back lightly on his feet. "Let's not beat about the bush and spend our time talking of little things like villages and people. Your offer must be better, Cadean, if you expect me to pick up your flag and put my own realm at risk."

He swung for my head with his sword, but I deflected the blow and slammed him in the shoulder with the flat of my axe. He staggered sideways, and I bared my teeth. "My own brother would bleed me dry, just like the vines."

Then the scent of honey and lavender rose in the air.

Samantha.

I stepped back and turned to face her. Her golden hair and leather riding clothes made her glow like the sun among the thousand shades of green around us. She moved like a lazy river, swinging her hips with every step. It reminded me of just how skillfully those hips could move.

I inhaled deeply as I took all of her in.

Then pain ripped through my arm. I dodged back out of the way of Auren's blade with a feral snarl. My brother had sliced cleanly through my shirt and left a thin red cut across the surface of my skin. Blood seeped from the cut and wicked into the cloth.

I glared at him. "What the fuck was that for?"

He could have taken my whole arm off, but he was a master swordsman, and the cut was exactly as deep as he intended.

Auren twirled his blade. "A grazing blow, and well earned.

You let your guard down and lost focus. Are you going to do that every time you see a pretty face?"

Just one face.

My brother wiped my blood from his blade with a cloth and slammed it down into his sheath. Then he looked over at Samantha with greedy eyes. "It occurs to me, Cadean, that there might be an exchange I'd consider."

My blood became an inferno. A raging wave of possessiveness devoured me, and I leveled my axe in his direction. "Stay away from her. She won't be part of any deal."

"Have it your way," Auren said.

I let my blade drop as Samantha drew close, flanked by her guards. Concern flashed across her face as she saw the wound. "I didn't mean to interrupt your duel."

"It's all right, we were just finishing up." I dismissed my axe back into the ether. "I've received worse scratches from riding in the forest."

"Or from fucking," Auren muttered under his breath.

Samantha blushed, and I spun on him. "I think you have other matters to attend to, brother."

He grinned broadly. "Kicking me out so quickly? You haven't even introduced me to your beautiful...acquaintance."

"And I don't need to," I growled.

He held out his hand to her anyway. "I'm Auren."

Her eyes measured him a second too long, and then she inclined her head slightly. "I'm Samantha."

There was something odd about their exchange, but I couldn't put my finger on it. That troubled me.

Auren gave her a rakish smile. "I must say, I can see how you captured my brother's attention—or wait, was it that my brother captured you? I mix the rumors up sometimes."

I shoved his shoulder. "Goodbye, Auren."

He backed away with a confident grin on his face. "I do hope we meet again, Samantha. You'll have to forgive Cadean. He can be a poor sport."

The way he let her name roll off his tongue made me want to cut it free with my axe. My neck heated, and every muscle in my body tensed, ready for a fight. A real fight. The last time that had happened, we'd nearly destroyed one of the towers of the citadel, and I knew that if the woman was involved, it would be far worse.

"We'll continue negotiations later," I growled.

Auren turned and walked off across the green. The sooner he was out of my realm, the better.

Samantha's gaze followed him as he departed, and my jaw clenched. What was I supposed to do with her? Wulfric had exploded with fury this morning after I'd told him what had happened.

You're playing with fire, Cade, and you're going to get us all burned.

But Samantha was impossible to resist. She'd awoken emotions in me that had been numb for centuries: jealousy, desire, and beneath it all, the need to be a better man.

I closed my eyes for a second and took a deep breath, drawing in the scent of the woods around me. My blood calmed.

Let Auren play his games.

42

———————

Cadean

Once Auren was around the corner, Samantha turned her attention back to me. "You call sword fighting negotiation?"

"Everything with Auren is a fight—just like with you. Structured combat keeps things more civil and prevents us from spilling actual blood."

"He spilled your blood."

I gave her a wry grin. "I was distracted by the most beautiful creature in my realm. It was well worth the scratch."

I took a step toward her, but she backed up as the color drained from her face. "It can't happen again, Cadean. Last night was a one-time thing, never to be repeated or even discussed."

Her words lanced through my chest like a frost-tipped spear. The ache bore down on me, crushing in from all sides. My throat tightened. Of course she felt that way. In her eyes, I was a monster, a murderer and despoiler.

"Can we talk in private?" she asked, glancing at her guards.

I waved them away, but I wouldn't be put off so easily. I reached out and brushed that ever-unruly strand of hair from her cheek. "Once would be a shame. There is so much more we could do."

Her cheeks flushed, and I could sense her rising desire, but she shook her head. "Cadean, I can't."

Every time she used my name, it sent pleasure rumbling through me. Whatever came next, our relationship *had* changed. I let my fingers trace down the line of her jaw. "You kissed me, remember?"

She drifted back from my fingertips, and her expression hardened. "I know. It was consensual, and I wanted to. But you need to promise me that nothing else will happen again."

"Why?"

"Because you're my enemy, and I'm your captive."

"I see." The shame of it burned through my soul, and I tightened my fist. She was right. I was nothing more than a ruthless, brutal, destroyer. And she was at my mercy.

"We're walking a dangerous line, and the magic I use to heal your wound is..." Her face flushed. "I need an assurance that it won't go beyond that. Otherwise, I don't see how we can move forward."

It was poison on the tip of a blade.

Her healing magic *was* enrapturing. Each time that she touched me, it sent blood pulsing through my body and devilish thoughts racing to my mind. And that paled in comparison to the strange magic that had passed between us last night.

"Do you understand?" she asked. "It never happens again."

My jaw ticked. Auren would be delighting in this if he were here. "I understand," I said, my voice grating against my nerves.

The tightness in her shoulders relaxed. She was ashamed of lying with me, her captor. Even beneath her lingering lust, I could taste the bitterness of regret.

The worst part was that I knew she was right.

Wulfric had hammered that much into me this morning.

She was dangerous. We didn't know what she could do with her magic. She clouded my judgement. She was a liability. She had the power to bring me to my knees. We had to protect the realm. He'd gone over a dozen reasons and beat them into my head with more fury than Auren had parried my axe. Yet it was almost impossible not to look at her, and if I looked, I would desire.

Easy, Cade.

We realized that we were staring at each other through the expanse of silence, and both of us looked away.

How the *fuck* was I going to make this work without losing my mind?

Be stronger than the beast within you. Be better.

Taking a deep breath, I gestured to the path winding through the dense foliage beside the green. "These are my gardens. Will you take a walk with me before I ride out?"

After a moment's hesitation, she nodded, and we headed into the deep, overgrown woods that bordered the green.

"This is a garden?" she asked skeptically as we slipped into the shadows of the undergrowth. The earth smelled of deep must and rotting wood. The ferns were thick, and mushrooms sprouted everywhere.

"In a way." I paused beside the decaying trunk of a tree and crumbled a little of the black wood between my fingers. Moss grew over the top, and small mushrooms and yellow fungus dotted the side. "For centuries, this was a favorite tree. When it died fifty years ago, I placed it here. Now it gives life to hundreds of beings that thrive in and around it. I prefer to watch nature do the gardening, and I just help shape it from the shadows."

We walked in silence as Samantha breathed in the rich scents around her.

"Last night, I asked you to help me with my magic," she said.

"I will."

She raised her eyebrows, and I shrugged. "I'm running out of time. You need to be able to draw on your power and control it. More importantly, you need to protect yourself. Will you give me three days? I have a few things to tend to."

I needed time to lay waste to the bastards who had sent the deathwings to Frostfall.

Samantha nodded. "Where are you going?"

"To defend the border. Every day, the vines push deeper into my territory, and the fae grow increasingly bolder."

I would teach them the cost of taking the lives of my people.

A long silence stretched between us again, but after a moment, she turned to me. "I want to do something to help."

I opened my mouth, but she held up her hand to silence me. "I know that the answer is to heal you, and I'm going to try. But I want to do more for those like Selene, like the villagers of Frostfall. I can't just sit here when attacks like yesterday's are unfolding."

Hope sparked in my chest. Was she really coming around?

"That would be welcome," I said.

"No killing. I don't want to be a part of this war. I just want to do what I can to help the people hurt by it. While I'm here."

As we resumed our walk, the truth coalesced in my mind. Mel had been wrong. There was no point in trying to convince Samantha that I wasn't a monster. She could see the beast inside me, even if the others had gone blind to it over the years. My hands had too much blood, and the things I'd done to protect my realm kept me from sleeping at night. And after what I had done to Samantha, and to her city, I was unredeemable.

But she was compassionate, brave, and pure. If I could make her fall in love with my people...*that* was something she could believe in. A reason not to betray me.

A reason to stay.

Frostfall had been the start. But there were so many other

villages that were struggling. She would have to see them. Get to know them. Invest in their survival.

I stopped and faced her, searching for a reason to hope. "If you're willing, I'd like you to assist Melanthe. She's responsible for restoring the wards that keep the vines out. Maybe she could teach you to help with that."

I kept my voice casual, afraid that any show of enthusiasm would make her suspicious and shy away.

She nodded. "I'd like that."

"We often ride out to bring supplies to border villages and treat the wounded. If you wished, you could ride along with me."

Getting out of the castle was always an easy hook.

Her eyes brightened. "Yes, I'd like that as well."

A tiny flame of hope flickered in my soul, shedding light despite the deep shadows cast by the unforgivable things I had done. If she saw what the war was like, met more of my people and learned to love them, then she'd see that they were worth fighting for, even if the monster that protected their lands wasn't.

We finished our walk in silence, and I had the guards escort her to Mel's workshop. It was a relief knowing that she'd be occupied and not wandering around the citadel. I didn't want her to witness what I was preparing to do. What I *had* to do to protect my lands.

I had to become a beast – a mask that horrified even me. I wouldn't be able to stand the weight of the guilt if Samantha knew the horrors I was capable of. But I was bound by war, and if I didn't crush the fae, they would take everything.

I headed down to the aviary, where the hands were preparing the griffstriders. The soft clanging of metal echoed through the air as Kass and Wulfric donned their weapons.

I summoned my axe and slipped it into the loop on my belt.

Soon, my friend, we will have our vengeance. We'll set the balance right—for Frostfall. For so many other places.

Everyone's mood was grim after the latest news arrived. Another fae party had breached the border last night and pillaged a town at the opposite end of my territory. Women, children, and men—all of them butchered like animals.

I would show the fae how to butcher men.

43

———

Samantha

Mel was bustling around the workshop when I arrived. There were bags under her eyes, and she looked completely exhausted.

"Are you okay?" I asked.

"Overworked. There's been a lot of fighting lately, and not all the people in our lands are shifters, so they can't heal on their own. Some are fae, though we have nearly every type of Magica living here. I've been making healing poultices, balms, and potions nonstop."

"Cadean sent me to help. What can I do?"

She paused in grinding a bunch of black pods, let out a long breath, and put on a weary smile. "Thank fates, I need it." Then she narrowed her eyes. "That's the first time I've ever heard you use Cadean's real name."

Heat flushed my face.

She put down the pestle and dusted her hands on her apron. "Glad things are smoothing out between you two. He was very impressed with you last night."

I looked away, wishing that I could disappear in the shadows like *he* could.

Mel raised her eyebrows. "By which I mean he said that you fought against the fae at his side, and that you'd saved three werefoxes on your own with your magic. Very impressive."

"Oh. That." I sighed with relief. She hadn't meant *that*. The Dark God obviously hadn't filled her in on *all* the details.

A very tiny, very treacherous part of me was disappointed. I wouldn't entirely mind if he was impressed for other reasons.

She gave me a quizzical look. "Why are you so embarrassed? Was there something else I should know about?"

I shook my head. "Nope."

Unfortunately, she probably had a good guess by now.

With a wry smile ghosting her lips, Mel walked over to one of the shelves and began laying things out. "Thank you for everything you did. Not many prisoners would have done something like that."

"I wasn't going to sit around and watch people die. That's why I'm here. I want to help."

"Good. We have potions to make, and I need help preparing the components I use to renew the wards. They're failing faster than ever. I don't know how we'll catch up."

Did that mean more towns like Selene's would be in danger?

She began pulling jars off the shelves and telling me what they were for. There was far more information than I could remember, so I grabbed a leather-bound notebook and starting jotting everything down. How had she ever managed all the work on her own?

It was almost impossible for me to find anything. Jars of components, magic scrolls, and oddities covered every available surface. While the Dark God's chambers were the den of a predator, meticulously organized and sensory, Mel's quarters were more like those of a hoarder who'd raided a flea market.

I'd thought it was cute until she made me start organizing it all. "If you're going to be helping me, I need you to be able to find things without asking."

She set me to work sorting herbs, roots, animal bits, mushrooms, and oozes. One jar was simply labeled: *Spores. Don't agitate.* Another was extract from the purple flowers that had almost gotten me killed in the fae glade. It was labeled as *Dream Lilies: micro dosing only.*

Apparently, someone had sleeping problems.

My best find was a copy of *Lady Curia's Tales of Court Debauchery* tucked inside a tattered spellbook with a broken spine. I definitely liked Mel's style, and I pulled the steamy book out for later—if I ever got a break.

I didn't. Mel was a ruthless taskmaster and kept me going. I spent the whole time covertly looking for anything that could help me escape, but my head was swimming by the time we wrapped up. As soon as I got back to my room, I collapsed into bed with my clothes still on and passed out in seconds.

The second day was a little easier. She even left me alone for a bit while she ran out with a delivery of potions. That gave me an opportunity to snoop around—or it would have, except the moment she was gone, there was a loud pop.

My heart skipped a beat, and I twisted around. The little bald goblin was standing on a shelf stacked with dozens of tinctures and herbs. I couldn't quite tell if he was giving me a toothy grin or baring his teeth at me in warning.

I smiled back and rose. "You brought me the window key. Thank you!"

He shrugged and began climbing along the shelf. Clutching one of the brown bottles, he popped the cork off and sniffed the contents—hopefully not the dream lilies.

"You'd better not spill anything," I said, pointing a wooden spoon at him. "And no stealing from Melanthe."

He scowled at me and slunk to another shelf, where he started rifling through other things.

I'd kept my tone light, as I didn't want to scare him off. It seemed the gobbo could get anywhere in the castle, and that could make him a crucial ally.

I returned to grinding some dried black pods into powder while he rummaged about.

Suddenly, the lock on the door clicked, and it swung open.

A wave of magic washed over me—ripe wheat and a summer breeze. The goblin's eyes went wide, and he vanished with another pop.

Auren stepped into the room, and I froze. He wore dark trousers and a linen shirt that did little to conceal a physique that could have only been crafted by the gods themselves. And he had a radiance about him that shimmered off his sun-kissed skin. He was strikingly gorgeous, but he wasn't Cadean.

"Hello, Samantha," he purred.

Auren was trouble—that much I was certain of.

I backed away. "I don't think your brother wants you anywhere around me."

I recalled how Cadean had exploded out on the training ground and looked like he might actually murder Auren on the spot.

The god laughed. "My brother *is* a jealous brute, but thankfully, what he doesn't know can't hurt him. He's away, and we're quite alone."

Alone with a very powerful god I did not trust.

My shoulders tensed, and my hand went to my neck—but of course, there was no collar there. I was in the citadel.

Where was Mel? She wasn't supposed to be gone long, and it had already been half an hour.

Auren took a step forward, but I backed away. With a warm

smile, he gestured to my chair at the table. "You don't need to be afraid. I'm a friend."

"A random deity just walked into the room. I'm going to be a little nervous, thank you very much."

I didn't sit. It was obvious Auren was up to something, but perhaps I could stall and pry some information from him until Mel returned.

"Where's Cadean?" I asked. "He said he was riding along the border."

Auren leaned against the table. "Oh, off killing fae, I suspect. Pillaging and burning."

My gut twisted. Deep down, I'd suspected he might be taking vengeance for Frostfall, but I'd hoped it wasn't against fae villages. Was I just fooling myself?

As if reading my mind, pity shone in his eyes. "Cadean wasn't always a monster, you know. But over the millennia, he's retreated into darkness, and all that's left of him now is a hollow shell of a god, hellbent on seeking revenge."

Damn. Auren did not mince words. Did he really think of his own brother the way I did? A spark of hope flickered to life. Could he be the ally I needed, or was he just telling me what he thought I wanted to hear?

Cautiously, I sniffed the air, but I didn't catch the scent of deceit. But then again, who could trust their senses around a god?

"You look so upset, Samantha. I hope you aren't harboring any sympathy for the crafty bastards. The fae have been draining my brother's power for years—though I'm afraid the noose is tightening around his neck. If you want my advice, you might watch out for your own."

My pulse quickened, and I swallowed. "What do you mean?"

"Well, you've been healing Cadean, haven't you? That puts a

target on your back. They already sent an assassin after you once—I wouldn't be surprised if it happens again."

My skin felt suddenly cold. An assassin?

Before I entered the sacred glade, Cadean had warned me that the fae sent someone to kill me, but I hadn't believed it.

Auren tilted his head, scrutinizing my expression. "Cadean didn't tell you he caught that fellow who recruited you? What was his name?"

"Sarion," I whispered.

"Of course, that's right. Rumor has it, he was tasked with bringing you back or killing you. Why do you think that was? What's so special about you that they'd take the risk?"

"I don't know." I slumped into the chair, no longer able to conceal my despair. "Why don't you ask Sarion yourself, or take me there and I'll ask, because I'd like to know."

An apologetic expression cut his face. "Unfortunately, Cadean won't let me anywhere near him. He managed to pull some information from the fae, but he won't tell me what it was. If—"

Suddenly, Auren stiffened, and he glanced back at the door. "Well, Melanthe's coming. I should go." He looked to me, his eyes flashing. "I'll find you again. In the meantime, I'll see what I can do to help you."

"Help me?"

He gave me a warm smile. "I hate to see such a beautiful thing in distress. And Samantha—" He paused, looking down at me. "Tell no one I visited. Don't trust Melanthe and the others. No one here is as they seem."

Magic trickled over my skin, and I felt a sudden compulsion to obey. Of course I wouldn't betray his trust. He was the first person in the Dark God's palace who was actually willing to help.

With that, he faded into the golden light that filtered

through the skylight, and I shook my head to clear the sudden fog.

Moments later, Mel walked in. Wrinkling her nose, she scanned the room before setting her gaze on me. "Was somebody else in here?"

"Nope. Why?" My stomach churned at the lie, but I had the distinct feeling that I shouldn't tell her about Auren.

She scrutinized me for an agonizing moment before crossing the room to a shelf. Bottles clinked as she searched for something. Suddenly, she turned back, holding up a perfectly smooth stone. "What is this? How did it get up here?"

Oh, shit, the little packrat had swiped something and replaced it with a rock—hopefully not the dream lily extract or the spores. I didn't want him to get hurt.

I raised my eyebrows. "I have no idea. There's a lot of stuff around here."

She frowned, and I went back to work, my mind fraught with questions. Who could I trust? The fae might want to kill me. Auren was definitely up to something. Mel was devoted to the Dark God.

And Cadean?

A mad part of me wanted to trust him most of all. To believe that he was more than a beast. That he was a guardian and protector, capable of more than bringing destruction and death. But I couldn't.

Auren had confirmed the truth. The Dark God may have once been a noble creature, but now, he was no more than a destroyer and villain, bringing chaos into the world.

No, there was no one in the citadel I could trust except myself.

~

The Dark God returned on the third day.

I watched him arrive from a high balcony. He looked weary, battered, and blood-stained.

He looked like a despoiler.

When I went to heal him that night, I made sure Mel stayed with me, despite Cadean's protests. It was hard to focus on healing him, as thoughts of burning fae villages and Sarion flickered through my mind.

I tried to remember the god that had saved Selene's village, and who cared so desperately for his people. The god who could turn autumn into spring and who'd called me beautiful.

At last, I was able to draw on my magic, but this time, the effect wasn't quite so potent, and it only healed his wound a little.

I went to bed that night with deep doubts churning my mind.

44

Samantha

The next day, the Dark God summoned me for a ride.

I found him in the courtyard checking Vega's saddlebags. Elowyn stood beside him, giving me a suspicious look as I headed down the stairs.

"Ready to escape the citadel for a while?" he asked.

"Is it that obvious?" Mel had worn me to the bone, and Auren's words kept haunting me. It felt like the whole place was constricting around me, trapping me in a web of danger and lies.

The Dark God smiled, though it didn't reach his eyes, and strode over. "Our agreement still stands. As long as we're beyond the citadel, you wear the collar."

"I know." I tilted my head back, exposing my neck to him.

Hesitating for a second, he removed his glove and traced his fingers over my skin. The iron materialized, heavy and cold. Yet with the thought of fae assassins and even Auren in my head, it wasn't quite such an anathema as before.

When Cadean stepped back, I thought I caught a glint of guilt in his eyes. "It's for your protection."

Turning away quickly, he swung up onto Vega's back. I held

out my hand for him to help me up, but he tipped his chin toward Elowyn. "She's agreed to carry you after what you did at Frostfall."

My eyes widened in surprise, and I turned around as the griffstrider bent her head and clawed the hard-packed gravel.

"I thought that maybe Kassian or Melanthe..."

"She's all yours," he said as half a smile broke across his lips. Elowyn clacked her beak, and Cadean chuckled. "She says you impressed her. That you're a brave warrior like her."

"You can actually speak with them?"

"Of course. I'm the god of the wilderness."

The griffstrider ruffled her feathers, and my heart began beating a little stronger. That was no light praise. I cautiously stroked the feathers on the top of her head like I'd seen Cadean do. "I was impressed with you, too."

Elowyn shook her head, gave a screech, and started preening, as if to say, *Of course you were. I'm a fucking griffstrider.*

I smiled, put my foot in the stirrup, and hoisted myself into the saddle. For a second, I held my breath, bracing for Elowyn to start bucking and spinning, but she didn't attempt to heave me off. She just stood, patiently waiting for me to get settled.

I patted her side. "Thanks."

She screeched, and my ears screamed in protest.

The griffstriders took off, running side by side across the bridge leading from the citadel. I savored the roll of Elowyn's gait and the chance to ride beside Cadean...though a treacherous part of me had looked forward to being squished in the saddle with him. It was all too easy to imagine his strong arms wrapped around me. Although sex was off the table, we might not always have to ride separately.

After an hour, we left the path and climbed through forested hills dense with oaks. The fog rose, and we passed into a new patch, this one full of marsh, and our striders had to pick their way carefully.

Eventually, I mustered the courage to ask Cadean the question raging at the front of my thoughts: "Did the fae send Sarion for me?"

The muscles of his neck tightened. "What?"

"Did you capture the fae who brought me to the Dreamlands?"

He choked up on the reins. "How did you hear about that?'

Now the tricky bit, to lie without getting caught. "When I was attacked in Frostfall, one of the fae used a glamor to look like him. I learned that Sarion was trapped here."

Two true statements placed side by side to make a lie.

The Dark God's signature flared, and suddenly, I felt like the entire forest was on fire. A black rage washed over his face, and the muscles of his forearms tensed. "Yes, he was here."

Was.

Nausea churned my stomach. Given the vitriol in the Dark God's reaction, I was certain the end for Sarion had been grim. But I had to know. "Did you kill him?"

Cadean measured my expression for a long time, before answering. "Don't concern yourself with him."

"I want the truth. I know he was your enemy."

The Dark God looked ahead, and then back with a glare. "Sarion is fine, and he has all his ears and toes. I strapped him to a horse and sent him back across the border with a message for his queen."

"What kind of message?" I had to know.

"Don't send anyone else, or I will seize every noble within fifty miles of the border and take their wings."

I tensed, but beneath the horror, relief still found its way through. Cadean hadn't killed him. I scrutinized his expression, searching for a lie.

"I'm telling the truth," he growled. "Why do you have any sympathy for that bastard? He had orders to kill you."

I really hadn't known Sarion, nor had I fully trusted him, but Cadean's words still stung. "Why didn't you tell me about him?"

"Because you didn't need to know." He paused and looked away. "Because you'd already been through enough."

We rode on in silence as I tried to sort out my emotions. I was surprised and relieved the Dark God had let Sarion live. But it seemed like I'd lost another ally, or that maybe I'd been in danger from the start. If I was going to escape, I was truly on my own—no different than it had always been.

After a few hours, our destination became apparent: a brilliant pillar of light rising into the air.

Burdened by my thoughts, I'd fallen behind Cadean and Vega in the woods, so I hurried Elowyn forward to ride beside him again. "We're headed to one of the Moon's pylons?"

"Yes."

Did he expect me to do something? To try to release him?

The Dark God glanced over, his expression hard but not unkind. "You told Mel that your magic felt like the Moon's. I thought that bringing you here might help you awaken it. I promised to help, didn't I?"

My mouth opened, but I didn't know what to say. He was agreeing to help me learn my magic, even though doing so threatened him. Was he beginning to trust me?

Excitement fluttered in my chest, but I glanced up at the glowing beam with concern. "I know the Moon's magic hurts you. Are you sure about this?"

"My situation is growing more dire. The fae are worse than ever before. I need my strength, and last night, the healing didn't work as well. You must find the cure. Try harder. Push. I'm running out of time."

I swallowed the tight lump in my throat.

We emerged from the forested foothills into a windswept moor. The beam of light rose from inside a ruined castle perched on a rocky outcrop. I recognized it instantly. It was the first of the pylons I'd visited with Savannah and Jaxson. How long ago had that been now? *A month and a half at least...*

We left our griffstriders at the base of the outcrop.

"There's no gateway. I can fly you up," Cadean said.

"Don't worry about that." I extended my claws, leapt on the wall, and began hauling myself up, hand over hand. I was a good climber and had no fear of heights. It had been a while since I'd climbed, and it felt good to stretch my muscles.

Cadean followed, extending his massive claws, and scaling the stone. I hastened my speed and was up and over the wall before him, though I wondered if he'd let me win.

I dropped down into the courtyard. In the center, an enormous stone orb floated freely above the ground. A column of light rose from the top—one of three that supported the dome of the Dark God's prison.

The Moon's magic was soft and warm, cool and light all at the same time. If flowed through me like early morning sunlight on a summer's day. I basked in the radiance and felt as if I'd never be full enough.

A hushed word brushed over me like a feather: *Samantha.*

I tensed and turned around. The voice had been like a whisper on the wind, but I'd heard it before.

Cadean's features hardened. "What is it?"

I sucked in a breath. "I thought I heard something, but it was just the wind. Are you okay? Feeling a little out of shape?"

A sheen of sweat lined his brow, and every muscle in his body was taut. He grimaced. "It's not the climb."

He was clearly hiding his pain. I'd seen him endure the tearing claws of deathwings without so much as batting an eye, but something about the Moon's magic was eating away at him.

"Don't worry, I'm fine. Concentrate on your magic. Not on me."

I bit my lip and looked back up at the column of light. "So, what do I do?"

His heat warmed my back as he stepped close. Between his searing aura and the Moon's magic radiating off the gray stone orb, I felt crushed by power—yet in a way, it was comforting, like a heavy blanket pressing in, or the depths of the sea.

Electricity snapped down my arms as he gently laid his hands on my shoulders. "I don't know how your magic works. For now, just try to feel. Absorb her power into you. See if it leads you to yours."

I closed my eyes and let the Moon's luminescence wash over me, wave after wave. I tried to imagine drawing it in with every breath I took—

Free us.

My breath caught.

"What is it?" Cadean asked.

"Nothing," I whispered, though I didn't know why. "I thought I almost had it, but it slipped away."

"Think of the kits you saved. What it was like to draw your magic, to wield it."

I nodded and tried to concentrate on that memory, on the broodlings and the terrified foxes, but all I could think about were his hands on me, holding me gently, yet tightly. In that moment, his touch was everything. I found myself craving it, along with his company. The realization terrified me.

"I think I might need a little space. To focus," I said quickly.

He cleared his throat and stepped away. "I understand."

Pushing the inner turmoil from my mind, I focused again, this time on the Moon's magic—the power rushing around me and buffeting my body. Pure light and cool warmth. A taste of every season. Sounds of a still night.

I didn't try to draw it in, but imagined myself like a fern, unfurling to catch the light of morning.

A tingling sensation spread along my fingers, and then along my arm. A building warmth radiated through me.

"It's working," Cadean said, and I opened my eyes.

My hand had begun to glow, and I stared down at it in shock. "I'm holding her magic. What do I do?"

"Try to make a sphere around yourself like you did before."

My heart thrummed with excitement as the collar grew warm about my neck. *Free us, and we will free you.*

Those voices...I didn't know what they meant, but I knew that this magic could be my ticket out of the Dreamlands. I reached for Cadean. "Give me your arm. Let me try to heal you."

Concern flashed in his eyes.

"This will work," I pressed. "For whatever reason, I can feel it."

Hesitantly, he unwrapped the bandages around his forearm and extended his hand. "Careful."

I took his arm and gently touched the marred skin. I envisioned him healing and poured all my hopes into him. Getting back to my mother. Getting home to Magic Side. It was just like the way I healed him every night, except instead of the meager magic I'd been able to draw then, I was brimming with light.

The heat in my fingertips swelled, and I felt the magic begin to flow between us. Could I heal him for good? Even if it was just a start, it was hope.

My heart thrummed, but I trained my thoughts on what I wanted, on what healing him achieved: my freedom. I thought of Jaxson and Savannah, and all the people I missed. Of Eclipse, where I'd worked too many hours, and my old apartment. Of Dockside. But even as my heart lifted, a darkness settled in.

All my memories were tainted by *him*.

When I imagined my city, it was now the burned-out ruins of

buildings. When I envisioned people I knew, they were screaming and running from the werewolves who'd been haunted by the Dark God's magic. And when I thought of my best friend, Savannah, it was her claws sinking into my flesh as he forced her to attack me.

The scar on my shoulder burned with silent anger, and a jolt of rage swept through me, lighting my blood on fire. Suddenly, a torrent of energy ripped out of me like crackling lightning.

Cadean roared and staggered back, clutching his arm. "What did you do?" he snarled, feral anger blazing in his eyes.

Fear and regret gutted me. I looked down at his right arm in horror.

A glowing network of bright blue lines twisted along his skin like the roots of a banyan. The curse had spread father than I'd ever seen it, entwining all the way up his arm.

My throat tightened to the point of choking. "I didn't mean do that! I was trying to heal you—I just lost focus."

I stepped forward, but he retreated with a scowl. "Am I supposed to believe that?"

The suspicion in his eyes was a lance through my heart. I shouldn't care, but I did, and a deep ache settled in my chest. "I swear I wasn't trying to hurt you. My focus wavered, and—"

But I couldn't bring myself to tell him how much I hated him, or how I'd been imagining all the horrible things that he'd done. I'd promised to help him, and I didn't want to admit a part of me would rather have revenge.

He gritted his teeth and pulled off his shirt. "Is it still spreading?"

"It's...it's all over your shoulder and a little of your back. But it's not spreading anymore." Guilt twisted in my gut. "Does it hurt?"

He shook out his arm and pulled his shirt back on. "Yes, it

fucking hurts. My flesh is burning from the inside out. The veins of light are like claws, tearing though my nerves over and over."

I reached out to him. "Let me try again. Maybe I can heal it."

"No. We're done here. We will never attempt this again."

The anger and mistrust in his eyes squeezed my chest. "I'll use Mel's balm when we return to the citadel."

He fixed me with an uncompromising stare. "I should've never brought you here."

45

Cadean

The next morning, I rode with Kass, Wulfric, and Mel out to the border.

Dire reports had flooded in overnight: the barrier had moved, and in some places, we'd lost miles of land. The fae had been quick to take advantage, and there'd been attacks along the north. Border towns had been displaced, and a wave of new refugees was headed toward the citadel.

What a fucking nightmare.

We dismounted in a small hamlet of a dozen houses. Once occupied by happy families, they were all abandoned now. A body lay in the middle of the street, and I could smell the scent of more.

Grief and rage pummeled me, and I tightened my grip on the axe.

The magical barrier cut straight through the center of town, a shining wall of light. The irony struck deep. Designed to protect the world from me, the barrier prevented me from defending my people.

The radiance of the Moon's magic was always difficult to endure but being so close made my wound burn like someone was shoving hot needles under my skin. No longer confined to my arm, the wound burned my shoulder and back as well, and the pain was far worse than it had ever been.

"How far did it move?" I asked Wulfric, flexing my aching hand.

He swung off his griffstrider. "According to my reports, it was a mile and a half further north yesterday. But it varies from place to place. Some places, it's worse, while in others, it hasn't changed location at all."

I stalked to the barrier until the pain in my arm and shoulder became too much. "Is it still moving?"

"No," he said. "Lucky for us."

That was something, at least. I returned to my councilors, a low growl rising in my throat. "We need to get on top of this."

Mel nodded. "You need a cure. It's no coincidence the Moon's barrier collapsed hours after Samantha exacerbated it."

"I thought the curse was like the blight of vines," I said. "Why is it affecting the barrier?"

"Both the blight and the curse are draining your power." Melanthe held up her fists and butted them together. "You and the barrier push against each other continuously, and the strength of your magic is the only thing keeping it back. The weaker you grow, the closer it gets. And unfortunately, Samantha weakened you significantly."

Kass twisted his dagger against his fingertip. "I told you she was dangerous. This is why the fae wanted her. We should have offed her ages ago."

I spun and stopped my axe an inch from his chest. "Don't even consider it. Not for a second."

His eyes widened. "Sorry, Cade."

Shocked at the ferocity of my response, I lowered my axe. "Yes, she's dangerous, but she's also the solution. If she can heal me, this all gets fixed."

"It seems like it's getting worse," the brave idiot muttered.

My anger flared. I buried the axe in the side of a tree instead of Kass's head. "She's trying."

"Is she?" he asked. "Or is she intentionally holding back, keeping you weak on purpose? It's what I would do if I were in her shoes. Keep you weak, and when you didn't expect it, dump whatever power I had into spreading the curse."

I spun on him. "She's not you."

Wulfric put a hand on my shoulder. "Obviously she's not Kassian, or I would have killed her already myself. However, we need to keep an open mind that she may be doing this intentionally."

I looked between Mel and my two generals. Did they think I was insane? I wrenched my axe free of the tree. "She was so close yesterday. I felt my wound changing—it was just for a second, but it was there. If she can harness that power instead of her anger..."

"Well, we've given her plenty of reason for that," Mel said.

Kass crossed his arms. "The problem isn't what her intentions *were*, Cade, it's what her intentions are going to be now that she knows she can wield the Moon's power and hurt you. She'll be looking for any opportunity to fry the skin from your bones. You can't let her go near the pylons again—or even the moonshard."

I nodded. "I'll consider that."

I stalked away, and dark thoughts twisted through me. Deep down, I knew she wasn't sabotaging this. Despite how much she hated me, she'd been trying to heal me. I felt it in my soul.

Of course, I had no doubt that she'd betray me in a second or flee if she had a chance, but the healing was different. During those moments, we shared a connection that I'd had with no one else. I couldn't explain it.

The urge to see her grew until I could no longer ignore it. Giving in, I closed my eyes and searched the shadows that hung across my realm, shadow-casting back to my citadel.

I could feel thousands of beings all around me, but her spirit burned brighter than all the rest.

She was in Mel's workshop. The shadows there slowly became windows, and I peered through. Her bare feet were propped up on Mel's worktable beside a scale with powders and a small, bubbling pot. Where she sat, the room was concrete and bright, but the farther away something was, the more ephemeral it became, eventually dissolving into shadow.

She was consumed in a book, and I was consumed by her. My gaze traced up her smooth legs to where they disappeared under the pulled-up hem of her dress.

Sound was even clearer when she was my target. I could hear her elevated pulse and the soft quakes of her erratic breathing.

And I could smell her, too…impossible. All the times I'd shadow-casted, I'd never been able to smell before. The sweet scent of her arousal lit a fire in my blood—

Why the fuck was she aroused?

Samantha nibbled on her lower lip, then spoke. "Have you *read* this?"

My heart froze. Who was in the room with her? Mel, Kass, and Wulfric were with me. No one else had access, or was powerful enough to get in, except…

Auren.

My grip tightened on the axe. I'd warned the bastard to stay away from her.

I moved to another shadow, sliding between them like I was peering through the windows of a house.

Samantha looked over her shoulder toward the far corner. "Yes, but the part about the mating ritual?"

And then I saw her companion, and shock rolled through me.

Rune. The fucking goblin was rifling through Mel's tinctures. The same goblin that had made my life a living hell. He was supposed to be dead or banished to whichever of the hells he'd sprung from.

Deep, forgotten anger awoke within me, and I curled my fist. "Rune, you bastard."

Samantha damn near fell out of her seat, and her head snapped to me, face pale with shock. "Oh, my god. Cadean."

She could see me? It wasn't possible. I should've been invisible. I was always invisible. What the fuck was going on?

I stepped to another shadow, and her gaze followed. My heart hammered in my chest. Had she awoken some new aspect of my power? Could she hear me as well?

"Enjoying your book, Samantha?" I asked.

She jumped to her feet, pulling the hem of her dress down. "What are *you* doing here? I thought you were riding the border with Mel."

Fates. She could see *and* hear me. My mind whirred with possibility.

"I am. I'm shadow-casting to you," I said, beginning to circle the room. "More importantly, what the fuck is *Rune* doing here?"

"Who the hell is Rune?" Samantha asked.

The goblin's head snapped toward her, its beady eyes wide. Clearly, the little demon couldn't see or hear me, otherwise he'd be halfway across my kingdom already.

"Rune, the fucking goblin." I reached up to wring him by the neck, but my fingers passed right through him. It was a metaphor for the past fifteen years of dealing with the wily bastard. Mel had promised me she'd taken care of him, so we were going to have to have a frank discussion once I returned.

"What are you doing? Leave him alone!" Samantha shouted.

Fear cut across Rune's face, and he disappeared, vanishing like an extinguished flame.

I stalked the edge of the shadows like a tiger in its cage. "So, you can see and hear me, but Rune couldn't."

She was looking at me with a mix of confusion and terror. "Can you please explain what the hell is going on?"

"When I shadow-cast, I'm usually invisible. But with you, everything is different—vibrant and alive. I could almost touch you…" I closed the distance between us and reached up to brush that loose strand of hair from her face, but my hand passed through.

She sucked in a breath, like she had felt my presence. "This has happened before. When you warned me about the dream lily in the fae glade, I thought I saw you for a second. I may have seen you back in Deerhaven, watching me. It was just a glimpse —I didn't even realize what I'd seen."

She shivered and stepped back into the beam of light streaming from the high window.

I tried to pursue, but I couldn't move into the light—so that much hadn't changed. I paced around her. "Why are you so nervous?"

"Because I hate the idea of you being able watch me at any moment, almost as much as I hate you."

"Liar." I gave her a wry smile and glanced at the book she'd been reading. *Lady Curia's Tales of Court Debauchery.* "Afraid of what I might catch you doing?"

She growled and seized the book off the table, clutching it to her chest. "Leave!"

The room around her dissolved into shadow. The last thing I

saw was her almost glowing in the beam of light, and then I was back in the woods on the edge of the bifurcated village.

"Cade?" Mel's voice caught me off guard. She and Kass were watching me with concerned expressions. "You stalked off, then just went into a trance," she said.

I shook my head. "I was shadow-casting to Samantha—but it was more than just being able to watch her. We could see and speak with each other. It's never worked like that before." I rubbed my suddenly throbbing forehead. "When I use my power to shadow-cast, I can see through shadows. When I shadow-step, I teleport through shadows that I can see. This was different, like something in between the two powers." I looked to Mel. "What do you think?"

She drew in a long breath and released it slowly. "I'm not sure. But between her being able to wound you, and now this... I'll look into it."

"There's something else," I said. "Rune is back."

A slew of curses left her mouth, and her face grew red. "I fucking knew it! I sensed that little rodent creeping around. Someone had taken a jar of elderwort the other day and replaced it with a stone."

"I thought you exterminated him years ago," Kass said, jabbing his dagger into the side of a tree. "If he steals one more thing from me..."

"I will deal with him," Mel snarled.

The corner of my mouth twitched up. She hated that little goblin more than I did. She'd spent years trying to catch him and banish him from the tower.

Good luck.

Rune and the change in the way my shadow-casting worked would have to wait. The hangman's noose was drawing tighter. The barrier was collapsing in on me, the fae were taking advantage, and we had a wave of refugees heading in.

I had to deal with them first. Then the fae.

46

———

Samantha

The following day, the refugees from across the north began arriving at Shadowstone. At first, it was a trickle, then dozens at a time. The great hall was soon teeming with families and loners and the lost, all huddled together.

By late in the day, I was dead on my feet, and my calves ached. Mel had rousted me from bed around eight, and I hadn't stopped moving for ten hours.

As I rushed by her with an armful of old blankets, she caught my arm. "Are you sure you're doing okay? I know you were up late."

I put on a smile to hide the aches. "I'm fine, happy to help. This chaos is nothing compared to a werefox feast."

It's far worse.

I hustled down the stairs into the large courtyard outside of the kitchen with Mel close on my heels. The scent of chicken soup and fresh bread wafted from the large pots heating over the fires.

Dozens of families crowded the space—some shifters, some fae, and some that I couldn't place. During the first few waves, many of the refugees had been wounded. Thankfully, the most recent group was fleeing the rumors of violence instead of battle itself.

According to Mel, the barrier had shifted inland last night, leaving several villages beyond the reach of the Dark God. The fae had swept in, and even with the moonshard, he couldn't be everywhere at once.

At least the violence wasn't as bad as I'd first feared. Only a couple of towns were attacked, and most of the refugees were fleeing out of caution, to wait out the storm until things settled down.

We hurried past a cluster of two dozen fae, who were an exception. They wore fine clothes that were tattered and covered with blood. Cadean's healers were busy tending to the worst of the wounds.

"What happened to them?" I asked Mel.

"A fae raiding party. The town was celebrating a wedding when they attacked. Most didn't make it."

Bile burned my throat. "Why would the fae attack their own?"

"It's not about species. It's about fealty. These people sided with Cadean and emigrated to his side of the border. Queen Ayanna likes to make examples of them when she can."

How could the Undying Court do this to their own kind?

I followed Mel to lines of tables arranged along a wall. Each was stacked with items—blankets, clothes, shoes, toys—whatever people in the surrounding areas had donated.

Many of the fleeing shifters had taken off their own clothes and donated them, adopting their animal forms instead. The kindness between strangers broke my heart.

One queue of refugees moved past the supply tables, while others moved past the food.

"What will happen to all of them?" I asked as I helped Mel restock. "Will they stay here?"

"They'll rebuild, or even return to their homes once the conflict dies down. In the meantime, they'll be housed in a camp. Cadean is in the forest now, using his magic to weave shelters from limbs and roots."

"Even for the fae?" I knew the answer deep down, but I wanted to hear it.

"Of course. Cadean will always fight for those who make his lands their home."

How was I supposed to reconcile the monster with the protector? The god who threatened to destroy my city with the god who was shaping trees into shelters for battered people?

I had no answers. Only questions.

Once we'd dropped off supplies, I took Mel by the arm and pulled her aside. "Did I have anything to do with this?"

"What are you talking about?"

"Two days ago I made Cadean's wound worse, and I couldn't heal it that night. Then, the borders changed, and the fae attacked...I'm just worried that by hurting Cadean I somehow—"

"Hey." Mel took me by the shoulders. "Did you attack these people or burn their homes? No. None of this was on you."

Guilt weighed on me as I licked my parched lips. "But did I make it possible?"

"Years of war and hatred made it possible."

She was dodging the question, which meant yes, wounding him had led to all of this.

"Samantha. Don't give me that woeful look. This is the fault of the fae, and right now, you're doing everything you can to help these people. In a few weeks, this will all settle down, and they'll go back to their lives."

"How?"

"The borders didn't change that much—we inspected them yesterday morning. Everything I heard from Kass is that only a couple villages were attacked, and they were in disputed territories. As bad as this looks, most of these people are here because they're scared and don't know what's going on. The borders will settle, and it will all blow over. We just have to weather the storm."

One of the healers hustled over to Mel and handed her a list. "I think we're past the worst of it, but we're running short on supplies for casting on-the-spot treatments. Can you help?"

She looked it over, then handed it to me along with her ring, which served as the key to her workshop. "I don't know where anything is anymore. Can you run up and grab everything from this list that you can find? I'll see if my magic can help in the meantime."

"On it." I slid the ring onto my finger, tucked the list away, and then rushed up the stairs and through the great hall. It was packed with people as well, and the steady drone of voices vibrated through the walls.

I hurried up the stairs and down the corridor to Mel's workshop but spun when a footstep echoed on the floor behind me.

One of the refugees had followed me up. He looked battle-tired and wore a traveler's cloak. His hood shrouded most of his features except for the jagged outline of a scar.

My fingers twitched. "Are you lost? If you're looking for food and supplies, you'll need to head back to the great hall."

He shook his head. "I've come for you, young princess. I need to get you away from here."

His accent was fae. And while there were fae refugees down below, this man was no refugee.

I began backing away. "I think you've got the wrong girl. I'm not going anywhere with you."

"There's no mistake. I know who you are, Samantha." He

took a step toward me. "I'm here to offer you refuge on the other side of the border. Come quickly, while the Wolf God is away."

My heart thundered in my chest. I wasn't wearing the collar. I could be free.

But there was no reason for me to trust this asshole. Had Queen Ayanna sent him?

Moving backward toward the door of Mel's workshop, I extended my claws. "Don't come any closer."

He stepped out of the shadows, and I memorized his face— coffee eyes, a sharp nose, and the wicked scar that cut from his temple to his chin. "A price has been put on your head, dead or alive. My pockets will be fuller if you come quietly."

I turned and dashed toward the door.

Before I reached it, the fae gripped my throat and slammed me against the wall. His fingers tightened, constricting my airway.

I brought my arm down on his, and his hold released, but when I aimed for his nose with my elbow, he danced back, a wicked grin on his face.

My blood ran cold. His fluid movements and the way he carried himself indicated he was trained to kill. And now he was between me and the door.

"Which one will it be, princess? Dead or alive? I'm running short on time."

"Your time's already up." I lunged forward and delivered two quick blows.

He ducked back out of my reach, then leapt forward, moving like lightning. But this time, I was prepared for his unnatural speed. I spun out of his grasp, and my claws slashed through the back of his coat.

His hood fell back, revealing the psychotic delight that shone in his eyes. "Fighting me is futile."

A rush of wind hit me as his palm slammed into my chest.

Blinding pain squeezed my lungs, and then my back hit stone, and I crumpled to my hands and knees.

Before I could gather a breath, fingers grasped my hair and wrenched me to my feet. "You're a practiced fighter, but your movements are slow and sloppy. Enough."

I threw my head back, then slammed my forehead into his. The crack drove him backward, giving me the space to drive a kick in his gut, sending him stumbling to one knee.

Was head-butting sloppy? Hell, yeah. But I was a pit fighter. I wasn't going for style points—I was fighting to survive.

The bounty hunter quickly righted himself with a growl and lunged at me. I blocked his fist and went for his neck, but before my blow landed, he seized my wrist and twisted. Blinding agony radiated up my arm, and I screamed. I tried to break his hold, but he kicked out my feet, and my back thudded onto the stone pavement. "You're testing my patience."

"Fuck. You." My skull ached, and the lights in hall swam, but I put venom into each word.

The man's lips twisted into a snarl. In a fluid movement, he yanked a short, curved dagger from his belt and pressed it to my throat. Fear squeezed my chest, and I fought under his weight, but the cold blade was death at my neck. I thrashed my legs, fighting to break his hold, but he was just as strong as he was fast.

"Last chance to live, princess."

For a moment, I glared back at him, and then I went limp.

A smile crossed his face. "An excellent choice for both of us."

He eased back slightly on the knife. It gave me just enough breathing room to knee him in the junk. The blade lightly grazed my throat as I batted his arm away. I gripped his wrist and slammed his hand into the wall, and the dagger clattered free across the floor.

He dove for the knife, but I drove my foot into his knee.

There was a pop, and he screamed, staggering back into the wall. As I leapt to my feet, he lunged for the knife, but I kicked it down the hallway.

Turns out that after years of being pinned by werewolves, I'd gotten pretty good at fighting from my back. Who would have thought?

The moment of satisfaction faded instantly, as he yanked another blade from beneath his cloak and launched himself forward.

Shit.

He was too fast to dodge, so I stepped inside his reach. The blade grazed my side, but I was able to rake my claws across his face, then slam his arm into the wall. The blade clattered from his hand as blood poured into his eyes.

I ripped into his face again, and he stumbled backward, temporarily blinded. I wasn't just sloppy. I fought dirty.

"The best thing about claws is they're always attached." I touched my neck where his dagger had been, and my hand came away coated in blood.

The world wobbled, but I took up a fighting stance and put it out of my mind. If the cut had been serious, I'd be dead already.

Teeth gritted, he wiped the blood from his face and snarled. "You'll fucking regret this choice."

Then he spun and dashed down the hall away from me at inhuman speed. As he ran, the daggers whipped through the air and back to his hands.

I chased after but skidded to a halt as a wave of magic exploded from behind me—burning fires and the rumble of an earthquake. *Cadean.*

The floor ahead of the bounty hunter buckled and churned as roots ripped their way through. He stopped short and dodged backward as the roots lashed out like the tentacles from some alien creature. With nowhere to run, he turned and charged toward me.

I raised my fists, but the Dark God stepped past, black smoke streaming from his axe. His rage washed over me in his wake, almost powerful enough to bring me to my knees.

He swung for the charging bounty hunter. The fae dodged, and faster than my eyes could track his movements, he rammed both blades into the Dark God's chest.

My heart stilled as terror rushed through me.

"Cadean!" I rushed forward, but the Dark God didn't even flinch. He seized the fae by his cloak and slammed him into the wall on the right, then whipped him across the corridor to the other side.

My jaw dropped. The stone walls had cracked each place he hit.

The fae, somehow still standing, staggered back. Roots wrapped around him, and then, with a roar of anger, the Dark God swung his axe around and buried the blade deep in the wall.

The fae's headless body slumped into the shadows boiling around Dark God's feet. Where the head rolled, I did not see.

I dropped to my knees in horror and relief.

Cadean turned around and strode to my side. He gave a low growl, and his signature flared, causing a cascade of shivers through me. "You're hurt."

"It's just a scratch," I said. "For a werewolf, at least. You took two blades to the chest."

My stomach lurched as my eyes drifted to the bloody gashes in his chest.

"I'm a god. The poison will wear off soon."

Poison? Shit.

I could feel the cuts on my neck and side healing already, but

Cadean inspected every part of me. His jaw tensed, making the sharp angles of his features even more pronounced. He was strikingly beautiful, like hurt-your-heart kind of beautiful. And those full lips that had devoured me the other night...

I shook my head. I'd nearly been abducted, and I was thinking about sex right after I'd just seen him behead a man? I was either concussed or had lost more blood than I'd thought.

Footsteps came racing down the hall. Mel. "What the hell happened?" She was huffing like she'd just run a marathon.

I pushed against Cadean's arms, but they tightened around me, holding me captive as a combustible mix of rage and protectiveness flashed in his eyes. His signature wrapped around me, and slowly, the shaking stopped.

"I'm fine, Cadean. You can let go now." I twisted in his lap, and he finally relented.

I stared at the headless body down the hall. The man had tried to abduct me, then kill me, but still, revulsion twisted my gut. The walls were sprayed with blood, and it still seeped from the open wound where his head had been.

I collapsed to my knees and vomited. Mel crouched beside me and held back my hair. "Who was that?"

"He was a fae assassin. Now he's a corpse." Cadean's voice was tinged with malice.

"Why did you do that?" I choked out. "I'd bested him. He was fleeing. You could've just captured him."

"I warned them what would happen if they attacked you again. A quick death was more than the bastard deserved. A mercy."

I rubbed my wrist across my mouth and rose. "You didn't have to do it like that."

"I'll destroy anyone who tries to harm you. And if I'd let him live, he would have returned."

Shaking, I turned away, but he caught my arm. I looked back at him, both thankful and angry.

Cadean let out a slow breath. "I'm sorry, Samantha. I saw you were in danger, and anger took over."

Ruthless beast and bold protector twisted into one, Cadean was too confusing to face. I shook my head. "It doesn't matter. It's done."

But I knew that both statements were lies.

Cadean gestured to Mel's door. "There may be more assassins lurking among the refugees. If you're not with me, I don't want you anywhere but Melanthe's workshop or your chambers. They're both warded with spells that will keep the fae out."

The freedoms I'd earned drained through my fingers like grains of dust, and bitterness stabbed into my heart. "Are you serious? You might as well throw me back in the cave."

His expression turned as hard and hammered as iron, though anguish vibrated beneath his firm voice. "I'm sorry, little wolf, but I can't risk anyone hurting you or taking you away from me."

Rage coiled within me, and I balled my fists. "I can protect myself. He was fleeing."

"It was too close," Cadean growled with shocking ferocity. "What if there are two attackers next time? Why didn't you use your magic?"

"I...I couldn't call it."

"Master it. I'll help you, but until then, you're in your chambers, in the workshop, or with me. No exceptions." He turned to Mel. "Make sure she has everything she needs. I will scour the citadel for any more intruders lurking in the shadows."

Mel gently pulled me into the workshop, but I glanced back over my shoulder. Cadean marched toward the body of the cloaked man, wisps of shadows coiling in his wake. He stopped to wrench his battle axe from the blood-covered wall, kicked the corpse aside, and continued on. With his axe at his side and his hair braided and knotted, he looked like a Viking god out of legend.

Or maybe like the god of death himself.

47

Cadean

I stalked Shadowstone for two days after the attack on Samantha, inspecting everyone and every crevice. I swept from the parapets to the dungeons and interrogated each of the fae that had taken refuge in the great hall.

In the end, I found nothing. But more killers would come, of that, I had no doubt. I would never let my vigilance down again.

Unfortunately, I'd killed the assassin too quickly in my rage and never had a chance to question him. I'd mounted him on a spike on the citadel wall as a warning, and I regretted that I hadn't done it while he was still alive.

Samantha chaffed at her confinement, so I had her train with Wulfric to blow off some steam.

Although the initial wave of attacks stopped, the lingering refugees were a constant reminder of what had happened. Anger and a thirst for vengeance churned within me, and while I wanted to sweep over the border and bring hellfire down on the fae, I needed to take care of my people first.

I ran my hand down Vega's feathers. The soft clanging of metal echoed through the aviary as Kass and Wulfric donned their weapons. I was consumed with visions of revenge, but the arrival of Samantha's honey and lavender scent pulled me from my bloody thoughts.

For as much as she infuriated me, she also calmed my soul.

I turned to her as she stepped into the aviary. She was dressed for a hunt in her riding boots and the fur coat I'd sent to her when the weather turned a few days ago. The cold had flushed her cheeks, and she was absolutely stunning.

A violent protectiveness for her surged within. There was no way I could take her with me.

I doublechecked Vega's tack as the griffstrider stamped. "What are you doing here? You should be with Melanthe."

"I heard you were riding out. I wanted to join. You said that I was confined to my quarters, the workshop, or your side—so here I am, at your side."

I sheathed a short dagger at my thigh. "You won't be joining us. It's too close to the border. You're already in enough danger as it is."

She strode across the space. "Is it a raid?"

"No. We're escorting a batch of refugees back to their village, along with supplies."

"When we were in the garden, you promised to take me with you the next that time you rode out to the border villages. I want to help. I can handle myself—you've seen it."

She was a strong fighter, but there were fae scouts in the area.

Frustration heated my blood as I mounted on Vega's back. "This is not a negotiation."

Samantha opened her mouth to protest, but Auren ducked into the aviary, wearing an embroidered gold tunic and trousers. "Don't worry, brother, I can keep an eye on her here. I saw she was training with Wulfric. It might be good if we got rid of any bad habits that she might have picked up from him. Or fleas."

"I don't need looking after," Samantha said, her voice sharp.

My blood heated, and I tightened my grip on the reins.

The last thing I was going to do was leave her alone, unsupervised with him. He always had an ulterior motive, and by the way the lecher looked at her, it wasn't hard to figure out what it was.

I urged Vega forward. "I don't want to burden my dear brother who's doing his best to help protect my realm. You'll come with us, Samantha."

Kass sighed and shook his head while Wulfric cast me a disapproving look. I passed it off and reached down to take her hand.

Samantha glanced at Elowyn. "Don't I get to ride her?"

"We're short fresh griffstriders. Wulfric is riding Elowyn today." I kept my hand extended. "Are you coming or not?"

She paused briefly but took my arm, and I pulled her up in front of me.

Vega lurched forward, clawing up the dirt beside Auren, and we tore out of the aviary, Wulfric and Kass on my heels.

About ten minutes out, we caught up with the train of supplies and refugees heading north—people returning to their homes, and hopefully, a little stability now that the barrier had solidified its position and the fae attacks had slowed. The refugees were stretched out in a long, haphazard line. Spirits were high, but the going was slow. We rode on the flanks as outriders, along with several packs of wolves.

Samantha's back was stiff as she leaned forward in the saddle, every muscle strained to keep from touching me. I slid my hand around her middle and pulled her to my chest. "I think we're beyond such reservations, little wolf."

"I hate being so close to you." Her tone was biting, but her pulse fluttered.

"Liar." I smiled, and with one quick tug, her bottom slid back against me. "I admit I rather missed this when you took Elowyn out."

She cursed but eventually eased back into me, and before long, our bodies moved in sync with Vega's strides. I caught myself leaning down and breathing in her floral scent. She was intoxicating, and that in and of itself should have been a warning, but for some reason, I couldn't help myself around this woman.

She was a drug, and the most addictive kind. The memory of our rapture haunted my nights, just as much as she haunted my days.

But I kept my desire locked down. I would not give in to the beast.

Once we'd left the forest and exited into the moors, Kass and Wulfric drew forward and flanked us.

"The wards aren't working," Wulfric said. "There are new vines in the forest. It's only been a couple days since Melanthe cast them. They should have lasted weeks."

Kassian shifted closer. "It's the same along the west. Reports from the mountains indicate the blight is spreading at an unprecedented rate."

Was it because Samantha had aggravated my wound, or something more? This wasn't the first time the blight had advanced so quickly. It spread like a sickness, sometimes lagging and other times surging for reasons still not understood.

I flexed my right hand, scowling at the constant pain burning beneath my skin. My own personal blight.

Samantha had tried to use the balm several times to undo the damage she'd done, but as delightful as her touch was, it only took away the worst of the pain. The tendrils of blue light still wound around my shoulder, searing my flesh from the inside. It was almost impossible to think with the constant buzz of pain in the back of my mind, and it was beginning to affect my judgement.

"Why don't you build a wall around your realm to keep the vines out?" Samantha asked over the howl of the wind.

"The Undying Court carved their kingdom from my lands. Although I'm trapped within this prison, my people aren't. They live and hunt on both sides of the border, as they have for millennia. If I built a wall to keep the blight out, families would be separated, and it would impede the migration of the animals they need to survive."

"Yet some fae defected to your side of the barrier?" she asked.

I leaned down, breathing in the sweet fragrance of her hair. "Not all fae are monsters. Some, I'm rather fond of."

She gave me a quizzical look, and her breath trembled as she inhaled sharply. Did she suspect?

Guilt tore at me. I desperately wanted to tell her, but I'd feared she'd run to them. Now that they'd sent assassins and she'd seen the horrors that Ayanna's warriors were capable of, it might be the time.

Still, it was a risk. She was a loose cannon.

Wulfric came up alongside us and threw me a warning glance. I was playing with fire.

Yet I'd have to tell her soon, or the truth would eat me from the inside out.

I sat back in the saddle. "The Undying Court are the worst of their kind. They take but they're never satisfied."

We rode in silence for a while when Samantha whispered, "I'm sorry."

I wasn't sure if she'd intended to speak those words, but guilt twisted into my gut like a blade. She was a prisoner with no stake in this war, yet she grieved for my people.

The Moon's fucking wall of light rose slowly in the distance, and I could see the fae-occupied land just beyond. The realm had been peaceful once, before they came. Although centuries had passed, at times, it felt like only yesterday that I'd walked freely in the forests beyond the barrier.

So much had changed. *I* had changed.

As soon as we neared the village, I heard cries of joy from the refugees, but my heart only tightened with fury. Many houses had been burned, and rubble and scattered belongings littered the streets.

"Will it take them long to rebuild?" Samantha asked softly.

"Maybe. But my people have become resilient over the years. Shifters will come from the south to help."

The caravan became a disorganized mess as people began running to check on their homes, while the supply carts tried to find room to pull off.

"Let me help distribute supplies," Samantha said.

She had so much compassion. These weren't her people, and yet she was driven by an almost desperate need to help. I smiled at her with admiration, tinged by sadness, and I let her down off Vega.

I hated that I had to keep her trapped here.

I circled through the ruins as my fury rose. At the far end of town, a pack of my scouts caught up with me. They burst from the cover of the shrubs, and one of the wolves shifted on the spot. "We spotted a patrol of fae riders and deathwings two miles east and followed them back to one of the border villages. It looks like they're planning to stay."

I wheeled Vega around to face him. "They're occupying one of the villages?"

"Making preparations to fortify, by the looks of things. They're planting vines and turning it into a base of operations. It's probably why they took out this town in the first place."

The bastards were relentless.

"How far on the other side of the barrier?"

"Maybe a mile—it would have been closer a few days ago, but the border shifted," the wolf said.

The fucking wound. That village had probably been on my side of the border a month ago. If I let the fae dig in, they'd harass this one now that the border was so close.

I had to take it out.

I spun my strider around and headed back to the caravan. "Wulfric, grab Samantha. Take her back to the Shadowstone immediately. Order your guards to protect the people and supplies. Kass, you're with me and the scouts."

Bringing Vega around, I circled Samantha. "Stay with Wulfric. Go back to the citadel."

She narrowed her eyes. "I'll stay here and help. If the fae come this way, I can help protect these people."

"But I won't be here to protect you. Go. It's not a negotiation."

If the fae were going to use the village as a base of operations, I couldn't let it stand. I didn't want her to witness what I was going to have to do, or the brutality of which I was capable.

Her heart was too good for that and it would only confirm what she knew already: that I was a monster.

I turned to the scout. "Take us there."

I kicked Vega in motion and charged for the border after the werewolves, with Kass on my heels.

We raced past the rubble of newly burned houses. Even after the heavy mist, some were still smoldering. The city smelled of death and despair.

My vision filled with faces of refugees spilling into my citadel, all scared, shocked, and wounded. How would my people ever rebuild with a fae outpost looming a few miles away?

I thought of Frostfall and the people there who still lived in fear. I thought of the assassin who'd come for Samantha.

Anger and the need for vengeance warred inside of me, consuming my thoughts.

The world turned red as shadows coalesced around me. I stole them from every patch of shade we passed until they clung to my shoulders like a massive, tattered cloak whipping in the wind. I would have vengeance for my people. I would become death, and I would restore the balance.

I pulled on the enchanted gauntlet Mel had made me. "Give me the shard."

Kass extracted it from his side pouch and handed it to me.

I grimaced as soon as I touched it. Despite the gauntlet, the magic made my wound burn worse than ever. Still, the pain was worth it. The moonshard was the only thing that gave me the power to strike back. To punish.

"Do you have a plan?" Kass asked.

"Same as always. Kill the soldiers. Drive the people into the hills. Reduce the town to ash. Make sure they have nothing to come back to and no reason to set up an outpost there again."

"Do you think you can push the barrier that far? It might be out of your reach."

I gritted my teeth. "I'll make it."

We were at the barrier in a matter of minutes, the werewolf scouts racing ahead. As we galloped into the shimmering wall, I held the moonshard aloft, pushing my magic into it. Like a prism splitting the sun, a rainbow of light poured forward, pushing the barrier ahead of us as a rolling wave.

The first hundred yards were easy, but by the third, my skin was screaming as a violent storm of shadow and light raged around me. Even if the Moon's magic burned the flesh from my bones, I would have vengeance for my people. I'd ensure their safety, no matter the cost to my soul.

I thanked the fates Samantha wouldn't be able to see what happened next.

Turning to Kass, I growled low. "Ride ahead and warn them I'm coming. Tell them to run. I don't want villagers there when I bring down the town."

"I don't think they're going to need a warning Cade," he said, looking up.

I followed his gaze. The sky above had darkened, and the shadows stretched out behind me like a black storm raging over the land.

Within seconds, the town came into sight. Overturned carts and open doors testified to the fact that the fae had fled before me.

But not all. Silver-clad warriors raised their bows as death-wings swirled in the air above them. A hail of poisoned arrows flew into the sky and fell on us, tearing into my skin.

I ordered Kass and the wolves to stay as I bore down on the archers. This battle was mine. Summoning my axe to my hand, I closed my eyes, letting whatever goodness that still clung to me fall away. Maybe if I was lucky, I'd find those pieces again when the balance was restored and the killing was done.

48

Samantha

Anger resonated through my bones.

Since the assassin's attack, Cadean had kept me locked in my room or the workshop, watching me constantly. And now, at the first sign of trouble, he was sending me back to my prison.

If this was all the use I was going to be, I should have stayed at Shadowstone with Auren from the start. At least that might have given me a chance to prod him for more information and see if he was willing to help me escape.

"We need to get going," Wulfric said, irritation thick in his voice.

I unloaded a box of rations, mostly wheels of cheese. "Let me stay here and get some of these people situated. If the fae show up, I promise to jump on the strider, and we can hightail it out of here."

"We go now."

I ignored him and swung around to the other side of the wagon. "I can't believe that he'd leave his most trusted general as my babysitter when all the wolves are out scouting. Seems like a waste of your talents."

"Cadean is a god. He's capable of far more violence in a moment than I could do in a year of campaigning. The best way for me to protect him is to keep you in check. That includes getting you to safety."

"Is that what you're worried about?"

He glared at me, wearing his resentment like a knife at his side. "I'm worried you're corrupting him. Making him weak, just like you did to his arm. The others may not see it, but I do. You're the curse."

My jaw tightened, and my cheeks burned like he'd slapped me across the face. It was too close to the truth. I knew that wounding Cadean had destabilized the barriers and caused part of this, but I wasn't the curse, was I?

A deep ache formed in my chest.

I turned and looked back in the direction Cadean had gone. A storm of shadows writhed above the trees, and the barrier was racing outward like the curl of a tsunami.

Every muscle in my body tensed. "He's going over the border. Why?"

Wulfric grabbed my wrist. "The fae have occupied a town within striking distance of this one. He's gone to level it and drive out the settlers. We need to go."

I resisted his grip. "Settlers? Like families?"

Wulfric's gaze homed in on me, his expression unreadable. "You sure you want me to answer that?"

My skin grew cold. "I always want the truth."

He smiled faintly and looked back across the border, the indifferent and frosty demeanor he usually showed me slowing peeling away. "He's trying to keep these people safe. Look what the fae did to this village. Think of it as a reprisal, a way to maintain the balance."

I released an angry laugh and pulled my hand free. "Balance.

Spoken like a true sycophant. I'm the one wearing the collar, but you're the one that follows him like a trained dog."

"How do you have any sympathy for them? They sent bounty hunters after you." Wulfric's signature flared with his outrage, and I ground my teeth as the sound of crushing stone and the scent of amber and peat overwhelmed my senses.

I backed away from him. "The Undying Court did. Queen Ayanna did. Not the people in that village. Condemning them simply because of who their masters are is fucking savagery."

"Who do you think feeds the soldiers and tends the vines?" He prowled after me, his expression lethal. "Who do you think raises the deathwings?"

"Innocent people with wicked lords."

A trail of smoke drifted above the trees in the distance. Then two more appeared, and another. Moments later, muted screams carried on the breeze. Nausea churned in my stomach. I couldn't just stand by while this happened.

I have to stop him.

"Enough of this. We're going," Wulfric growled.

No fucking way.

I needed to disable him, but he was wider and several feet taller than me. I was tough, but he was built like a brickhouse and an elite warrior. He'd kicked my ass over and over in training.

"I know what you're thinking, little wolf. Don't do it. I will hunt you down faster than you can realize what a mistake it was."

My wolf surged in my chest at the challenge, while a rising rage simmered under my skin.

He lunged and seized my arm. I jerked, but his claws raked over my skin, and I shouted in pain. Before he could get another hand on me, I pulled my dagger and rammed the butt into the side of his head.

His grip weakened as he grunted and staggered to the side.

Wolfman can't catch me if he had a concussion. Probably.

Pandemonium suddenly broke out around us, and I tore free. I ducked into the crowd of refugees, but Wulfric shoved his way through. I heaved a stack of crates over on top of him, and then I darted toward Elowyn.

"Take me to the Wolf God," I shouted as I hooked my boot in the stirrup and swung up on her back. "I have to stop this."

With a screech, she charged forward and leapt over the scraggly bushes that dotted the open landscape separating Cadean's kingdom from the fae. The closer I got to the iridescent magic barrier, the more easily distinguishable the cries and screams became.

I didn't have a plan—just a desperate need to do *something*. Even if that was just to see the truth with my own eyes, no matter how difficult it was.

We galloped through the barrier, and the cold thrum of the Moon's magic tickled my skin. I glanced over my shoulder, noticing the dark figure of Wulfric barreling out of the ruined town toward me. Fuck.

I spurred Elowyn, and we picked up speed, slipping into the forest. Into fae territory.

I could hear Wulfric crashing through the trees behind us. He'd be more maneuverable and might be able to overtake us in the dense woods. I had to throw him off.

I leaned down low over Elowyn's neck. "Keep going for a mile, then head back to where we started."

She screeched, and then I stood and seized a low branch flying by overhead.

My arms screamed with the impact, but I dug my claws in and used my momentum to flip me up on top of it. I scrambled to the other side of the tree and waited.

Wulfric came crashing through moments later. He stopped for a second but didn't look up.

I held my breath, praying he couldn't hear my heartbeat and was following Elowyn's scent instead of mine.

He darted forward and was gone.

After counting to thirty, I dropped to the ground. Shrugging the fur coat off my aching shoulders, I slipped out of my clothes and stashed them under a bush.

The cool wind chilled my bare skin. My wolf stirred, and I let the shift take hold. My bones and tendons snapped and stretched, and a moment later, I shook out my fur and dashed into the forest.

The focus of my wolf eased my nerves.

I was much faster on four legs than two. My senses were also sharper than in human form, and I followed the scent of smoke and the occasional wails that cut through the dense vegetation.

I squeezed through a large thicket, hoping Wulfric would be slowed if he turned around and picked up my scent. It paid to be small and nimble. Brambles and thorns tugged against my fur, but before long, I was out.

I silently padded forward until the trees thinned and the outlines of wooden thatched structures appeared. I took shelter beside a thick juniper bush, hoping the aromatic branches would obscure my scent.

My heart pounded as I absorbed the devastation before me.

Whatever the fae had done to the Dark God's village, this paled in comparison.

The houses were not burned-out husks, but piles of rubble and dust. It was like a tornado had ripped through the village. The lifeless bodies of two men lay in the churned dirt thirty feet away. Not deathwings or broodlings, but fae soldiers in shining armor. I stared at the blood that soaked the earth around them, a numbness settling over me. But other than the soldiers, the place was a ghost town. No cries of terror. No piles of corpses or screaming people. No warriors or armies.

Only ruins.

And *him*.

49

———

Samantha

My throat clenched as the Dark God stepped out of the billowing smoke at the far end of the village. His brown hair was pulled back and knotted, and a sheen of sweat coated his neck and forearms. He held the glowing moonshard like a beacon, though its light seemed weak in the shadow of his presence. He swept his axe in an arc through the air, and in its wake, a wave of destruction ripped through the last remaining houses, leveling them.

Horror rolled through me, followed by a deep dread that felt like it was seeping into my heart.

He was the tornado—a compassionless force of nature unleashed on the living world.

When he turned and met my gaze, the only thing I saw was the iron face of a heartless killer. Nausea rooted in my stomach. I didn't recognize him anymore. He was far worse than anything I had ever imagined.

As the Dark God strode toward me, roots and green vines rose from the earth behind him, covering the desolation. Soon, it would be like there had never been a village here at all.

He wasn't just death. He was annihilation.

Had Sarion been right all along? Or maybe there was no one with a soul in the godsforsaken Dreamlands.

I turned to run, but strong hands seized the scruff of my neck from behind. I fought, slashing back with my jaws, but Wulfric's hands were like steel.

"I told you to watch her," the Dark God growled, his eyes never leaving me as he slipped his axe into its loop.

I clawed and snapped my jaws, but Wulfric only tightened his grip and pushed my head down in submission. "Yeah, well, she nearly cracked my skull open."

"I've got her," the Dark God said. "Find Elowyn and her damn clothes. Now."

Wulfric shoved me forward.

Hatred blossomed in my chest, and I couldn't bear it. I lunged forward and ripped into Cadean's chest with my claws.

He growled and staggered back, giving me the space to dart past him. I ran as fast as I could, oblivious to the thorns and branches that tore at me. I knew I couldn't outrun the Dark God, but the terror was in control. I stifled a mournful howl and pushed on.

The trees and brush ahead of me uprooted and moved to block my path. The ground churned beneath my feet, and I tumbled and slid across the dirt.

"Stop running, little wolf."

The Dark God's signature flowed over me, thunderous and cold. I ground my teeth against the press of it, but then my body contorted as I was caught in the throes of a shift. It was futile to fight it, and seconds later, I was on my hands and knees in the dirt, naked and human. I sat up and covered my chest with my arms, my skin pebbling from the chill in the air.

The Dark God prowled forward and growled. "What am I to do with you, Samantha?"

I looked up at him, my heart skipping a beat. Sunshine filtered through the trees, casting him in light and shadow. A monster who could take my breath away with a single look.

"Let me go, you bastard," I said.

"I'm afraid I can't do that."

I knew it was pointless. The beast was never going to let me go willingly. He had to have been lying the whole time. He'd twisted my thoughts and made me think that there was something redeemable in his dark heart, a sliver of kindness. That maybe he even felt something for me.

It was all illusion.

I leapt to my feet as he advanced with the moonshard glowing in his hand. I could feel the tingle of its magic calling to me. Pulsing within me.

I thrust my hands out, and light arced from my palms. For a second, a brilliant shield of light flickered around me, forming a barrier between us.

But almost as quickly as it had formed, it faded.

The Dark God pulled the fur cloak from his shoulders and held it out. "You can summon your shield for *me*, but not for an assassin?" His tone was laced with violence and anger.

"You're worse."

He paused. His jaw tensed, but his gaze never left my face. "I would never hurt you, little wolf," he said, sounding almost pained.

"Look at the wreckage around you. Look at what you did to Magic Side. You already have."

He stared back at the ruins, shrouded in shadow and billowing ash. The ruined dreams and the bodies of fae warriors. For a second, remorse flickered in his eyes, but it was quickly consumed by anger.

He thrust his cloak toward me. "You're shaking. Despise me all you want, but take this."

I wanted to throw it on the ground, but the wind was ice. I seized the cloak from his hand and draped it over my shoulders, momentarily delighting in its warmth. It smelled of smoke and fire, and also of him—a deeply earthy musk that stoked something primal and brutal inside me.

"I hate you," I snarled.

He dipped his head, and his nostrils flared as he inhaled. When he looked back at me, his pupils were dilated, and his lips pulled up in a faint smile. "Liar."

Tears burned my eyes, but I refused to let them fall in front of him. "How do you live with yourself?"

Something dark flashed behind those brilliant pale eyes. "We're leaving." He whistled for Vega, and the griffstrider cantered out of the woods.

Frustration and anger and helplessness boiled up inside of me, tearing me apart. My eyes dropped to the short dagger strapped to his thigh, and I tensed.

In a fluid movement, I wrenched the dagger from its scabbard and whipped my arm forward. Moving faster than I'd ever imagined possible, Cadean spun around and caught the blade in midair with his bare hand.

Fuck.

Blood dripped from his palm down his arm, matching the dried gashes I'd left on his chest. "What do you think your little blade would do to me, Samantha?"

My pulse quickened, my breaths shallow, but I managed to speak. "Some of the people in this village could have been *innocent.*"

He flung the blade to the ground. "No one is innocent in war, little wolf. Once, this was my land. The fae drove my people off and settled it."

I backed away. "And now, there's nothing left but ash and bones."

"I've shown more mercy than the fae ever have. I slayed the soldiers, but I let the people who tried to settle here flee. Those who chose to stay made their choice."

He may have spared some of them, but did it matter in the end? He was a warlord propagating strife. The fae would just retaliate and strike back.

The cold wind whipped around us, but we stood glaring at each other amid the wasteland.

I threw my hands wide. "This is where the fae soldiers come from, Cadean. Where deathwings come from. You create them by doing this. Those who fled today will never forget this, and when their children grow up, the only thing they will have left from here is hate."

His gaze fell to the wreckage around us, and for a long time, he was silent. "I know."

His voice thrummed with guilt and anger and rage, and for a second, I saw a hint of the man trapped behind the monster.

It wasn't enough.

Eventually, Wulfric returned, riding Elowyn. As soon as he did, I tossed the Dark God's cloak on the ground and put my clothes back on.

Cadean mounted on Vega's back and held out his free hand.

I glared up at him. "I'm not riding with you."

"You are."

Suddenly, that old battle felt pointless. I was tired and frozen, and going back to the citadel one way or another.

Too hollow to fight, I let him pull me into the saddle. Shivers racked my body, and I didn't even protest when he tugged me closer and wrapped his arm around my waist. I hated him, but I wasn't going to freeze to death out of principle.

His breath heated my cheek and neck, and I closed my eyes, cursing the way his touch and power affected me.

"I'll never stop fighting you," I whispered.

"I know." He dipped his head down, and I felt his smile against my temple. "I wouldn't expect anything less."

His voice was gravelly and thick, and it sent a shiver down my spine.

I promised myself that one day, I was going to stab him through the heart.

50

———

Samantha

After we returned, Cadean didn't remove the collar, and I didn't leave my room for two days. They brought food, but I rejected it. And when Cadean sent messengers to summon me, I refused to heal him.

Mel even checked in, but I drove her away. Eventually, they left me alone to sit in the dark.

I could still smell the hotcakes and sausages the servants had placed on the little table. They'd gone cold hours before.

I would've rather had a sopping wet bag of jerky and bread. At least then there'd be no illusion about what it was: prison rations.

Leaning back, I let my skull *thunk* against the wall.

I was trapped. Not just by the collar that Cadean insisted I wear or by the walls or the Dark God himself, but by the war and my inability to stop what was happening.

Occasionally, I'd leap up, throw open the curtains, and check the horizon for plumes of smoke. Although none ever appeared, I knew that one day, he would take the moonstone and strike across the border again. Destroy another town, whether to remove a threat or in revenge.

There was nothing I could do. If I tried to escape, he'd just hunt me down or draw me back with the collar.

So I sat in the dark, trying to summon my power. Nothing came. It never came when he wasn't around—except once, when I'd protected the kit foxes. But that had been amid terror and fear, and I'd never been able to do it again. I was powerless with him, and powerless without him. It was worse than having Magicuffs on my wrists.

What was my way out?

After a few hours of brooding and plotting, my skin began to tingle. A low vibration rolled over me, and my muscles tensed as I caught the scent of fire and the taste of chocolate. I tried to block out the sound of wind rustling through pines, but his signature only strengthened.

Then I heard his heavy footsteps in the corridor. They stopped, the lock clicked open, and he stepped in, shutting the door gently behind him.

My sensitive eyes allowed me to make out his features in the darkness. Powerful shoulders. His strong jaw. Glacial eyes that always made my heart beat a little faster. Why was I condemned to suffer at the hands of a beautiful monster?

Cadean dropped to a knee beside me, and I closed my eyes, wishing I could melt into the stone floor.

His fingers brushed the hair from my face. "Are you unwell?"

A shiver of delight ran down my spine, and I wanted to scream in fury at the way my body still reacted toward him, even after everything.

I turned my head away from his touch.

"Little wolf." His voice was soft and gentle. "Look at me."

I swung my head back and glared at him with all the hate and rage and anger in my soul. "I despise you."

While the expression of concern on his face didn't change, I saw the spark of pain in his eyes.

What did he care?

The Dark God dropped his hand. "I'm sorry about what happened across the border. Is that—"

"This is about you keeping me prisoner," I said. "It's about all the lies. It's about what happened across the border happening again, and again, and again."

His brow furrowed, and he watched me intensely. "I'm trying to protect my people."

"Then you're failing. You're drowning them in a cycle of violence and vengeance."

He winced like I'd ripped my claws across his face. I didn't feel the least bit guilty.

"We haven't launched any new attacks across the border," he said.

I tilted my head and gave him a scathing look. "But there will be, won't there? I've heard the whispers echoing in the hall. You're gathering your warriors."

His momentary hesitation told me everything I needed to know.

"Get out," I growled.

He rose, and what I saw in his eyes caught me off guard. Sadness, guilt, and agonizing shame. "Do you think I relish the killing?"

Standing, I strode to the door. "It's clear you do. I've seen the battle lust in your eyes."

I wrenched the door open to the surprise of the guard standing outside.

Cadean tightened his fists, and the guilt in his expression was replaced by rage. "I will not apologize for doing what I must to protect my people."

I gestured to the exit. "Then you have no soul at all."

He hesitated, and then, shaking with frustration, he stormed out. I slammed the door behind him.

The moment he was gone, I began pacing back and forth.

I had to get out. He was never going to let me go. His promises were lies. Even if I healed him, he'd likely never release me. I'd be a prisoner for the rest of my life, and I'd have to stand idly by while he murdered thousands of innocents.

Fuck that.

Somewhere between the fancy room and the dancing and the feasts, I'd forgotten that I was the prisoner of a vicious warlord. A bastard who'd killed members of my pack and decimated my city.

How had I become so lost? Or had I just been broken from the start?

I rested my forehead against the cold stone wall and closed my eyes. The truth was, getting out wasn't enough anymore. It hadn't ever been.

Haunting visions of the ruined fae village flickered through my mind. Escaping wasn't enough.

I slammed my palm against the wall. "I need to stop him from doing it ever again."

But what could I do?

I could try to deliberately spread the curse, weakening him as far as I could. It had been an accident at the pylons, but if I really tried...

The thought of intentionally hurting Cadean made my insides churn. I grasped the bed to keep my balance as vertigo swept over me. My heart ached, and in that moment, I realized I'd never be able to hurt him, no matter how much I hated him.

That's not who I am.

Deep within Cadean, there was a sliver of good, a man who protected his people. I'd seen it. Selene and her people were counting on him to defend them. If I spread the curse and weakened him, her village and all the others along the border would be in danger.

Then what could I do?

I closed my eyes, unable to imagine anything but the image of him, standing amid death and destruction, the moonshard glowing in his hand.

The moonshard.

That was the solution to everything.

Without it, Cadean couldn't raid the fae villages, and losing it wouldn't stop him from protecting the people on his side of the barrier. It wouldn't stop the war, but maybe it would restore the balance. Maybe it would help stop the cycle of violence and reprisal.

Slowly, certainty set in, like the heavy air of an approaching storm.

I had to steal the moonshard. The problem was, how to get it and get away?

Panic began to set in, but I braced against the bed. *I have to tackle this one step at a time.*

The first thing to do was to figure out where the damn thing was. Kass always carried it in his saddlebag, but the Dark God had called it his most prized possession—he would probably keep it in a treasure vault.

Would he keep it close? In his room?

I'd always felt its cool-warm presence when we were out riding, even when I was far from Cadean. Had I felt it in his chamber when I went to heal him?

I closed my eyes and racked my mind, trying to recall every sensation. The room was always filled with his power—the deep vibration of the earthquake and the rustle of wind in the pines.

But was there something else? Another presence drawn out? I could almost feel it tickling the back of my memories, just out of reach. When I'd healed him, was it possible I'd started drawing energy from the moonshard hidden nearby?

Maybe. I couldn't be certain, but if I could get into his room, I might be able to feel its presence. Of course, that was easier said than done. The front door would be sealed and warded, but perhaps his balcony might provide access.

I was pretty sure he was gone. After he'd left my room, I'd heard him descending the spiral staircase to the lower levels. There was no way to know how long he'd be away, but I could at least test my plan of breaking and entering.

I rushed to the drawer and pulled out the little key Rune had brought me. I unlocked my window and stuck my head out. The tower curved off to the side, but I could still make out the lip of his balcony about a hundred feet away.

I could make it. All I had to do was climb along the side and not fall to my death.

I was good at free-climbing, and there were plenty of cracks in the stone for my claws to dig into. If I ever was going to try to escape out the window, I'd have a much longer descent, so even if there was no way in from the balcony, it would be a good practice run. And if I could get in, fates only knew what useful information I could find.

I levered myself halfway out the window and kept my eyes trained on the rock ahead.

All I had to do was not look down.

Or get caught.

51

———

Cadean

After checking in on the little wolf, I'd gone down to the courtyard to meet Mel and Kass, who'd just returned from riding the border. Between Auren and the fae, I was certain it was no longer safe to speak in public, so I led them back to my chambers.

At least Auren would be gone soon. With the mounting fae threat and assassins, I'd told him to wrap up his affairs and take his leave. He was a complication I could not afford, and didn't entirely trust.

Once we reached the top floor, I wove a spell of silence around us so we could talk as we walked past the little wolf's room.

"You've finished renewing the wards?"

"I can't say how long they'll last, but with your blood this time, they should keep the blight at bay for longer," Mel replied.

"Good."

"I could use Samantha's help, but she hasn't returned to the workshop. Or been willing to speak to me for days. What happened out there? I thought you were just escorting refugees back home."

"The fae had occupied a village on the other side of the barrier and were going to use it as a base for raiding," I said, anger tensing my jaw. "I leveled it. We were also able to destroy the roots of one of the vines. It should free up miles of this land from leeching death. I have no qualms about what we did."

"Then why do you look so guilty?" she asked as we reached my room.

I stopped with my hand on the door. "Because I didn't want Samantha to see that side of me. She hates me enough as it is, and I'm afraid I've done irreparable damage."

I shoved through into my chambers, and the others followed. My chest felt tight. I could still smell Samantha's scent from the last time she'd healed me, lingering in the room, yet it was as fresh as if she'd just been there.

It might have been the last time.

Whatever bridge I'd been building, I'd burnt it to the ground just as surely as that fae outpost.

It had been a foolish hope from the start.

"I don't understand what she was doing over there. You should have never brought her along," Mel said.

"Yes, well, I'm a fool." I dismissed the spell of silence around us.

"It would have been fine if Wulfric had done a better job of babysitting," Kass said.

I'd been meaning to ask Wulfric why he'd allowed her to escape. He was the fiercest warrior in my realm. The only reason she'd managed to flee was because he'd allowed it.

I stepped to the edge of the balcony, on the seam between the sunlight and the deep shadows of my room. I stared out across my domain and at the wall beyond.

Kass put a hand on my shoulder. "The girl is becoming a

problem, Cadean. Aggravating your wound, the assassin, stealing a griffstrider and charging over the border. You must deal with her or lock her away permanently."

"I will not," I growled, and shrugged off his hand. "Never ask it again."

"You've always told me to tell you if your judgement is compromised," he pressed. "It's compromised. You're blinded by the hope that she can heal you."

But it wasn't just that. The things I felt, I could never explain to him.

I leveled my gaze. "Maybe I'm blinded by hope, but you're blinded by fear. She has a good heart. She could make a difference here."

"Yes. By curing the Dark Wolf God and weakening him so much that the barrier collapses in on us all," he muttered.

Turning my back on my Master of Information, I glared out across the balcony at the fates-damned wall of light rising into the sky. It was closer than it had ever been. Rage burned through me like a viper's venom. I *knew* she could heal me. If I could just find a way to draw her magic out, everything would go back to the way it was.

Then a revelation dawned.

The anger and frustration in my soul hardened into cold iron, and I turned to my councilors. "After she wounded me, the barrier shrank. You're not seeing the opportunity that creates."

Kass raised his eyebrows "Are you talking about the exciting opportunity to have our realm restricted to a single tower in the middle of the Dreamlands? It's cute, but it's not going to hold all four of us."

"This realm is barely big enough to hold your ego as it is," Mel sniped.

Ignoring their endless fencing, I stepped back into the shadows to join them. "Each time the barrier moves, the fae push forward. They build settlements and plant vines. They move their outposts closer so they can punch deeper."

"Right, we're fucked," Kass said.

I shook my head. "You're not looking at the problem right. What happened to the border when Samantha exacerbated my wound at the pylon?"

"The barrier shrank, and we lost miles in a day," Kassian said.

"It's because I'm not strong enough to hold back the Moon's magic. But what would happen if Samantha were able to heal me completely this time?"

"You're hoping the barrier will move back out?" Melanthe offered.

I hurled my axe across the room, and it embedded itself in a bookshelf with a resonant crack. "Back to where it was months ago. In a single instant."

Kass stopped toying with his dagger, and his eyes narrowed. "Their entire front line would be in our territory. You'd be able to attack wherever you want."

I nodded. "Right now, they think they're safe from me. Their border towns will be preparing for invasion, not defense. We could catch them by surprise and wipe out their ability to wage war for decades. I'll take the moonstone and ride as far as I can into their territory, and wipe out any outpost or village that's a threat. They'll have to go into full-on retreat."

Kass whistled low. "Fuck."

I tightened my fist. "Our people could have peace for a while."

The blood had drained from Mel's face. "This all depends on Samantha being able to heal you."

"She's close. I can feel it—even the other day when she burned me. If I can teach her to love our people, she'll do it.

She'll find the strength. She's a protector at heart, despite how much she hates me."

Mel cocked her head to the side. "And what will you do with Samantha then? Will you let her go?"

The thought of losing her made my chest ache. "I don't think I'll ever be able to let her go."

I couldn't. I'd find a way to convince her to stay. I'd find a way to atone, and somehow make her fall in love with my lands and people. I'd help her discover her power and master her magic.

Somehow, I would find a way to show her the man hiding within the beast.

52

Samantha

My claws ached from digging into the stone below the Dark God's balcony, and my heart was pounding so hard, I was terrified it would shake the stones of the tower loose.

I don't think I'll ever be able to let her go.

I'd heard it from his lips, drifting through the archway. The charade was over; the Dark God meant to keep me a prisoner for the rest of my life.

I was fucked.

Not only that, but as soon as I healed him, the barrier would move back out, and he would sweep through the fae villages, burning them to the ground. I could still see the rubble and ash every time I closed my eyes.

Trembling, I looked around, then began making my way carefully along the wall.

The climb itself wasn't difficult. I'd spent many weekends climbing at Red River Gorge back home, and there were plenty of seams in the stone. The three-hundred-foot drop from the top of the tower, however, would be deadly, even for a werewolf.

I kept my eyes on the rock ahead of me and didn't look down.

I checked over my shoulder toward the balcony, but the Dark God hadn't emerged from the room. Why had he returned so quickly?

Finally, I reached my open window, threw my hands over the ledge, and hauled myself halfway through.

"Hi."

The unexpected voice sent adrenaline racing through me, and I froze, eyes wide. Auren sat in the armchair across from my bed.

"Are you mad? What are you doing in my room?" I asked, struggling to pull myself up and in.

"I think the question is, what are you doing hanging halfway out of your window? Up to no good, I presume. Do you need a hand?"

I heaved myself the rest of the way through. "I was getting some fresh air. Everywhere else in this claustrophobic tower is packed with guards, lackeys, and gods. Are you going to rat me out?"

"I won't tell Cadean you slunk out the window if you don't tell him I slunk into your room—he'd imprison you, but he'd probably try to take my head. He's the jealous type and very possessive of you."

I touched the collar around my neck that was now a permanent part of my attire. "So I've discovered. How in the hell did you even get in?"

"I wouldn't worry about your safety. The room is strongly enchanted against the fae. I just happen to be a god—we're very hard to keep out of anything."

The sunlight from the window cast him in an unnaturally golden light. He was the polar opposite of Cadean, civilized and charming. While Cadean was a brutalist statue, breathtaking in his harsh beauty and feral power, Auren was refined and elegant, a Greek sculpture carved from soft marble.

Why wasn't it him that I wanted to kiss?

"Why are you here?" I asked.

"I heard that you'd locked yourself away after what happened across the border. I wanted to see you and make sure you were okay."

"I'm not. It was awful. If I'd known the circumstances, I would have stayed back."

Auren nodded sympathetically and paced to the window with an air of practiced casualness. "I'm sure it was horrible seeing them kill your kin. They may live under the Undying Court, but still, they're your people."

The air went out of the room, and my stomach knotted. "What do you mean, *my people*?"

When he glanced over at me, his expression was unreadable. "You don't know? They didn't tell you?"

"I have no idea what you're talking about."

He slowly turned toward me, an expression of sorrow on his face. "You're part fae, Samantha. I thought you knew. I thought Cadean told you when he found out. I—I'm sorry."

"That's impossible," I said. "I'm a wolf shifter."

He shook his head. "But also part fae. Why else would you be able to do magic?"

"It's not possible.

I suddenly felt dizzy, and Auren reached out to steady me. "I'm sorry, I shouldn't have said anything. I don't want to get between you two—"

I seized his arm and dug my claws in. "Tell me everything you know."

Auren's face was inscrutable, but at last, he looked away. "Cade had his suspicions after Melanthe tested your blood, but it was confirmed when you were able to enter the glade with the moon blossoms. Only the fae can enter the glades."

I was fae. And Cadean had known the whole time?

My world spun off its axis, and my stomach heaved. My mother was a wolf, but my father...I'd never met him. I'd assumed he was a wolf, too, but he'd abandoned my mother when she was pregnant. Could he have been fae? Had my mom even known? I felt like if she had, she would have told me. We shared everything. Except this.

My heart was drumming a million beats a minute, and my skin had gone cold and clammy. I could sense the truth of his words. The evidence was clear now that I knew what to look for. The creature in the glade had even called me a traitor to my own kind.

She'd meant a traitor to the fae, not the shifters.

"What else do you know? About my past? My magic?" I pressed, mind reeling. There were many fae out there and countless courts.

Auren shook his head. "Nothing. Maybe Cade or Melanthe know, but they play their cards close to their chest."

Fae.

Had Sarion known? Was that why they wanted to recruit me? I hoped I wasn't related to someone in the Undying Court. They were fucking monsters, just as bad or even worse than the Dark God.

But their people weren't monsters. Not all of them.

I released Auren's arm and leaned my head against the wall, closing my eyes. It was too much. The death. The lies. The horror of what might come next. The corners of my eyes began to burn.

Auren placed a hand against my back. His touch was warm but practiced. "I'm sorry to drop this on you. I thought you knew. Clearly, it is a shock. I'll give you some space to process it, and maybe I can find a way to visit you one more time before I leave in a couple days."

He stepped back, and terror flashed through me. "You're leaving? Why?"

He held my last sliver of hope for escaping. I just wasn't sure if he would betray his brother to help me, and more importantly, if I even trusted him. If he refused, he'd likely tell Cadean, which would only make my situation worse. I was running out of time.

"It seems I've worn out my welcome." Auren winked. "Maybe he's afraid I'll steal you away. But more likely, he's planning an attack and doesn't want me to know the details."

My last potential ally was leaving. I'd be on my own.

As he turned, I grasped his wrist. "Take me with you. Help me escape."

His features softened as he looked down at me, and he reached up and brushed his fingers along my jaw. "I can't betray my brother, no matter what my desires are."

My breath caught. What were his desires?

Auren was striking and handsome, and I'd be a liar if I said I wasn't drawn to him. He was full of light, and there was always a smile on his face. I felt safe when I was around him, but when he departed, it left me with the feeling that I'd missed something important—I just could never put my finger on what.

What I felt with Cadean...that was different. That was consuming and spellbinding, like he was both destroying and liberating me all at once. And even after everything he'd done, there was a part of me that kept hoping there was some good inside of him.

That part of me was a fool.

"Please," I begged. "There must be something you can do."

Something flashed in his eyes, a cold spark beneath the warmth. Then he brushed his fingers over the cool metal around my neck. "I wish I could, but you wouldn't get far with this collar."

The collar was the key to everything. No matter if I escaped with Auren or found my own way out, or was even captured by the fae, Cadean could always pull me back.

"You're a god. There must be a way to break it."

"Only Cadean or a magic that can counter his can remove it—and unfortunately, my own powers are too close to his."

"Who could counter it?"

"Well, considering the Moon has been able to keep him trapped all these years, her magic might do it. But I don't think she'll be coming for a visit any time soon."

The Moon. Fuck.

"Is there nothing else? What about the fae?"

He snorted. "Maybe. But they would just as likely snap a collar of their own on you. You may share blood, but they are not to be trusted. If you ever escape, do not run to them."

I rubbed my face and ran my hands through my hair. "Fuck. There must be something I can do."

Auren stepped to the window and paused. "You've harnessed the Moon's magic twice now to wound my brother. Maybe you can use it to break the collar."

That seemed improbable. I swallowed the swelling lump of defeat that rose in my throat.

"Cadean loves to watch you. I should go before he catches me here. Take care of yourself, Samantha."

I nodded because I knew that if I spoke, tears would follow.

There was the scent of summer wheat and amber, and then an explosion of light wrapped around him. He transformed into a sparrow and fluttered out the window.

Of course that was how he'd gotten in—shapeshifting, just like Cadean could.

I slumped down onto the bed. I was alone. Truly alone.

My body felt heavy and cold, and my heart ached. I hadn't really known Mel or the others, but I'd grown used to them, and sometimes, I'd enjoyed their company. The laughs and banter, Cadean's kiss—it was all a pack of lies.

How had I opened myself to them? And Auren, was he even my friend? If so, why had he waited so long to tell me?

The truth was, I had to get the moonshard and get free, and I had to do it on my own. Just like always.

53

Samantha

I paced the room, heart racing.

Auren had hinted that I might be able remove the collar if I harnessed the Moon's magic. I'd drawn power from both the moonshard and the pylons, but could I do it on my own?

Might as well try.

I knelt on the floor, grasped the iron collar in my hand, and summoned my power. I focused on drawing in that feeling of cold and warmth that I called on to heal the Dark God.

For a moment, there was nothing, but then a soft glow of cool light built up within me. I pushed it through my fingers and into the iron collar around my neck. Slowly, the collar began to warm, then burn. My arms quaked, and I strained, pushing every ounce of power I had into the damned thing.

And then the power was gone, like someone had pulled the cord on the TV. I collapsed onto my palms, weighted down by sudden exhaustion and an overbearing sense of failure.

I slumped against the wall as despair flooded my heart. "I need some fucking help."

But I was alone. Nothing had changed.

The beautiful room, the bed, the clothes—they were all illusions. I was still in shackles in that dark cave deep beneath the citadel. I closed my eyes, fighting off the tears, then put my face in my palms. "I'd trade my left tit just to get out of here, just for something, anything to go my way."

There was a wet slap on the stone floor, and the scent of fish.

I dropped my hands and opened my eyes. It *was* a fish, still alive and gulping for air. Standing behind it, like a small, green, ugly knight in shining armor, was Rune.

The godsdamned little bandit himself.

Rune the noble. Rune the bold. Rune the little beastie who'd been tormenting the Dark God for years, and still hadn't gotten caught. He was like an ugly little Robin Hood, and just the hero I needed.

My mind reeled with possibility, and for the first time in weeks, I felt a spark of hope. "You're here to help?"

He shrugged, then slapped the back of his hand into his palm a couple times.

"For a trade, of course." My knight in shining armor was also a mercenary. What could I give him?

I knelt in front of him. "You hate the Dark God, don't you?"

Rune barred his teeth and made a rude gesture.

I inched forward. "And you like me, right?"

He shrugged again. Okay, well, it was better than the finger. "If you help me escape, it will drive him insane."

Rune gave me a malicious grin but rubbed the tips of his fingers together. The problem was, he could just as well steal anything I could trade him.

I closed my eyes and racked my brain, then peeked one eye open. "I can give you something that you can't steal, and that no one else can take."

He leaned forward, drumming his little knobby fingers together with excitement.

I smiled. "My eternal friendship."

His fingers stopped, and he gave me an incredulous look. Okay, that wasn't what he had in mind, but it was worth a try. With a snort, the little mercenary waved his hand dismissively and walked away.

Fuck.

There had to be something I could give him that no one else could.

I leapt to my feet and tugged on my collar. "You can have this!"

He looked over his shoulder, and his eyes sharpened.

"No one can remove it, and nobody else has one. It's unique. If you can help me get it off, it's all yours."

I knelt again, and he walked forward and tentatively reached his hands out and traced the iron whorls.

"It's very nice," I coaxed. "And if the Dark God realizes you have it, his mind will implode with fury."

Rune wore a delightedly malicious expression. Then he grabbed the collar and yanked.

I gagged and tumbled sideways, laughing for the first time in what felt like years. "It's going to take more than that!"

He held up his hands.

"I don't know! Let me think."

I began pacing back and forth, and Rune mirrored me, hands behind his back.

"The Dark God carries a key for it. Do you think you could sneak it out of his pocket?"

Rune gave a distraught squeak and shook his head.

Then the only other option was breaking the spell with the Moon's magic. I'd failed on my own, but what if I used the moonshard?

The whispered words came back to me: *Free us, and we will free you.* Had it been the moonshard speaking? Did it want to be free of the Dark God just as much as I did? Perhaps the magical stone could somehow help me get out.

I sucked in a sharp breath and glanced at Rune. "It's fucking worth a try."

He nodded vigorously, then cocked his head to the side, as if to say, *What is?*

I kneeled and grabbed Rune by the shoulders. "Do you know every inch of this castle?"

He rolled his eyes, which I interpreted as, *Yes, duh.*

"The Wolf God has a piece of stone that glows with soft light. It's about six inches long." I let go of him and tried to approximate the knife-like shape with my hands. "Do you know where he keeps it?"

Rune shrugged, but in an affirmative way this time: *Of course, so what's it worth to you?*

"I want it. It might be what I need to remove the collar. If it works, the collar is all yours, forever."

Rune's beady little eyes dilated so that they were like obsidian marbles, and he nodded slowly. Then he held up a finger and waggled it.

"What's the problem?"

He mimed turning a key in a lock, and then opened his hands like doors.

"He keeps it locked in a vault. Do you know where the key is?" I asked.

He shrank down, shoulders hunched, and I caught the scent of his fear.

I nodded sympathetically. "The big bad wolf has that key as well, doesn't he?"

Rune tapped his hip, and my heart began beating faster. "He keeps the key on him."

I snatched a quill and piece of paper off the writing desk. "Can you draw what it looks like?"

Despite his many wonderful qualities, Rune was not an artist. The resulting illustration was a crooked stick with a blob on the end.

"Ah," I said as disappointment took me.

He pointed at me and drew a finger across his throat.

"Yeah, it's dangerous. But then again, I'm desperate."

I laid down on the soft bed for the first time in days and began thinking. How to get the key?

I stayed there for hours, going over everything I knew about the Dark God—his personality, his powers, the citadel, and even the legends of our packs—ones he'd laughed at.

But that's where I found my answer.

I sprang out of bed, heart racing. To trap the Dark God, the Moon Goddess had drugged him with the waters of dreams, putting him to sleep.

Could I do it again?

It was a supremely dangerous and foolhardy plan. But I had to get the moonshard, not only to free myself, but to stop the Dark God from ever crossing the border again.

I pounded on my door. "Tell Melanthe that I'm ready to go back to work."

That afternoon, I rejoined Mel in her workshop and set to work prepping components for the spells that kept the vines at bay. After an hour, she looked up from her pile of notes and smiled. "It's good to have you back. I've grown accustomed to having you around."

I forced a smile and continued grinding malachite into a strange-smelling powder.

She came around the table opposite me and leaned against

it, her expression fraught. "What's up with you? You've been so quiet."

"I'm being held against my will by a murderous bastard." I dropped another bulb in the mortar and crushed it. "Isn't that reason enough to be in a bad mood?"

Mel shook her head. "It's the raid, isn't it? I don't know what possessed Cadean to take you along. I'm sorry you had to see it."

"It would've happened whether I saw it or not," I muttered.

She sighed. "He's fighting a war—"

"Like that justifies anything," I said sharply.

Mel put her hands on her hips and cocked her head. "It very much does if it stops the fae from attacking villages like Frostfall."

I paused my work and fixed her with a piercing stare. "But will it? When the fae attack, he makes a reprisal, and they retaliate. It's not going to stop until all the innocents living in the Dreamlands are dead."

Mel's brows pulled together, and she looked upset. "Maybe you can't see it, but he's fighting for the life of this realm. He's done and will continue to do things that might seem questionable, but if you could just understand—"

I slammed the pestle on the table. "What's there to understand? It's not going to stop. Once he's done wiping out the entire Undying Court, then what? Will my home be next? What about after that? He was locked away because he wanted to destroy mankind."

She spun away from the table. "Have you stopped to think that those legends were created by the same people who locked him away? I don't know what he was like a millennium ago, but I've spent my adult life watching him fight for the shifters here."

I shook my head sadly. "Whatever good he's done, he's still a monster, Mel. I've seen it."

She looked at me with an expression as hard as iron. "Some monsters just need to be tamed."

My heart squeezed, and hot tears burned my eyes. I grabbed the pestle and began grinding again, refusing to give in to my emotions.

Mel leaned against the bookshelf, her back to me. "I'm sorry, Samantha. For everything. Cadean. This place. What you've seen, and what's been done to you. All of it."

Her scent was a cocktail of regret and frustration, and I realized that she was captive to her loyalty, as I was to the collar.

I sighed. "I know."

She turned, and I saw the struggle in her eyes. She was torn between Cadean and me, and as much as I wished that she'd side with me, I knew she wouldn't. Couldn't.

"Just give Cadean a chance," she said. "He's better than you think."

A deep ache lodged in my throat. *Never.*

We didn't speak much the rest of that day or the next. I knew she wanted to, but I just didn't know what to say. What had been close between us had been stretched thin, though it was still there.

I avoided Cadean. When I wasn't in my room, I was in Mel's workshop, helping prepare the spell components she needed to recast the wards around the borders. Some were traps. Others were alarms. I didn't understand the nuances of the magic. But what was clear was that they were failing faster and faster. At least I knew I was helping protect the villages like Selene's, and it didn't require me to kill.

Was that how Mel saw her own work? A way to help without bloodshed? Well, technically, with quite a lot of bloodshed—she was a blood sorceress, after all—but it was willingly made.

I pulled petals from flowers, wove spiderwebs into thread, extracted mercury from cinnabar, and a dozen other numbing and potentially dangerous tasks. It allowed my hands to work and my mind to plot.

Conceptually, my plan was simple.

I would dose the Dark God with dream lily extract when I applied his balm. He'd told me at the glade that the only creatures immune to the effects of the flower were the briarwitches. I was hoping that included him.

I would use a lot, just to be safe.

Once he was unconscious, Rune would help me find where he kept the moonshard, and I'd use it to break the enchantment on the collar around my neck. Then I'd flee to Frostfall, where I knew there was a portal.

A million things could go wrong in between. Frankly, it was extremely unlikely to succeed. But I had to try.

If we could get the moonshard, it would be enough—even if I couldn't get the collar off. I could give the shard to Rune, and he could hide it or dispose of it, or maybe even take it to Magic Side if I got caught. At least I'd know the borderlands would be safe from the Dark God.

It was something to pray for.

54

———————

Cadean

Mel followed me into my quarters the next evening. I was too tired to protest, so I let her in, then slammed the door.

"Cade," she said sharply. "We need to talk about this."

I pulled my axe out its scabbard and tossed it on the couch, my hands and forearms streaked with dried blood of the vines.

"There's nothing to talk about," I growled, catching my reflection in the mirror across the room. My hair was pulled back and knotted, coated with blood like the rest of my body and soul.

Samantha was right. I was a fucking monster—and one that was rapidly losing control. My frustration had been building for weeks, and I could barely contain it. Everything was closing in around me. The barrier, the fae, my own mind.

And at the center of everything, there was *her*. I couldn't stop watching, couldn't stop imagining, couldn't stop thinking about her.

I'd ridden hard all day, hunting fae scouts along the border. I'd brought the moonshard and planned to cross over and ambush their patrols. Yet somehow, I couldn't bring myself to do it. Instead, I'd unleashed my fury on the vines until a scream of deathwings arrived to defend them.

Mel poured a glass of summer wine and handed it to me. "You're hurting, Cadean."

I kicked the leather satchel with the moonshard across the floor. I'd return it to the vault once she was gone, but I didn't want to be anywhere near the damned thing.

"Of course I'm hurting," I growled. "My realm is collapsing. The blight is advancing. And the only person who can heal the wound at the root of it all despises everything I am. Do you have any idea what it's like to live with ceaseless pain?"

"Is it the pain that's hurting or how she looks at you?"

I stood and strode out on the balcony. "I don't care what she thinks of me as long as she heals me."

Mel joined my side. "That's a lie that even I can smell. You care what she thinks. You care for her. I see it in everything you do."

Mel was the closest thing I had to a sister, but the way she was prodding me right now made me want to exile her to the far ends of the Dreamlands.

I gave a grunt. "You heard the oracle. Heads, she has the power to save me, tails, she has the power to bring me to my knees. I thought I was getting somewhere, but now she hates me more than ever. That coin is going to land tails up."

"You don't care about the oracle. You care about *her*. It's obvious to everyone but you. Even Wulfric knows."

Who wouldn't care about her? She was strong and fierce, and her presence drew the air from my lungs. But she loathed me with a hatred strong enough to span eternity.

My breaths were unsteady, and I itched to put my fist through the wall. "So what are you saying? Stop dancing around it and speak."

"You're obsessed with her, and you have been since the

moment your paths crossed. When you shadow-cast, she can see you when no one else can. And she's also the only one who can cure your wounds."

I thrust my arm before Mel. "Because *she's* the one who cursed me."

Mel shook her head. "I don't think the balm is doing anything, Cade. She can heal you because she is your mate."

The blood drained from my heart, and the room slanted as fury shot through my veins, stronger than any of Mel's brews. "You can't be fucking serious."

"Somehow, the fates have entwined your souls," she said flatly. "The oracle. The wound. Your magic."

"She's a mortal, and I'm a god. Not even the fates are that cruel."

"Are you certain?"

"I'm not going to listen to this."

"Fine, whether you believe me or not, you need to consider the possibility. If she's your mate and if Queen Ayanna gets her hands on her..."

My head snapped to her, and anger coiled around my heart as violent thoughts rose. The room shook as a wave of energy surged from me.

"If Ayanna so much as touches a single hair on Samantha's body, I'll tear the continent apart and leave nothing but bones and ash of the Undying Court."

Mel adjusted her hair after the wave of force passed, and a wry smile formed on her lips. "And you feel this protective for most women? For me?"

I dragged a hand through my hair. "It's not possible. We're connected some way, but it can't be that. She's mortal."

Mel nodded. "That means you don't have much time to act the fool."

I braced against the wall as everything around me became a dizzying haze. Was she truly my mate?

She despised me, believed I was nothing more than a beast and a monster. Whatever chance I'd had, I ruined it.

I hung my head. "If it's true, I'd just taint her with my darkness. I'd destroy her."

Mel put her hand on my shoulder. "Or maybe she'd take some of the burden away. Perhaps that's why the fates have bound you together."

How could I place that burden on her?

55

Samantha

My opportunity came two days after I returned to work. Mel had to ride out with Wulfric to repair one of the wards on the western border, and after some begging, she let me keep busy in the workshop.

Unfortunately, she left me under Kass's supervision. He was an absolute headache, but at least he had no idea what I was planning and wouldn't know what to look for.

I'd prepared a batch of healing balm partway. All I had to do was slip in the flower extract and mask its smell.

While Kass lounged on the sunbed, flipping through a book on hallucinatory plants, I bustled around the room doing my normal work. But during a moment when he seemed particular engrossed, I made my way to the shelf where Melanthe kept her tinctures.

Where are you?

I shuffled through the glass bottles until I found the one I was looking for. It was clear glass with six dried purple flowers suspended in a hazy liquid—dream lilies, identical to those I'd almost touched in the fae glade.

"Do you enjoy drugs?" Kass asked absently, and my hand froze in the middle of pulling the bottle from the shelf.

"What?"

He paused mid-page turn and looked up at me with a grin. "You don't peg me for one to let loose. I bet you're a goody two-shoes. A real princess."

Had he met me at all?

A grin split his lips, and my neck heated with frustration. He was having a go at me, of course.

When I didn't answer, the vampire continued, "A pretty princess in a tall tower."

I suddenly longed for the days I'd been stuck in that godsforsaken cave, alone and in silence.

He sat up and inspected me. "Is everything all right over there, Samantha?"

My temples throbbed, and I knew he could hear my heartbeat a mile away. I needed a cover. I grabbed a tiny brown bottle and tossed it to him. "Here. If you like to party, you might enjoy this."

He snatched it out of the air and inspected it. "What is it?"

"Powdered mandrake root. It helps with..." I extended my finger, then made it droop. "I'm not saying you should use it. But you know."

Kass narrowed his eyes. "Maybe I'm wrong. You were probably a rebel."

I didn't want to think back to my days of growing up. I'd been a rebel in my alpha's eyes, and I'd had to fight tooth and claw to survive.

I finally found the scent neutralizer that Melanthe used for particularly stinky potions and drifted across the room, leaving it and the bottle of dream lily extract on my workbench. Then I grabbed a small wooden box off a high shelf and took it over to Kass.

He lifted one of his brows. "What's this?"

"Mushrooms."

He grinned. "Are you trying to impede my ability to keep an eye on you?"

Well, it would have been nice.

I just smiled. "I swear to the fates, Kassian, I'm not trying to drug you."

He sniffed them as I headed back to my workbench, then closed the box. "You tempt me, but I can't be irresponsible. Anyway, I usually prefer to have someone else indulge on my behalf. The rush is so much nicer when infused in blood. You aren't interested, are you?"

I calmly sat down at my workbench and uncorked the scent neutralizer. "Keep your fangs to yourself."

He shrugged. "Maybe next time. Anyway, whatever you just opened has put me off. I don't think my nose is going to work for a while."

Keeping my breath steady, I uncorked the bottle of dream lilies. I had no idea how many of these it would take to knock out a god, but from what Mel had said, they were extremely potent. Using a pair of tweezers, I pulled out three blossoms and dropped them in the mortar with the moon blossom bulbs I'd already begun to mash.

Kass had gone back to his book.

Trying to act casual, I returned the bottle to the shelf, making sure to conceal it behind the others.

"Are you almost done?" he asked, and my heart skipped a beat.

"Almost. You're quite impatient." Hoping that my panic wasn't as obvious as it felt, I sat down and began to carefully grind the dream lilies until they were mixed into the mash of moon blossoms.

He let out an emphatic breath. "I'm impatient because you've grown exceedingly dull lately—sitting around and playing with your potions."

I eyed the mash on the end of the pestle and pondered whether it would be worth testing the potency on the vampire. Gods, it was tempting. "As opposed to what?"

"Feisty. Violent." He smiled, and this time, the bottoms of his fangs were visible. "I much prefer you like that. And though Cadean may not admit it, I've no doubt he's of the same opinion."

Ignoring Kass's gaze, I cautiously spooned the mash into a brass bowl, then finished adding the rest of the ingredients. *I could show him violence.*

"Your heart is pounding, Samantha."

"I was just visualizing driving a stake into yours." It wasn't entirely a lie.

He tilted his head back and laughed. "Now, that's interesting. Any time you'd like to try that, just let me know."

When the balm was ready, I carefully scooped it into a jar, keenly aware that getting even a drop on me would knock me out, or possibly even kill me. There were probably enough dream lilies in the balm to put the entire castle into a coma.

I sniffed it. It didn't really smell like the normal balm, but it didn't smell like dream lilies, either. It would have to do. *Fates, please don't let Cadean notice until it's too late.*

I stoppered the jar and sealed the edges with a bit of wax, then scrubbed the residue off everything.

Go time.

My heart began beating irregularly, and my chest felt like it was going to crack. Trying to get some sort of control over my mind, I focused on the rhythm of the scrub brush and my breathing, in and out. Was I really doing this?

I wished there was something more I could do to be

prepared, but the truth was, I just needed speed and luck. And Rune.

I turned to Kass. "I'm done. I'll see the Dark God now."

He threw the book aside. "Thank fates. I was literally getting ready to stake myself through the heart."

I took the jar and a smooth metal applicator to apply the balm and waited for him at the entrance. Kass unlocked the door but paused with the key still in the lock. "You're quite nervous."

Shit.

I tossed my hair and gave him the most condescending look I could muster. "I'm always nervous. Your master is a savage, murdering beast who's built like a titan. Do you think I forget that when I'm rubbing this on his skin?"

For what felt like hours, Kass kept his eyes trained on me, scrutinizing every feature of my face. Finally, he pushed the door open. "I should certainly hope not. It's always good to remember exactly who you're dealing with."

I gave him a weak smile. *Touché.*

56

Cadean

Standing on the balcony, I took in the velvet darkness that shrouded the landscape, broken only by the stars and the shimmering light of the Moon's fucking cage.

I inhaled deeply, noting the rich scents carried on the wind. Signatures of my land, along with the trace of something else: decay. The rot of the fae.

Queen Ayanna was always out there, a viper hidden in shadow, waiting to strike.

If only Samantha would come around. I'd hoped to win her to my side, but that had gone terribly wrong. I'd thought she would understand what was at stake, but now she hated me more than ever.

I deserved it, of course. I wasn't blind to the monster I had become—I was just less at ease with it now that she was around.

How could I ever atone? I knew Samantha's heart well enough to know that nothing I could say would make up for what had happened in Magic Side. And I couldn't give up my war against the fae. As long as they kept pushing, I had to find ways to strike back, harder and faster, to keep them at bay.

My people needed me to be that monster.

I growled and strode into my chamber, frustration clawing to get out. I needed to run my beast and clear my mind, but anymore, even exertion couldn't free me from thoughts of *her*.

We were bound, one way or another.

My chest ached with frustration and despair. Could she really be my mate? It would explain so much, but I'd thought the fates had learned not to twist together the lives of gods and mortals long ago. The consequences were always cruel—one doomed to die, the other to watch.

A knock sounded on my door, and I froze as I caught the scent of *her*.

"Come in," I said, unbinding the arcane locks on the door with my magic.

It swung open slowly, and light silhouetted a graceful form that always made my heart race. She was wearing riding attire, and it suited her so perfectly that I wondered why anyone would ever wear a dress.

She stepped in hesitantly. "I didn't mean to disturb you. I can come back—"

My gaze drifted from her lips down to the balm in her hands, and hope sparked in my chest. Had she come around? Perhaps all wasn't lost.

"I wasn't expecting your company, but I'd welcome it." I sent Kassian away, then pulled out a bottle of wine from the Summerlands from the rack. "Care for a drink?"

She nodded, her unease painfully apparent.

I uncorked the bottle and filled a goblet of wine for her. "I'm glad you're here, though I can tell, you're still upset."

"I'm furious," she said, almost whispering. "But fighting won't do any good. You promised me that if I could heal your wound, you'd let me go, so I'm going to keep trying."

The thought of not having her around had almost become

impossible to imagine, and my fingers constricted around the bottle.

She took a sip of wine. "This is very good."

I poured some for myself. "I used to be able to travel. Now, the wine is the only thing I have that can remind me of what the Summerlands smelled like—the rich scent of the earth and the bite of the minerals washed down from the mountains."

She looked down. "I'm sorry."

Her voice was tinged with pain, and it made my soul hurt.

"I'm glad I can share it with you," I said.

Distress haunted her face. She gulped the wine and set the glass aside. "I should get to work."

Fair enough.

I downed my glass and pulled my shirt over my head. She glanced away when I caught her gaze lingering on my chest. Grinning, I took a seat. "Nothing you haven't seen before, little wolf."

Her cheeks flushed, and I heard the uptick of her pulse. "It's hard not to look."

"You may look all you want."

I watched her closely as she stepped forward, noting the way the sconces brought out the golden flecks in her eyes. Gods, she was beautiful.

She set the lid of the jar on the table and dipped a spoon into the balm. I frowned at her. "Am I suddenly too painfully good looking to touch?"

Her breath faltered momentarily. "No. I increased the potency of this batch. I'm hoping it will work better this time, but I'm not sure what it would do to me, so I'll apply it with a spoon."

I watched her cautiously but sensed no deceit. "Are you sure it will work without your touch?"

"I'm hoping so."

I leaned back as she gently applied the balm to my wound. It stung, but my wound was already on fire. The agony of application was always worth the relief.

"Tell me something about yourself," I said, my jaw tensing at the pain.

"What do you mean?" She seemed shocked and unsure.

Was it really so hard for her to talk to me? I grimaced. "Right now, my arm feels like it's being flayed, and I could use a distraction. Tell me something. About you."

"Oh." She wrinkled her nose as she smeared more balm on. After a moment, she said, "I play roller derby, mostly in the summer."

"Roller derby?"

She nodded. "A bunch of girls on skates, zipping around a rink and trying to knock each other over. We wear tight outfits and helmets. It's kind of silly, but also brutal. I don't know how many times I've broken my nose."

I couldn't comprehend what it must be like. Considering the way she'd fought the deathwings and the fae, she had to be a formidable opponent. She'd probably broken more noses than she received.

"The Bitches with Bite. That's the name of our team. We're all werewolves," she added.

"Fitting and fearsome." I couldn't help the grin that formed.

As the silence stretched between us, my muscles relaxed. "We should run your wolf tomorrow," I said, fighting off the tug of a yawn. "With everything that's happened, the two of you have been cooped up too long."

"That would be nice."

"I'll take the form of a stag. It's one of my favorites."

"What's it like being able to turn into different animals?" she asked.

It was hard to concentrate. She had moved to my shoulder,

and it felt like someone was driving nails into my flesh. I thanked the fates for the wine, which dulled my thoughts as well as the pain. It must have been strong, though the wine from the Summerlands always was.

"It keeps me sane. I've been trapped in this place for too long. I learned every inch of it as a wolf and as a man. And when it got too claustrophobic, I learned it as a hawk, and then a mouse. Every new form taught me a new way to love this place."

Samantha's hand paused, and when I looked up, sadness brimmed her eyes.

"That's why I fight so hard to protect it—it's not just about the shifters and fae and creatures that look like us. Each patch of forest is a home to thousands of creatures too small to defend themselves."

My foggy thoughts washed in and out like waves, along with regret.

She'd taken a step back, and there were almost tears in her eyes. "And yet, across the border, you were a god of destruction..."

I wanted to defend myself. To justify my actions by pleading the case of my people. I wanted to explain that I wasn't only bound by the Moon's barrier, but a thousand years of belief, by the dark power I'd had to embrace to save my lands. But I knew that every justification would ring hollow, so I simply nodded. "I was."

Samantha said nothing but kept working.

I had to find a way to rebuild the bridge between us. It was about more than the healing. Seeing her heartbroken was like a noose around my neck, strangling me and choking my breath from my lungs.

But after all that had happened what could heal her heart? I had to offer her something.

Could it be the truth? Of what she was? Of what we might be? Or would it just drive her further away?

I opened my mouth but suddenly felt tongue-tied, like my brain was drifting, my thoughts awash. It had to be more than the wine. "I need to tell you something that I've been keeping from you."

My hand slipped off the edge of the chair, and I shook my head as confusion muddled my thoughts. "How many moon blossoms did you put in this balm?"

"The same as normal," she said, applying more to my back. "What did you want to tell me?"

Her scent told me she was telling the truth, but something wasn't quite right. "The same? I thought you made it stronger."

I grasped for the jar of balm, but my clumsy fingers knocked it to the floor. It shattered.

Samantha stepped back, but there was no look of surprise on her face. Realization dawned like a thunderbolt. I rose, but the muscles in my legs spasmed, and my knees buckled. "What have you done?"

She narrowed her eyes, and although I swore I saw a flash of guilt, her tone was as sharp as a blade. "I won't be your prisoner, Cadean. I told you at the village that I will *never* stop fighting you."

Anguish cut into my heart even as the rising delirium clouded my senses and impeded my movements.

She'd betrayed me. She'd *poisoned* me.

Rage poured through my body, but my limbs wouldn't respond. I called on the shadows to entwine the deceitful little wolf, but the only shadows that came were ones around the edges of my vision.

"Wherever you go, I will find you," I growled. My voice was gravel in my throat, my words laced with bitterness.

She knelt so she could look me in the eyes. "Not if you're stuck in this cage."

I slammed my palms on the floor, dragging myself forward. "You will regret this, little wolf."

57

———

Samantha

The Dark God growled and pulled himself toward me, but his hands slipped, and he fell still.

I didn't breathe.

I watched him like a hawk, and when I was certain he was down for the count, I let out a long, slow exhalation. I thought that I'd feel triumph, but guilt and anguish flooded me instead. What had he been about to confess? That I was fae?

I took an uneasy step forward and knelt, holding my hand in front of his mouth. Relief flooded me as his breath warmed my hand. The bitterness was there, too.

Why did I care for him? He'd kept me prisoner and was using me to wage a war that was killing innocents, many of them his own people. I shouldn't feel guilt. I'd done what I must to protect them.

A soft grunt from behind made me jump. Rune stood on a ledge of the bookshelf, leaning against the spine of a red book and looking annoyed.

We had one shot, and we had to make it count. I'd sort out the guilt later. Once I had the moonshard, he'd never be able to cross the border again. There would be no more fae villages burning in my dreams. It wouldn't solve all the problems, but it would have to be enough.

I knelt by Cadean and searched his pockets. No key to a vault, and no key to my collar. I cursed and looked back at my little accomplice. "Where's the key?"

Rune pointed to the axe.

Huh?

I grasped it and heaved it up, but it was so heavy, I could barely hold it. How in the hell did the beast of a man swing it so effortlessly?

Grunting, I turned to Rune. "I hope your plan doesn't involve me breaking in with this."

Rune tugged the red book out an inch, then lifted it and knocked it twice. Suddenly, a section of the shelves swung open, revealing a dark chamber.

My heart raced. "Rune, you're brilliant."

Before I stepped inside, I glanced over my shoulder, checking that Cadean was still out cold. He was, but his warning wouldn't release my thoughts: *You will regret this, little wolf.*

Not if I made it out of here.

My eyes adjusted to the dark, revealing a stone pedestal in the center of the cylindrical room. It had a huge slit in the center.

Rune pointed toward the axe. *It* was the key.

Even with werewolf strength, I strained just to heft the axe up and slam it down into the slot. There was a deep and resonant boom when it slipped in.

Then the dark walls began to dissolve like long morning shadows retreating before the rising sun. They revealed shelves filled with treasures and strange objects, but I only cared about one thing: *the moonshard.* It sat in a niche along the far wall, softly glowing.

I let out a shaky breath as relief rushed through me. "Rune. You are a genius. Thank you."

He bowed and started rifling through all the Dark God's shit. If he'd been able to lift the axe himself, I was sure the vault would have been emptied fifteen years ago.

The moment my fingers wrapped around the moonshard, a flurry of pinpricks worked up my arm, filling me with the sensation of champagne bubbles. The Moon's magic gave me with a sense of warmth and rightness I hadn't felt in a long time.

And the whispers returned: *Free us.*

My breath caught. What were they? The voice of her magic? I'd heard it at the pylons and several times before. But there was no time to consider what it meant—I had to free myself first.

I closed my eyes and focused on the feel of the Moon's magic. The pulse of heat and cold, the sensations of infinite sky and of falling among the stars. I drew it in, and slowly, the glow blossomed in my hand.

Stepping back into the room, I found a mirror and pressed the shard against the ornate collar around my neck. "All right, let's hope this baby works."

I closed my eyes and said a prayer to the Moon Mother: *Free me.* I poured every ounce of focus into that thought, letting the Moon's magic pulse and thrum through my body. The flutters under my skin swelled, and then the shard heated as I felt a strange energy moving between my palm and the stone.

The collar grew warm, then hot. It started to move.

My heart stalled and my eyes flew open as the intricate branches of the collar untangled themselves. Then the living iron slid from my neck and clattered to the floor.

Shock rolled through me. I was free.

I glanced over at Cadean. He was still out cold, though very much alive. His breathing had quickened, and I decided not to dwell on the implications of that.

Scooping up the collar that had been my prison, I held it out to Rune. "Thank you for everything you've done. As promised, this is yours."

He held it above his head, triumphant, like it was the World Cup.

I beamed. "We'd better get going."

Rune looked at me, shook his head, and vanished.

Oh.

I glanced around the empty room for the little rogue. "Okay, I'm on my own, then?"

He didn't respond.

"Well, this is bye, I guess..." I kept looking around, hoping he'd reappear, but there was no sign. He was probably smart. This was where the plan got dicey.

Or had that been when I drugged a god?

I shuddered. Even now, the Dark God's magnetism pulled me toward him. His head was turned to the side, his brown hair in waves framing the hard but heavenly features of his face. I dragged my gaze across his now familiar tattoos and the strong contours of his bare chest, and my heart squeezed.

This was not the monster I knew. The shadows were gone, and his face was peaceful. This was the brave protector, the man who would do anything to defend his people and his realm.

The glowing blue veins twisted around his arms and over his shoulder just as badly as they had after the pylons. I was going to leave him weak and consumed by the curse.

Guilt and sorrow tightened my throat.

What would happen to Selene and her village? And all the other shifters and fae who made his lands their home?

I gripped the moonshard and squared my shoulders as the weight of duty and determination settled over me.

I couldn't stop the war. But maybe I could restore some semblance of balance and turn back the clock to the time before

I'd wounded him and caused the barrier to constrict. Maybe even to before he'd taken the moonshard. The balance as the Moon Mother had intended in the first place.

I knew he'd planned to attack when the barrier changed, but he was out cold. Hopefully, it would give the fae a chance to realize what was happening and pull back. He wouldn't be able to surprise them or cross the border to press his advantage.

I wanted to do more, but this was the best I could manage. I had obligations to both sides. And to him. Perhaps if I took away some of his pain, the darkness would go away.

I knelt beside the beautiful god and clasped his hand in mine. Even asleep, his energy sparked inside of me, igniting feelings of warmth and need.

I closed my eyes and entwined my fingers with his. And then I called my magic.

It came instantly. At first, it was a trickle, cool and warm over my skin, like a gentle breeze on a summer day. Then the power flared as the moonshard came to life in my hand, adding its strength to my own.

A deep glow began inside of me, swelling with hope and power and belief. *Heal.*

I brought the Dark God's hand to my lips. "Heal, Cadean. For the sake of Selene, for the sake of all the people in your realm. For the sake of the goodness that's lost somewhere deep within your soul, heal so that you can protect this land."

For a moment, my words hung in the air. And then the dam burst, and radiance poured through me. My body shook and my muscles strained as my magic exploded out of me and into him.

My eyes flew open, and I gasped. The blue veins that covered his body glowed with silver light, burning the curse away.

I was going to leave, but I could leave him with this. "Heal, Cadean. Heal for me."

His body arched, and the white veins of light crackled away, disappearing from his shoulders and then down his arm, leaving an expanse of pure skin in its wake.

The torrent of power collapsed inside of me, and I released his hand to brace myself against the floor. My breaths came in heavy bursts as a wave of exhaustion rolled over me.

My shoulders trembled as I looked down. Almost all traces of the curse were gone except a tiny speck of blue light.

I'd done it. Fucking fates, I done it.

And now it was time to go.

"I fulfilled my part of the bargain," I whispered. "Now I'm going to fulfill yours. I'm taking my freedom."

For a moment, my heart warmed as I looked down at the beautiful man he might have been, but then it chilled again as I thought of the wreckage of my home. Of the flattened fae village. Of all the lies.

Of my mother and my family back in Magic Side. If he had his way, I'd never see them again.

"Samantha," he whispered, and I froze.

The Dark God's eyes flickered open, and I leapt back. Had my healing magic woken him, or was it just that he was a god and could shake off the stings of deathwings?

It didn't matter—it was time to get the fuck out.

Cadean rolled to his side. "Don't do it, little wolf. Don't leave."

To hell with that. As much as I'd grown accustomed to the kind and noble side of him, I still hated the Dark God.

Stumbling over the furniture, I darted for the balcony.

"Where are you going?" he rumbled, his voice so deep and low that it sent shivers straight through me.

I extended my claws, grabbed the edge of the balustrade, then flipped myself over the stone railing and glanced back at the Dark Wolf God one last time. "Good-bye, Cadean."

He was still incapacitated by the balm, but his eyes blazed with betrayal.

A mix of emotions battered me—relief, guilt, hope, and concern—but I pushed them down, focusing on the next task at hand: scaling the three-hundred-foot stone tower.

Like an idiot, I glanced down.

Whoa, boy. Sure, I'd been out here before, but this made climbing Red River Gorge seem like I'd been playing on a jungle gym.

I sank my claws into the seams between the smooth stones, but in some places, the stones were so large that I had to drop a few feet before catching a hold. My fingers strained from the impact each time, and I could smell the keratin as the stone filed away at my claws. I was way out of practice.

A hawk soared overhead, alighting on the balcony above. One of Cadean's scouts?

I gave up on finding handholds and began a controlled skid down the side of the tower. I dropped a little, then drove my claws into the next crack. The impact ricocheted through my arms and body, and I groaned, certain that I'd almost dislocated both shoulders. But a burst of magic from the moonshard kept me holding on.

I did two more skids, growing more confidant each time with the Moon's magic strengthening my grip. Glancing down, I calculated that I was halfway there. Just a couple more drops.

Taking a breath, I retracted my claws and fell. The stone whizzed by, and then I rammed my claws into another gap about twenty feet above the ground. For a second, it held, but then the stone crumbled. My arms flailed for an instant before my feet hit and my back found the ground.

The air whooshed from my lungs, and the stars overhead swam...and then I heaved myself onto my knees and forced myself to my feet.

Pain shot through my body, and I gasped. Broken ribs and a cracked leg. I stumbled back down, stifling a cry of pain. I'd pushed way past the limit of my werewolf resilience.

I have to escape.

Suddenly, heat flared in my pocket as the moonshard surged. Its magic coursed through me. My broken bones cracked and popped, and the nausea of the pain left me. In seconds, the agony eased, and I sucked in a breath.

Having the moonshard was like having a battery with an endless supply of magic.

Free us, and we will free you, the voices whispered.

What did that mean?

With no time to consider that, I checked my surroundings, then took off toward the aviary with renewed strength like I'd never felt before.

The night was brisk and quiet. I ducked behind the corner of an outbuilding as a sentry crossed ahead. Thankfully, the wind was blowing toward me, and he couldn't scent me. Moving as quickly and quietly as I could, I dodged between the trunks of the gigantic trees that ringed the towers as I made my way toward the aviary. I paused to catch my breath and scan the surroundings. I scented the griffstriders, but no one else.

The masters lived on the second floor of the aviary, but they'd be inside at this hour, probably having dinner. If not, I was prepared to do what I had to.

I crept into the darkness cast by the tower overhead and crossed the open court. The aviary doors were unlocked, but when I peeked my head in, I didn't see or scent anyone. I'd figured as much. The griffstriders were deadly enough to prevent anyone from breaking in, and if there was a fire, it was better if they could escape without tearing the whole building down.

I slipped inside the back door, closing it quietly. The smell of hay and raw meat—traces of the striders' dinner—turned my stomach. I was so close, I could taste my freedom.

I opened the gate to the cave where Elowyn slept.

The griffstrider lifted her head and dug her clawed forefoot into the dirt. The tattered remains of an animal lay close by—leftovers from dinner, and a good reminder of what would happen to me if I fucked this up.

I stepped forward and rested a steady hand on her feathers. "Shh, it's just me, Elowyn. I'm getting out of here, and I need your help. Can you take me to Frostfall? I'll free you afterward. You can go wherever you want."

She raised her head again and let out a hot puff of air. *No.*

My chest grew tight as worry and panic flooded my system. "Please, Elowyn. I wouldn't ask if my life didn't depend on it. Don't you want to be free of this place?"

But the strider only dug her taloned foot into the dirt again, her stark expression making my heart drop: *I'm no prisoner or traitor.*

A breath loosened from my chest.

Fuck.

Despair pulled at me, but I refused to give up. I'd have to go as a wolf. The question was, what route should I take? I could head to the closest barrier, then make my way south to Selene's village. It would be a roundabout way of getting there, but it would get me out of the Dark God's grasp sooner, in case he woke up.

It wasn't a great plan, but it was all I had to work with.

I stepped close to the griffstrider and brushed the soft feathers along the side of her head. "Thanks for carrying me and helping me get away from Wulfric. I'll miss you."

She clacked her beak.

I turned to leave, but Auren's voice froze me in my tracks: "What are you doing here, Samantha?"

58

Samantha

My breath caught as I met his cross expression, and my racing pulse returned. He'd always given me counsel. Would he stop me now and hand me over to his brother?

There was no hiding what I was doing. "I'm leaving."

I crossed toward the door, but he stepped forward and caught my arm. "Don't be a fool." When I tried to pull my arm free, he pushed me against the wall. "This is madness. He'll hunt you down, you know that, right?"

"He's incapacitated, and I broke the collar."

Auren stiffened, his gaze going to my bare neck. "What? How did you manage that?"

"With this." I shoved him back and pulled out the moonshard, brandishing it like a knife. The Moon's magic surged through me, and for just a second, I felt invincible. "Now get out of my way or help me."

His eyes flared, as did his signature.

I knew in my heart that if he wanted to take me down, there was nothing I could do. He was a god with strength and power beyond comprehending.

"The moonshard..." he whispered, eyes almost glistening with lust.

I tried not to let my terror show. "You said that you had pity for me. That you'd help me if you could. Well, now's your chance. I've lost the collar, and Cadean won't be able to cross the border in pursuit."

He stood there on the knife edge of decision, deciding whether to betray his brother or condemn me to a life of imprisonment.

The door to the aviary slammed open. "Well, well, well. What the fuck do we have here?"

Kass strolled in, a ferocity to his features I'd never seen before. His gaze scoured me, then settled on Auren. "You fucking traitor."

He drew his sword and pointed it at us. "Are you insane? Did you think Cadean would let you two just leave?"

"This isn't what it looks like," I said.

"Oh, really?" he snapped. "Then please, pray tell."

Auren took a step forward, aligning himself between me and the vampire. "Don't you have better things to do, Kassian?"

The air pulsed around us as a wave of sunlight and power filled the room.

Kassian's eyes rounded at Auren, and his fangs slipped out. "You just tried to *glamour* me? I'm a fucking vampire! That doesn't work. Even for gods."

Oh, shit.

Kassian moved in a blur, thrusting with his blade. Auren threw out his hand and unleashed a blast of magic that knocked Kassian back into the far wall. His head cracked on the stone, and his body slumped to the ground.

My heart clenched. "You didn't kill him, did you?"

I dashed toward Kass, unsure why I felt an ounce of concern for the bastard.

"Not yet," Auren growled as he strode forward. "But we'll need to get rid of him."

I blocked his advance. "No. Don't kill him."

"I'm not going to have him ratting to Cadean. We'll use him as a hostage if we need."

"Does that mean you're coming with me?" I asked, heart clenching in my chest.

"No darling, you're coming with me, and so is that sad sack of a vampire. I have no choice now, do I?" Auren strode across the aviary and opened a gate. He clicked his tongue, and a golden griffstrider stalked out. "The vampire will presume that I was complicit, and my brother will believe him. If I kill him, my brother will still know I had a hand in this mess."

"I'm sorry. I didn't intend to get you caught up in this."

He lifted a brow at me, and it reminded me so much of the way Cadean did the same. Guilt and a glimmer of regret rose in my chest.

"What's done is done." He hauled Kassian up with ease and tossed him over the strider's rump. "The truth is, my brother is out of control and has been for some time. Between that stone you're carrying and the magic power you seem to possess over him, there may be a way to rein him in. I never thought it possible." He turned and met my gaze. "Well, what are you waiting for?"

He didn't have to ask me twice. I tucked the moonshard away and joined his side.

Auren checked the ropes he'd used to secure Kass, then climbed onto his strider and extended his arm to me. "You're going to make my life very complicated, Samantha. I hope you're worth it."

He pulled me up in front of him and kicked the strider into gear.

"Thank you," I said over my shoulder. "I owe you one."

Auren's hand slipped over my stomach. "I'll remember that."

I couldn't help the unease I felt being close to him. I'd grown so used to riding with Cadean that this felt wrong. Guilt tightened my throat, but I pushed it away.

I was getting the fuck out. There was nothing that could stop me now.

The golden strider tore at the earth, and I didn't bother looking back. The cold air lashed at my cheeks, and the ride was much rougher than when I'd rode Vega and Elowyn.

Unlike the Dark God, Auren didn't seem to have the power to move trees, so his strider had to leap over roots and duck around vegetation. I'd never focused on the subtle way Cadean manipulated the woods around him.

Or the subtle way he'd manipulated me.

Cadean

Cold, hard stone.

I rolled onto my back, and my vision swam. Shadows and blurs of color flowed in and out before my eyes.

My thoughts were sluggish, not quite connecting.

I lifted my arm, and wonder overwhelmed me. The curse was nearly gone. The pain was gone.

She healed me.

Shock and elation and gratitude rushed through me. But why was my head so foggy? Was that a side effect of her magic?

"Samantha?"

No response. I shoved myself partway up. There was a broken jar of cream lying on the floor next to me. Samantha's balm. As the last of the fog drifted away, the memories came rolling back.

She'd betrayed me.

"Fuck!"

Adrenaline poured through me as I forced myself to my feet. Purged by my powerful healing abilities, the last of the poison rapidly released its hold, replaced by an almost paralyzing anger.

The traitor. I snapped my hand up and pulled on the collar around her neck, but there was nothing.

Had she lost consciousness? Even then, I would have still been able to feel the bond with the collar. But it was gone. She couldn't have possibly broken the spell over it, could she? It was impossible.

I closed my eyes and searched the shadows for her.

The brilliant flame of her spirit drew my vision to her in an instant. Shadows and colors whipped past my eyes, and then I saw her. She was moving quickly on a griffstrider—held in the arms of my brother.

The vision collapsed as an inferno of rage ignited within me. I roared as my magic exploded through the room. Bottles of wine shattered, books were torn from the shelves, and the furniture ripped itself to shreds, leaving only desolation.

The fucking bastard had stolen her right out from under me. I should have known he was plotting something, or that they were plotting together. How else could she have gotten the collar off?

I called for my axe, but it resisted, pulling me toward my hidden chamber.

No. It can't be.

Not even my brother knew about that.

I rammed my claws into the wall and ripped the door to the secret chamber off its hinges.

My stomach twisted with shock and horror. My axe was embedded in the pedestal, and where the moonshard was supposed to be there was a dead, silver fish. For one second, my thoughts flatlined, and then an anger like I'd never known consumed me.

"Rune!" I charged toward the balcony and hurled myself into the air.

My body tumbled, and I seized the form of a giant eagle. Beating south on my wings, I shot toward the border of my brother's realm. Had this been his plan all along?

No. It had been *her*.

Auren was calculating and meticulous. This was reckless and bold—the act of someone with nothing to lose and the bravery to look death in the face. I had to admire Samantha for that. She was a wolf at heart.

Closing my eyes, I reached out for her with my mind, feeling the subtle tug. I turned to follow the sensation, soaring toward the barrier.

They were drawing close, but I was right on their heels. I scanned the forest until I spotted the gaps in the canopy that followed the old road.

There was a flash of gold between the leaves—Auren's strider. I could feel his signature thrumming below. But over the top of that was honey and lavender, and the relentless pull on my chest.

I couldn't let her escape. Between her and the moonshard, I would lose everything. Hell, I would have gladly traded the moonshard just for her.

The flickering barrier of light rose into the sky, racking my body with pain even at a distance.

It was now or never. Heart thundering, I flexed my talons and tucked into a dive.

59

Samantha

I felt him before I saw him, a low rumble of power sweeping over the land like an avalanche. The bitter taste of chocolate on the tip of my tongue and the sweet scent of cedar logs burning in a hearth.

A shudder of terror and delight ran down my spine, and I sucked in a sharp breath. His signature sang to my body, and I hated every shiver of desire.

"He's coming!" I shouted.

Auren spurred his strider to a maddening pace. "I know! We should have crossed the border by now, but it's moved again...outward!"

Shit. Healing Cadean had moved the barrier, making our escape just that much harder.

I bit my lip. Nothing I could do about it now.

At least we were close. The barrier's iridescent light glinted through the trees ahead, and the cool tingle of the Moon's magic beat back the dark presence of the god on our heels.

I tried looking behind us, but the path was clear. Even so, he felt dangerously close.

The moonlight beaming through the canopy flickered as a shadow rushed by overhead.

I craned my neck to follow. "He's above us!"

Suddenly, the trees ahead tore themselves from the ground and crashed down, blocking our path.

"Fuck!" Auren snarled. "We're going over!"

The strider bounded over the fallen trees, dodging the grasping limbs and splintered wood. The entire forest closed in. We were so close.

Then there was a brown blur, and a heavy branch slammed into my chest. Agony ripped through me as the impact drove the wind from my lungs and flung us from the saddle.

I crashed to the ground, Auren beside me.

Gasping, I rolled over.

The strider reared, then charged forward toward the wall through the writhing forest with Kass still bound to its back. Auren staggered to his feet and shouted, but the beast didn't turn around.

He pulled me to my feet. "You're bleeding."

I glanced down. My chest was covered with blood, but it was just scratches from the tree branches. "It'll heal. We've got to go."

The forest rumbled and groaned as the trees shifted back.

A massive eagle screamed down out of the sky like a dark meteor. Seconds before impact, it turned into a mass of shadow, and took the form of a massive wolf.

My heart stilled as I tried to comprehend what I was seeing: a giant beast stepping straight out of legend.

The Dark Wolf God made Jaxson and every alpha I'd met seem like pups. His fur was like wisps of shadow fading with the wind. He was at least ten feet tall at the shoulder, and his jaws had been shaped to rip out the throats of dragons. With every step he took, his muscles tensed with lethal strength.

This was the monster he hadn't wanted me to see: his true form.

The Dark God's glacier-blue eyes flared with anger and hatred and possessiveness. It felt like his gaze was scouring the flesh from my body. He was judging every inch of me and finding me wanting.

Traitors! his voice roared in my mind, shaking me to the core. *How could you betray me like this, brother?*

Auren advanced without fear. "Stand down and let us pass, *dear* brother."

Never, the black wolf boomed, shaking the leaves of the trees. *You have what is mine.*

A cruel smile crossed Auren's lip. "You only possess what you're strong enough to hold, and you're too weak to hold your domain together. Your realm is spent, and you are spent. Stop grasping at straws."

Growling low, the giant black wolf stalked forward through the collapsed trees. His fangs were long enough to pierce clean through the chest of a man. Even Auren's.

For a second, they stared each other down. Then the Dark God lunged, and my heart seized.

Auren leapt back, and in a burst of light, he transformed into a golden wolf the size of his brother. The two charged and met midair, snarling and biting. They rolled and crashed against the trees, clawing and biting and slamming into each other with terrifying ferocity.

I backed away. I was a fighter, but this was a battle between gods.

The Dark God pounced, but Auren rammed him with his shoulder, sending him tumbling across the ground. Auren's golden wolf was on top of him in a second, and he sank his teeth into Cadean's neck.

I cried out before I could stop myself and almost swore I

could feel the pain in my own neck and shoulder. Fear for Cadean cut through me, though I couldn't justify why. He was my enemy and trying to imprison me. I should be rooting for him to die, but a part of me couldn't stand to see him suffering.

With a feral snarl, the Dark God heaved himself up and flipped his brother. He sank his teeth in and hurled the golden wolf backward against a tree. The trunk snapped, and Auren collapsed to the ground.

With a swirl of magic, the Dark God returned to the form of a man. His features were as hard as iron, and his muscles glistened with sweat. Striding toward Auren, he drew his black axe. Sinister shadows began to boil from the blade like flames.

Auren slowly staggered to his feet, but the Dark God lunged in for the kill.

No.

I leapt forward with an outstretched arm, and a wave of light ripped through me like the aftershock of an earthquake. My heart crashed against my chest, and the power exploded out around me, forming into a glittering shield between him and Auren.

The Dark God's axe slammed into the wall of my magic with a blinding flash of light. He roared as I collapsed to one knee with my hands held high. Black flames streamed off the blade of his axe as it cut into the shield, and my arms shook with exertion, but the barrier held.

Closing my eyes, I pulled every ounce of strength I could from the moonshard.

He yanked his axe back and brought it down, sending a shockwave of force cascading through me.

"I don't want to hurt you, little wolf!" he growled. "Get back!"

"*You* get back!" With a scream of fury, I released the magic I'd been holding. As it exploded outward, crackling lightning leapt across his skin, the force throwing him into a tree.

Holy shit. I dropped my trembling arms, totally spent.

I glanced over my shoulder as Auren shifted back into the form of a man and pulled himself to his feet.

Then Cadean's hand clamped around my left wrist. "Care to try that again, little wolf?"

How had he moved so fast?

"Let go!" I pulled away.

"Never," he snarled. "You are *mine*."

That single word—*mine*—pierced through my heart with both terror and delight. His desire and possessiveness were like a drug, but I would not be tamed.

With a single motion, I wrenched the moonshard out of my pocket and rammed it into his breast. His eyes went wide as its magic flared, searing his skin. The Dark God staggered back and dropped to one knee, clutching his chest.

I looked down at the glowing shard in my hand. It was soaked in blood. *His* blood. Crimson rivulets spiraled down my arm.

Horror filled me, and my stomach clenched. I took a step toward him, but Auren seized my arm and yanked me toward the barrier. "Run!"

I hesitated for a second, but then I turned and ran.

The trees lashed out at us, but we dodged and twisted out of the way. It was almost like the barrier was rushing toward us— whatever was happening, I thanked the fates.

When I heard a roar behind us, I glanced over my shoulder.

Cadean was barreling after us in his wolf form. Terror cut through me, and I stumbled, but Auren yanked me to my feet.

And then there was a wall of light, and the sensation of cool warmth, and tingling magic.

We were through the Moon's barrier. Safe.

I skidded to a halt alongside Auren, and we looked back.

The Dark God slammed into the barrier, and ripples of force

cascaded over the surface of the wall. He thundered but kept fighting. His fur looked almost as if it was on fire, and he began to glow with a white light.

It hurt me just to watch it. The searing agony that he felt tore at my heart.

Finally, he wheeled around and stalked away from the wall. He paused and turned, glaring back at us with his piercing ice-blue eyes. They were utterly paralyzing.

Was he finally going to let me go?

A memory flared to life in the back of my mind. He couldn't cross the barrier, but he *could* manipulate the forest. That was how he'd grabbed me when I'd been with Sarion.

Shit.

Before I knew what I was doing, I raised the moonshard and summoned its magic. A wave of light burst out of me just as the trees ripped their roots free and lashed out at us from across the barrier like striking cobras.

As my pulse of magic hit the barrier, it crystalized for a second, and the thrashing vines rebounded. I kept pouring my magic through the moonshard, absolutely stunned as the wall became like glass, repelling the Dark God's magic.

"How are you doing that?" Auren asked, wonder in his voice.

I had no idea, and I grasped for understanding. While Cadean had been able to use the moonshard to bend the barrier, I'd just made it impenetrable—*exact opposites*.

"How long can you maintain it?" Auren asked.

"No fucking idea. Let's get out of here."

"Agreed." Raising his hands to his mouth, he called for his strider. It burst out of the woods ahead with Kass still hanging awkwardly over the back. Auren leapt into the saddle and reached down to me. "Let's go."

I froze as the Dark God's voice rumbled in my mind. *You betrayed me, little wolf.*

I turned, certain he could hear me. "I healed you, and I left. That was our bargain."

You stole from me, he growled.

"I restored the balance. I healed your wound and put the barriers back where they belong. I stole the shard so you can't cross again. Protect your people, and do not enter my world or the lands of the fae."

You only restored my prison.

"It's the one you deserve." With that, I turned and grasped Auren's hand. He pulled me up into the saddle, and I settled in.

I took one last look at the Dark God stalking back and forth behind the walls of his shimmering prison. The murderer. The destroyer. The architect of my captivity.

I was free.

Yet as we galloped away, I swore I heard his voice echoing in my mind: *This is not over, little wolf. You are mine.*

I trained my eyes on the path ahead. *Not anymore.*

60

Three days later, in the depths of Auren's dungeon...
Samantha

Kass clenched his hands around the bars of his cell. "He'll come for me, and he'll come for you."

I grinned and slipped the moonshard out of my pocket. "Not without this, he won't."

Kass's hand dropped from the bars. "How the fuck?"

I twisted the tip of the shard against my fingertip like I'd seen him do so many times before with his dagger. "Wouldn't you like to know? What's important is that your master can no longer push past the border. He can't sack fae villages, and he can't come after me. Or even you."

"He'll send Wulfric and the others. He will never stop hunting you."

I smiled. "Maybe. Or maybe he's learned that this bitch has bite."

Kass pushed against his bars. "Don't be a fool. I can't believe you're throwing your lot in with that asshole Auren. You can't fucking trust him."

"I'm right here, prick," Auren snarled.

"I know," Kass said. "You have no idea what you're involved with, Samantha."

"I'm more interested in what *you're* involved with, Kassian." Auren grinned. "Which is why my people are going to be asking you a lot of questions."

A pang of sympathy twisted my gut. I placed my hand on Auren's arm and glared back at the vampire who'd caused me so much misery. "Make sure his rations are soggy. And if you have to move him, put a bag over his head. But don't hurt him. The masochist would just enjoy it."

Auren laughed and led me out of the dungeon. "Don't tell me you have a tender spot for that bastard."

"Only for where I want to ram a stake."

It was a lie, but one I had to force myself to believe. I'd grown fond of Mel and Wulfric and even Kass during my captivity, but I had to let those feelings go. I had to let my feelings for Cadean go. That was beginning to seem more and more impossible.

I followed Auren up the stairs and through a myriad of hallways with servants rushing everywhere. Auren's palace was so different than Shadowstone, almost baroque with white walls and gilded decoration.

I was followed by a cadre of guards everywhere I went, and he'd provided maids to help with my clothes and hair. Auren had even sent me a dozen dresses to replace my tattered riding clothes. I'd chosen the red one with silver trim. It was breathtaking—and entirely not me.

It was like living in a fairy tale, like all the stories shoved deep beneath my bed back in Deerhaven. Yet for some reason, a part of me still longed for the Dark God's hall, with its living pillars and scent of deep woods. And the scent of *him*.

That was madness, of course. Maybe it was all too much, too fast.

I went to tuck the moonshard back in my bodice—a great

advantage of cleavage when you didn't have pockets—but Auren stopped my hand. "Are you sure you don't want me to put that in my vault? It makes you a target."

"No," I said, quicker and more harshly than I intended, and I stepped back.

He bowed his head. "I completely understand."

"Sorry...I didn't mean to sound like that. I'm still trying to learn my magic, and it's connected to the moonshard somehow."

I didn't mention the voices that called to me whenever I held the shimmering stone. *Free us.*

That was a mystery I didn't yet feel safe enough to ask about.

We strolled along a veranda that looked out over his lands. I'd been his guest for three days, but it was time to get a move on. "I appreciate everything you've done for me Auren, but I need to get back to Deerhaven—or if that's not possible, to Magic Side. I've been gone for nearly four weeks, and my mother needs someone—"

Auren took me by the shoulders and smiled. His power flowed over me, warm and inviting, and suddenly calmed my nerves. "Give me a few more days until we know it's safe. Cadean will be expecting you to run back there, and his forces will by lying in wait. I'll send someone to look in on your mother. There's so much for you to do here. As you pointed out, you need to learn how your magic works."

"Yes, but I need to get home."

"Is home enough? You did so much more than escape. You healed my brother and seized the moonstone. You restored the balance here, but there's so much more that you can do."

I stared at him, a flicker of unease settling in my bones. "I need to go."

"I watched you control the barrier, Samantha. That could change everything about this war, for the lives of those caught on all sides—but not if you leave. Not if you go back to being Samantha the bartender."

I opened my mouth to protest but closed it again. Samantha the bartender. Samantha, queen of the ring.

The truth was, I couldn't go back to being that girl from Deerhaven. She'd died seven weeks ago at the hands of her best friend. I had no idea who it was the Moon had brought back from the darkness, but I knew that my old life wasn't enough. Not anymore.

That life had been built on lies. I wasn't just a werewolf. I was half fae. I had magic. Power. The ability to change things here. I even had the strength to stop a god in his tracks.

Auren was offering me a new chance at life—one that Deerhaven had never given me, or Magic Side, either. A chance to find who my father had been, to discover my magic, and to find out who I was.

"I'll let you think about it," Auren said, strolling away. His guards stayed behind with me, a wall of silver and gold.

I stepped to the balcony and gazed out across the Dreamlands.

As always, mist separated the patches of golden forests, green marshes, and even the rocky red outcrops of mountains. Beyond that, the white towers of the Dark God's citadel looked like claws tearing up through the heart of his land.

I knew he was watching.

Over the past three days, every time I walked past a shadow, I'd felt his eyes tracking me relentlessly. Perhaps it was my imagination, but I could almost hear the wind rustling in the pines and taste the rich flavor of chocolate each time it happened.

I took a deep breath and focused on the shimmering barrier that kept him at bay.

I knew the truth now: there were two gods trapped behind

that wall. One was a destroyer, a monster that swept out of legend, burning villages and spreading darkness and death. He was the bastard who had nearly killed me, who'd threatened everything I held dear.

The other was a warrior who would stop at nothing to defend his people. A god who could turn autumn into spring. A god who had saved my life again and again. It was *him* I'd healed, and him I trusted to protect Melanthe and Selene. He was the one who'd traced his lips across mine and awoken desires I could barely admit. And each morning when I was drowsing in my bed, it was him for whom my fingers were searching.

And he was imprisoned forever.

My chest rose and fell with aching breaths. Was there any way to separate the beast from the prince? A way to rescue the sliver of good residing in the god that haunted my dreams?

I touched my neck. I'd gotten away, and the collar was gone. But deep in my soul, I knew another truth: somewhere along the way, the Dark God had captured me, and he would never let me go.

Thank you for joining Samantha and Cadean on the first leg of their journey! *Hunters Kiss*, the second book in the series will be here in the new year, but you can preorder it now (https://mybook.to/Hunters-Kiss)

Are you wondering how Cadean reacted to Samantha's escape? We wanted to end with Samantha's point of view, but you can sign up for our newsletter to read a bonus deleted scene: https://dl.bookfunnel.com/hotnnhrwfe. (We never spam and you can unsubscribe at any time).

Samantha first appears in the *Wolf Bound* series, so if you would like to learn more about her and the events leading up to *Wolf God*, you can read it here: http://mybook.to/Wolf-Marked

Thanks for reading!

HUNTER'S KISS

SAVAGE GODS: WOLF GOD BOOK 2

VERONICA DOUGLAS

HUNTER'S KISS

RUTHLESS GODS: WOLF GOD, BOOK 2

I can't escape the truth.

I broke out of the Dark Wolf God's realm, but I know he's always there, watching me from the shadows. I should hate him, but I can't deny that I'm drawn to the ruthless beast, and the heat between us is only growing stronger.

Am I a fool for thinking there's a chance he can be redeemed?

He's pulled me into a war between the shifters and the fae— the two halves of my secret heritage. Both sides are hunting me, but I refuse to be a pawn in their games.

With the fate of the Dreamlands hanging in the balance, I'll need to master my magic and face the truths that could tear me apart.

Preorder now: http://mybook.to/Hunters-Kiss

ACKNOWLEDGMENTS

Thank you to all our readers and friends—you've been so supportive throughout this long and winding journey!

Thank you to Maggie Shayne and Ash Fitzsimmons for your patience and amazing editing skills! You are incredible and really helped bring this story to life.

Thank you to the amazing readers on our advanced review team, especially Amanda, Gwen, and Katy for your sharp eyes!

Many thanks to Lauren Gardner for all of your hard work. You are absolutely a lifesaver! And thanks to Caethes, for all your efforts to keep us rolling. We'd be lost without you both.

And finally, a huge shoutout to JoY Author Design for creating the beautiful character art and covers that truly inspired our writing!

ABOUT VERONICA DOUGLAS

Veronica Douglas is a duo of professional archaeologists that love writing and digging together. After spending an inordinate amount of time doing painstaking research for academia, they suddenly discovered a passion for letting their imaginations go wild! A cocktail of magic, romance, and ancient mystery (shaken, not stirred), their books are inspired, in part, by their life in Chicago and their archaeological adventures from around the globe.

COPYRIGHT

This is a work of fiction. All reference to events, persons, and locale are used fictitiously, except where documented in the historical record. Names, characters, and places are products of the author's imagination, and any resemblance to actual events, locales, or persons, living or dead, is coincidental.